High October

High October

ELENA GRAF

PURPLE HAND PRESS

Purple Hand Press, an imprint of Castle Hill Media LLC
www.purplehandpress.com

Trade Paperback Edition
ISBN-13 978-1-7334492-0-5
Kindle Edition
ISBN-13 978-1-7334492-1-2
ePub Edition
ISBN-13 978-1-7334492-2-9

09.14.20

To Sheila, as always

FIVE YEARS AGO

Chapter 1

As Liz Stolz sat in the drive-up line at Awakened Brews, she wondered if the day would bring any interesting cases. Family practice could be monotonous, but when the summer visitors came to town, anything could happen.

The intercom stirred to life. A young male voice asked for her order.

"Good morning, Billy. It's Dr. Liz." That was all she needed to say. By the time she drove around to the window, her coffee was prepared exactly the way she liked it—extra large, dark roast, double cream, no sugar.

The young man stuck his skinny, muscular arm out the window to put the cup directly into her hands. "Careful, Doc. It's hot," Billy cautioned as he did every day. Liz handled the cup gingerly, mindful of the temperature. People said it was hot enough to melt a fishing hole in Sebago in the dead of winter.

Liz paid cash and added a few extra dollars. "Keep the change."

Billy's face visibly brightened, although tipping was Dr. Stolz's habit, and everyone at Awakened Brews knew it. Liz liked knowing that her generosity was appreciated. She liked that she knew the young people who made her coffee. One mowed her lawn in summer, another raked the leaves in fall and shoveled the snow off her garage roof in winter, but she could call on any of them to help her haul heavy things to the dump or stack firewood.

Liz liked everything about the town of Hobbs, where she'd settled after she'd bought the family practice on Beach Road. Hobbs boasted more miles of sandy beach than any town in Maine. Despite its popularity with the tourists, Hobbs was a real town with a supermarket, a movie theater, and a high school. Less than ten thousand people lived there year-round, but in the summer, the population swelled to four times that size. When it reached its peak three weeks before Labor Day, traffic on Route 1 came to a standstill.

At five thirty in the morning, the route to the beach was mostly clear.

Liz parked her truck and settled on a bench near the fence to wait for the sunrise. A storm had come through during the night, and the wind off the water was brisk. The banners in front of the T-shirt shop were flapping furiously, making a fierce racket.

Tourists from the beachfront motels had their phones poised to snap photos of the famous Hobbs sunrise. Finally, a sliver of orange light appeared on the horizon accompanied by bands of incandescent pinks and brilliant lavenders.

By the time the sun had risen, the crowd had dispersed and Liz's coffee was gone. She pitched her empty cup into the rusted oil barrel and headed down the stairs to the beach. Walking along the water's edge, she set a brisk pace to the estuarine preserve. The occasional splash of cold ocean into her rafting sandals didn't bother her. The water would never be warmer than it was in August.

She recognized some of the beach walkers and nodded a greeting as she passed. Some stopped for a brief chat. Liz always planned for these interruptions. Without them, the walk took exactly forty-three minutes, with conversations, an hour. Either way, she was back in her truck in plenty of time. She tried to tamp down her wind-blown hair, almost impossible now that she had let it go completely gray. She covered the unruly curls with her favorite baseball cap from the Dead River Bait Company. The fabric on the bill was fraying, but she liked the visual pun of the fish skeleton logo.

After unlocking the back door to the office of Hobbs Family Practice, she took a very hot shower before the front office staff arrived. While the nurses drew blood, she reviewed the morning's appointments—follow-ups for blood work, a child with a nasty summer cold, a couple of emergencies: two UTIs and a sprained thumb. One of her partners was on vacation, so Liz had double duty, which meant a busy day.

The afternoon was for physicals. It was Friday, so Liz let her office staff go home early while she examined the last patient. She entered her notes into the system and locked up the office.

Liz's usual Friday evening routine in warm weather included a lobster roll and slaw at the beach. During the day, it was almost impossible to find parking. At dinner time, the tourists jammed into the restaurants along Route 1, and the beach lot was empty. Liz pitched her sling chair on the jetty and positioned it for the best view of the harbor. She took a deep breath and filled her lungs with sea air.

Life doesn't get any better than this.

The stiff wind that had been blowing since morning hadn't let up. Eventually, Liz moved her picnic into the cab of her truck to enjoy the last colorful gifts of the sky. After the sun set, she headed home.

She planted herself on the sofa in the media room with an IPA from a new brewery in Kittery. She listened to the end of PBS evening news while she scanned her emails. The IPA was crisp and hoppy, but it made her sleepy, so she punched up a throw pillow and rolled over to take a nap.

She awoke with a start to the sound of her phone dancing on the table. Her eyes were gluey as she tried to focus on the screen. Webhanet Playhouse? What could that be about? Liz answered with her doctor voice: "Elizabeth Stolz."

"Liz? It's Tony." Liz sat up and shook her head to clear it.

"Tony? Hey," she said with a conspicuous lack of enthusiasm.

"I hate to bother you, but my lead actress fell and really hurt her leg. Urgent care is closed."

"So? Bring her down to Southern Med."

"Liz, it's Friday night in the summer. It will be a madhouse. She's in a lot of pain. Please."

"Oh, for fuck's sake, Tony." Liz rubbed her eyes. "Really?"

"Liz, you owe me for all those tickets I give your friends."

"You owe me for all those house calls I make to your theater." Resigned, she got to her feet. "Meet me at my office. I'll need an x-ray to see if it's fractured."

Liz grabbed her cap from the hook near the garage door. As she hauled herself into the cab of her truck, she realized she had no idea what was playing at the Webhanet Playhouse. She avoided town during the summer season because of the traffic and hadn't seen the marquee in months.

She arrived before Tony and unlocked the front door before heading into the back to turn on the lights. She found a stethoscope in her desk and hung it around her neck.

"We're here!" The sound of Tony's booming actor's voice was accompanied by shuffling and soft moans of pain.

Liz came into the waiting room. "Hey, Tony."

The assistant director of the Webhanet Playhouse was in his forties, deeply tanned, and pencil slim. He had thick brows and a bushy moustache, which unintentionally gave him a Groucho Marx look. "Thanks so much for coming over," he said.

Liz nodded and tossed her ball cap on the check-in counter. The patient, a pretty, middle-aged blonde raised her eyes and stared at her. Liz decided that the woman was older than she first looked, so she took her pulse and gave her heart a quick listen. Normal heart sounds. She looked vaguely familiar, but then so many actresses look familiar.

Liz knelt on one knee and gently prodded the puffy area around the woman's ankle. The rapid swelling could mean a sprain or a fracture. Ankles could be so finicky with all the tendons and ligaments in the vicinity. Liz always x-rayed lower extremity trauma to be sure.

"Okay, Tony. Help me get our patient down to the x-ray room."

The woman grabbed a carelessly painted, neon-green cane that had probably been a prop in a Webhanet Playhouse production. With Tony's help, she succeeded in limping into the x-ray room.

The x-ray showed a fracture of the lateral malleolus of the right fibula, minimally displaced. Liz reasoned that she could reduce it with manipulation, but it would be agony for the patient. "The small bone in your leg is broken right above the ankle, but I can set it."

"Tony says you're a surgeon," the woman said.

"Yes, but orthopedics isn't my specialty. Fortunately, this is reduction 101. Any medical student could do it, but it will be painful. If you want me to go ahead, I'll give you a fast-acting painkiller by injection."

"Yes, all right," said the patient. Saying that much had taken effort. She'd been holding her breath because of the pain.

Liz touched her hand. "Try to breathe normally or you'll get lightheaded." The woman nodded. "Tony, can you please help our patient into the exam room across the hall?"

Liz went into her office to unlock the safe and remove a pen injector. When she returned, she stabbed the woman in the thigh right through her costume, an aqua jumpsuit of a slinky, shimmering material. "We need to wait a couple of minutes for the painkiller to work." Liz rolled away on her stool to have another look at the x-ray. She glanced at her watch to gauge how long to wait. "Just another minute or two." She smiled to reassure the patient, who now looked even more familiar. *She's at least my age,* thought Liz. *She's not a natural blonde, and that stage makeup is covering a multitude of sins.* It annoyed Liz that she couldn't place her. Former patient? Hospital staff? Someone she'd seen on TV?

The woman closed her eyes and sighed. "The pain is just fading away." She opened her eyes and managed a little smile. "What did you give me?"

"Morphine. Old-fashioned, but it always does the trick."

"She gives good drugs," volunteered Tony.

Liz shot him a filthy look. "That's enough, Tony." He was joking, of course, but the Feds were keeping a watchful eye on opiate use, and Liz didn't know anything about this woman.

She glanced at her watch. "Lie down for me, please." She helped the woman bring her legs up on the table. "I'm going to pull and push at the same time. Despite the painkiller, it's going to hurt quite a bit. I promise to be quick. Ready?"

The woman nodded. She attempted a brave smile, but she let out a sharp yelp as Liz pulled the bone back into place.

"All done. You're a real trooper." Liz slid her arm under the woman's shoulders to help her sit up. "I'll be right back."

Liz went to the supply room to see what cast materials were left after the busy tourist season. Summer visitors came in with the most amazing injuries, so they always had plenty of splints and elastic bandages on hand. Liz rummaged around on the bottom shelf and found a brand-new walking boot still wrapped in plastic and the cotton socks to go with it. There were also some pneumatic splints for lower extremities. She took one of those too.

"We're in luck," she announced, returning to the room. "You can put weight on a closed fracture like this, so a walking boot will do fine. Now, we're going to take a little stroll down to the x-ray room, so I can make sure everything is lined up correctly. If it is, you can probably skip a visit to an orthopedic surgeon…if that matters to you."

"I have a high deductible, so yes, it matters. Thank you."

The x-ray showed the bone ends met perfectly. Liz came in to help the woman put on the boot again. "It looks fine."

Tony solicitously held the woman's arm as he helped her down the hall to Liz's consulting room. "See? I told you she'd fix you right up. Isn't she fabulous?"

The woman gave Liz a brief, curious look.

"All kidding aside, thank you sooooo much." Tony patted Liz's shoulder.

"Don't thank me yet. No stage work for your star until that bone heals. And she can't drive for at least six weeks." Liz sat down behind the desk and pulled a prescription pad out of the drawer. "I can write a script for Percocet, but ibuprofen is better if you can stand the pain."

"Don't you need my insurance card?" The woman looked flustered. "Usually, that's the first thing they ask for."

"Yes, I guess I do." Liz's front-office staff was so efficient, she hardly thought about paperwork, but there would be hell to pay if she let a patient leave without getting her insurance information. "Yes, please give me your card, and if you could fill out a new patient form, my staff will contact you for the other information. One minute."

Liz located a new patient form and a clipboard at the front desk. By the time she returned to her office, the woman had found her insurance card. Liz went into the business office to copy it. She always tried to address patients by name, but she'd been in such a hurry to stop the pain, she hadn't thought to ask. After she copied both sides of the card, she picked it up and read the name: "Margaret Mary Krusick."

Krusick? That name sounded so familiar.

"No! Can't be…"

Chapter 2

After she filled out the medical form, Maggie was curious to see where she'd landed. At first, she couldn't believe the woman who'd come in wearing shorts, hiking sandals and a worn baseball cap was really a doctor, but it was after hours and she had come at a moment's notice.

As Tony had raced up the back roads from the Playhouse, he'd sung the doctor's praises, explaining she'd bought the family practice on Beach Road after retiring as chief of surgery at Yale New Haven. All Maggie could think about was the pain and had barely heard a word he'd said. After the doctor set the broken leg with a snap of the wrist, she understood why he was so impressed. Not many GPs would do that in the office, especially nowadays.

While the doctor was photocopying her insurance card, Maggie looked around the consulting room—modest as doctor's offices went, small but efficient, just a desk and some visitor's chairs that weren't very comfortable. The art on the walls was soothing but surprisingly sophisticated. Her eyes traveled to the framed diplomas and certificates. Columbia Physicians and Surgeons. Good school. Yale New Haven surgical residency and a Hopkins fellowship. Impressive. Unfortunately, Maggie's contact lenses weren't always the best for distance reading. She had to squint to make out the name on the certificate: Elizabeth Anne Stolz, M.D.

"Oh…my…God!"

"What's the matter?" Tony looked concerned.

"I know her!" Maggie whispered.

"You do?" Tony's bushy, black brows rose in surprise. "From where?"

"We went to college together. Forty years ago!"

"You've got to be kidding!" As usual, Tony's exaggerated reaction was over the top, probably the reason he'd failed as a serious actor. His performances had always been more in line with a drag revue than legitimate theater. Small wonder he'd given up acting and turned to directing and theater management.

The doctor returned and handed the card back to Maggie. Now, she could see the resemblance of this tall, lanky woman with wavy, iron-gray hair and penetrating blue eyes to her college roommate. Clearly, she was no longer the stooped, flat-chested girl Maggie remembered. Now, she had perfect posture, attractive curves, and discernible breasts. Very nice breasts, as a matter of fact. Maggie's eyes lingered on the gentle rise in her T-shirt. There were fine wrinkles around the blue eyes, now regarding her with curiosity, but despite a deep tan, which made the blue of her eyes brilliant, her face was fresh and unlined. Meanwhile, her mouth twitched, barely hiding a little smile that let Maggie know she'd been recognized too.

Sitting behind the desk, Liz looked much more doctor-like. She briefly scanned the patient history form. Apparently, she found nothing interesting because she set it aside. "My office will call on Monday to get the details. Can you be reached at the number on the form?"

"Liz..."

"Yes, I know, it's a big surprise, but we can catch up later. First, we need a plan." That was pure Liz, her predilection for order trumping her curiosity. "You'll be immobilized by this fracture. Where are you staying?"

"At the Windward B&B in Webhanet."

Liz frowned. "But they don't have an elevator there, do they?"

Maggie shook her head. "No, just stairs, and my room is on the third floor."

"Can you switch to another room?"

"The place is packed to the gills," Tony said, raking the dark hair that always fell on his face away from his eyes. "Most of the cast is staying there."

"Can you find her something else?"

"I'm sure everything's booked solid until after Labor Day. You know how it is in August."

Liz drummed her fingers on the desk. Finally, she looked up at Maggie. "It may not be your first choice, but I have a bedroom and full bath on the first floor."

The idea of being Liz's house guest after a separation of forty years was nothing short of stunning. "Really, Liz, I couldn't possibly impose on–"

"Really, it's nothing, and it wouldn't be the first time I've taken in a stray. Right, Tony?"

Tony barked a little laugh. "Right." He turned to Maggie. "If you stay at Liz's place, you'll have much better accommodations than at the Windward."

Maggie glanced at Liz, trying to size up the situation. It seemed she had no alternative. "Thank you, Liz. It's very generous of you."

But Liz wasn't listening. "Just how did this accident happen?" she asked, peering at Tony.

"We were trying to recreate the scene in the movie where Donna jumps up and down on a bed, so we came up with the idea of using a trampoline."

"That's idiotic! Especially, if you're hiring aging actresses for your plays."

Maggie swallowed her indignation at the remark, remembering that Liz could sometimes be so tactless. Obviously, that hadn't changed.

Tony shrugged. "It went fine in rehearsal."

Liz gave him a disapproving look and turned to Maggie. "We'd better get you home before the morphine wears off. Tony, can you spare that cane until she can pick up one at the pharmacy?"

"Sure, and no rush. I can't even remember which show we used it for."

Maggie managed, with their help, to get down the stairs to the parking lot. Tony walked with her to the truck, while Liz sprinted ahead to open the door and push the passenger seat all the way back. "Put your rear in first, then pull yourself up. There's a grab ring just inside the door near the windshield. You can hang on to that. I'll help you." Maggie was startled to feel strong hands around her waist literally lifting her into the seat. Liz helped her swing her broken leg into the cab. With the boot, it was a tight fit. Liz yanked down the seat belt and reached around Maggie to clip it. That was unnecessary, but Maggie could see Liz was on a mission and didn't dare interrupt. Tony sang out his goodbyes through an open window as he drove by.

Liz climbed into the driver seat and turned the key in the ignition.

"Fancy meeting you here." Ignoring the camera display on the dash, she looked over her shoulder to back up the truck. "I always thought I might bump into you at the hospital when you were living in Connecticut. A lot of my old friends showed up there. Unfortunately."

"Fortunately, I've been pretty healthy and so was Barry." Liz made a face, so Maggie quickly added, "We're divorced now."

"It happens." Liz's indifference toward her marital status surprised Maggie, especially considering how controversial it had once been. She provided some context to encourage more of a response. "He went off with his much younger female assistant on the West Coast. He lives in California now."

"Unfortunately, male menopause breaks up a lot of marriages."

Maggie wondered if Liz already knew her marriage had ended. Although Maggie had sworn their roommate to secrecy, she wasn't sure Claudia had always honored her promise. "I suppose Claudia told you."

"Nope. I haven't talked to Claudia in years. Not since she got married and moved to Vermont. We message on Facebook from time to time, but that's about it."

Then there was silence. After a gap of forty years, it was hard to know where to begin.

Liz's hand rested casually on the bottom of the steering wheel as she drove the big truck, navigating effortlessly along back roads that took them deeper and deeper into the woods. Maggie had no idea where they were going, which made her apprehensive until she realized she trusted Liz implicitly, or she never would have accepted her invitation.

"It's so dark up here at night," said Maggie, staring out the window.

"We have laws against light pollution. Up north, you can still see the milky way. Sometimes, you can even see the Northern Lights."

"Have you ever seen them?"

"No, but I'd like to someday."

"Me too."

Liz turned into a driveway almost hidden by the trees. The house was set so far back from the road that it couldn't be seen until you were practically on top of it. It wasn't a big house, but it was three stories tall. Wood was neatly stacked on the porch that ran along the front.

"Five steps up to the porch. One step into the house. I'm sure you can manage that."

"I'll try."

"Don't worry. I'll help you." Liz reached up to help her out of the truck. "Put your hands on my shoulders. Then slide down. Easy does it." Maggie liked the solid feel of Liz's shoulders. She followed the instructions and ended up in Liz's arms, which felt surprisingly good. Liz seemed to have no reaction, focused as she was on helping Maggie keep her balance. "You okay?" Her hands remained on Maggie's waist to steady her.

Maggie nodded. The warm hands moved away, but one returned to support her back as she tackled the stairs to the porch and the step into the house. The boot was awkward, but Maggie was adapting to the odd syncopation of the heel-toe gait.

As she entered the house, she took in the décor along the way. The living room was casually furnished in a style suited to a Maine resort town. There were hints of a North Woods camp motif—mounted antlers, an L.L. Bean Hudson's Bay point blanket thrown casually on a leather club chair. A wood stove stood in the corner. In a display cabinet and a special glass-top table were colorful rocks. *Minerals*, Maggie corrected herself, *not rocks*. Liz had been collecting them since she was a girl. Maggie still had the cluster of quartz crystals Liz had given her. It occupied a special place on Maggie's desk. When she had writer's block, she fondled it, testing its pointed edges, which always made her think of Liz with her razor-sharp intellect and quick tongue.

"Do you need the bathroom?" Liz asked.

"Yes, and it's torture getting out of this costume."

"This way." Liz opened the door to a large room with a queen-size bed covered with an old-fashioned quilt.

"A floral pattern? I never took you for a floral kind of girl," said Maggie, gratefully sinking down on the bed.

"Jenny bought it."

"Who's Jenny?"

"My ex."

Liz pointed to a door. "There's the bathroom. Do you need help getting out of that costume? It looks pretty tight. I could cut it off with bandage scissors."

"No, I don't think Tony would appreciate that. Can you help me get it off?"

"Sure." Liz rummaged in a chest of drawers. "I keep old clothes in here for surprise guests, mostly people who've imbibed too much and need to stay the night. Help yourself to anything you find." She threw an oversized Kennebunk Brewing Company T-shirt and a pair of men's gym shorts on the bed. "Okay for tonight?"

"Works for me."

"Tomorrow, I can run down to Webhanet to pick up your bags."

"How long do you expect me to stay?"

Liz shrugged. "I don't know. As long as you need to, I guess."

"Thank you." Maggie was moved to tears by the kindness of this woman, who didn't owe her a thing and had every reason not to be kind. The sudden rush of emotion surprised her. Maybe it was a side effect of the morphine.

Liz frowned as she studied the situation. Maggie knew she was making one of her famous plans. "First, we'll open the zipper, then take the top down to the waist. You stand and we'll pull it down as far as we can. Then we'll take off the boot and pull the damn thing off."

Liz's strategy worked perfectly. Soon Maggie was sitting on the bed, wearing only her flesh-colored body slimmer.

"I hate to ask, Liz, but I think I'll need help with this too."

Liz raised her lower lip and emitted a long sigh. "I never thought when I undressed you again, I'd be peeling you out of a body slimmer."

"Nothing you haven't seen before." Maggie reached into her crotch to unfasten the snaps. "I think it might be easier to get it off over my head."

"Like undressing a toddler. All right. Hands up!" Liz reached down to pull up the body slimmer. Her face, at the level of Maggie's breasts, was obviously turned away. "Ready? One, two, three!"

That part didn't go as planned, which Maggie had expected. Putting on the body slimmer had been a torturous process of stretching, wiggling, and tugging. After another attempt, Liz sighed in frustration. "Let me cut it off. I'll buy you another one. I promise." She didn't wait for an answer before leaving to get the scissors. A few minutes later, she freed Maggie from the tight suit, cutting it down the back as if it were sausage casing. "In the emergency room, we often have to cut off people's clothes to get to trauma." She turned her back while Maggie shrugged on the old T-shirt and pulled on the running shorts.

"I'm covered up now. You're so funny, Liz."

"I didn't want you to think I was staring at you while you were naked."

"Believe me. It's not that exciting. My figure's not what it used to be."

"Whose is...especially at our age?" Liz patted her belly. "We have amazing craft beers up here."

Maggie realized she was only calling attention to her own imperfections to make her feel better. "A big improvement over that anorexic kid I used to know."

"I wasn't anorexic, just really thin," said Liz, making it clear the technical difference was important to her. "I'm going to make myself some chamomile tea. Would you like some?"

"Chamomile tea sounds wonderful."

Liz's quick, slightly off-center grin reminded Maggie so much of young Liz that her heart lurched a little. Yes, young Liz was still in there. Somewhere beneath the iron-gray hair, the fine wrinkles, and those beautiful breasts, was the skinny girl she remembered. Maggie had to admit the breasts were a nice improvement. She gave them another admiring look.

"You can sit in the living room and put your leg up while I get the tea ready," said Liz. "Elevation is important or that leg will swell even more."

Liz took her arm as she directed her to the living room. Maggie liked the reassuring feel of her hands easing her down on the leather sofa and carefully lifting the broken leg to rest on the hassock.

"Are you cold? I can make a fire."

Maggie shook her head, but Liz brought over the Hudson's Bay blanket and laid it beside her. "Just in case… It can get pretty chilly up here at night. I'll get you some ice for the leg."

She left. In a moment, Maggie heard the rumble of an ice maker. Liz returned with a Ziplock bag of ice cubes. "I have one of those reusable gel packs around, but the hell if I can find it." She unfastened the Velcro straps of the boot and eased it off. She draped a towel over the injury, followed by the ice bag. "You can have the boot off as long as you don't put weight on that leg. Tonight, I'll put on a pneumatic cast. You'll have to wear that at night for a couple of weeks. Do you sleep through the night or do you usually get up to urinate?" Maggie would have said "pee," but of course, Liz would use the correct medical terms.

"I'm a sixty-year-old woman. What do you think?"

"Annoying as hell, isn't it? I'll leave you a pair of crutches. Do you know how to use them?"

"Yes, I learned how for a play," Maggie said proudly.

"Using them for real is a little different." Liz glanced toward the kitchen. "The water must be hot by now. Be right back."

While Liz was preparing the tea, Maggie took the opportunity to look around. The prints on the walls, graphic pen-and-ink drawings of old barns, although stark, were somehow soothing. The leather furniture was comfortable and probably expensive. Wood was neatly stacked in a cast-iron ring by the wood stove. There was a hammered brass bucket of kindling beside it. Everything was tidy and devoid of clutter. It was exactly the kind of décor she would expect Liz to choose.

"You have a very minimalist style of decorating," she called to Liz in the kitchen. "Almost monastic."

"I like to keep things simple." Liz came in carrying a tray with a pottery teapot and two matching mugs. "You don't approve?"

"I didn't say that. In fact, it suits you perfectly."

"Jenny tried to pretty up the place. She likes the country look, the floral quilts, lace curtains. Pigs on sticks." Liz mocked a shudder. "Not my style."

Maggie tried to sound less curious than she felt. "So, you live alone?"

"Yes. And you?"

"I've been seeing someone."

"A man, of course," said Liz without a hint of judgment.

The neutrality of the response made it easier for Maggie to say, "Yes."

Liz sprang up from her seat. "I need to get you some ibuprofen. After the morphine wears off, you'll really need it." She left and returned with the pills and a glass of water. "You're sure you don't have cardiovascular disease or stomach problems?" Liz asked, holding back the brown pharmacy bottle. "I didn't hear anything unusual when I listened to your heart."

"As I said, I'm pretty healthy."

"That's good." Liz shook two pills into Maggie's hand. "If you get up during the night, take another one. It's easier to prevent the pain than to treat it once it gets started."

"You make a very good nurse." Maggie instantly regretted saying it. Being a doctor, Liz might not take it as a compliment.

"Doctors make terrible nurses. Nurses pay attention to details much better than we do."

Maggie leaned forward and took Liz's hand. "Liz, I want you to know I'm sorry, really, really sorry about what happened."

Liz withdrew her hand. "It's late, and you've had trauma. Let's hold off on any big conversations. All right?"

"But it's hard to accept your generous hospitality without at least an apology."

"Later, Maggie," said Liz shaking her head. "Don't spoil it."

Chapter 3

Liz went to the basement to look for the shower chair her mother used during her visits. Time would be short in the morning, and she wanted to make sure Maggie was all set up before they went to bed. She passed the bookcase filled with old books deemed unworthy of a place in her office upstairs. Among them was a row of maroon college yearbooks. She pulled out the volume from sophomore year, quickly searched the index, and found Maggie's name among the Fs. She flipped to the page.

The photographer had caught Maggie slouching on a bench near the library, smiling fully as she looked up from her book. Her blond hair looked white in the photograph as it nearly was in life, a platinum color produced by a monthly ritual of bottles and vinyl gloves. The natural color of Maggie's hair was dark honey. At one point, Liz was so besotted, she'd even agreed to participate in the monthly ritual of touching up the roots.

Maggie's eyebrows were a bit wild, an untamed look that was between fashions at the time. Her eyes were hazel, actually quite pale, but they could be dark, stormy, or petulant, depending on her mood. She had a small, upturned nose. Her lips just covered the slightest overbite, but her most distinctive feature was a small, square chin with a cleft that Liz loved to test with her finger. In this photograph and in life, Maggie was almost deathly pale. Felicia, their roommate from Puerto Rico, once quipped, "She makes the white walls look colorful."

Liz turned a few pages to the next photo. Here, Maggie was standing, another candid, this time outside the dormitory. The shot unfortunately emphasized her wide hips and narrow shoulders. Another photo showed Maggie at nineteen, the star of the campus theater company with a major role in every production. That was how Liz remembered Maggie as her brain began churning up memories—illuminated by a spotlight in the perpetual night that is a darkened theater.

Liz stared at the photo. This woman had broken her heart. She had been her first love, the first heart-stinging love of youth. Now, she was sitting in her living room.

With a sigh, Liz returned the book to its place on the shelf and resumed her search for the shower bench. She found it exactly where she had left it, carefully wrapped in plastic, on the shelf in the back room. Liz sprayed it with antiseptic and vigorously scrubbed it in the laundry sink. She'd been trying to moderate her surgeon's compulsion for cleanliness, especially during the harsh Maine winters when the constant washing left her hands chapped. She maintained the hygiene regimen in the office, but in real life, she was trying to learn to tolerate a little dirt.

"I thought you'd left me," said Maggie when Liz returned.

It was on the tip of Liz's tongue to say, "No, I don't do that. You do," but she caught herself just in time. Their unexpected reunion was going well. *Don't spoil it*, Liz told herself, echoing the advice she'd given Maggie only a few minutes ago.

"I brought up the shower chair for you, and I adjusted the hand shower on the bar, so you can reach it."

"Thank you. You're so kind." Maggie reached out her hand. "Sit next to me."

Liz shook her head. "Our tea must be steeped by now. Let me pour it." She filled two cups from the pot and handed one to Maggie. Then she took a seat in the club chair. "I like to see people's faces when I talk to them," she explained unnecessarily.

Maggie took a sip of tea and smiled. "I love chamomile tea."

"I remember."

"I haven't had it in years. Why have I been depriving myself?"

"I don't know. Only you know the answer to that."

Maggie set down her cup. Her little frown indicated she'd perceived the double meaning. "I thought about you many times over the years. I thought about reaching out, but then…"

Liz nodded. "I found you on the NYU faculty page and your Facebook page. I sent you a friend request. When you didn't respond after a couple of days, I deleted it."

"I saw it. I debated whether to respond. When I finally decided, it was gone."

"Don't tell me what you decided. I don't want to know." Liz blew on her tea to cool it.

"I didn't know where to begin. It had been so long since we talked. When Claudia and I were still close, she kept me up to date. I knew when you were accepted into medical school, when you took the residency at Yale, when your father died…. I was sorry to hear that by the way."

"Thank you." Liz said it because it was expected, but her father had been dead for nearly thirty years, and it felt strange to accept condolences so long after the fact.

"Both my parents passed. Dad's heart gave out. Mom didn't know what to do without him. The breast cancer came back." Maggie looked pained.

"Unfortunately, it often does."

"That was your specialty, wasn't it? Breast surgery?"

"I'm a general surgeon, but yes, I did a lot of breast work. Jenny got me into it after reading Susan Love's *Breast Book*. She said, 'You know, you could do something for those women besides lopping off their breasts like you were pruning roses.'"

Maggie smiled fondly. "You haven't changed a bit. Still trying to change the world. Still rescuing damsels in distress."

"I don't rescue damsels anymore," said Liz, shaking her head.

"What do you call inviting me into your home?"

Liz raised her shoulders. "Being practical?"

"Of course, but thank you for rescuing me, even if it wasn't your intention." Her relaxed smile told Liz that Maggie's theatricality was easing. When she was anxious, she retreated into her art.

"I need to start reading my mail from the Playhouse," said Liz. "I had no idea you were starring in a production this season."

"I had no idea you'd moved to Maine."

"As I said, I always thought we might bump into one another at Yale New Haven."

"Oh, I was there often enough."

"You were? Why?"

"Fertility treatments."

"Claudia mentioned you were having trouble getting pregnant."

Maggie sighed. "I suppose Claudia told you everything."

"No, she said very little. If you recall, you told her not to."

Maggie gave her a hard look. "Liz, I had to cut you off after you tricked my brother into giving you my number. It felt like you were stalking me."

"Stalking you?" Liz took a deep breath, then burst into laughter.

Maggie looked profoundly indignant. "Well, it did!"

Liz finally stopped laughing and assumed a serious expression. "I'm sorry my persistence seemed so threatening. I just wanted to talk to you."

"You don't understand. My parents insisted I stay away from you, or they wouldn't pay my tuition. My education was very important to me."

"That part, I do understand. When I came out, my parents disowned me. When I was in medical school, it was tough for me financially. It took years to pay off the debt."

"But you had the courage of your convictions." Maggie gazed at her thoughtfully. Her indignation had passed and her expression had softened. "It was very hard to leave you. You have no idea how hard. My feelings for you were very strong. They were putting all my plans for my life in jeopardy. I had to turn you into some kind of psycho to justify keeping you away." Maggie stared at the floor. "My parents wouldn't let me speak to you again. Barry made it a condition of our marriage."

Liz studied Maggie's face for a long time before she said, "But you went along with it."

Maggie still wouldn't look at her. She nodded.

"Thanks for finally being honest." Liz drained her cup and put it on the tray. "Finish your tea and let's go to bed. You've suffered trauma, and I have to work tomorrow."

"You work on Saturdays?"

"All family docs have weekend hours. We treat people who can't afford to take time off from work. The good news is I have Monday off. I can show you around Hobbs, if you feel up to it."

"You expect me to still be here on Monday?"

Liz shrugged. "Are you in a big hurry to go somewhere?"

"No, but I don't want to overstay my welcome."

"You just got here." Liz rose to move the tray with the tea cups out of the way, so Maggie could get up from the sofa. "Come on, old girl. Time for bed."

"Thanks for reminding me about my age," grumbled Maggie as she struggled to get up. Liz helped her to her feet and handed her the neon green cane.

When they reached the guest room, Maggie gratefully plopped down on the bed. "Can you show me how to take this thing off?"

"You need to learn to do it yourself. Just open the Velcro straps and pull out the front piece." Maggie carefully followed the instructions.

When Liz pulled off the cotton sock, Maggie visibly winced at the sight of the swelling and the developing bruises.

"On a scale of one to ten, how bad is the pain?" asked Liz.

"Six, but I can live with it."

Liz nodded. "The morphine is wearing off, but the ibuprofen should kick in soon." She slipped the plastic air cast over the foot and inflated it with a little hand pump. "How's that? Too tight?"

"It's tight," said Maggie through gritted teeth.

Liz let out some air. "I want it a little tight," she explained, "to keep down the swelling but not so tight that it cuts off the circulation to your toes. Lie down and relax. I'll check the color of your toes in a minute."

Maggie pulled herself up on the bed. "Comfy bed."

"Only the best for my guests. Do you think you can sleep? Or do you need a sedative?"

"Don't you remember? I sleep like the dead. No, I'm sure I'll go right out once you turn out the lights."

Liz leaned over and checked her toes. "The pressure is good. Your little piggies are all healthy and pink. Do you need to use the bathroom before I go up to bed?"

"Oh, Liz. That, I can manage!"

"Just in case, I'll hang around until you get back." Liz rose to get the crutches. "I left a pack of make-up remover pads on the counter. I'm sure you'll want to get rid of that stage make up."

"You think of everything."

"I have a lot of guests."

Maggie maneuvered the crutches under her arm pits. "My lens case and glasses are in my bag."

"I'll get it."

When Maggie emerged from the bathroom. Liz couldn't hide her reaction fast enough.

Maggie nodded an acknowledgement. "Yes, I look faded without makeup…and old."

"So do I," Liz instantly replied.

Maggie smiled sadly. "But you're not wearing any make up. And you have a beautiful tan."

"And I am two years younger."

"Don't rub it in." Maggie hobbled toward the bed.

Liz took the crutches from her and balanced them against the wall, positioning them carefully within Maggie's reach. She picked up Maggie's cellphone from the bed stand. "I'm putting my number in your contacts. If you need anything during the night, just call me. I always sleep with my phone next to the bed." Liz pulled up the covers. "All good?"

"Just one thing, but you need to come closer."

Liz put her hands on her knees and leaned down.

"Closer," said Maggie, beckoning with her finger. Maggie placed her hands on Liz's cheeks and squeezed gently. "Thank you so much for your kindness." She pulled Liz's face closer and kissed her forehead. "And thank you for your warm welcome. I don't deserve it, but I really appreciate it."

"You're welcome." Liz stood straight. "Don't forget to use the crutches to get to the bathroom."

Maggie rolled her eyes.

"I mean it. It's easy to forget during the night when you're half asleep."

"Good night, Liz."

Liz went back to the kitchen to wash out the teapot and cups. She switched on the light above the stove. When there were guests in the house, she always left it on, so they could find their way around.

After Liz trudged up the two flights of stairs, she remembered she could have taken the elevator. She seldom used it because it seemed lazy. The architect had insisted she add it to the design, so she could "age in place." When she'd renovated the house, that had seemed so far off, but now that she'd seen Maggie again, she realized the years had blasted by while she wasn't looking.

Liz sighed as she climbed into bed. She was so bone-weary she expected to go right to sleep, but she couldn't, knowing Maggie was just downstairs. The fact that she hadn't recognized Maggie disturbed her. Of course, Maggie had changed but not that much. Maybe it had been the distraction of the injury or the tantalizing possibility of reducing a fracture, a procedure Liz hadn't done in years. As a surgeon, it was so easy for her to get caught up in a challenge and forget the patient, although she thought she'd cured herself of that when she'd gone into general practice.

She needed to get some sleep. The alarm would go off early, and she couldn't be late to open the office. She rolled over and closed her eyes. The quick view of Maggie's breasts came to mind. Her physician's eyes were like a camera that took incredibly detailed photographs. Her fingers had a memory of their own. She recalled the feel of Maggie's bare skin when she'd helped her out of the body slimmer—warm and a little sticky with perspiration.

Once, she had loved that body and known every inch of it—the little mole on the inside of Maggie's thigh and her genitals, as pale and compact as the pink rose buds they'd exchanged when they'd said goodbye on that summer day so long ago. Liz forbade her mind from imagining more details of Maggie's body. Otherwise, it would be too hard to face her in the morning.

After forty years, how could she still want this woman so much?

Other memories wafted into Liz's mind. She remembered the smell of freshly cut grass. Liz had paused her mowing to check the mailbox. While they'd been apart, Maggie had written every day, but for almost a week, there had been no mail. At the back of the box was a small envelope, instantly recognizable as Maggie's pale blue stationery. As Liz ripped it open, she had no way of knowing it would be Maggie's last letter. It explained that she had decided not to return to New York. The reasons were designed to appeal to Liz's practicality. Living at home would allow Maggie to save money. Her father had gotten her a part time job to help pay her tuition, which was lower at the small, local college. How could Liz argue with that? But she did. She had argued and pleaded and begged. The toll calls to Syracuse were expensive. Her telephone bills consumed all of her allowance.

Finally, Maggie told her not to call again.

The room seemed stifling after that recollection. Liz got up to open the sliding door to the deck. A barred owl hooted softly in the distance. Another owl replied. Then a third. It became a chorus. Combined with the gentle whoosh of the wind in the pine trees, it made a perfect lullaby. She wondered if, downstairs, Maggie was listening too.

Chapter 4

The soft knocking at the door roused Maggie from a sound sleep. She almost jumped out of bed, but the drugs had worn off, and the pain in her ankle sharply reasserted itself. She wasn't going anywhere without crutches.

"Come in," she called.

Looking much too cheerful for that hour, Liz popped into the room and laid something on the foot of the bed. "It's a little chilly this morning. Here are some workout pants and a heavy sweatshirt."

Maggie pulled herself into a sitting position, which only reminded her how much she needed to pee. She'd lacked the confidence with the crutches to negotiate her way to the bathroom during the night.

"How's the leg? Mind if I take a look?" Without waiting for permission, Liz flipped up the blanket and gave Maggie's toes a brief inspection. She deftly deflated the air cast with one hand. "I did show you how to let the air out? Squeeze this little valve. It vents the air."

"Liz…"

"What?" Liz looked slightly annoyed that her demonstration had been interrupted.

"Good morning."

"Oh, right. Good morning," she said, looking chastened. "Sorry. I've been living alone too long. I forget the social amenities sometimes."

"Social amenities are important." Maggie put on her glasses so she could see and gave Liz a quick once-over. "It's cold in here, and you're standing there in shorts."

"I'm a Mainer now. I'm used to it." Liz unzipped the sweatshirt. Maggie thrust her arms into it, grateful for the warmth. "Your leg doesn't look bad. How does it feel?"

Maggie glanced down at her ankle. It was swollen to twice its size and had bloomed like an angry orchid into multiple shades of purple and magenta. "It feels like it looks. Terrible."

"It's natural for a broken limb to swell," Liz explained. "It's nature's way of splinting a fracture."

"Thanks, Doctor, but can I get up and pee before the lecture?"

"Of course." Liz brought the boot to the bedside but made no attempt to help her. "Go on. You need to figure this out for yourself."

Maggie put on the boot correctly, but Liz pulled the Velcro tighter.

"I want to show you how the coffee maker works and a few other things before I go."

"What time is it?" Maggie asked.

Liz turned the bedside clock. "Six thirty-five."

"It's criminal that you're so cheerful at this hour."

"I would have let you sleep longer, but you don't know where anything is. I want you to be comfortable here while I'm gone."

Liz helped her to her feet. As Maggie hobbled into the bathroom, she realized how much she liked feeling Liz's touch.

The bathroom was equipped with bars for the handicapped, and Maggie gratefully used them to lower herself onto the toilet. What a relief to pee! She raised her arm and gave her armpit a tentative sniff. She could use a shower. This version of *Mama Mia* was choreographed to be very active, and all the anxiety about the injury hadn't helped. She'd wait to shower because Liz seemed to be in such a hurry.

Maggie found her way into the kitchen, an enormous open room with gleaming appliances, granite counter tops and cabinets made of gorgeous wood. Liz gestured to a stool at the island. "Or you could sit in the breakfast room and look at the garden."

"No, here's fine." Maggie was pleased to have gotten that far in the ridiculous boot. She hiked herself up onto the stool.

Liz demonstrated how to fill the little plastic pod with coffee and brew a cup. She filled another pod, evidently to reinforce the lesson. "I love the convenience of a single-serve coffee maker but hate the plastic waste." The coffee gurgled through the pin hole into a pottery cup decorated with a moose. "Up here, we separate our trash into three categories. Four, including compost."

Liz slid a pad from a Habitat for Humanity appeal in Maggie's direction. "I wrote down some information for you." Maggie glanced at the pad. Each item had been carefully labeled: WiFi password, Hobbs Family Practice office number, the front desk at The Windward Inn. Liz pointed to the last number. "Tell Lorna, I'll pick up your clothes around twelve thirty, unless I get stuck with a patient or run into traffic. This is one of the busiest weekends of the summer."

She gestured toward a counter near the refrigerator, where a toaster and breakfast items had been set out: old-fashioned bulk butter, strawberries and blueberries, jam, English muffins. "The hard-boiled eggs in the fridge are fresh. I made them this morning. There's yogurt and cheese. Help yourself to anything you find."

"You're going already? Can't you have a cup of coffee with me?"

"Sorry, but I have to open the office this morning."

Maggie scrutinized Liz, who was wearing khaki Bermuda shorts made of some high-performance fabric, a violet polo shirt, and hiking sandals, but at least today, she had on some makeup. "You're wearing that to the office?"

"Why not?" Liz glanced down at her clothes.

Maggie tried to moderate her look of disapproval. "It's not very professional. When I first saw you, I couldn't believe you were a doctor."

Liz looked surprised. Then she laughed. "Maggie, you're in Vacationland. No one thinks twice about what I wear. And if they do, I don't give a flying fuck." Liz glanced at the breakfast things on the counter. "There's more coffee in the cabinet over the coffee maker. Anything else you think you might need?"

"No, I'm fine. Really. Thank you."

"Oh, and there's a landline phone in the hall. All the short dials are listed there too, including my cell."

"Liz, go! I can manage." Maggie gave her a quick kiss on the cheek and a little shove.

After Liz left, Maggie brewed more coffee. She knew she would need more than two cups. The morphine and ibuprofen had left her groggy, and her rhythm had been upset by working in theater again with its late nights and dinner after the show. She found the coffee—some locally roasted blend with a blue lobster on the bag—and sat listening to the high-end coffee maker gurgle and spit dark, aromatic liquid into the moose cup while she assessed her situation.

She realized she was now the prisoner of the woman whose heart she had broken forty years ago. How was that for irony? Maggie compressed her lips. Yes, it was strange justice. Yet, how lucky she was to have fallen under the care of the head doctor at Hobbs Family Practice. Another GP might never dared to set the bone in the office. Nowadays, specialists did everything, but Liz had always been a cowboy. As far as she was concerned, rules were made to be broken.

Maggie remembered sitting behind her friend on her candy-apple red Triumph, terrified as Liz tried to outrun the policeman who'd caught her riding a motorcycle without a helmet. That was illegal in New York, even in those days. Liz drove the bike into a field and left the officer yelling and gesticulating at the side of the road. When they were out of sight, they got off the bike and laughed until they fell into the high grass, where they made love. Maggie still remembered the sweet smell of the grass and the feel of Liz's gentle fingers inside her.

Bad Liz was young Elizabeth Stolz's secret identity. Otherwise, she was the sort of daughter who would make any parent proud—a whiz kid who'd skipped two grades before high school, volunteer paramedic, Phi Beta Kappa, double-major pre-med student, who was always on the dean's list. In her scarce free time, Liz tutored poor kids in math and science.

But Liz had a rebellious streak. It was in fashion then, along with student sit-ins and war protests. Liz never wore dresses or skirts, only fraying bell-bottoms and T-shirts with anarchistic messages. The motorcycle boots had really frightened Maggie's mother. "Stay away from that girl," she'd cautioned. "There's something strange about her."

Maggie had tried to keep their long-ago romance lost in the past, written off as a youthful mistake, like some women write off abortions or failed early marriages, but Liz was a secret that refused to be kept. Maggie had been foolish enough to tell Barry about Liz the same day she'd told her mother. Barry was her confidante that summer when she'd felt so alone, terrified of the desire that threatened her carefully planned life.

Barry was sympathetic. He held her against his hard-muscled, football player's body and reassured her. She begged him, after three years of denying him, to take her virginity. She needed him inside her, so that she could be absolutely certain that she was "normal." After it was done, she bled a little, as a virgin should. He beamed at her from those proud, blue eyes. He had made her his, and now, her stake in the American dream was secure.

After they were married, whenever Maggie turned away from him in bed, she wondered if he thought Liz was the reason. The anxiety made Maggie receptive even when she felt no desire. In the end, she hated him and hated herself for the trap she had set, a trap ready to snap shut at any moment.

No, she had never completely escaped that time with Liz or forgotten the possibilities it raised. The thought of Liz returned whenever she refused Barry, and that look of veiled concern crossed his face. Or when Claudia inadvertently dropped information about their mutual friend, then bit her lip like a guilty child for failing to censor herself. The irony and injustice stung Maggie. The more she tried to forget and live the virtuous life of a model wife, the more she thought of that too brief, wonderful year with Liz Stolz.

If only a child had come. Maybe then, the sacrifice would have been worthwhile. God knows, they had tried. Their bed stand was always littered with fertility charts and thermometers. Poor Barry. She had used his body like a stud animal, climbing on his penis with only one purpose in mind. After years of trying, she'd turned from him. He had given her everything else that she had been brought up to expect—a center-hall Colonial in an upscale suburb, financial security, and membership in the country club, but he could not give her a child.

Whose fault was it? That had never been determined absolutely, but Maggie was sure that she was to blame. She was, in that horrible Biblical expression, *barren*. No matter how hard she tried, nothing would grow in her.

Maggie shook off the thought as she got up to get cream for her coffee. Opening the refrigerator, she was surprised to see how well stocked it was—full of vegetables in special reusable bags, fruit, expensive Scandinavian yogurt, cheeses wrapped in paper, and healthy snacks like hummus. She noticed a pork tenderloin. If she felt up to it later, she'd cook Liz a nice dinner to thank her for her kindness.

That brought back memories of the communal dorm meals they'd shared in college. The student apartment in the newly-constructed dorm off campus was spacious and modern. It had a full, state-of-the-art kitchen, complete with "Harvest Gold" appliances. The four roommates pooled their food money and made weekly runs to the grocery store in the old station wagon Liz's father had given her so she wouldn't be stranded on campus. There was a local grocery store, but the suburban supermarket only a few miles away had much better prices.

Maggie was the budding gourmet cook. Felicia, their Puerto Rican roommate, prepared exotic Caribbean dishes. When their turns came, Liz and Claudia cooked more pedestrian fare, edible but uninspired. They had less time for culinary pursuits because they were always busy studying. Claudia was a physics major concentrating on particle theory. Liz was always solving chemistry and physics problems and reading strange things like Hegel's *Phenomenology of Mind* for her second major. What an odd, intriguing girl she was in those days. So serious.

Although Maggie usually wasn't hungry until much later in the morning, she had missed dinner the night before and was suddenly ravenous. She ate a hard-boiled egg and some berries with yogurt. She avoided bread if she could, trying to hold on to what figure she had left, especially now that she'd returned to acting. After finishing her minimalist breakfast, Maggie put the perishables in the refrigerator. She listened to its hum in the enormous kitchen while she figured out what to do.

The break was in her right leg, so the rental car, parked in the lot be-hind the Playhouse, would be useless. Later, she'd call Tony to have some-one return it. She'd wait a bit to call him. Most theater folk were night owls and would still be asleep at that hour. She'd need to call her agent, of course, to let him know that she couldn't continue in the production. Her contract still had three weeks to go, including Labor Day weekend. Fortunately, it had an exit clause for unforeseen calamities. Breaking a leg would certainly qualify.

Maggie rinsed the breakfast dishes and loaded them into the dishwash-er. After that, she had no idea what to do. She couldn't check her messages or email. Her charger was back at the Windward, and her phone was pretty much dead. She fetched the cane from her room and set out to explore.

She discovered Liz's office first. It was a large room with a sleek desk and a leather executive chair that looked like it belonged in a modern hospital. Maggie studied the plaques and photos that covered the walls. There was Liz in an elegant evening dress, posing as she received an award. Another showed her in her professional garb, a tailored power suit. Carefully groomed and coifed, she stood in the center of a large group. Liz was tall enough to dominate the photo, but it was more than her height. She had a sure look of authority and confidence in her eyes that clearly announced she was in charge. The caption read: "2007 Department of Surgery."

During her visits to the hospital for fertility treatments, Maggie had often been tempted to ask for Dr. Stolz, but she'd always stifled the tempta-tion because she'd promised Barry she'd never speak to her again. Then, she saw a tall woman with short, chestnut-brown hair exit the elevator while she was going in and wondered if that could be Liz. She wanted to run after her, but it had been so quick. The elevator door closed, cutting off the view of the departing figure.

Afterwards, she wondered what she would have said to Liz. *I'm sorry? I never meant to hurt you? I had to cut you off because I could no longer bear to hear the pain in your voice?* Yes. She would have said all that and more. Now, she would also say, *I've never loved anyone the way I loved you.* Maybe she'd have the opportunity to say those words, if only she could get her to listen. Liz seemed so determined to put the past behind her.

On the top of a file cabinet, Maggie found a scrapbook full of newspaper clippings announcing even more awards and professional events. They stopped around the mid-90s, probably stored digitally after that. As Maggie flipped the pages, she concluded that Liz must have been quite a professional powerhouse, someone Maggie would have been proud to show off to her Connecticut neighbors.

There was a laptop on the desk, but it was password protected, and there was no guest account. Maggie carefully lowered the lid. She noisily made her way down the hall, where she found a large room dominated by an enormous TV mounted on the wall. There was a carefully placed sound system with high-end speakers. She remembered that Liz liked action movies and classical music played as loudly as in a concert hall. Maggie explored the collection of CDs. Being an audiophile, Liz would have CDs, of course, but there were also vinyl records and a turntable. The remaining walls were lined with floor-to-ceiling bookcases crammed with books.

Maggie noticed a Martin acoustical guitar standing in the corner. Maggie strummed it. It was out of tune. She wondered if Liz ever played it now. In college, she had played very well. Maggie tuned it and played a few chords. It had a nice, warm tone conducive to the music Maggie liked to sing, mostly folk and Broadway.

As Maggie continued her exploration of the first floor, she was surprised to find a small elevator at the end of the hall. She toyed with the idea of going upstairs and looking around. No, that would be an invasion of her hostess' privacy. *Let her invite me…if she wants me to see.*

Instead, she went back to the media room, found the remote, and after a few false starts, figured out how to turn on the giant television. She found a cable news program and stretched out on the sofa to listen. The leather was cold against her skin, so she pulled up the Hudson's Bay blanket.

Chapter 5

Liz walked her last patient to the front desk and leaned over the counter to speak confidentially. "Ginny, can you close up today? I have an errand to run in Webhanet."

"Sure, Liz. Right behind you." Ginny inserted Mrs. Landon's credit card in the machine. When the payment had processed, she handed it back with a genuinely warm smile. "Thank you, Mrs. Landon. Have a nice weekend."

Ginny kept the practice running like a well-oiled machine. She argued with the insurance companies on behalf of their patients. She banished the pharmaceutical reps trying to peddle their wares despite the sign on the door that banned them. Most of all, she made sure Liz stayed on schedule and got her paperwork done.

"You're the best," called Liz over her shoulder as she headed down the hall to her office.

Liz unlocked her office closet and grabbed her bag off the shelf. The distressed buffalo-leather shoulder bag was one of Heat Packing Mama's latest offerings. It was heavy for its size because there was a 9 mm pistol in a hidden compartment.

Liz had never considered carrying a gun until some yahoo in a pickup truck flying a Confederate flag had followed her right to the door of the supermarket. It wasn't as if she'd flipped him the bird or said anything to provoke him. Waiting in the left turn lane for the light to change, she'd glanced over at him with a frown. Evidently, looks of disapproval were now considered insults.

The experience was enough to scare her into buying a pistol. She did it by the book like everything she did, signing up for the gun safety class and applying for a permit, even though it was no longer required. Now, she was a certified safety instructor herself. Liz never did anything halfway. Some of her friends, especially the women, were horrified when she told them she carried a gun, so she'd stopped telling them. To those who continued to lecture her, she made excuses about being alone in an office where they kept controlled substances.

As Liz pulled into southbound traffic, she despaired of ever getting to the Windward by one o'clock. Lorna had left a message that she needed to leave by then to do a store run for breakfast items. Liz cut over on 9B to Route 9 in the hope of making better time. It was the long way, but in mid-day, bumper-to-bumper traffic, it was the fastest, if not the shortest, route.

She just missed Lorna, but the front desk clerk, one of the many "guest workers" who did much of Webhanet's seasonal work, unlocked the closet where Maggie's bags were stored. "Mrs. Grayson hopes that she packed everything," the young woman said in heavily accented but grammatically correct English. "There were things everywhere. Do you wish to check the room to see if anything remains?"

Liz shook her head. She wasn't surprised to hear Maggie had left a mess. Apparently, that aspect of Maggie's personality hadn't changed. Liz remembered the layers of clothing that accumulated on every surface of their dorm room. Maggie slept under the pile of clothes on the bed. Yet she always looked perfectly put together and unwrinkled when she went out on a date with one of her many male admirers.

Liz handed the clerk two twenty-dollar bills. "Please give this to Mrs. Grayson for her trouble." The clerk carefully put the money into an envelope under the cash register tray while Liz watched. Liz fished a ten out of her wallet and gave it to the young woman. "Thanks for your help."

There were two large suitcases, a duffle bag, and a smaller bag that was surprisingly heavy. "What the hell!" Liz exclaimed as she slung the strap of the small bag over her shoulder. She remembered from vacations with Maggie, that she never traveled light, whereas Liz could spend two weeks in Europe and live out of a carry-on.

There wasn't a cloud in the sky, so Liz opened the tailgate and tossed the luggage into the back of the pickup. The traffic on Route 1 looked a little better now, so she decided to chance it with the idea of picking up some chowder along the way. She debated whether it should come from the Webhanet Deli or Shelly's Clam Shack. The Deli sold the creamy, thick soup that tourists called chowder. Shelly's offered the real thing—thinner and milky, but chock full of diced potatoes and coarsely chopped quahogs. There was a long line at the window at Shelly's. Although Liz was impatient to get home, she waited because she wanted Maggie to have the authentic experience. Even though she'd had a lobster roll just the night before, she ordered two chowder and lobster roll specials.

***

"Where have you been?" asked Maggie, looking anxious when Liz came through the door at nearly two o'clock.

"Traffic," explained Liz, bringing their lunch into the kitchen. "Let's eat. Then I'll bring in your luggage."

Maggie made a little face.

"What's the matter?"

"There are things in my bags that probably shouldn't sit out in the sun."

"Oh, for fuck's sake." Liz grimaced.

"Liz, please don't swear. I don't like it."

Liz stared at her. "You're kidding."

"No."

"Well, shit." Liz turned around to get Maggie's bags. She brought in the big suitcases first, then the smaller bags. Liz dropped the bags in the hall outside Maggie's door. "What's in this one? Rocks?"

"Makeup," replied Maggie in a matter-of-fact tone.

"Figures." Liz rolled her eyes. "Come on, let's eat before our chowder gets cold. Or chowdah, as we say up here."

Maggie followed her into the kitchen. "Forget it, Liz. You'll never be a Mainer. Even I can do a better Maine accent."

"You're an actress, so that doesn't surprise me. But can you say, 'Heayuh's the beeyah?'"

"What does that mean?" Maggie looked puzzled.

"'Here's the beer.'" Liz opened the refrigerator. "Want one?"

"No, thanks. I'm not a beer fan."

"More for me." Liz snatched a beer off the door of the refrigerator and grabbed the bag from Shelly's. "Come on. We'll eat out on the screen porch."

Liz enjoyed Maggie's look of wonder at her first sight of the cottage garden behind the house. In mid-August, it was in full bloom. The old-fashioned hollyhocks, bee balm, coreopsis, cone flowers, and butterfly bush created a riot of color. The plants in the raised beds were heavy with tomatoes, peppers, and eggplants. There was also a densely planted herb plot.

"Do you have a gardener?"

"No. That is, none except me. A landscaper built it, but I keep it going."

Liz distributed the sandwiches and handed Maggie a plastic spoon. She hated reusable plastic utensils, but they kept giving them out, so she figured she might as well make use of them. She flipped the lid off her chowder container and dug into it.

"I see you found the elevator," Liz said between mouthfuls.

Maggie looked up quickly. "How did you know?"

Liz tapped her phone to launch the security video of Maggie staring curiously at the elevator door. A ghostly, gray image of her face came close to the camera, then moved away.

"But I didn't go upstairs," Maggie quickly explained.

"Yes, I know. If you'd tried, it would have set off the alarm." Liz showed Maggie a fob on her key chain. "This sets the security system automatically when it leaves the perimeter. I doubt you'd enjoy having six Hobbs police cars in the driveway and an officer pounding on the door."

Maggie stared at the key fob. "I admit I was tempted, but I decided you're entitled to your privacy."

"That's nice of you." Liz shrugged. "I don't care if you go upstairs. I have nothing to hide. No Gretchen doll under the bed. However, there might be a dildo or two in the night stand." Maggie's eyes widened, which made Liz laugh. "Come on, Maggie. Don't give me that shocked look."

"I'm just not used to you like this. The Liz I remember was so quiet and shy."

"That was a long time ago. You don't succeed as a surgeon by being shy." Liz took a break from the chowder and turned her attention to her lobster roll. "What else did you find in your exploration of my house?"

"I was in your office looking for a computer to get on the internet," Maggie admitted. "I saw all those awards."

"If you think that's something, you should see what's in the closet. I was going to throw out that crap when I moved, but my mother said she would kill me. Jenny said she would kill me. I prefer being alive so…. It was Jenny who hung up the stuff in my office."

"You were still together?"

Liz shook her head. "No. She was just visiting. Although I think she was surveying the scene to see if she wanted to join me up here."

"*Did* she want to join you?" asked Maggie, focusing on her chowder. Her tone only sounded casual. Liz could tell she was very curious.

"For about five minutes, yes, but she wasn't ready to make such a big move. A shame. We could really use an OB/GYN of her caliber up here."

"Do you miss her?"

Liz chewed her lobster roll while she formulated a response. "Sometimes. I miss the conversation at dinner…someone to talk with about medicine." She drained the rest of her chowder by drinking the last drops straight from the paper cup. "Pardon my manners or lack of them. Living alone will do that to you."

"Maybe you need someone to civilize you."

Liz gave her a warning look. "Don't get any ideas."

Maggie shifted in her chair like an artist trying to find another perspective. "I could see you settled down with someone. Why not Jenny?"

Liz shrugged, not about to give Maggie more information than she'd already squeezed out of her.

"Is she attractive?" Maggie asked casually.

Liz put down her sandwich and gave Maggie a hard look. "Maggie, why are you interviewing me?"

"I haven't seen you in forty years," protested Maggie in a righteous tone. "I don't know anything about you!"

"Not jealous, are you?"

"How could I be jealous?" Her face had reddened a little. Liz studied her carefully and decided that her question hadn't been that far off the mark.

"Yes, Jenny is attractive, not like you, but a good-looking woman."

"I see." Maggie went back to her chowder, but Liz could sense that she wasn't done with this topic. She'd only put it on hold.

Liz decided that flipping the interrogation was the best way to deflect more questions. "What about you? You said you were seeing someone."

"Tom. Yes. He's also a professor at NYU."

"Will he expect a call about the accident?" Liz finished her sandwich in two bites.

"I doubt it. Before I left, I told him it was over between us."

"Ah," said Liz, nodding. "A broken leg and a broken heart."

"You've got the wrong idea. My heart's not broken. Neither is his. We'd just run our course. Like you and Jenny."

'That's good."

Maggie gave her a questioning look, but Liz had no intention of explaining. She waited for Maggie to finish her sandwich. Then she cleared away the papers and containers from their lunch and brought them into the kitchen.

She heard Maggie call from the porch: "I'd like to take a shower now that I have clean clothes to put on. Would you mind...?" Liz went back to the porch door and gave her a puzzled look. Maggie pointed toward the hall.

"Oh, you want your bags brought into your room. For a moment, I thought you were asking me to help you take a shower."

"You wish."

"Maybe I do," called Liz over her shoulder as she went out to move the bags. "But in all seriousness, I will help you, if you need help."

"I'm sure I can manage," Maggie called back.

***

Maggie returned with a towel wrapped around her head turban-style. She sat next to Liz on the wicker love seat.

"Put your leg up," said Liz without looking up from her iPad. With a groan, Maggie hauled her leg up onto the hassock.

"You're a hard taskmaster, Dr. Stolz."

"I hope you're keeping it up when I'm not here," said Liz, peering at her.

"Mostly," Maggie admitted, "not always."

Liz assumed her doctor's scolding look, a neutral stare guaranteed to trigger the patient's own feelings of self-recrimination. "It's important to keep it up. It reduces the swelling and the pain. After I finish reading this, I'll get you some ice."

"What are you reading?"

"About how measles is making a comeback. Measles! I thought we were done with that decades ago. Fucking anti-vaxers."

"Liz..."

"Yes, I know. The language." She closed the cover of her iPad. "Feel better? Now that you're clean?"

"Much, but I feel like I'm keeping you from enjoying your weekend. I hope I haven't spoiled any plans."

Liz shrugged. "I was thinking about driving up to Baxter State Park and doing some hiking tomorrow, but with you here, that won't work."

"I'm sorry to show up without any warning."

"It's not like you planned to break your leg. What a stupid stunt! What was Tony thinking?"

"I had my doubts too, but he's the director." Maggie laid a warm hand on Liz's bare thigh. It tingled where it lay. "You were going to get ice."

"Yes, I was." Liz got up and headed to the kitchen. In a few minutes, she returned with a bag of ice and a towel. She took off the walking boot and carefully arranged the ice pack over the break.

"I must give this infirmary a five-star review. The service here is excellent." Maggie gave Liz a warm smile. "Thank you for all you do for me." She reached up and brushed Liz's cheek with her fingertips.

Liz stood up quickly to get away from the gentle fingers. "You're welcome," she said gruffly. She picked up her iPad and sat down in one of the wicker chairs instead of returning to her seat beside Maggie.

Maggie frowned, evidently having gotten the message. She retreated into theatrical poise. "Let me make dinner for you tonight. I saw you have a pork tenderloin in the refrigerator."

Liz looked doubtful. "Are you sure you're up for that? I don't mind cooking."

"No, let me. It will give me something to do."

✻✻✻

For dinner, Maggie roasted eggplant and peppers from Liz's garden to go with the tenderloin. She made a tomato salad with balsamic vinegar glaze and fresh basil. It was a simple meal, but Liz savored it because it was such a treat to have someone cook for her. She loved to cook, but lately, it had become merely a chore to provide herself with nourishment. Sometimes, she invited company just to have an excuse to cook something other than grilled meats and vegetables.

After Liz cleaned up the kitchen, she sat with Maggie on the porch in the gathering twilight. "This is one of my favorite times of the day," she confided to Maggie.

"It's so peaceful here. It was so quiet last night I almost couldn't sleep."

"Did you hear the owls?"

"Yes. Wonderful. Haunting."

"I was hoping you heard them."

Maggie gave her a warm smile. "Really?"

Liz nodded.

"Liz, do you mind if I play your guitar?"

"No, of course not, but I'm sure it's out of tune."

"I tuned it today."

"Hmmm. Checking out my office, my fridge, my elevator and now, tuning my guitar. Should I worry?"

"Please get it."

Liz left and returned with the guitar. She strummed it, then tightened a peg. She tested the strings again and tightened another peg. "It's been sitting a while. I'm not surprised it won't stay in tune." She handed the guitar to Maggie. "Go on, my chanteuse. This is how I remember you best."

Maggie strummed some chords. "What would you like to hear?"

"You pick. You're the one who wanted to play."

Maggie began to play the opening chords to something very familiar. "Who Knows Where the Time Goes?" The melancholy, reflective song instantly catapulted Liz across forty years to their dorm living room where that Judy Collins album was constantly playing.

At the end of the song, Liz's eyes were stinging. She swallowed the lump in her throat and tried to sound cheerful. "Maggie, you still do the best Judy Collins imitation I've ever heard."

"Thank you, but I'd like to think I'm doing my own interpretation, not imitating her."

"She's still singing. She comes up every year for a concert at Nathan's. In fact, I think she'll be up here on Labor Day weekend. I could see about getting tickets."

"I couldn't possibly stay that long."

"Why not? You have someplace else to be?"

Maggie lazily strummed the guitar while she considered the question. "No, I guess not," she conceded.

"So, I'll get tickets?"

"Only if she sings this." Maggie began to sing, "That's No Way to Say Goodbye."

Liz felt a sudden clutching sorrow, as if Maggie's sweet voice had reached across the decades and squeezed her heart.

"Please stop," Liz said.

"No, sing it with me."

"I can't." Liz got up and went inside, leaving Maggie alone in the dark.

Chapter 6

Maggie awoke to opera. The volume was carefully modulated but loud enough to wake her. She let the air out of the cast, exchanged it for the walking boot, and threw on her robe. The rousing soldier's chorus from Faust emanated from the kitchen, where Liz sang along in a tenor voice that was perfectly on key but completely androgynous.

Maggie stood just outside the kitchen door to listen. Liz continued to sing as she poured batter into a cast iron muffin tin. She exchanged the spoon for a spatula to scrape the bottom of the bowl. She shoved the pan into the oven and paused her singing to set her watch. The chorus continued. Liz, unaware that she was being observed, sang along with gusto. When the selection switched to the duet from *Don Carlos,* Liz, hand on her heart, sang the hero's part with equal passion.

Maggie applauded from her hiding place and came into the kitchen. "That was superb! I hate to break it to you, Liz, but you're not a tenor."

"Oh, Maggie, don't spoil my fun!" Liz reached for her phone to cut off the music. "Did I wake you? I tried to keep it down, but as usual, I got carried away."

"It was time to get up." Maggie lumbered into the kitchen on the awkward boot and put her arms around her tall friend. Liz briefly tensed but then relaxed into the embrace. If Maggie slouched a bit, her breasts slid under Liz's instead of colliding. Their profiles fit together like puzzle parts. "I'm sorry if I upset you last night," she said, pulling Liz closer. The feel of her body was so different now. She felt like a woman. Maggie luxuriated in the softness of her flesh.

"You didn't upset me. It was the memories. I could practically smell your dinner cooking in the dorm kitchen and see Claudia studying on the other sofa."

"I've sung those old songs so many times since. I have other memories overlaid on them." Maggie sighed and gave Liz a good squeeze. "This is what I miss most about not having a partner. Hugs."

"In that case…" Liz gathered her up and hugged her enthusiastically, stopping just short of a bone-crusher. Obviously, the years had not diminished her strength. "But no more apologies or heavy conversation today. The weather is going to be spectacular, and we are going to the beach!" Liz untangled herself from Maggie's arms. "Sit. I'll make you coffee."

"No, let me do it. And I should be making you breakfast to thank you for your kindness. What are you baking?"

"Popovers! With Maine butter and wild blueberry jam."

Maggie attempted to sit at the counter, but Liz banished her to the breakfast room. "And put that leg up!" Maggie took a seat at the breakfast table and put her leg up on the neighboring chair. Liz arrived a moment later with two mugs of coffee.

"I could get used to this wonderful service. Then, you'll never get rid of me."

"There are worse things." Liz poured cream into her coffee. "By the way, I ordered those Judy Collins tickets. The concert's on Friday of Labor Day weekend."

Maggie stirred her coffee. "So now you're stuck with me. I could fly home and come back for the concert."

"That's ridiculous," said Liz with a dismissive wave of her hand. "Besides, who's going to help you get around?"

"In case you've forgotten, we have taxis in New York. And I can have my groceries delivered."

"Yes, but here, you have beautiful accommodations…" Liz raised her arms expansively. "… a comfortable bed, home-cooked meals, and your very own physician in residence?"

"A pretty good deal, but I don't want to overstay my welcome."

"Impossible. You're in the Stolz B&B, where we always extend hospitality. I have visitors all summer. You just happened to arrive at a good time." Liz checked her watch. "Thirty minutes for popovers."

"You're one of the few people I know who still wears a watch." Maggie reached for Liz's wrist to have a closer look. "Pretty fancy."

Liz gave the watch a critical glance. "Cartier. Not real gold. Plated stainless steel. A little pretentious, but I wear it because I have to time things like pulse beats. They gave it to me when I retired."

"Why did you retire so early?"

Liz visibly tensed. Maggie sensed she might be probing too deeply, but Liz answered without hesitation. "Because the administration only cared about the bottom line and the public image of the hospital. I'm a surgeon, not a PR agent. But the final straw was a ridiculous malpractice suit. The day I was cleared of any wrongdoing, I announced my retirement."

"Wow," said Maggie, more in reaction to Liz's vehement tone than the story.

A moment later, a little buzzer sounded on Liz's watch. "It even has a timer. Cool, huh? The popovers need to come out." Liz got up and took the cast iron pan out with oven mitts. She put the pan on a slab of wood. "That's a cutoff from my shop." Maggie had no idea what Liz was talking about, but she noted that the wood was beautiful. Liz plucked two popovers from the tin with her bare fingers and dropped one on each plate. "Enjoy." She pushed the enormous hunk of butter in Maggie's direction.

"You're spoiling me."

"Enjoy it while you can. My patience for pampering invalids is limited."

Maggie realized that she *was* enjoying the attention. Usually, she was the one catering to someone. That's how it was with men. They expected women to take care of them.

She watched Liz happily slather butter on her popover and felt a sudden stab of guilt. "How can you be so kind after what I did to you?"

"It's in the past. Let's leave it there."

"But I want you to know that I–"

"Maggie, stop right now. I won't have this perfect day spoiled with confessions or apologies. I'm glad you're here. Let's just enjoy it." There was the hint of protesting too much in Liz's voice, but Maggie reluctantly let the subject go.

"Your popovers are delicious." Maggie wiped melted butter off her chin with the back of her hand. "I could eat them all!"

"Go right ahead. They don't keep well."

"In that case…" Maggie reached for another.

Liz put down her coffee cup. "Maggie, I have an idea. You can say no, if you don't feel up to it, but I've been meaning to invite Tony and his partner over for dinner. There's no show at the Playhouse on Sunday nights, so they should be free. What do you think?"

Maggie didn't think for more than a moment. She liked Tony and felt she owed him something for rescuing her after the injury. Of course, she wouldn't have needed rescuing if he hadn't come up with that idiotic trampoline stunt, but that was another subject. She agreed it sounded like a nice idea and listened while Liz called Tony from the kitchen.

"They'll be here around seven," Liz reported when she returned to the table. "Meanwhile, would you like to go to the beach?"

"But I burn like a piece of bacon. Remember our canoe trip in the Adirondacks?"

Liz's eyes widened with remorse. "That was the most amazing sunburn I've ever seen, and you can believe I've seen a lot of them."

"But you couldn't understand why I didn't want to make love."

"What can I say? I was a horny kid. All I could think about was sex. But don't worry. I have plenty of sunscreen and a beach chair with an awning. You can wear my fishing hat with the wide brim."

"You have a solution for everything."

"Of course, I do!"

Maggie hadn't thought to bring a bathing suit when she'd packed for this gig. During summer stock, she usually slept in after the late nights at the theater. By the time she got up, it was nearly time to go to the theater again. Fortunately, she found a pair of cotton shorts and a sleeveless T-shirt she'd thrown into her bag at the last minute. There was also an oversize white blouse to use as a cover against the sun.

She sat on the front porch while Liz loaded the truck. The promised awning chair was packed along with Liz's fishing poles and buckets. Liz easily swung herself up into the back of the pickup to tie down the fishing gear and the cooler.

Their first stop was the bait shop, where Liz bought frozen mackerel and added it to the cooler. "You put your bait in with our sandwiches and drinks?" asked Maggie, incredulous.

"It's just fish, and it's wrapped up tight."

When they arrived at the beach, Liz parked Maggie a few feet from the walkway, so she wouldn't have to trudge through the sand. She raised the awning on the cleverly-designed beach chair and set up an inverted five-gallon bucket so Maggie could elevate her broken leg.

Maggie's eyes followed Liz as she headed to the jetty with her fishing gear. From behind, she could be mistaken for a much younger woman. Her long legs were youthful, beautifully tanned and well-muscled. She strode with confidence across the sand, weights and swivels dangling from the lines, another five-gallon pail in tow to hold the bait fish and net. She easily ambled up the rocks to the jetty.

Maggie let her book fall in her lap, so she could use the telephoto lens of her camera to watch Liz walk along the rocks. She was as confident of her footfalls as a cat. When they were young, some said Liz was awkward and unfeminine, but she'd always had an easy way of moving that defied preconceived notions of grace.

Maggie turned the camera to video and captured the exact moment Liz pulled up the big fish of the day to the congratulations of the other fishermen on the jetty. Liz's childlike pleasure in reeling in a "keeper" was endearing. She posed proudly as Maggie focused the shot of her holding the big striper.

The fish, Liz explained, was barely legal at exactly twenty-eight inches. She grumbled about the change in the legal-size limits and needing a salt-water fishing license since the new regulations. Maggie nodded without absorbing any of the information. She was completely caught up in Liz's pleasure in the catch because it reminded her so much of young Liz, whose innocent delight was contagious.

On the way back from the beach, they decided to add a fish course to the dinner menu. While Liz drove, Maggie searched on her phone for recipes.

"Do you have fresh oregano in your garden?"

"Do I have fresh oregano in my garden?" Liz repeated in a mocking voice.

When they got home, Liz went out to the garden to cut the herbs on Maggie's list. She washed and chopped them while Maggie prepared the marinade. They worked well together, which Maggie considered a good sign. She made the dressing for an arugula, sweet onion, and blueberry salad and playfully slapped Liz's hand when she tried to filch a few leaves to sample it.

"Out of my kitchen," Maggie ordered.

"It's my kitchen."

"Out!"

Liz snatched more arugula leaves out of the bowl and snickered like a cartoon villain as she walked away.

From the window over the kitchen sink, Maggie watched Liz clean and filet the fish, thinking how ironic it was for a surgeon to wield a fish knife, but she wasn't surprised when the filets Liz brought into the kitchen were absolutely perfect.

"Liz…don't be offended, but you need to shower. You smell like fish."

Liz sniffed her arm. "You're right." She headed toward the door, but before she left the kitchen, she turned around. "You've become very bossy, you know."

"I have?" asked Maggie anxiously.

"Yes, but I don't mind."

❖❖❖

Maggie was used to spending time with gay men. The theater world was full of them. She had instantly bonded with Tony, who adored women's clothes. When they'd met, he'd carried on about her outfit, instantly winning her heart. As Maggie put on a clingy summer dress and carefully styled her blond hair, she told herself she was dressing to impress him, but in her heart, she knew she was really dressing for someone else. Fortunately, Liz's comfortable downstairs guest room had a vanity table with good light.

Maggie doubted she could put on makeup in the bathroom with only one good leg to stand on.

There was a knock at the door. At Maggie's invitation, Liz stuck her head into the room.

"Oh, you're getting dressed up." Liz looked distressed.

"Well, I am an actress. I'm expected to put on a show." Maggie turned around. "You can come in, you know."

Liz stepped into the room and sat down on the bed. Her admiring look reflected in the mirror instantly brought Maggie back to Liz standing in the doorway of the dorm bathroom. At first, Maggie thought she was trying to learn something about makeup and tried to teach her, but Liz wasn't interested.

"Remember how you used to watch me put on my makeup?"

In the mirror, she saw Liz nod. "I thought you were the most beautiful woman I'd ever seen."

"You were in love."

"Yes…poor, young fool that I was."

Maggie put down the mascara brush and turned around. "You weren't a fool. I was in love too."

Liz's expression instantly changed from dreamy admiration to frank discomfort. She rose abruptly. "I'd better change into something dressier, so I don't embarrass you." She was instantly out of the room.

"Liz, wait!" Maggie wanted to run after her, but she had to put on the boot first. By the time, she made it into the hallway, Liz had gone upstairs.

When Liz reappeared, she was wearing black pants, a stylish top, jewelry, and makeup. Maggie tried not to look shocked by the transformation, but she blurted out, "Oh, Liz. You look beautiful!"

Liz scowled, but she blushed a little. "Thank you. I can put on a show too when I have to, but I don't really enjoy playing grown up anymore. I still have a whole closet full of clothes I never wear."

"Well, maybe you should. You're a beautiful woman. When you dress up a little, you're absolutely stunning!"

The doorbell rang. "Let me get the door," said Liz, looking anxious to get away.

There were hoots of surprise and appreciation when Tony and Fred came in. "Oh, Maggie, what have you done? You've been here for two days and you've reformed her!"

Maggie joined the scene in time to see Liz playfully punch Tony on the shoulder. "I had nothing to do with it."

"Oh, I doubt that." Tony opened his arms to Maggie. "And you look gorgeous as always, my dear." He enthusiastically kissed her on both cheeks. "A vision to behold!"

Tony's partner, an equally slender man with a shaved head approached and kissed her too. "Hello, I'm Freddie, Tony's better half. You haven't met me yet, but I designed your costume for *Mama Mia*."

"*You* designed that ridiculous jumpsuit?" asked Liz in an incredulous tone.

"We were trying for that disco look." Freddie opened his palms in a plea for understanding.

"It was so tight I was ready to cut her out of it, but she stopped me. She said you'd want it back."

"I do. I spend a lot of time on those costumes!"

Tony held Maggie at arm's length and gave her a thorough once-over. "Darling, you look so much better than the other night. Your doctor must be very good for you." He bent so he could speak near Maggie's ear. "And obviously, you're good for her too."

"Let's hope so," Maggie whispered back.

"Hey, no secrets here," said Liz, trying to wrest back some control of the situation. "Let's sit out on the porch and enjoy the nice weather. She herded her guests through the hall to the porch. After everyone had a seat, she rubbed her hands together. "Martinis?"

"Of course!" said Tony and Fred in chorus.

"Maggie? Sorry. No alcohol for you."

"Seltzer. Thanks, Liz."

Liz disappeared. She returned a few minutes later with iced martini glasses, a pitcher of martinis, and a glass of seltzer for Maggie. "We've had a slight change of menu. I caught a striper today."

Tony and Fred cheered. "You go, girl!" Fred said, enthusiastically clapping.

"Maggie prepared it, and I hope I do her recipe justice. But first, a toast." She poured the martinis and distributed the glasses. "Madam," she said with a little bow as she handed Maggie her seltzer. She raised her own glass. "To the fish!"

"To the fish!" they agreed with a clink of glasses.

Liz took a seat next to Maggie on the wicker settee. Opposite them, Freddie delicately crossed his legs. "So, Maggie. Tony tells me you and Liz went to college together. I want to hear the whole story…every last detail!"

Maggie and Liz exchanged a look.

"Oh," said Tony with a canny smile. "It's like that!"

"Like what?" Liz affected an innocent expression.

"They want us to think we haven't guessed," Tony said in a loud stage whisper.

Liz quickly changed the topic to politics. "Did you see the latest poll? They say Michaud is ahead, but I think LePage is going to get in again."

There was a chorus of boos. "No way," said Fred.

Liz shook her head. "Michaud should never have come out. Northern Maine voted against gay marriage in the referendum."

"Maybe someone threatened to out him," Fred wondered aloud.

"Who knows what the real story is?" said Tony.

Maggie knew nothing about Maine politics, so she went into the kitchen to flip the fish in the marinade.

❈❈❈

The striper course was a hit. Maggie enjoyed watching Liz bask in the compliments. "Thank you, but we have to thank Maggie for the recipe and the excellent preparation." Liz put her arm around her.

Freddie elbowed Tony. "They make a cute couple, don't they?"

Liz instantly withdrew her arm. Maggie saw that she was blushing to the roots of her hair. *She still has feelings for me, not just the feelings old friends have for one another.*

The martinis had left Liz garrulous, and she fell into animated conversation with Tony about how operetta had "degenerated" into musical theater. Maggie half-listened because the ideas being exchanged could be useful in the book she'd been writing on the history of musical theater, but she contributed little to the debate. Her mind was preoccupied with her earlier discovery.

The rest of the dinner party proceeded at a leisurely pace. Outside, the light faded. Liz streamed soft jazz through the sound system. They watched it grow dark outside and listened to the music. The conversation about everything and nothing wandered aimlessly. Maggie felt at ease and relaxed. These people were so different from Maggie's friends in New York with their frenetic pace, their compulsion to occupy every moment of their time, to be awake at any hour, day or night.

There was rustling in the compost heap.

"Aha!" said Liz, jumping up to look. "Something's discovered the fish guts."

Liz and the two men rushed to the window. Maggie, stuck in her chair with an ice pack on her raised leg, listened to them speculate about the identity of the creature feasting on the fish entrails. "Do you think it's a bear?" asked Tony in a loud whisper.

"More likely a raccoon," Liz whispered back. "They love fish."

They listened intently until the animal wandered off, crushing dry leaves underfoot as it made its way through the woods.

"We need to get going soon." Tony reached out for Fred's hand. "Maggie has a broken leg. I bet it still hurts."

"I'm okay," volunteered Maggie, although she was grateful that she'd taken a double dose of ibuprofen before dinner. "Don't worry about me."

Fred gave her a sly look. "I'm sure you two would like some alone time."

Liz, still a little tipsy from the alcohol, let out a little snort of amusement. "We have plenty of time. She's stuck with me for six weeks."

"I am?" asked Maggie sharply. "That's not what I agreed."

"Come on, Freddie. Let's go," urged Tony. "They're about to have a spat. Knowing Liz, it won't be pretty."

Liz saw them to the door. When she returned, she sat next to Maggie on the love seat and stretched her arm across the back. Her skin barely contacted Maggie's bare shoulders, but where it did, it was warm and gently stimulating.

"How did they know?" Liz wondered aloud.

"You dressed up for me."

"I did not!"

"What a liar you are."

"All right. I dressed up for you."

Maggie hesitated for a moment. "And the way you look at me."

"How is that?"

"Like you find me attractive."

"I do."

"I know." Maggie turned in her seat to face her. "I find you attractive too."

Liz withdrew her arm. Maggie felt a chill where it had been.

"I'll do the dishes," said Liz, springing to her feet.

Chapter 7

Liz heard the walking boot clomping across on the tiles of the kitchen floor. She checked her watch. Seven thirty. Early for Maggie to be up and around. Liz listened to the coffee machine gurgle. A moment later, Maggie came out on the porch wrapped in a bathrobe, her hair all askew, and her glasses perched on her nose. Pale from sleep, she looked every minute of her sixty years. Liz mentally pinched herself for the unkind thought.

"Good morning," said Maggie, taking the seat beside Liz on the wicker love seat.

"Good morning. You could have slept in."

"I know, but I want to talk to you."

Liz felt a twinge of anxiety at the stern note in Maggie's voice and the ominous crease between her brows. She closed the cover of her iPad and set it on the table. "What's on your mind?" She took her feet off the hassock and sat up to show Maggie that she had her attention.

Maggie took a sip of her coffee, extending the pause and Liz's anxiety. "I think I should go home," she finally said.

"Why?"

"Because I'm imposing on you and your life."

"You are not!" Liz protested.

"I am. I'm parked here, and I need a lot of help because of this stupid leg. You've already gone above and beyond. You came at a moment's notice when I broke my leg."

"I'm a physician. It's my job."

"It wasn't your job to invite me into your home."

"No, actually, that was pretty unprofessional."

Maggie rolled her eyes. "Oh, Liz! Sometimes, you are so thick I could shake you!"

"What about the Judy Collins concert?" asked Liz anxiously. The tickets had been expensive, not that it mattered so much as the fact that she'd been looking forward to the concert and to showing Maggie that they had good entertainment in Maine. No, it wasn't New York, but in the season, there were some great shows.

"I can come back for it. Or you can take someone else."

"No! I only got the tickets because you're here. They're for *you*."

Maggie sighed in exasperation. "Don't you see that my being here makes you uncomfortable?"

"No, it doesn't!"

Maggie turned in her chair. Her hazel eyes earnestly studied Liz's face. "Liz, I'm an actress. I observe people's behavior and reactions so I can reproduce them on stage. In fact, I'm probably better than most shrinks at reading people. My being here has thrown you off balance."

"So? Maybe I needed a little shaking up."

"Maybe you did, but you didn't choose it. I just showed up out of nowhere."

Liz sprang out of her chair and went to look out the window. The idea of Maggie leaving was far more upsetting than she'd expected. She tried to distract herself with the beauty of her garden. A monarch butterfly danced lazily in the patch of milkweed she'd planted just for them. A hummingbird zipped by so fast it could only be heard, not seen. There was the low murmur of bees feasting on the monarda. As beautiful as the flower beds were, the vegetable garden looked a bit sad. The eggplants needed to be picked and the herb plot should have been weeded weeks ago.

"My garden needs attention."

"Liz, look at me."

Reluctantly, Liz turned around.

"It's perfectly natural for us to have feelings for one another. You were the first woman I ever loved. I was your first lover. That's very special, and it wasn't just a roll in the hay. It was passionate and powerful, so powerful that I couldn't face you again. But I never forgot you. I still–"

"I need another cup of coffee for this." Liz dashed into the kitchen.

When she returned, she felt Maggie's eyes following her to her seat. After she sat down, she could feel her eyes boring into the side of her head.

"See? You can't even talk about it."

"What do you want me to say?" Liz crossed her arms on her chest.

"Oh, Liz. I don't blame you. It was a shock to see you. I'm sure it was a shock to see me. Maybe after the dust settles, we can get together under more normal circumstances and catch up. After I wake up a little, I'll check the flights to New York."

Liz tried not to sound as desperate as she felt. Maggie was leaving, and all Liz could think of was that summer forty years ago. She forced herself to speak calmly. "No, please. I want you to stay. Aren't you comfortable here?"

"It's wonderful. You're a great hostess. It's beautiful here, like the best vacation I never knew I needed."

"Then why do you want to leave?" asked Liz, frustrated.

Maggie got up and hobbled over to where Liz sat. She put her hands on her shoulders. "Look at me, Liz."

Reluctantly, Liz looked up.

"You still have feelings for me and that upsets you."

"I'm sorry my feelings are so obvious."

"You're not the only one with feelings."

Liz let the words sink in. She swallowed hard.

"But you're straight."

"I chose to be with men."

"So why are we having this conversation?" Liz shrugged off Maggie's hands and moved to another chair.

"Because I care about you, and I never want to hurt you again." Maggie shook her head. "I'll check on flights. Is Boston an option?"

"It's fine." Liz's tone was surly, not because it was well over an hour to Boston or she had anything special to do, but because Maggie was insisting she had to leave.

Maggie went back to her room. Liz sulked as she finished her coffee. Finally, she got up and knocked on Maggie's door.

"Come in."

The suitcases were open on the bed, and Maggie was laying out her clothes to pack. Liz stood in the doorway instead of coming in. "Maggie, I don't want you to leave."

"I know you don't. And I don't want to leave either. I'm enjoying it here." Even as she said this, Maggie continued to pack, carefully folding her clothes into tidy piles. Evidently, when she wanted to be neat, she could be.

"Please stay."

"I just can't. Please try to understand."

Liz sighed. "Okay. Let me get dressed, and I'll drive you to the airport."

Before Liz went up to dress, she retrieved her coffee cup from the porch and put it in the dishwasher. She heard Maggie's boot clomping down the hall.

"Liz…?"

Liz turned around.

"I'll stay until the Judy Collins concert."

"You will?" Liz hugged Maggie so enthusiastically she knocked her off balance and had to steady her. "What made you change your mind?"

"I was looking forward to the concert, and I'm enjoying our visit, but I don't want my being here to make you uncomfortable. If it does, I'm going home. Understood?"

"Absolutely. Now, come out to the porch. I'll make you another cup of coffee."

When Liz returned with the coffee, Maggie said, "This waiting on me hand and foot has to end. I broke my leg, but I can walk, thanks to you. And I intend to pull my weight. On the days you have office hours, I'll take care of dinner."

"Then make a menu, and I'll pick up what you need."

"And you don't have to entertain me while I'm here. I have plenty of work to do on my book."

"Tell me more about this book," said Liz, relieved to have a neutral topic of conversation, something that didn't have to do with the past or their feelings.

Maggie explained that she'd outlined the book two years earlier and had a positive response from an agent, but the whirlwind of her last year of teaching and an off-Broadway play had prevented any extended work on the project. "I wanted to get in some theater gigs before the sun sets on my career. There aren't many good roles for older women, so it's not easy finding parts."

"You're still damned attractive."

Maggie gazed at Liz with a look half between sadness and gratitude. "To you, maybe, but you're biased. I don't have the phenomenal talent of a Meryl Streep or Glenn Close, who can get away with unconventional beauty and still be successful in their later years. That's one reason why I opted for being an academic instead."

"I bet Barry preferred that too." The words had just flown out before Liz could stop them.

Maggie gave her a suspicious look. "Yes, he liked my being an actress so long as I was only the star of community theater and occasional summer stock. My being a college professor suited him better than stage work."

"Too many eyes on you as an actress."

Maggie looked mildly annoyed. "I know you're not a Barry fan, but he was very supportive when I said I wanted to go back to school. In fact, he encouraged it. I was getting restless, and he thought graduate school would give me focus."

"Good strategy. Keep wifey happy but under control."

"Liz, stop it! You'd hate any man I married, but you're wrong about Barry. He was very good to me."

"So why didn't you just overlook his little affair?"

"It wasn't a little affair. They were in pretty deep when I found out. I was furious and had an affair in retaliation."

Liz couldn't keep her eyebrows from shooting up. "You did? That doesn't seem like you. You're such a good girl."

Maggie looked away. "She was the director of the play I was doing that summer."

"She? A woman!" Liz's eyebrows rose higher and her mouth gaped open.

"Oh, Liz, don't look so surprised. Yes, a woman, a very special woman. And I can't tell you her name because you may have heard of her, and she's still in the closet."

Liz finally closed her mouth. "Was it serious?"

"It only lasted the run of the play. A month, but yes, it was powerful."

"Have there been other women?"

"No. She was the only one."

Liz sat back and stared at Maggie while she took stock of what she'd learned. Why should she expect Maggie to be the dutiful Catholic girl she remembered from college? Of course, she'd changed, just as she had.

"Well, I'll be damned."

"So now you know."

Liz's stomach began to growl, and she realized she was hungry. She'd been so absorbed in the conversation, she'd ignored the twinges. "Do you want to go out for breakfast? I know a place where they make the best lobster benedict."

"Lobster benedict? That sounds interesting...and very fattening." Maggie studied Liz. "Are we done with true confessions for the moment?"

"Yes, I think so. Give me a chance to absorb it all. I'm sure I'll have more questions, but now, let me take you out for breakfast. I'm starving."

Maggie struggled to her feet. "All right. I need half an hour to shower and put on my face."

"I'll wait," Liz said and picked up her iPad to finish reading *The New York Times*.

When Maggie returned, she looked like a different woman. She was wearing a colorful, sleeveless sundress with a floral design. Her makeup and hair were perfect, but true to her word, it had taken only half an hour.

Liz gazed at Maggie with frank admiration. "You're gorgeous."

"Thanks. You're not so bad yourself...especially, when you make some effort."

The comment hit Liz the wrong way. She forced herself to speak in a neutral tone. "Maggie, I had to dress for success for thirty-five years. Now that I'm retired, I will dress exactly how I choose. Can you understand?"

"No," said Maggie bluntly and gave her a critical look. "You're so gray. I didn't expect that."

"I used to dye my hair while I was still at Yale. The men can get away with being gray. It makes them distinguished, but a gray-haired female surgeon just looks like a little, old lady."

"That could be reassuring. Don't people associate little old ladies with kindness?"

"Not when she's your surgeon. They expect her to be sharp, which means young. And you can't look like an old lady when you have to put snotty, young surgeons in their place."

They went outside. Liz reached out to help Maggie into the truck. She had to lift her a little so she could get in. "I don't know why I'm putting you through this. We could take the Audi."

"You have another car?"

"Yes, do you want me to get it?"

"No. I'm in now," said Maggie, strapping herself in. "Let's go."

When they arrived at the diner, there was a line out the door into the parking lot. Liz went in to see what their prospects were for getting a table. The morning counter waitress caught her scoping out the place and called to her, "Don't worry, Liz. Come to the counter. There's a couple at the end who have their check."

Liz elbowed her way through the crowd at the door and helped Maggie onto the counter seat. She carefully stowed the green cane in the corner, so no one would trip.

"Who's your friend, Liz?" the waitress asked as she slapped down paper place mats that showed a map of Hobbs and its businesses. Liz always checked to make sure Hobbs Family Practice was listed.

"Paula, meet Maggie Fitzgerald."

Paula stood straight, hands on hips and gave Maggie the once-over. "Oh, I know who you are. You're playing in *Mama Mia* at the Playhouse."

Maggie looked flattered to be recognized but appropriately modest. "Yes, but I'm sidelined now. I broke my leg in a trampoline accident."

"I heard about that." Paula shook her head. The red hair dye was fresh, so it was brighter than usual. "Those guys are too ambitious. Still dreaming of Broadway productions when it's just summer stock. I'm really sorry, honey. What can I get you today?" She glanced at Liz. "I already know what you want. Two eggs over easy, rye toast, don't break the yokes."

Liz laughed. "Well, Paula, today, I'm going to surprise you. In honor of Maggie's visit, I'm going to order the lobster benedict."

"Maybe there's hope for you yet. Coffee?"

Liz made a face. "Oh, I think we've had enough coffee to float away."

"Paula, thank you. I'll take some coffee." Maggie shot Liz an irritated look.

"Sorry. I have a bad habit of deciding for other people."

Maggie lightly touched Liz's thigh in a gesture of forgiveness.

"Did you hear about that big accident on 109?" Paula asked when she returned to pour Maggie's coffee.

"No, I didn't. I'm surprised I didn't get called in."

"Why would they call you, Liz?" Maggie asked.

"I'm on call for surgical emergencies. I haven't given up surgery. I'm a part time surgeon in a practice in York."

Liz caught sight of the police chief at the other end of the counter. "Brenda! What happened on 109 last night?"

A middle-aged woman with blond hair in a French braid looked up from her meal. "Kids drag racing in the middle of the night." The police chief left her breakfast and came down to where Liz sat to speak more discreetly. "One car overturned and burst into flame. The driver burned to a crisp. Doubt he'll make it."

"Holy shit!" Liz cringed as she visualized the burn victim after that kind of fire. "Anyone I know?"

Brenda leaned over to whisper the name into Liz's ear. "Billy Chase from Awakened Brews."

"Oh, no! His mother will be crushed." Liz took a deep breath to suck in her shock and grief. She thought of Billy, his cheerful voice in the morning, his solicitous warnings about the heat of her coffee, his quick grin when she added a few extra dollars to his tip.

Brenda nodded sadly. "I know. It's terrible. I'm surprised you didn't hear all the noise from your house. Called out three fire departments."

"Didn't hear a thing. I was out cold."

Brenda glanced at Maggie. "Hey, who's your friend?"

"Maggie Fitzgerald, this is Brenda Harrison, our police chief."

"Maggie Fitzgerald." Brenda repeated, studying Maggie's face as she tried to place the name. "Wait! I know. I saw you in *Mama Mia*. You were fantastic!" She glanced down at Maggie's boot. "A shame about the accident. Doc taking good care of you?" she asked in a confidential tone.

"The best."

"Maggie's an old college friend," said Liz as if compelled to explain the connection.

"Hey, watch how you throw around the word 'old,'" warned Maggie.

"Right?" Brenda laughed and patted Maggie's arm. "Nice to meet you, Ms. Fitzgerald. Enjoy your stay in Hobbs. Excuse me, but my breakfast is getting cold." She glanced at Liz. "Catch you later."

"Does everyone in this town know you?" Maggie asked when the police chief had returned to her seat.

Liz lowered her voice. "A lot of the full-time residents are my patients. Obviously, the police chief and I are tight because of emergencies."

The lobster benedict arrived, heaps of picked lobster meat over spinach on toasted English muffins. It was topped by a poached egg and swimming in homemade Hollandaise sauce.

"Looks wonderful. I can feel the pounds coming on just by looking at it." Maggie put a forkful in her mouth. She chewed with an expression of profound pleasure. "It's incredibly delicious."

"Told you so."

While they ate, they discussed plans for the day. They talked about going up to the wildlife park in Gray until Liz remembered that the terrain was extremely hilly. Maggie would find it challenging with her walking boot, and Liz doubted she'd tolerate being pushed around in a wheelchair.

"Maybe we could go up to Portland and take the afternoon ferry cruise around Casco Bay," Liz suggested. "If we leave now, we might just make it."

"Maybe we should stay home, so you can relax before you have to go back to work. Didn't you say you had projects to do around the house?"

"I have to weed the herb bed."

"That should keep you out of mischief for a few hours."

Liz smiled. "Don't count on it."

***

Slathered with super-blocking sunscreen and wearing Liz's wide-brimmed fishing hat, Maggie sat outside on the lounge chair while Liz weeded the herb bed, yanking out Canadian Mayflowers by the dozens. Maggie browsed *The New York Times*, the paper weighed down with a rock because it was so breezy. Liz had agreed to pick up the paper edition on the way back from the diner although she subscribed to the online edition and took a dim view of cutting down trees for newspapers. "It does help the Maine economy," she conceded, "...the few paper mills left up North."

After a few hours, Liz cursed her age and paused her weeding because there was a spasm in her lower back from bending too much. As she stretched, she saw that despite all their precautions, Maggie's fair skin was turning bright pink.

Liz climbed out of the herb bed. "I think I've had enough for one day. How about you?"

Maggie looked up and glanced at her arms. "Yes, I'm starting to burn."

"I probably shouldn't encourage you to spend so much time in the sun. With your pale skin, you're a skin cancer case waiting to happen."

"But you love the outdoors, and I like to spend time with you," said Maggie in a warm voice.

"I'm glad, but I don't want anything to happen to you on my watch. We need to pace ourselves." Liz bent to pick up her tools. When she stood up, she saw that Maggie was admiring her backside.

"Yes," Maggie agreed. "We need to pace ourselves."

While Liz was putting away her tools in the garden shed, she finally picked up on the innuendo.

"I need a good scrub and a shower," Liz said when she returned. "Would you like to see upstairs?"

"You're going to let me into your private domain?" Maggie's eyes were big with exaggerated surprise. "What about the security cameras?"

"They've been off since I got the video feed of you checking out the elevator."

"You mean you haven't been watching me dress and undress?"

Liz felt her cheeks flame. "What kind of pervert do you think I am? Of course not! There are only cameras in the hall and the elevator."

Maggie laughed and squeezed her arm. "Only kidding."

They took the elevator up to the second floor, where the Maine theme pervaded throughout. In one room, the walls were covered with light-house art; the next room had scenes of the North Woods, straight out of the Cabela's catalog. The beds were covered with colorful moose quilts. The third room had a seashore motif, complete with lamp bases made of col-ored glass like old-fashioned fishing floats. The last room had two futons and a big TV. Liz explained that it served as a sitting room for guests and a spare room for overflow.

"You must get a lot of company."

"All summer long. I had to dig a new well to accommodate all the new bedrooms."

"So, you didn't build this house?"

"The original house was the footprint you see downstairs. The architect determined that the foundation and the first-floor framing were strong, so we built up, not out. Come upstairs. I'll show you why."

Liz pressed the button to open the elevator door. "After you," she said with a little bow.

When they reached the third floor, they walked down a short hallway. Liz opened a door. "My bedroom." She enjoyed Maggie's look of amaze-ment as she took in the view through the floor-to-ceiling windows that spanned the entire wall.

"You can see the ocean!"

"The water is in the distance, but yes, you can see it. My neighbors weren't too happy when I cut down all the trees on this side for the view."

"It's absolutely spectacular!"

"Would you like to sit out on the deck while I take a shower?" She led Maggie out to the deck where she could sit on a lounge chair and keep her leg elevated.

"Being up so high would take some getting used to," said Maggie, looking down.

"I was worried that my fear of heights would keep me from enjoying the deck, but I'm fine as long as there are railings." Liz thumped the rail. She gave Maggie the local paper to read while she took a shower.

As Liz scrubbed her dirt-encrusted fingernails with a surgical brush, she took unexpected pleasure in the fact that her house had impressed Maggie. Although Liz no longer felt the need to flaunt her wealth, there was a time when professional success had been very important to her. The big house in Connecticut and the three performance cars in the garage would certainly have appealed to the young Maggie Fitzgerald's social ambitions. Liz wondered if tangible signs of success still meant so much to her.

After her shower, Liz dressed in the bathroom and headed out to the deck. "Ready to leave?"

Maggie turned and smiled. "It's so beautiful here, I don't know if I'll ever be ready to leave."

"Well, then maybe you shouldn't."

Chapter 8

Liz was long gone by the time Maggie awoke the next morning at a little past nine. She put on her glasses and the ridiculous walking boot. Now that her leg was beginning to feel better, the boot had become a real annoyance. The ankle was still livid, every color a bruise could imagine. The swelling had gone down, although the profile of the ankle bone was still only a memory.

When Maggie had asked Liz how the fracture was healing, she'd gotten far more than the simple explanation she'd expected. Liz had shown Maggie her x-ray and a little video animation of the bone healing process. Maggie was fascinated. She'd never had any doctor explain any medical condition in such detail. During all the years of enduring fertility treatments, she'd simply nodded and gone along with the doctors' recommendations. Barry was the one who'd asked all the questions on the rare occasions he came along for the appointments.

When the clock in the hall chimed nine thirty, Maggie decided she really must get up. It was a warm morning, so she didn't bother with a robe, and after all, she was alone in the house.

When she came into the kitchen, she nearly screamed. A young, red-haired woman was busily wiping the stove top. "Oh hello," said Maggie, trying to recover some poise. She was glad that her nightgown was fairly modest. "And who are you?"

The young woman pulled out her ear buds and smiled. "I'm Ellie, Liz's housekeeper. She called to tell me she had a guest in the downstairs guest room, so I was trying to do quiet things until you got up."

"Evidently, she forgot to tell me."

The young woman looked apologetic "Did I wake you?"

"No, I was awake. I just came out for some coffee."

"I see she left two filled coffee pods for you." Ellie nodded toward the counter where the coffee maker stood. "You go ahead. Don't mind me. I'm almost finished in the kitchen."

Maggie made herself coffee and took it out to the porch while she read *The New York Times Book Review* left over from Sunday's paper. A short while later, Ellie poked her head through the door. "Will it bother you if I vacuum?"

"No, of course not."

"Liz said I need to be quiet because you're writing a book."

"I am, but you need to do your job."

"You're not in my way." She smiled. The sweet-faced young woman had profuse freckles on her pale face. *Ethnic Irish*, Maggie decided. She'd heard there were many of them in Maine, and if the number of Irish pubs on Route 1 was any indication, the rumor was true. "I saw you in *Mama Mia* at the Playhouse," Ellie proudly confided. "You were fantastic!"

"Thank you." It pleased Maggie to know that so many of the locals supported the theater.

"I volunteer as an usher on my days off," explained Ellie. "That's how I got to see the show. I was sorry to hear about your leg. I guess that means you're out of the show."

Maggie nodded. "The audience doesn't pay to see an actress with a broken leg."

"Liz said you'll be staying with her until your leg heals."

"Oh, did she, now?" That's not what they had agreed, and the fact that Liz was spreading a deliberate exaggeration was interesting. However, that wasn't any of the young woman's business, so Maggie wasn't about to set her straight.

"I'd better get back to work. I have another house to clean this afternoon. Nice chatting with you, Ms. Fitzgerald."

"Fitzgerald is my maiden name. I still use it on the stage. Now, it's Ms. or Dr. Krusick."

"Oh, you're a doctor too?"

"I'm a professor, or I was…before I retired. Not a medical doctor."

"Liz has a lot of doctor friends. Dr. Carson visits every year. Sometimes, she brings her nieces and nephews and their children, a real houseful! And

Liz's niece brings her kids. Good thing, there's so much room in this house. It's like a B&B here in the summer."

"That must make a lot of work for you."

"It does, but Liz pays me extra. She's very generous." Ellie glanced at the clock. "I really must get back to work."

Ellie left and Maggie wondered if the "Dr. Carson" who visited was Liz's ex. She knew from lesbian friends on the NYU faculty and in the theater that lesbian relationships often continued long after the sexual relationship was over.

After Ellie vacuumed all the common areas, she asked if she could clean Maggie's room.

"Just do whatever you'd normally do," replied Maggie indifferently, crossing out the paragraph she'd just finished writing. This was her fifth attempt to open the new chapter. No matter how she tried she couldn't get into it today, and it had nothing to do with the noise from the vacuum.

"Do you have any laundry for me to do?" asked Ellie. "I'll throw it in with Liz's."

"I've been using the hamper in the bathroom." The direct question forced Maggie to pay attention. "Don't worry. I can take care of my laundry."

Ellie glanced at the walking boot. "Really? I don't think you'll make it down to the basement with that boot on. Why don't you let me see what's in the hamper?"

Around noon, Ellie came in to say she was leaving. "It was nice meeting you, Dr. Krusick. A real honor. I'll see you next time." She offered her hand.

Maggie decided after Ellie left that it was high time to shower and get dressed. She went into her room to find that Ellie had picked up all the clothes heaped on the furniture and hung them neatly in the closet. The bed linens had been changed, and her clean laundry lay carefully folded on the bureau. She was embarrassed that Ellie had seen the state of her room. But Lorna at the Windward Inn had also seen her mess. What must these people, who knew Liz well enough to call her by her first name, think of her friend from New York?

***

Maggie made herself lunch, and while she was looking in the refrigerator, she hunted for something to make for dinner. She found the extra striper filets in the freezer along with some containers of what appeared to be homemade tomato sauce. With rice and a salad, it could make a tasty meal. Maggie looked up recipes for fish prepared with a light tomato sauce while the filets defrosted in the refrigerator.

When Liz came home, Maggie instantly perceived that something was wrong. Liz offered a cursory greeting, then took a bottle of whiskey out of a cabinet and poured herself a generous portion. Frowning, she stood in the kitchen, while she gulped down the whiskey. She poured herself another glass and headed out to the porch.

"What's the matter?" asked Maggie, following her out, annoyed that the boot slowed her pursuit.

"The mother of the boy who burnt up in the accident came to see me looking for tranquilizers. He died on the way to the burn unit in Boston."

Maggie rubbed Liz's shoulder. "I'm so sorry," she said in a soothing voice.

"He was such a nice kid. I really liked him. I don't usually go to the funerals of my patients, but I think I'll go to this one." Liz cleared her throat, and Maggie knew it was to mask strong emotions. "I've been at this a long time, but it's still hard sometimes. It's especially hard with the young ones."

"I can imagine."

"No offense, but I don't think you can."

"Do you need time alone?"

"No, it's fine." Liz forced a smile. "It's nice to have company." She reached out for Maggie's hand. "Sit down."

"I can sit only for a moment. I'm getting dinner ready."

"What a nice surprise to come home to someone cooking dinner for me."

"Didn't Jenny cook for you?"

Liz made a little face. "Jenny wasn't much of a cook, and her schedule was stranger than mine. Unless I cooked, we ate out."

Maggie sat down next to Liz for a while, but Liz had very little to say. She sipped the whiskey and stared out the window. Maggie reached out and gently stroked her arm. Liz turned and gave her a sad look. "Thank you," she said.

***

The poached striper recipe was such a success that Maggie decided to bookmark it to her favorites. She enjoyed watching Liz eat the food she cooked because she truly savored it. Her eyes closed and she made little sounds of appreciation as she tasted each part of the meal. "My God, this is amazing," she exclaimed. It was especially satisfying to hear Liz's compliments because she certainly had the means to eat in some of the very best restaurants.

They had just finished eating when Maggie's phone rang in the kitchen. Maggie could hear it vibrating on the granite counter top. "Let it ring," she said. She disapproved of devices ruling everyone's life and deliberately refused to affirm their dominance by jumping every time her phone rang. Eventually, the ringing stopped but then instantly began again.

"If they're calling twice, it might be important," said Liz, glancing in the direction of the kitchen.

"It's my daughter. She usually calls around this time of night on a Tuesday."

"Your daughter?" Liz asked with a puzzled frown.

"Yes, I have two of them." Maggie anxiously scanned Liz's face to judge her reaction. She hadn't meant to withhold this important fact. She simply hadn't felt the need to make an announcement.

"I thought you couldn't have children," said Liz, narrowing her eyes.

"I couldn't, so we gave up trying and adopted two older girls from Romania. They were sisters. The adoption agency wouldn't separate them, so we took them both."

"Those Romanian orphanages were supposed to be a horror."

"You have no idea," said Maggie, averting her eyes because she didn't want Liz to see the emotion the memory evoked. "I'm so glad we could help those poor little girls. There were challenges at first, but they grew up to be good people. Sophia is a resident in oncology at Baylor Medical Center. Alina is the local news producer for the NBC affiliate in Florida."

"Impressive."

Maggie knew the remark was sincere, but she felt the need to underscore a point. "You might not believe it, but I am a real feminist. I insisted on the best education for my girls, and I encouraged them to be anything they wanted to be."

"I'm sure you did." Liz patted Maggie's hand as she got up from the table. "You should call your daughter, or she'll be worried about you. I'll do the dishes." She picked up the plates and headed to the kitchen. She returned with Maggie's phone.

When Maggie's daughter answered she sounded harried and tired. "Are you okay, Mom?" asked Sophia anxiously. "You just came up on my Google crawl. You broke your leg! Why didn't you call me?"

"Don't worry, Phi. I'm being looked after by a very good doctor. She's an old friend from college."

"Really? Someone I know?"

"You never met her. Her name is Liz Stolz."

There was a dead spot in the transmission, or maybe it was deliberate silence. It was hard to tell. "Elizabeth Stolz, the surgeon?"

"Yes. Do you know her?"

"*The* Elizabeth Stolz?"

"Yes, I guess so," Maggie confirmed anxiously. What did Sophia's reaction mean?

"Mom, she's a legend!"

"Really?" asked Maggie, listening to Liz rinse the dishes in the kitchen.

"She revolutionized breast cancer surgery. We read her book and her case studies in our training."

"You did?"

"Wow," said Sophia, drawing out the word. "She's your friend?"

"Yes, from college."

"Why didn't you ever tell me?"

"We lost touch…a long time ago. It was an accident that we met. Literally, an accident." At least, that was the truth.

"Oh, my God, Mom. Elizabeth Stolz! How cool is that?"

"Would you like to say hello?"

"Can I? Can I really?" asked Sophia in an excited, childlike voice.

"Let me ask." Maggie muted her phone and called into the kitchen. "Liz, will you say hello to my daughter? She's one of your admirers."

The water cut off in the kitchen. Liz came out to the porch. "Really? I have admirers? Who knew?" She laughed gently.

"Hold on, Sophia. Here's Liz."

"Hello, Sophia," said Liz cheerfully into Maggie's phone. "Yes, I'm holding your mother hostage until her leg heals. I hope you don't mind." Now Liz was spreading her propaganda to her daughter.

Whatever Sophia said in reply, Liz laughed heartily. "No, I'm used to the exploding suitcase. I lived with it in college."

"Sophia is a neat freak," Maggie whispered. "So is Alina, my youngest. Go figure."

Liz nodded as she listened to what Sophia was saying on the other end. Maggie enjoyed the smiles and a wink, a little stunned by the instant bond between her daughter and her old friend. Liz muted the phone to address her. "Is it okay to tell your daughter about your injury and how I'm treating it? Privacy laws, you know."

"Of course, you can tell her everything."

Maggie understood very little of the conversation that followed, an abrupt shorthand filled with medical terms that sounded like a foreign language. Liz looked thoughtful as she patiently answered Sophia's questions.

"Well, thank you," said Liz, obviously winding down the conversation. "And I promise I'll take good care of her…. Yes, she's very special to me too." She handed the phone back to Maggie.

"Oh, Mom. How cool that I got to talk to her!"

"So, you're satisfied I'm in good hands?"

"Seriously? If I could fly up right now and pick her brain, I'd be there in a heartbeat."

"Maybe some other time." As much as Maggie loved her daughter, she didn't want anyone upsetting the delicate balance of her renewed friendship with Liz. There was still so much ground to cover and so much to say.

After she ended the call, Maggie listened to Liz whistling an air from *Aida* while she finished cleaning up the kitchen. Sophia had said she was a legend. What did that mean exactly? When Liz was out of the house, Maggie would certainly give the awards and news clippings in Liz's office a closer look. She'd also try to find out about Liz's book. Maybe Sophia could give her more information.

Chapter 9

Liz tried to be discreet about glancing at the clock while Mrs. Riordan went on about her autistic grandson, Most of Liz's time as a family practitioner was spent listening, completely opposite of how she had managed her patients as a surgeon. Then, she'd been a firehose of information describing procedures, possible outcomes and rapidly answering patients' questions. When she became a family practitioner, she had to teach herself to listen. It was excruciating at first. She always wanted to jump ahead and finish her patient's sentences, but slowly, she'd learned that context was essential to treating a whole person. Sometimes, seemingly inconsequential bits of data were important, especially those minor complaints patients tended to gloss over.

But there wasn't anything medically useful in Mrs. Riordan's gushing over her grandson. It was Liz's attention she wanted, so Liz continued to smile and nod despite the clock counting down the minutes. Today, she'd hoped to leave early or at least on time. She had made dinner reservations for six, so they could eat a leisurely meal before the concert. The seats closest to the stage were reserved for patrons who bought the dinner package. Nathan's was pricey, but Liz didn't mind. The chef had justifiably earned the restaurant's five-diamond rating by featuring locally-sourced food, preparing it simply, and presenting it beautifully.

Mrs. Riordan flipped open her wallet and proudly showed a picture of her grandson. "See? He doesn't even look autistic."

"A very handsome boy," replied Liz in a genuinely admiring voice.

"Yes." Her patient sighed.

"I'm afraid I need to get home a little early tonight, Mrs. Riordan. I have tickets to hear Judy Collins sing at Nathan's tonight." Liz rarely confided anything about her personal life to her patients, but she needed to convey the urgency of leaving...soon.

Mrs. Riordan quickly put her wallet away. "So sorry to keep you, Dr. Liz. You go to your concert."

Liz walked her patient to the front desk. "Six months for a blood draw and an office visit, Ginny."

Ginny was giving her that look that said, "Get out of here *now*."

"Enjoy your holiday weekend, Mrs. Riordan," said Liz.

"You too, Dr. Liz." She reached up to give her a hug. "I really hope you enjoy the concert. Tell me all about it when I see you next time."

Liz promised that she would. She made an effort to preserve her dignity by walking to her consulting room at a reasonable pace, but as soon as the hall was clear, she grabbed her bag and headed out the back door.

She decreased the pressure on the gas pedal as she approached the intersection. The Hobbs police liked to lurk behind the old TV repair shop and pounce on speeders in the completely unnecessary 35-mph zone. They had stopped Liz a few times, although none of the officers dared to give tickets to Hobbs' most popular M.D. Even the newest members of the force knew to issue only warnings, which Liz stacked in her glove box like old grocery receipts. She carefully watched her speed past the old building. As soon as she was out of the danger zone, she leaned on the gas pedal and allowed her mind to wander.

What to wear to this event had been a worry since she'd reserved the tickets. Maggie, of course, would look stunning, as she did on every occasion. Liz had finally chosen an unconstructed black linen blouse with a low neckline that showed a bit of cleavage. With skinny pants and black heels, the outfit would be chic but casual enough for an evening of folk music.

Maggie's door was closed when Liz came in. "I'm home," Liz called out as she bounded up the stairs. "I'm going up to change."

She began stripping on the way to the bathroom, where she wiped off all her makeup and started from scratch, aiming for a dramatic, evening look. She checked the time on the clock over her shoulder while leaning in to apply eyeliner. It smudged. "Fuck." For emphasis and good measure, she repeated it, louder this time. Finally, she flicked a crisp line across the lid. She took time with the mascara because her hands were shaking. As a surgeon, she'd always taken pride in her steady hands. Tonight, for some inexplicable reason, they shook.

Liz jumped into her clothes. She couldn't run down the stairs in heels, so she took the elevator. She paced as she waited in the entry hall for Maggie. Finally, her patience wore thin. "We have reservations for six," she called through Maggie's door.

Maggie emerged, wearing a black dress, accented by a colorful scarf in peacock colors. She looked every bit the glamorous actress.

As she took Liz in, her eyes widened. "Is that really you?"

"I don't look that different!" Liz's surly tone was intended to fend off further compliments, but it didn't work.

"Yes, you do," said Maggie, appreciatively touching the shoulder of Liz's blouse. "I hardly recognize you. But I definitely approve."

"Thank you," said Liz with genuine modesty. "You look pretty amazing yourself, but you always do." Liz handed her a box.

"What's this?"

"Your fracture is so close to the ankle, you can get away with a shorter boot, especially now that the bones are beginning to knit."

Maggie opened the box to find a short, black boot with Velcro ties. Of course, it was ugly, but much less obvious than the gray plastic, full-leg boot she had been wearing.

"Sit down. Let me show you." Liz removed the other boot and the inner sock and replaced them with the ankle-fracture boot.

"My dress boot," said Maggie, raising her foot to show it off. Liz handed her a new cane finished in mottled blue and black metallic. "The latest for the well-dressed invalid. I feel positively elegant!"

Liz asked her to wait on the porch while she pulled out the Audi.

"You're really going all out tonight," observed Maggie, as Liz helped her down the stairs. "I'm honored."

"The parking is extremely tight at Nathan's."

"Liz, let me believe it's all for me," said Maggie as Liz opened the passenger door for her.

As they waited at the light on Route 1 to make the turn, Maggie said, "Remember our date for my twentieth birthday?"

Liz remembered it well. She'd spent a fortune on tickets for a revival of *A Streetcar Named Desire* at Lincoln Center because she knew Maggie loved Tennessee Williams. Maggie had worn a long dress and Liz, a black silk pantsuit. Before the performance, she took Maggie to dinner at an expensive Manhattan restaurant for which even she'd needed to save to afford the bill. She anxiously held doors for Maggie, pulled back her chair in the restaurant, and confidently paid the exorbitant restaurant tab. After the play, they went to an upscale bar and ordered cognac in crystal glasses. They looked so comfortable in their grown-up clothes no one questioned the fact that, at seventeen, Liz was underage.

Liz slid down in her seat a little as if she could hide from the memory. "God save us from our youth."

"Not at all. You were charming that night, so debonair and gallant." Maggie reached out and patted Liz's thigh. "I cherish those memories of you." She allowed her hand to linger a moment, stroking the fabric lightly with her fingertips. "Tonight is like a date."

"Yes, I suppose it is," agreed Liz reluctantly.

"You don't like that idea?"

"It's fine, I suppose."

Liz parked in a handicapped spot at the restaurant, knowing her M.D. plates would stifle any objections. She tried not to abuse the privilege, and, in this case, her passenger was legitimately disabled. She offered Maggie her arm to help her negotiate the stairs to the dining room.

"You haven't changed a bit," said Maggie. "Still playing the attentive gentleman."

"Stop it, Maggie. You're embarrassing me." Liz glanced over her shoulder to see if anyone had heard.

"Oh, I doubt it. Besides, the role suits you perfectly."

The waiter arrived to ask for their drink orders. "The elderberry martini is nice," suggested Liz. Maggie agreed to try it, so Liz ordered two.

"The sculpture in the garden is so interesting," said Maggie peering at the rusty, steel figures in the rock garden outside.

"It's very clever. See? Your eye is drawn to the elements of the garden instead of the dilapidated building on the other side. Like stage illusions in the theater."

"Remember when you were stage manager for *Antigone*?"

"I remember." Liz looked up from studying the menu. "You made a stunning Ismene, but you should have gotten the lead."

"That director wanted a dark-haired actress for *Antigone*. One of the few times my blond hair was a liability."

Liz frowned. "I always wondered why he encouraged all that touching between Antigone and Ismene. He was suggesting not only lesbianism, but incest."

"It was the time. All that weird experimental theater was in vogue. I'm sure he thought it very edgy. He said we were too reserved and needed to be loosened up."

"He was a pervert."

Maggie laughed. "So you said. You certainly didn't like him. But I learned a lot from him, and he did offer me a part in his off-Broadway play. Remember when you offered to quit school and get a job so I could become an actress?"

"That was an idiotic idea. I can't believe I ever said that."

"You were in love, Liz, but I could never have deprived you of your dream of becoming a doctor."

"I almost didn't become a doctor."

Maggie's mouth parted in surprise. "Why?"

"I was a complete basket case after you left. My grades suffered because I hardly ever went to class. I was such a mess I considered dropping out."

"Oh, Liz. I never would have forgiven myself if you dropped out."

"My campus housing situation was a disaster. Claudia and Felicia had moved out of the new dorm. When you didn't show up, I was assigned a new roommate. She always wanted me to sleep on the couch, so she could fuck her boyfriend. I got an apartment off campus and hunkered down. I never went out except for classes I couldn't miss and to buy food."

"That's why Claudia said she never saw you."

"No one saw me. Not even my parents. When I started having suicidal ideation, I knew I was in serious trouble."

Maggie's eyes widened. "My God. I had no idea it had gotten that bad. Why didn't you get help?"

"I couldn't go to a shrink. In those days lesbianism was still on the books as a mental disorder. And the least hint of psychiatric issues could keep you out of medical school or prevent you from getting a license."

"So you suffered alone?"

"Pretty much. What else could I do? I didn't know anyone like me. I knew they existed, but how would I find them? Then one day, I saw an ad in *The Village Voice*. A support group for lesbians coming out. That probably saved my life. Eventually, I pulled myself together. I ended up with a few Bs to spoil my perfect record, but I graduated magna cum laude and got into medical school."

"Oh, Liz. I'm so sorry," said Maggie with a sigh.

Liz shrugged. "It wasn't just you. It was everything. I lost an entire year of my life, but I survived."

Maggie studied Liz's face. "I never wanted to hurt you. Never. *I loved you.*"

"I know. You were scared. You were used to being the popular girl everyone liked, so you caved to religious and social pressure to conform. I see that now."

Maggie leaned on her hand. "What do you think would have happened if my mother hadn't interfered?"

Liz gazed into her water glass as she considered the question. "Who knows? We might have broken up and moved on to other lovers. First loves seldom last."

"But sometimes they do." Maggie looked directly into Liz's eyes.

Liz held Maggie's gaze. "Then why didn't you call me after your marriage ended?"

"I was afraid of your anger."

"But now you're not?"

"Oh, I am. I'm sure it's still there...deep down."

"Don't worry. I'm not a vindictive person."

"But you're afraid," said Maggie, searching her face.

"Aren't you?"

Liz was relieved when the waiter arrived to deliver their drinks, which diverted Maggie from the previous conversation. The martinis were deep red in color and had a pleasant foam on top. "I'm not a big fan of flavored martinis, but these are exceptional. Did you know elderberries have antiviral properties?"

Maggie tasted hers and smiled. "It's delightful. Maine has been full of interesting and wonderful surprises. I've really enjoyed being here, but soon, I need to figure out how to get back to New York."

Liz felt uneasy. Maggie had agreed to stay until the concert, but until now hadn't mentioned a word about going home.

"When you talked about driving down to see your mother, I thought I might hitch a ride."

"That probably won't be until next weekend. I have office hours."

"I know." Maggie sat back in her chair and studied Liz. "I can wait until you can bring me home. You seem to enjoy holding me hostage. You tell everyone I'm staying until my leg is healed."

"I figure if I say it enough, it will become real."

"Are you sure you don't mind? I've been here for three weeks."

"I don't mind at all. I've been enjoying your company. In fact, I was going to ask if you'd like to go camping in Acadia once your leg is healed. We have an Indian summer when it's warm enough to go without a jacket, but the nights are crisp. The old Mainers call it 'High October.'"

"I don't think I'm up for camping these days. My back couldn't take sleeping on an air mattress."

Liz laughed. "Neither could mine, but the place I have in mind is quite civilized. They have little cabins with real beds and linens, a full bath, even WiFi."

"You make it sound so enticing. Let me think about it. I've been imposing on your hospitality for a long time."

"Impose away. It's pretty quiet up here when all my summer visitors leave."

Maggie gave her a penetrating look. "Are you lonely, Liz?"

Liz gazed back into the hazel eyes. "No, but sometimes the winters are hard. I keep myself busy. I'm involved in a lot of things."

"What about sex?"

Liz blinked. Maggie was asking her about sex. "Are you offering?"

Maggie laughed softly. "I don't know. Are you?"

Maggie's steady gaze was making Liz anxious. She said in a breezy voice, "Don't worry. Plenty of women are interested in me. I'm considered quite a catch, you know." She wiggled her eyebrows suggestively.

"I'm sure you are." The gleam in Maggie's eyes was equally suggestive. "And they're right. You are quite a catch."

***

They each drank another elderberry martini during the show. On the way home, Liz streamed Judy Collins songs through the Bluetooth in the car, and they sang along.

"What an amazing performance!" Liz said. "Hard to believe she's closing on eighty."

"Her pipes are not what they used to be, but she did a great job of modulating her voice to make the best use of it. I have to do that sometimes. Menopause changes women's voices. Our throats get dry just like our vaginas."

Liz was silent as she considered the information.

"You're a doctor. Why am I telling you?" Maggie wondered aloud.

"Yes, but I never thought about it that way. See? I learned something tonight."

When they arrived home, Liz gratefully took off her shoes. She almost never wore heels anymore, and she'd always hated them. On stocking feet, she headed to the kitchen. "Would you like a glass of wine?" she called to Maggie. "I'm too keyed up to go straight to bed."

"Yes, that would be wonderful. We can sit on the porch and listen to the night sounds. It's so relaxing."

Liz brought the wine and sat down beside Maggie on the wicker love seat. Maggie moved closer. Where their thighs touched, it tingled.

"I'll really miss this when I go back to New York," mused Maggie with a sigh.

"The city has its own night sounds."

"Yes, but this is very special." Maggie put down her wine glass. She took Liz's glass out of her hand and set it down too.

Liz smiled, getting the idea. With the lightest touch under Maggie's chin, she gently turned her face.

"I was wondering when you would finally get around to this," whispered Maggie.

"Do you mind?" asked Liz.

"Do I mind?" mocked Maggie, closing her eyes and moving closer. Liz could feel her sweet breath on her skin. Liz took Maggie's face in her hands. Maggie's lips against hers were velvety soft and warm. They parted, welcoming her inside. Maggie's mouth was tangy with white wine. Her newly washed hair smelled grassy like a summer field in June. They explored one another's mouths as if it was the first time, the desire just below the curiosity and the slight hesitation, in case it all went wrong.

But it didn't. Maggie responded with equal enthusiasm, gently filling her mouth with her tongue, teasing. She molded her hand around Liz's breast. Her fingers lightly traced its curve ending at the nipple, which instantly responded to her touch. Maggie smiled and released Liz's lips. "Who taught you how to kiss?" She asked, allowing her fingers to graze Liz's cheek.

"You did."

"I did a damn good job."

"Yes, you did." Liz reached out for her again, but this time, Maggie only gave her a quick, friendly kiss.

"Not tonight, Liz. It's too soon. We're not ready."

Liz swallowed her desire.

Maggie got up. "Good night, Liz. Thank you for a lovely evening."

"Glad you enjoyed it."

"I did. Every bit of it."

Liz remained on the porch to finish her wine. The evening had stirred up so many memories she had tried to forget. That production of *Antigone* was the last of the season before summer break. It was hot in the theater, and under the spotlights, Maggie visibly perspired. Liz remembered the sexy feel of her sweaty body through her costume—sheer evening pajamas with wide-legged pants. When they kissed in the wings between scenes, Liz boldly went up the pant leg and took what she wanted.

The director had suggested that the young actresses dispense with underwear. They'd agreed to go braless but wore nude panties to preserve their modesty. After all, it was a Catholic college. As Liz watched in the wings, she could see Maggie's pert nipples through the thin fabric. When Maggie came offstage, Liz pulled her behind the traveler so that she could caress them.

What were they thinking? It had been such a risk. Anyone could have come upon them fondling one another behind the curtain. If they'd been discovered, who knows what the administration would have done? They'd expelled students for less.

The memory of Maggie's sweaty body recalled the night Liz had helped her out of the body slimmer. The feel of her bare skin had been enough to bring back all the lust Liz had felt on those hot nights in the little, student theater.

Liz touched her lips as she thought about the kiss they'd shared. She imagined Maggie in bed in the downstairs guest room and the sexy nightgown she wore to bed. Liz had caught a glimpse of it when Maggie had left her robe open one morning.

Liz could knock on the door.

No, she couldn't.

Maggie was right. It was too soon. They weren't ready.

Chapter 10

Maggie yawned and stretched. *Like a cat*, she thought, *Maggie the Cat*. She'd once played the role in Cat on a Hot Tin Roof. She adored Tennessee Williams' plays—Streetcar, Glass Menagerie, Iguana, Suddenly Last Summer. Tortured, lonely, eccentric people who can only reveal the truth of their lives under duress. One would never know from looking at the image Maggie presented to the world, but she was ideal to play Tennessee Williams' faded heroines. On the surface, she'd seemed the perfect wife and perfect mother, but below the surface lay the secrets.

She turned the alarm clock so she could see the time: nine thirty-five. She hadn't intended to sleep so late, although there was no place she had to be, and Liz would be at the office all morning. Maggie lay in bed listening to the sounds outside the window: birds singing, of course, but also the chipmunks chattering to one another, the hum of a bee foraging in the zinnias in the flower bed below her window. When she'd first arrived, she'd thought the woods were so quiet, and they were, compared to the noise of traffic in New York City. In truth, the land around Liz's house was vibrating with sounds and full of life.

She closed her eyes again and thought of Liz's kiss, which instantly returned her to their darkened dormitory room four decades ago. It had taken weeks of furtive embraces, caresses on the cheek, kissing one another on the hands and face before mustering the courage to kiss on the lips. How different it had been to kiss a girl after enduring the rough-faced boys, who had clumsily poked their sloppy tongues into her mouth. Liz's face was bright and smooth and her skin so soft. Like baby's skin. She kissed neatly, like she was sucking honey from a spoon.

Maggie smiled to herself. Grown-up Liz kissed with more confidence, but she still kissed like she was tasting honey, slow and easy but with obvious pleasure, sometimes even a little smile of delight. There was no doubt Maggie had been excited by that kiss. She imagined how it would feel to be caressed and probed by her friend's strong, competent hands. Maggie imagined Liz stroking her and opening her with her fingers. The thought so aroused her that she reached under her nightgown and touched herself.

The orgasm, when it came, was deep and satisfying. Maggie brought her fingers up to her face. Her own female scent excited her. Maggie lay in bed thinking of Liz. Did she ever imagine making love to her? Did she remember their last time together in Maggie's tiny bedroom in her parents' house? Maggie remembered every detail vividly. She had come home from a date with Barry, guilty at leaving Liz alone to go out with him to the movies. Liz was surly and standoffish when she returned. Seducing her had taken effort. Maggie had blown gently into her ear, which was guaranteed to excite her. When she'd gently flicked Liz's clitoris with her tongue, she'd come within seconds. Afterwards, all was forgiven, and they'd lain in one another's arms, pledging to love one another forever.

After reliving the memory, Maggie was tempted to make herself come again, but it was getting late. She finally got up and put on the new boot. Liz had been thoughtful to bring it just in time for the show. The ankle boot was less conspicuous and much lighter. It was certainly easier to get around without that enormous brace on her leg.

In the kitchen, she found two filled coffee pods and a note beside them to remind her there was lemon-blueberry bread for breakfast. She was listening to the coffee lazily streaming into the cup when heard her phone ringing in the distance. In a moment of panic, she realized she had no idea where it was. Then she remembered she'd left it on the table in the porch and hobbled out to get it.

She grabbed the annoying thing right before the call went to voice mail. Without checking the identity of the caller, she spoke impatiently. "Well, hello!"

The male voice on the other end laughed. "Maggie, it's Tony. I'm sorry if I woke you."

"You didn't. And I'm the one who should be sorry. That was rude. I don't wake up well, and I couldn't find my phone."

Again, he laughed. "I called to invite you to breakfast. You must need a break from Liz by now."

In fact, she couldn't spend enough time with Liz, but she'd never admit that to Tony. "She's not even here."

"I know. Saturday office hours. Fred has an appointment with her at ten, which reminded me I haven't seen you since our little dinner party. Let's get some breakfast at the Omelet Mill, then hit the consignment shops."

"Give me an hour."

"Okay. Pick you up at eleven."

❋❋❋

The Omelet Mill was Webhanet's most popular breakfast spot. Even at half past eleven, there was a line for a table.

"If Liz were here, she'd whisper sweet nothings into the hostess's ear," said Tony. "We'd get a table right away."

"Yes, she has a way with hostesses and waiters."

"The whole town knows her. That helps."

The hostess waved in their direction. "I'm sorry," she said. "We really try our best to accommodate the handicapped."

Maggie bristled at the remark, despite being grateful her broken leg had earned them a place to sit down. Her leg was much improved, but it still hurt when she stood on it too long. The people lined up for a table glared as Maggie and Tony passed on their way to the front. She wanted to point to her boot and say, "See? I really am handicapped."

They were shown to a tiny table next to the kitchen door. The door constantly swung open and shut as wait staff carrying heaping plates of breakfast food passed by in a steady stream.

"They have lobster omelets here," said Tony. "They're very good."

"No, thanks. I've had enough lobster to last a long time. Liz would eat it at every meal if she could."

Tony nodded. "But she paces herself. She's very disciplined. Very German," he said in an exaggerated German accent.

Maggie laughed, realizing Tony had Liz pegged perfectly. "How did you two meet?"

"She'd been coming up here on vacation and became a fan of the

Playhouse. We had a heart attack one night during a show, and she an-swered the proverbial question, 'Is there a doctor in the house?' She's a big donor. We need to keep her happy."

A harried, young woman in tight jeans and a black T-shirt barreled up to take their order. She looked disappointed when they ordered only eggs and bacon instead of something more exotic and expensive. Besides its three-egg omelets, the restaurant was known for its Belgian waffles loaded with whipped cream, fruit syrup, and native Maine berries.

"Okay. Now that you're my captive, I want the whole story," said Tony. "And I mean, all of it!"

"What are you talking about?"

"There's obviously something going on between you and Liz."

"Don't be crazy."

"Honey, I'm not crazy. I can see how she looks at you." He stuck out his tongue, held up both hands to his chin, and aped a puppy, complete with the panting. "And you look at her the same. You stare at her ass. Now, I know she has a nice ass and great legs, but really! I thought I'd have to mop up the drool!"

"Tony!"

He threw back his head and laughed, making Maggie want to sink into her seat.

Fortunately, the waitress arrived to deliver their coffee. "Friendly, isn't she?" said Tony, following the waitress with his eyes. "We could have gone anywhere for a meal like this, but the food is always good here." He poured cream into his coffee. "Usually, it's not this busy, but this is high season, of course. The Playhouse has been absolutely packed."

Maggie silently cursed the injury that was keeping her off the stage. She'd been counting on this opportunity to help launch a comeback. "How's the show going?"

Tony shrugged. "Melissa is doing a great job, but they paid to see you."

"I don't know why. My one claim to fame is that road show of *Les Misérables*, and that was years ago."

"Don't undersell yourself, Maggie. You have lots of fans. People love off-Broadway and comeback stories."

"I blew my comeback opportunity by going to graduate school."

"Well, don't blow this one. You have a great second-chance career ahead of you. Get that leg healed, and I'll sign you for *Carousel* in the Spring." Tony flexed his black eyebrows. "Interested?"

"Maybe. Tell me more."

"It opens on May fifteenth. Rehearsals start in April. Maybe Liz will let you stay with her until then, but winters in Maine are long, dark, and bleak. Sometimes we get over a hundred inches of snow. And ice...you should see the ice."

"What makes you think I'd want to stay with Liz?"

"Well, you haven't left yet."

"She asked me to stay until my leg heals. I think she's lonely."

"Not a chance. She's involved in everything: chamber of commerce, food pantry, mineral club, hiking club, handgun classes."

"Handgun what?"

"She's a certified gun safety instructor. You didn't know?"

"No," Maggie admitted.

The waitress plopped down their plates in front of them. Tony sprinkled pepper on his eggs until they looked like ants had invaded.

"Don't think I'm going to let you get away without telling me your story, Maggie the Cat." He looked at her intently and wiggled his eyebrows for emphasis.

"It's not that interesting, I promise."

"Let me be the judge of that!"

"We were roommates in college, but I left after sophomore year, and we lost touch."

"That's all?"

"Not exactly."

"Were you lovers?" Tony stopped eating and watched her face carefully. Maggie tried to deadpan, but she knew she couldn't fool him. "I knew it!" he declared with glee. "Fred was right."

Maggie rolled her eyes. "Tony, keep your voice down. You don't have to tell the whole world."

"Who cares? We're in the gay capital of Maine."

"But I'm not gay."

"Are you sure?"

"No, I'm not sure, but I was married for over twenty-five years."

"That doesn't mean anything. There are lots of late bloomers. Especially among you ladies."

"There was one other woman besides Liz," Maggie admitted.

"Then you're bi."

"Yes…I mean, no. I mean, I don't know."

"Yes, that about sums it up, doesn't it." Tony reached across the table and patted her hand. "It's okay, honey. You'll figure it out eventually." He'd finished his coffee and was looking around for the waitress to refill his cup. "Tell me about college. You left her."

"Yes, and it broke her heart. She wouldn't let it go. She kept calling me. Finally, I had to cut her off."

"And she's still carrying a torch for you after all these years. How romantic."

Maggie sighed. "It's scary, actually, because I have feelings for her too. Maybe I should go home."

"Do you want to go home?" asked Tony with a sympathetic frown.

"Honestly, not really. It's beautiful up here and so quiet. I've gotten a lot of work done on my book. Liz is great company. And…"

"…and you're curious to see where this will lead."

"Yes. But I want to make sure it's more than curiosity. I can't hurt her again. I just can't."

"No, that would be terrible. You were her first. Those feelings run deep, real deep. She'd never forgive you if you hurt her again."

"I know," Maggie agreed with a nod. "That's what I'm afraid of. If we move too fast, that will be the end of our friendship. I don't want that."

"Just take it slow, and don't hop into bed the first chance you get."

"No, I don't want to ruin it before it even gets started." Maggie carefully stacked the toast she had decided not to eat. "She obviously doesn't want me to leave. She keeps coming up with reasons for me to stay. Last night, she asked me to go camping in Acadia."

Tony laughed heartily. "You? Camping?"

"Stop it. I used to go camping when I was a girl. I enjoyed it."

"Knowing Liz, she'll take you up to Cabela's or Freeport and outfit you from head to toe. I can just see you in pink hiking boots, little shorts." He wiggled his hips in his seat in imitation of a sashay and then roared with laughter.

"Stop it, Tony! You're so loud!"

"I'm a failed actor. My voice is trained to project."

"Well, try to modulate it…a little. Anyway, I haven't agreed to go…yet."

"But you want to go."

"Maybe it's selfish, but I want to see how our story ends or doesn't."

Tony nodded thoughtfully. "It's very seductive playing the 'what if' game, isn't it? Most of my exes were such bastards, I'd never want to see them again, never mind get involved. But if I were a woman, and I had an ex like Liz, I would be very curious."

"But I can't hurt her again."

"No, you can't, and if you do, you'll have to answer to me," he said, wagging his finger.

After Tony paid the bill, they headed back to Hobbs and the consignment shop near Beach Road. Although Tony adored women's clothes, he had an ulterior motive for trolling the thrift shops. Sometimes, he found items to use as props or costumes for his plays. He held a scarlet, sequined dinner dress against his slender torso.

"This would be perfect for you, Maggie," he called across the store. All the patrons turned around at the sound of his booming voice. Maggie hobbled closer to answer.

"Only with a body slimmer, maybe. And I don't like sequins. They fall off all over the place."

"Well, maybe we should look for something more practical. Especially, if you're going to winter up here."

"I didn't say that!"

Tony ignored her as he headed to the rack of jeans and women's casual blouses. "Look at this! Flannel is in again, or so they tell me."

"It's a pretty color," she agreed. The plaid had muted lavenders and blues, shot through with hunter green. She agreed to try it on.

They spent almost two hours in the shop and left with half a dozen pairs of jeans and as many casual long-sleeve shirts, turtlenecks, a couple of hoodies, and a winter parka. "The L.L. Bean parka is a fantastic buy," confided Tony in a low voice as they waited for the clerk to ring up Maggie's purchases. "You'll need it if you're going to Acadia in October."

Tony loaded their purchases in the back of his SUV. "I can run these through the commercial washer down at the Playhouse and bring them over another time. Want to hit another store, or have you had enough?"

"I'm willing, but my leg isn't." It was protesting not only with pain, but also swelling.

"Another day, then," Tony agreed, opening the passenger door for her.

✳✳✳

When they arrived at the house, Liz swung open the front door and glared at them. Without a word of greeting, she stepped aside and pointed into the doorway.

"Uh oh," said Tony in a stage whisper. "We're in trouble."

Maggie instantly sensed Liz's anger, but she was amazed at her self-control. Her face was completely devoid of expression.

"Didn't you get my messages?" Liz asked.

"No." Maggie took her phone out of her bag and saw the green text icon with the little red balloon in the corner. She tapped it and saw the message: "Are you okay???" The time sent was one thirty-six, about the time Liz usually got home after weekend office hours. There were also two missed phone calls. "I don't always hear my phone when it's in my bag," Maggie explained.

Tony gave Liz a sheepish look. "I think I should go," he said quietly. "Don't blame Maggie, Liz. It's my fault. I put her up to it."

"I don't blame anyone," Liz said in a humorless voice. "I was worried." She glowered at Maggie. "You left the door unlocked."

Maggie caught her lower lip with her teeth. How stupid! How could she have done that—she, who had three locks on her door in New York? "I'm sorry," she murmured.

"See you later," said Tony, slinking away.

Liz closed the door. "You don't have to answer to me, Maggie, but I was worried about you, especially when I came home and found the door unlocked."

"I'm really sorry."

"You could have left a note, sent me a text, called the office–"

"Liz..."

"What?"

"I need to sit down."

Maggie marveled at the instant change of expression—from tightly controlled anger to professional concern. She needed to remember that in case she ever played a doctor character again. "Let's go out to the porch and sit down," said Liz, taking her arm.

Once Maggie was seated in the wicker love seat, Liz sat on the hassock and pulled Maggie's leg into her lap. She ripped open the Velcro straps and pulled off the boot.

"This short boot is so much better," Maggie said, hoping to get more than a few words out of her angry friend. "Thanks for bringing it."

"You're welcome." Liz's stern tone indicated that breezy words of gratitude wouldn't improve the tenor of the conversation.

"I'm sorry."

"I accepted your apology. Just don't do it again. I..." Liz looked flustered as if she'd almost said something, but caught herself just in time. "I don't want anything to happen to you."

"I'm sorry."

"Stop apologizing," said Liz impatiently. "I heard you the first time."

Liz delicately touched the puffy ankle. That was the only sign of the injury now. The color of the leg had mostly returned to normal, which was dead white, even in the summer because of Maggie's sensitivity to the sun. Liz's touch was sure but gentle. She tentatively explored the areas around the instep and the arch with her fingertips.

"It looks fine," Liz reported as she gingerly touched the area around the break.

"You have such gentle hands," said Maggie with a warm smile and found herself imagining those hands elsewhere. She could feel the blush rising at the thought.

Liz grunted. Intent on her examination, she hadn't noticed the color of Maggie's cheeks. "You can be sure that if I touched the wrong place too hard, I'd have to scrape you off the ceiling." She gave Maggie a firm look. "You need to pace yourself. You were on your feet too much today." She lifted Maggie's leg as she got up and placed it on the hassock. "Keep it up for a while. I'll get you some ice."

While Liz was in the kitchen, Maggie realized how deeply Liz's concern had moved her. It had been a long time since anyone had worried about her comings and goings, and it felt good to have someone care again, even if the price had been enduring Liz's scowls and lectures.

Liz returned with an ice bag and a towel and carefully arranged them over the break.

"Thank you."

"You're welcome." Liz's tone was still stern, but Maggie could tell that her anger had mostly passed.

"And I will go to Acadia with you."

Liz stood up and smiled as broadly as a fifth grader in a class photo.

Chapter 11

Liz gazed wistfully at the photo of the campfire with the water lapping almost up to its edge and studied the floor plan again. The only cabin available was billed as a waterfront studio that featured a screen porch, a kitchen, and a full bath. Apart from a tiny bunk room clearly meant for children, there was only one bed. The main part of the cabin was separated from the bunk room by a pocket door, which would afford some privacy. The arrangement was less than ideal, but there was no other option. Liz clicked the reservation button and whipped out her credit card to pay the deposit.

She shut down her laptop and locked up the office. It was a tropically warm night with high humidity rolling in from the ocean. Liz found herself wishing for an icy drink, so she headed to the IGA to pick up some tonic water. Local musk melons were on sale. Heavy and fragrant, they still had some of the dirt of the field on their mottled rinds. She added a couple to her basket and headed to the register.

As she passed the urgent care, she noticed an ambulance park in front with all its lights flashing. She crossed her fingers against the possibility of being called in for an emergency. The last few weeks had been so busy with stupid accidents. On Labor Day, a teenaged boy had slipped off the jetty while trying to reel in a fish. It had taken her hours to clean out all the abrasions and suture the jagged wounds.

As she approached the house, she was surprised to see a car parked in front of the garage. No one she knew owned a Hyundai sedan. Surviving year-round in Maine required four-wheel or all-wheel drive. The plates were from Florida, which threw her for a moment, until she figured out the driver had probably picked up the car at the airport. Why hadn't Maggie let her know she was expecting a guest?

Liz left the quinine and melons in the truck while she investigated. Just in case, she loaded a round into the chamber of her pistol. Through the garage door, she could hear loud voices coming from inside the house.

"What made you think I'd want you to come?" Maggie's voice sounded both anxious and angry.

"I just wanted to talk to you," replied a raised male voice.

Liz tried the door and found it unlocked. *Dammit, Maggie. I told you to keep the doors locked!* Liz hung her bag on a hook by the door and put the pistol in her pocket. She quietly opened the door and stepped into the house. Maggie and the man seemed completely unaware as she approached.

"What's going on here?" Liz demanded.

At the sound of her voice, they both swung around and stared at her. Maggie looked overwhelmingly relieved to see her. The man looked alarmed.

"Maggie, who is this?" Liz asked, eyeing the middle-aged man standing beside her. Mostly bald, completely gray, and barely as tall as Maggie, he looked more pathetic than threatening.

"You must be Dr. Stolz." The man attempted a smile, but it came out as a grimace.

"And who are you?" Liz stepped into the room. Her hand remained in her pocket, ready to draw her pistol if the man proved to be dangerous.

"I'm Tom Meier, a friend of Maggie's from New York." He extended his hand, but when Liz made no move to take it, he quickly withdrew it. Her hand remained firmly on her pistol.

"Maggie, do you know this man?"

"Yes," said Maggie in a frustrated voice, "but I didn't invite him."

"I only came up to see her play." Meier nervously shifted from one foot to the other. "That's when I found out about the accident. The woman in the ticket office told me she was staying with you."

"I don't appreciate your showing up at my house unannounced." Meier took a step back at the threat in Liz's voice. Liz maintained her grip on her pistol. "Maggie, do you want this man to leave?"

Maggie looked conflicted. "He did come all this way."

Liz's eyes never left Meier's. "I'm fine with him staying as long as you are."

Maggie sighed. "He can stay."

Liz slowly released her grip on the gun. The heavy pistol dragged in the pocket of her shorts, making an obvious gun-shaped outline in the thin, high-tech fabric. Out of the corner of her eye, she saw Maggie stare at her pocket and give her a worried look.

"Maggie, are you sure everything is all right here?"

Maggie nodded. "Yes, Liz. I'm fine."

Liz gave Meier another warning look. "All right, then." She went into the garage to retrieve her bag. She replaced the pistol in its holster.

The conversation sounded decidedly friendlier, when Liz returned with the grocery bags.

"Dr. Stolz, can you recommend a restaurant? I'd like to take Maggie out for dinner."

Liz eyed him suspiciously. She was not about to let Maggie go off with him unless she was clear about her intentions. "Maggie, do you want to go out to dinner with Mr. Meier?"

"Professor..." corrected Meier.

Liz shot him a withering look.

"If not, you could invite him to stay for dinner. We have plenty."

Maggie looked conflicted again. She anxiously glanced at Meier. Finally, she said, "You're welcome to stay, Tom..."

"If you really don't mind..." Meier said. "Thank you, Dr. Stolz."

"It's a hot night. I'm going to make myself a gin and tonic. I have some very nice craft gin made here in Maine. Any takers?"

"Sounds wonderful," said Meier.

"Wine for you, Maggie?"

Maggie nodded. Liz went into the kitchen, where she prepared a tray with local smoked cheddar and crackers and fixed their drinks. After she served her guests, she returned to the kitchen to scrub sweet potatoes and cut up vegetables.

Meier seemed to enjoy Liz's cooking. After the meal, he pushed back from the table. "That was absolutely superb." Liz frowned because she knew the meal was an ordinary weeknight dinner, unworthy of such praise. "I don't often get home cooking," Meier added.

"Oh? Doesn't Maggie cook for you?"

"Not often. She's usually too busy."

"I'm surprised. She cooks for me."

Meier shot Maggie a brief, quizzical look.

"We take turns," Maggie quickly explained. "Liz is in the office, seeing patients. I'm home all day."

Liz's ear instantly caught the word, 'home,' and she liked hearing the sound of it coming from Maggie's mouth.

"I always look forward to coming home to good conversation and a delicious dinner. Maggie is a wonderful cook."

"Maggie was telling me you used to cook together in college," said Meier, obviously trying to open a conversation.

"Yes."

Undaunted, Meier tried again. "Maggie said you read Hegel. You don't meet too many primary care doctors who would admit to that."

"I've also read Schopenhauer, Kant, Heidegger, and Fichte. I minored in philosophy."

"I teach German literature. I suppose Maggie's told you that."

"Actually, Maggie hasn't said much about you," Liz replied with a smirk. If Meier perceived the not so subtle dig, he didn't let on.

"It must be pretty boring up here for you with such an interesting background."

"I'm never bored," said Liz. "Only boring people are bored."

"Liz wasn't always a family doctor," interjected Maggie. "She was chief of surgery at Yale New Haven."

"Really?" Meier looked impressed. "So why are you up here practicing family medicine?"

"It's my little retirement project. To keep me occupied in my dotage." Liz refilled all the wine glasses, which emptied the bottle. "I'll open more wine."

As she screwed the opener into the cork, she overheard Meier tell Maggie, "We could fly back to New York together. I bet you can still get a seat if we call tonight. Those early morning weekend flights are never full."

Liz stopped working the corkscrew and cocked an ear to listen to Maggie's answer.

"No, thanks, Tom. I have another trip planned. I'm staying here until then."

Liz nodded in approval. While she cut up some musk melon for dessert, she listened to Meier's efforts to persuade Maggie to return to New York. To her credit, Maggie never wavered.

Before she served the melon, Liz went down to the wine cellar to find another bottle of pinot grigio in case the night ran long. When she returned to the kitchen, the conversation in the dining room had shifted.

"No, I'm not interested. Thank you for coming all this way to see my show. Sorry you were disappointed."

"Why didn't you call me when you broke your leg?"

"Why should I? We broke up. Remember? It was your idea."

"I know, but I've changed my mind."

"Why? Did your graduate student dump you? I'm so sorry," said Maggie in a voice that oozed sarcasm.

Liz loudly cleared her throat to warn of her approach before returning to the dining room. Meier and Maggie exchanged an anxious look when she came in.

"I didn't plan any dessert, but I found this wonderful local melon in the supermarket. I admit to sampling it in the kitchen, and it's absolutely delicious."

"Not for me, thanks." Meier tossed his napkin on the table. He pulled back his chair and got up. "I think it's time for me to go." He glowered at Maggie, who refused to look at him. "Thank you for your hospitality, Dr. Stolz."

"I hope you don't mind if I don't see you to the door," said Maggie, sticking out her leg to demonstrate her excuse.

"Never mind. I can see myself out."

Liz followed him and opened the front door. "Have a safe flight home." She deliberately left her hand at her side rather than offering it. Meier eyed it but decided not to offer a handshake either.

"Thanks," he muttered, frowning. "And thanks for dinner. My apologies for intruding."

Liz returned to daggers shooting from Maggie's eyes. "What were you thinking inviting him for dinner?"

Liz shrugged. "If you had said so, I would have happily shown him the door."

"Bastard! They're all bastards! I don't know why I even bother with them."

"I don't either," Liz agreed. "It's their biology. They can't help themselves."

"And you!" said Maggie in an accusing voice.

"Me? What did I do?"

"What was that thing in your pocket?"

"Nothing."

"Don't tell me it was nothing, Elizabeth Stolz. It was a gun, wasn't it?"

Liz averted her eyes from Maggie's accusing stare. "Busted."

"Are you crazy!" Maggie shrieked. "What were you going to do? Shoot him?"

"If he was attacking you? Raping you? Yes."

Maggie stood there, glaring at her. "You're just like all the other yahoos up here."

"Excuse me?" Liz's voice went up a note. She was insulted.

"You heard me."

"You have no idea what you're talking about. There have been home invasions here, people out of their minds on opioids. People know I'm a doctor. They might think I keep drugs in the house. Why do you think I have the security system?"

"I thought Maine was a safe place."

"It is safe, much safer than New York where you can get shot through your window sitting there minding your own business. And I am not a yahoo."

"You gun nuts are all yahoos. Do you carry that thing all the time? Even when you're with me?"

"Yes."

"Guns scare the hell out of me. They really, really scare me."

Liz realized Maggie was trembling and put her arms around her. At first, Maggie accepted the attempt to comfort her but then abruptly flung off Liz's arms. "I don't know you anymore," she said in an accusing voice. "I have no idea who you are!" She hobbled off to her room.

"Fuck," said Liz aloud as she went into the kitchen to clean up. "That went well." She cleared the table and rinsed the dishes, glad that a grilled meal left few dishes or utensils that couldn't go into the dishwasher. The hand-blown wine glasses were an exception. She filled the sink with soapy water and carefully washed them. After she set them in the drainer to dry, she remembered the propane tank was still open, so she went out to the deck to close it.

The night air was very appealing after the oppressive heat and humidity of the day, so Liz sat down in one of the Adirondack chairs to listen to the night sounds. She allowed herself a long, deep breath as she sat back to watch the moon rise.

"Liz?" a voice called from the dark of the porch. "Do you mind if I join you?"

"Of course not."

Maggie, already in her nightgown, came out on the deck, one foot bare, the other in the ankle boot. She sat down beside Liz. "I'm sorry I lost my temper. It had nothing to do with you. I was upset because that bastard had the temerity to show up here. And now you know."

"Know what?"

"That he left me. It's so humiliating."

"Why be humiliated by some asshole running after a younger woman?"

"Well, I couldn't hold his attention. Not my husband's either."

"Their loss. You're beautiful and very sexy. If they can't see that, they're idiots."

"Thank you, but you're biased."

"That may be, but I'm not blind."

Maggie reached out her hand. Liz took it. Their fingers intertwined.

"Let me get you a glass of wine," said Liz, getting up. She went into the house and brought out the wine bottle and glasses.

"Liz, you're so kind. It was very generous of you to ask Tom to join us for dinner. Did you know right away who he was?"

"It took me a minute, but I recognized the name and connected the dots. I should have asked privately if you wanted me to invite him."

"You didn't know the whole story."

"There are many things I don't know about you."

"I could say the same. When did you become a gun nut?" Maggie's voice had lost its edge of accusation. Now, it was merely curious.

"I am not a *gun nut*. I fervently believe in gun control and gun safety. That's why I became a safety instructor."

That seemed to mollify Maggie. She nodded. "I know you're not a nut. You grew up with guns. Remember when you tried to teach me to shoot your shotgun? My shoulder was sore for a week."

"If you had tucked it into your shoulder like I told you..."

"I know. I didn't listen." Maggie sat back in her chair and gazed up at the stars. "You were always trying to turn me into an outdoorswoman."

"There's still hope. I reserved the cabin in Acadia today. It was the last one, so I took it."

Liz considered how to explain the sleeping arrangements. She played up the cabin's location by the water, the amenities that would make it seem much less like roughing it. "It only has a queen-size bed. I'm sorry, but I was afraid I'd lose it if I didn't reserve it on the spot."

"Are you planning a seduction?"

Liz swallowed her wine in a gulp. "No, of course not! I'll sleep in the bunk room."

Maggie smiled. "Are you sure?"

Sure about what? The seduction or sleeping in a tiny room meant for children? Liz tried to decide which question to answer. She chose the less controversial one.

"Sleeping in a bunk will be fine, more like camping."

Chapter 12

Liz brought her laptop out to the porch to catch up on her paperwork. She was glad to have remote access into the office system so she could work from home. She was also glad that Cathy Pelletier, her partner, had Saturday office hours that weekend.

Although Liz was supposedly working, she was surreptitiously watching Maggie give herself a pedicure. It made no sense that Maggie had a broken leg and still couldn't walk very well, yet she felt the need to paint her toenails lavender. As Liz continued to watch, she found the entire process from soaking the toes to shaping the cuticles mystifying and ridiculous.

"Don't lean too hard on that heel," she cautioned with a frown.

Maggie didn't look up from carefully slicking on the polish. "I thought you were working."

"I am working."

"No, you're not. You're watching me. I can feel it." Maggie glanced at Liz's bare feet. "You should let me give you a pedicure. Your feet are frightening."

Liz inspected her toes as she wiggled them. "Thanks, but no thanks." She stuffed her feet into her Crocs to hide them.

Maggie raised a brow. "I know you hate girly things."

"That's not completely true. I like them on you."

"I know you do." Maggie looked up and smiled.

"It seems very intimate to be touching someone's feet."

"Nail salon workers do it every day. They even get paid for it."

"Still," Liz insisted, "it feels like an invasion of privacy."

Maggie laughed. "Liz, my fingers have been inside you, and my tongue has been on your clit, and you're worried about me touching your feet?"

Liz found it both shocking and exciting to hear Maggie talk so openly about sex. She deflected by saying, "My feet are incredibly ticklish."

"So?" Maggie gazed at her with raised brows. "Go get your manicure tools and fill that basin half full of warm water. Add exactly one drop of dish liquid. Go."

For no reason that she could divine, Liz followed Maggie's orders. Perhaps it was a holdover from their college days, when Maggie, being older and more sophisticated, had assumed the role of teacher, and Liz had deferred to her.

Liz returned with her manicure kit and handed it to Maggie.

"Nice set," said Maggie looking it over. "I wouldn't dare use my own tools. I'm guessing, Dr. Stolz, that you sterilize these after every use."

"I do."

"Of course, you do. All right now, soak those hooves in the basin until my polish dries." Maggie read the newspaper while her nail polish dried. After about ten minutes, she said, "I'm ready for you." Liz brought over a chair from the table and sat across from Maggie, who patted a place on her lap. "Let's have your foot." Dutifully, Liz landed her foot in the location Maggie had indicated. "You can read, so you don't have to watch what I'm doing to you."

"I'm curious now."

"Don't tell me fibs, Liz. You're squirming inside."

How had she known? Liz wondered, but she affected an attitude of calm and tried to restrain the impulse to writhe. It was true that her feet were ticklish.

"Why do women paint their nails?" Liz asked.

Maggie shrugged. "To be pretty."

"To be more attractive to men?"

Maggie shook her head. "No, for themselves. Women like to be pretty for themselves and for other women. They know other women are judging them."

"So, it's about status. I've read that the Chinese noble class began growing their fingernails to prove they were wealthy and didn't need to do manual labor."

Maggie looked pensive. "Maybe status is a tiny part of it, but for me, it's really about being pretty for myself, like wearing a favorite dress or a revealing negligee. It makes me feel more attractive and sexy."

"Affirming your self-image."

Maggie looked up. "Liz, you think too much. Just sit back and enjoy it. Doesn't it feel good?"

It was relaxing to be touched by Maggie's gentle hands, and if Liz was willing to admit it, very stimulating. Then Maggie poked a little too hard at her cuticle with the orange stick, and Liz jumped.

"Sorry. I didn't mean to pinch you." Maggie smiled. "That really didn't hurt that much. You're just out of your comfort zone, aren't you?"

"A little. I doubt I'd let anyone else do this."

"So, why are you letting me?"

"I must trust you. I've let you do other things to me, put your fingers inside me and your tongue on my clitoris." Liz grinned. She knew she was being fresh throwing Maggie's words back at her. "I even gave you my virginity."

"Technically speaking, you didn't," said Maggie, focused on shaping the cuticles. "Have you ever slept with a man?"

"See? I told you touching feet was too intimate. Now, you're invading my privacy."

"Well? Have you?"

Maggie's hazel eyes were curious, but she was hiding it well.

"Yes, I slept with a couple of my male friends…for the experience."

"And…?"

"It was disappointing."

Maggie nodded. "I know what you mean."

"I thought if I did it enough, it would get better, but it never did. So I stuck with women."

"At least you figured that out. I never did." Maggie frowned. "Well, I did, but I wouldn't admit it to myself."

"I don't want you to put polish on my nails," said Liz to change the subject. They were getting in a little too deep.

"Oh, I will, but it will be a natural color." Maggie smiled her cat smile. "One step at a time."

"Here we are like two female primates bonding through a grooming ritual. Among female bonobos, that can lead to sex, which they use to cement relationships and define status. Or sometimes for no reason at all except pleasure." Liz wiggled her eyebrows suggestively.

"Is that so? First, I'll ask you to reciprocate on the grooming. My roots need a touch up."

Liz rolled her eyes.

"Don't roll your eyes at me, Liz Stolz. It's hard for me to do because I can't stand on this stupid leg in the shower. And if you want sex, you'll have to do your share of the grooming."

"I *don't* want sex, Maggie."

Maggie gave her a hard look. "Sometimes, you're such a liar."

"All right, I *do* want sex, but not *just* sex."

Maggie sighed. "Other foot." Liz switched and put her other foot in Maggie's lap. "It would be too easy to fall into bed with you and wreck everything. I want to do it right this time."

"This time?"

"Yes, if that's where this is heading, and I think it is."

"Then maybe we should stick with the grooming part."

"That works for now. You can do my roots after your polish dries." Maggie raised her eyes from Liz's toes and gave her a little smile. "I'll take a rain check on the sex."

Chapter 13

From the window over the kitchen sink, Maggie watched Liz come out of her woodworking shop with her phone pressed to her ear. In the sharply focused September sun, her gray hair shone like a silver halo around the head of an unlikely saint. Sitting on the stone wall that ran along the path from the barn, Liz was animated as she talked. She hardly ever talked with her hands. The one exception was on the phone, as if she needed the emphasis of gestures to make her point to a person she couldn't see. The broad smile on Liz's face as she headed toward the house told Maggie she was happy to hear from the caller.

"So, you'll be here by dinner," said Liz, coming into the kitchen. "See you, then." She ended the call with a tap. "We're going to have a house guest." She plucked a nectarine from the fruit bowl. "Jenny Carson is coming." Grabbing a paper towel to catch the juice, Liz leaned over the sink as she bit into the nectarine. "These nectarines are delicious. We need to get more."

"I'll put it on the list." Maggie wondered why the quality of the nectarines was suddenly more important than a visit from Liz's ex.

"She's four hours away, so I suppose we should plan something for dinner other than leftovers."

"Does she come here often?" Maggie asked, trying to sound nonchalant.

"She comes every summer for a few weeks. And she does this from time to time…decides she needs to get out of Dodge, so she jumps into her car and heads to Maine."

"And she assumes she's welcome?"

"She does call first, unlike your friends."

"That's good. Otherwise, she might get shot," said Maggie, not to be outdone.

Liz ignored the barb. "She knows she's always welcome. As you know, there's plenty of room here for guests."

Maggie glanced at the little trail of sawdust footprints behind Liz. "Ellie will kill you for dirtying her kitchen floor. She just washed it yesterday."

"I know." Liz took the last bite from her nectarine. "I'll sweep it up."

"Try taking your shoes off first."

"Good idea." Liz flung the nectarine pit into the compost pail under the sink. She took off her shoes and carefully swept up the sawdust.

"What are you building out there?"

"A Chippendale highboy. It was supposed to be a wedding gift for my niece. At this rate, it might be finished by the time her daughter gets married, but it's coming along. When you can walk better, I'll take you down to see it."

"I'd like that."

Liz nodded. "I might need some time alone with Jenny to talk about business. She wants to sell the land we bought in North Carolina."

"Why would you buy land *there*?"

"Jenny always said Asheville was an oasis in the land of the Philistines. We'd talked about building a house there when we retired. I don't know what I was thinking. I could never live in the South. Too fucking hot."

"So why buy it?"

Liz shrugged. "At the time, I thought Jenny and I would go on forever, and the land seemed like a good investment."

"That's how you make decisions? Whether it's a good investment?"

Liz compressed her lips and looked pensive as she considered the question. "Most of the time, but not always. Sometimes I do things for no other reason than I want to, like moving to Maine." She grabbed another nectarine from the bowl and headed back to her shop. Maggie watched as she walked down the path.

She was both overwhelmed with curiosity and nervous at the idea of meeting Liz's ex. Liz wasn't the kind to have photos around the house, so she had no idea what Jenny Carson looked like. Other than saying Jenny was a successful gynecologist in her early fifties, Liz had provided few details. Supposedly, their relationship was in the past, but it was beginning to sound like there were plenty of loose ends.

***

It was close to seven thirty when Jenny came through the door. "My God, what a trip!" she complained, dragging an enormous rollaboard over the threshold. She flung her arms around Liz and kissed her on the mouth. "I've missed you so much!" She glanced at Maggie. "Is this your friend? When you said you went to college together, I always assumed you were the same age."

Maggie winced at the remark, despite Liz's warning that Jenny could be blunt. She gave her a critical look and Jenny returned the inspection. Jenny's short hair was fashionably gray. Her figure was trim except for her prominent breasts. She had a pretty face, but her eyes were unmistakably her best feature. They were the most amazing shade of blue Maggie had ever seen. She wondered if Jenny wore tinted contacts to enhance the color.

Jenny's warm smile after the thorough once-over made her seem almost maternal. She was an OB/GYN, and mothers were her business. Maggie wondered if motherly behaviors had rubbed off on her, especially when Jenny opened her arms wide and caught Maggie in a full-body hug. "Hello, Maggie. Welcome to the family." Maggie glanced at Liz for an explanation, but she just shrugged and rolled her eyes.

"Liz, I'll just take my things upstairs. I need a few minutes, if you don't mind. I desperately need to get out of these sweaty clothes."

Liz gestured toward the hallway that led to the elevator.

"I hope you put me in the seashore room again," said Jenny. "It has the best view!"

"Take any room you want," said Liz. "The linens are clean on all the beds."

"Not that it matters," said Jenny with a wag of her hip.

What was that supposed to mean? Maggie wondered. She didn't dare ask.

Once the elevator door closed, Liz's eyes pleaded for understanding. "I know she can be a bit much, but she's harmless really and very funny once you get to know her."

"How long did you say you lived together?"

"Fifteen years."

"There must have been something between you to last that long."

Liz looked thoughtful. "Well, she didn't mind my ridiculous hours because hers were worse. She's wicked smart, and she likes toys."

"Toys?" asked Maggie, puzzled.

"Yes, you know. Sex toys. Dildos?" Maggie tried to modulate her shock but her eyes widened and Liz laughed. "I wasn't kidding about the dildos in the night stand, but no sex doll under the bed. I promise." She winked.

"You like sex toys?" asked Maggie, horrified but consumed with curiosity at the same time.

"With Jenny, I did. She's very inventive, and she knows a lot about female anatomy. The sex was amazing."

Maggie glanced toward the elevator door where Jenny had disappeared and wondered about the "amazing sex" part. How could she ever compete? Her experience with women was so limited. Would Liz find her lovemaking quaint and naive? And toys? Maggie had to admit she found the idea titillating, but did Liz *need* toys? That's not what Maggie had imagined, not at all.

Liz had gone into the kitchen to put the pizzas together. Maggie followed her in to help, but Liz seemed to have everything under control. Liz always laid out her cooking utensils and pans beforehand, almost like she was preparing a surgical tray. She cut everything with precision—meat, vegetables, fruits. All the ingredients for the pizza were lined up in careful rows, making a rainbow on the plate.

Jenny's favorite wine was open on the counter, an aerator in the neck of the bottle. The label was all in French. Maggie pointed to the papal tiara and the keys of Peter molded into the brown glass.

"What's this?"

"That's the seal of the Avignon popes. That wine comes from the former papal estates," Liz explained. "That's why it's called Châteauneuf du Pape."

"Is it any good?"

Liz handed her a wine glass. "Taste it and tell me."

Maggie poured a few dribbles into the glass and sipped it. It was so dry it made her mouth pucker, and it smelled like feet after a heavy workout in the gym. "Jenny likes this stuff?" She screwed up her face and stuck out her tongue for emphasis.

Liz laughed. "It's her favorite. I'm not a big fan of French wines myself."

"How much does it cost?"

"About fifty dollars a bottle. Sometimes, I can get it on sale in New Hampshire for less."

Maggie tried not to look shocked, although she couldn't imagine spending that kind of money on a bottle of wine. "An expensive habit," she said casually.

Liz shrugged. "Jenny can afford it."

Jenny returned wearing cotton capris and a snug, low-cut T-shirt that revealed her considerable cleavage. She was barefoot and moved around the kitchen as if she lived there. She opened the correct cabinet on the first try and took out a wine glass.

"Did you try the wine?" she asked Maggie. "What did you think?"

Maggie puckered her lips. "A bit dry for my taste."

"Oh, but it's divine. Love that dirty socks smell!" Jenny sidled up to Liz and put her arm around her waist while she watched her arrange the ingredients on the pizzas. "Looks amazing. Liz makes the best grilled pizza." Jenny glanced over Liz's shoulder. "Have you had it yet, Maggie?"

"Yes, she made it the first week I was here."

"Did she make it with goat cheese, arugula and caramelized onions? Oh, my God! That's my favorite!"

"Sorry, Jenny, that's not on the menu tonight," said Liz impatiently. "I didn't have any goat cheese. Be glad for something to eat."

"Oh, I am. I'm always happy when you cook for me." Jenny planted a quick kiss on Liz's cheek. She turned around and leaned against the counter. "I can cook, Maggie, but I don't unless I have to. Liz *loves* to cook."

"That's because I love to eat," said Liz, arranging the pizzas on a tray. "I only wish what I eat didn't love me back."

"Yes, dear, you're getting quite a little beer belly." Jenny patted it affectionately. Watching Jenny casually touch Liz as if she owned her irritated Maggie more than she was willing to admit.

"If you liked beer, you'd understand," said Liz.

Jenny grimaced. "Swill. All of it."

"You just lack appreciation for the finer things in life," called Liz over her shoulder as she headed out to the grill on the deck.

Their banter was rapidly giving Maggie a headache. She looked for a way to escape.

"We should keep her company while she cooks," Jenny suggested. "She likes that."

"No, thanks. I'll let you two catch up. I want to ice my ankle and put it up."

Jenny frowned with concern as she studied the leg. "Still swelling? That shouldn't be. You should let Liz take a look at it."

"She looks at it every day. I've never had such an attentive doctor."

"Yes, she can be a little overbearing at times. But I'll leave you to your ice and elevation," said Jenny with a little condescending smile that Maggie found extremely annoying.

Maggie passed on the ice because it had merely been a ploy to get away from Jenny. In the media room, Maggie closed the door. It had a lock that she was momentarily tempted to engage but decided it was not her place to lock doors in someone else's house. Grateful to be alone, she put her leg up on the hassock.

She sighed and sat back to assess her situation. She felt like she'd been hit by a speeding truck. For a moment, she considered packing her bags and calling a cab to take her to a hotel. No, she told herself, Jenny Carson wasn't going to force her out of Liz's house. She had every right to be here. What she needed to do was pace herself and limit her exposure to Jenny. But how dare that woman call Liz overbearing!

A few minutes later, Liz opened the door and poked her head in the room. "We're ready to eat."

"I'll be there shortly," said Maggie sullenly.

Liz came into the room and closed the door behind her. "Are you all right? I'm glad to see you have your leg up. Is it bothering you?"

"It's not the leg…"

Liz nodded. "Yes, I know. Jenny is quite a character."

"She certainly has you figured out," replied Maggie in a tart voice.

Liz compressed her lips. Maggie could tell she was trying very hard not to say something. "Come get your dinner before it gets cold."

After a few minutes, Maggie became anxious that it would look rude if she didn't come to the table, so she got up and went out to the porch. As she sat down, Liz shoveled a brightly colored pizza onto her plate.

"Is your leg feeling better?" asked Jenny. "Liz, you need to look at it. It shouldn't still be swelling."

"What the hell do you know about fractures?" snapped Liz.

"Very little beyond what they taught us in medical school," Jenny admitted.

"Then stay out of it."

Maggie gave Liz a wary look. She could see that Liz was tired from working in her shop all day and having to hold dinner. Her effort to be sociable was wearing paper thin.

Jenny began talking about some new painkiller. Soon, she and Liz were deep into a discussion of its properties. Liz apologized for leaving Maggie out and tried to steer the conversation toward plans for the weekend, but Jenny kept circling back to medical topics. Bored silly, Maggie offered to clean up the kitchen.

She wondered as she undressed for bed if Liz and Jenny would sleep together. She slept fitfully, waking to the vague recollection that there was a stranger in the house. She forbade her mind from imagining Jenny in Liz's bed, but the more she tried to block mental images of them intertwined, the more vivid the scenes became.

She was irritable the next morning and desperately needed a cup of coffee. When she came into the kitchen, she found them hip to hip in front of the coffee machine. Jenny's hand lazily rubbed the small of Liz's back. They spoke in murmurs, chuckling from time to time. It was clearly a conversation between two people who had been physically intimate. The question was, how recently?

"Good morning!" said Maggie brightly to alert them to her presence.

Liz turned around and smiled. "Good morning. Would you like a cup of coffee?"

Jenny gazed at Maggie with an annoying smile. "Liz had to remind me how her coffee machine works."

I bet, thought Maggie.

"Go sit in the breakfast room, Maggie," said Liz. "I'll bring you some coffee."

Jenny followed her out. "We're talking about taking the ferry cruise around Casco Bay, but Liz is worried you can't manage all the walking with your bad leg." Jenny glanced at her leg with an exaggerated expression of sympathy.

"That won't be a problem," replied Maggie without hesitation.

Liz came in, bringing her coffee. "Are you sure, Maggie?" Her little frown of sympathy was genuine. "It's quite a walk between where we park and the ferry launch."

"No, I can do it."

Jenny and Liz exchanged a look. Jenny shrugged. "It's your call, Liz. You're her doctor."

"We could take a drive around Sebago instead," Liz suggested.

"No, you've been talking about this Casco Bay cruise since I got here. I want to go."

❊❊❊❊

As Liz had predicted, it was a long walk from the parking lot to the boarding line for the ferry. Jenny and Liz held their place on line, while Maggie sat on a bench nearby. She had resisted sitting down as long she could bear it, unwilling to show any weakness in front of Jenny.

Liz left the line to check on Maggie. "Are you all right?"

"Fine." In fact, her leg hurt from the walking and standing.

"You don't look fine. You look pale as death. You know, we don't have to do this. We can go back. You can rest while I get the car."

"I said I'm fine," insisted Maggie. She glared at Jenny whose look of sympathy was totally inauthentic. *I'll be damned, if I give in to myself in front of you.* She shot Jenny a brilliant smile.

They finally boarded. Liz located the elevator to the top deck and found three seats in a shaded area near the bow. Liz was wedged so tightly between Maggie and Jenny she begged them for some space. "Talk about being in the middle," she muttered under her breath. Restless, she got up and went forward.

As Liz leaned over the bow rail to watch the crew ready the ferry for departure, Maggie admired how her legs met her buttocks. Jenny spoke directly into Maggie's ear, "I agree. She does have nice legs." The heat instantly rose in Maggie's cheeks. She imagined the white spots that always peeked out whenever she blushed.

When the ferry began to move, Liz came back and insinuated herself between them, flexing her shoulders to open up more room for herself. "Everybody happy?" she asked.

Maggie rolled her eyes.

The wind and water spray off the bay was refreshing. The boat stopped at an island to offload passengers and freight. Liz got off to get them old-fashioned ice cream Drumsticks in the little general store.

"This was a good idea," said Maggie, chasing the melting ice cream with her tongue as it ran down the cone. "Very relaxing."

After they docked, they ate at the best seafood restaurant in the Old Port, a place where piles of whole fish and shellfish lay on mountains of shaved ice, and the tables were covered with newspaper. Liz put away almost a dozen oysters by herself, sharing a few with her companions, and then went on to eat a whole lobster.

"Liz, remember your metabolism isn't what it used to be," Jenny said, watching her.

"I'm being virtuous. Except for the butter, it's all protein, and I'm not having any beer."

When everyone had finished their meal, Jenny picked up her spoon and gently tapped her water glass. "Your attention, please. Let's raise a glass to Elizabeth Anne. Happy Birthday, dear friend, and many more."

Maggie flamed with embarrassment. "Happy Birthday, Liz. I can't believe I forgot."

Liz shrugged. "It's okay. I didn't expect you to remember, but now have a drink for me since I'm abstaining."

Maggie raised her glass and joined the toast.

Liz hiked back to the parking lot to get the car. Jenny played with her phone while they waited, which suited Maggie, who had nothing to say to her.

On the way back to Hobbs, Jenny fell asleep in the back seat. Maggie reached out and patted Liz's thigh. "Thanks for that. It was fun."

"I'm glad you enjoyed yourself, and it wasn't too much for you."

"Oh, I didn't say that. It was a lot of walking."

"But you did very well."

"I wasn't about give in to myself in front of your friend there," said Maggie, nodding in the direction of the back seat.

Liz chuckled. "I knew that."

***

Jenny left after breakfast the next morning. After cleaning up the kitchen, Liz came out to the porch and sat down. "I always feel a little guilty being off when the rest of the world is back to work." She reached for her iPad, but Maggie touched her arm.

"Before you get started on that, I want to talk to you."

Liz flipped the cover closed and crossed her arms on her chest. Now that she had Liz's attention, Maggie didn't know how to begin. The closed body language didn't help.

"Well? What is it?" Liz prodded. Her frown made her look even more inaccessible.

"I thought you and Jenny broke up."

"We did."

"You have a very cozy relationship for people who aren't together anymore."

"We broke up as partners, not friends."

"Friends with benefits?"

Liz let out her breath slowly, obviously making an attempt to be patient. "Occasionally." The frown deepened into a scowl. "How is this any of your business?"

"It's not."

Liz studied Maggie's face for a long moment. "It's complicated."

"I bet."

"We were together a long time. Our families and friendships are intertwined. We still own the house in Connecticut together. We got it for a good price. Neither of us could afford to buy it again, even in this down market. That's why we decided not to sell it when we split up, and I moved up to Maine."

"You mean she lives in your house?"

"It's *our* house," replied Liz with emphasis. "That's why she wants to sell the land in North Carolina. To use her share from the sale and a mortgage to buy me out."

"That's good."

Liz's shrug seemed like more than indifference to her opinion. "I'm in no hurry for the money. I don't really need it now."

"But selling the property would simplify things between you."

"Yes, it would, but that's less complicated than managing her portfolio, although I think I finally persuaded her that she needs a real financial advisor, not just me, an amateur who gets lucky most of the time."

"You manage her investments too?" Maggie's surprised tone seemed to catch Liz off guard.

"Yes. As a friend," she said cautiously. "I don't charge her for it."

Maggie gave Liz a hard look. "I guess you're not done with her yet."

"Oh, I am. It's just complicated." Liz returned Maggie's firm look. "Why is this so important to you?"

"Liz, did you sleep with her?"

Liz blushed a little. Maggie turned in her seat so Liz couldn't read the dismay on her face. "Never mind. I don't really want to know." But she did want to know, because if Liz was still sleeping with her ex, it was probably time to go home.

Maggie was reluctant to ask outright, so she kept to herself for most of the day. Liz was evidently doing the same. After lunch, she disappeared into her workshop. Maggie didn't see her again until dinner time.

As usual, Liz praised her meal, obviously savoring every last bit of the braised lamb shanks Maggie had prepared.

"Better than any French bistro," said Liz pushing back from the table with a satisfied smile. "I should hire you as my personal chef."

"Then I'd have to live up here."

"You could. Winter rentals are really cheap." So, they had gone from not so subtle hints about moving in to cheap rentals nearby.

"Yes, I'm sure you'll need that downstairs room for someone else." Maggie got up to clear the table. "I wouldn't want to be in the way."

"You're not in the way." Liz rose to help her.

"Oh, I think I was when your friend, Jenny was here."

"I'm sorry she was so mean to you. I've never seen her behave that way to one of my friends. I have no idea what got into her."

"She wasn't the most pleasant person, but you were the one making me feel uncomfortable."

"Me? What did I do?"

Maggie stared at her.

"I swear nothing happened," said Liz, raising her hands.

"Then why the guilty look when I asked you about it? You turned beet red."

"You asked if I slept with her, and I did. Jenny couldn't sleep, so she came upstairs to see if I was still awake. We sat in bed and talked about why she needs a financial advisor. Honestly, money talk bores her. When she fell asleep, I didn't throw her out. Technically, I did sleep with her, but nothing happened. So, now you know." Liz continued loading the plates into the dishwasher with more than the usual clatter.

"Thank you for telling me the truth. But I'm not sure you're done with Jenny if you let her sleep in your bed."

"I'm done with her as a lover, but not as a friend."

"No one's asking you to give up her friendship."

"That's good because we've been friends for over twenty years, and I'm not throwing her away because you happened to show up." Liz turned off the water in the sink. She quickly dried her hands with a dish towel, then angrily flung it on the counter. "I'll finish later," she said, heading to the porch.

Maggie found Liz sitting in the dark and took a seat opposite her. "Liz, I'm not asking you to give up your friendship with Jenny, but I need to know where I stand with you. I'm not getting into a relationship with someone who's still involved with another woman."

"Jenny and I are friends. Our only involvement is financial. And aren't we getting ahead of ourselves talking about a relationship?"

"But I thought…"

"You thought you could waltz back into my life, and I'd want you back. Of course, you did. You're Maggie Fitzgerald, the star. Everyone wants you. You can't imagine anyone not wanting you."

Maggie cringed. The words landed on her like pointed stones. After a moment to recover, she responded in a coldly theatrical voice, "Apparently, I had the wrong idea. I'm sorry. I'll make arrangements to fly home tomorrow."

As Maggie got up to leave, Liz caught her hand. "No, I'm sorry. And you don't have the wrong idea."

Maggie brushed off her hand. "Good night, Liz. I'm going to bed now."

"Maggie, please!" Liz jumped out of her seat and ran after her.

Maggie hadn't gotten far, still hobbling on the ridiculous boot. Standing in front of her, Liz's tall body blocked the light and the path to her room. Maggie felt constricted and anxious.

"Liz, please let me pass. I need to go to bed."

"Please. I'm sorry I said that. Let's work this out. I'd hate for you to go to bed angry," Liz pleaded with a worried frown.

Maggie sighed. "Liz, we still have a long way to go," she said, gently touching Liz's cheek. "Go to bed. We'll talk tomorrow."

Chapter 14

It was chilly in the house when Maggie got up the next morning, the first shocking harbinger of the Maine winter to come. She found a pair of workout pants among the old clothes Liz kept for guests. Wearing pants required balancing on one leg to put them on, so she tried to avoid them, but now that it was getting cooler, she'd need to reconsider. Being Liz's castoff, the pants were too long, so Maggie rolled them up. She put on the heavy sweatshirt that Liz had given her that first morning after she'd arrived.

As Maggie hobbled into the kitchen to get her coffee, she felt a waft of warm air coming from the living room. She smiled. Liz had made a fire in the wood stove before she'd left for the office. She was such a good hostess. No wonder her house was full all summer.

Maggie took her coffee to the living room and despite the pleasant heat from the wood stove, she was still cold. She pulled the Hudson's Bay blanket over her legs.

While she drank her coffee, she revisited the argument with Liz. It wasn't a big, loud quarrel like the kind she used to have with Barry. At one point, she'd moved out of the house, taking an expensive rental in town for exactly one month to get away from him. Her daughters were horrified, and Barry had panicked once he realized that he was now responsible for their care. In the end, they had agreed that the best thing for everyone was for Barry to move out.

Maggie would be too embarrassed to tell Liz that things had gone so wrong in her marriage. There were early signs. Maggie had felt adrift, even after Barry got her a job doing corporate communications at his company. In the beginning, her feminist instincts to prove herself kept her going, but after a while, the corporate grind wore her down.

She vividly remembered the night Liz called after having tricked Kevin to get her telephone number. She could tell Liz was slightly intoxicated from the odd cadence of her speech. Maggie knew Barry was listening the whole time. He gave her suspicious looks while she made vague responses and desperately tried to end the call.

The argument afterwards was loud and stunning. She'd seen hints of Barry's temper all along, but he'd kept himself pretty much in check. That night, he shouted and threatened her with his fists. Fortunately, he never laid a hand on her, but he insisted on sex, despite her refusal and easily overpowered her. Now, she knew to call it what it was—marital rape. The next day, she got a post office box and opened a separate bank account, but she stayed with him for another twenty-five years.

Maggie finally felt warm enough to get up to make another cup of coffee. When she pushed the brew button, she finally noticed the sticky note pad near the coffee maker.

> Let the wood stove burn down or it will be too hot later. Thanks.
> Love, Liz.

She smiled when she read the closing. These little clues to Liz's feelings always touched her. Liz was never effusive. Her affection was low key and incremental, although its expression could often be deeply symbolic. They seldom argued when they were college lovers, but once, after a fight, Liz went home to her parents' for an entire week. When Liz returned, she brought a single pink rose that was so perfect, it looked fake, but it wasn't. They sat side by side and marveled at its perfection. Then they made love, and it was so perfect that Maggie felt her edges were merging with Liz's, and there was nothing separating them.

As Maggie headed to the refrigerator to get cream for her coffee, she noticed that some of the boxes of tomatoes, eggplants, and peppers on the floor next to the pantry were gone. Liz had said she intended to take them to the food pantry. Her plan was to process the remainder into sauces and dinners to be stored in the freezer. When Maggie opened the refrigerator, she saw the stacks of packaged Italian sausages and the tubs of ricotta cheese. Liz hadn't asked her to get involved in this project, but now, Maggie saw an opportunity for a productive day, never mind an excuse to avoid working on her book. She put up a big pot of water to boil, so she could scald the tomatoes in preparation for making sauce.

Liz called around noon. Maggie could tell from her cheerful tone that she'd rather just forget about the argument and move on, but then she said, "How about we go out to dinner and continue our discussion from last night?"

"Oh, Liz. The kitchen is a disaster, and I just made a vat of sauce and five trays of eggplant rollatini. I thought we could have some for dinner."

There was a long pause. Did Liz disapprove of her taking the initiative?

"You didn't have to do that," she finally said.

"I know, but I'm home and you're busy, so I thought I'd help out."

"I guess that means you're staying a while."

"I guess so. And, Liz, bring home some Italian bread—a semolina or that nice ciabatta with roasted garlic."

"I thought you didn't eat bread."

"I do on special occasions." Maggie allowed a brief pause to elapse. "And I do want to continue our conversation from last night."

By the time, Liz got home from the office, Maggie had finished processing the tomatoes. She'd made both plain and Italian tomato sauce and packed it in the plastic containers Liz had set aside.

"Not bad for a city girl," Liz said, coming up from the basement after putting the sauce in the freezer. "You even remembered to leave room for expansion when it freezes."

"I'm more competent than you think."

"I never doubted it."

"Sit down. Dinner is ready."

Maggie smiled as she watched Liz demolish a plateful of rollatini. "My God, Maggie. This is so good! How did you become such a good cook?"

"When I first got married, I had a lot of time to practice. It took me a while to get a job. Barry didn't want me to work. He liked the idea of a stay-at-home wife, but finally, he got me a job at his company."

Liz nodded, absorbing the information. She frowned a little. "You didn't cook for Meier. Why not?"

"Because he expected it."

"You cook for me."

"You don't expect it, and you enjoy it so much. I love to watch you eat what I cook. Your compliments make me feel appreciated."

"I do appreciate you...very much." Liz picked up a piece of ciabatta and dipped it into the little dish of olive oil. "Relationships change over time. Everything is wonderful in the beginning. The parties are on their best behavior."

"Are you on good behavior, Liz? Are you suddenly going to start grunting at the dinner table and ignore everything I say?"

Liz laughed. "God, I hope not. Jenny and I ran out of things to say after a while, but that's because our relationship was mostly about sex."

"That's why I don't want to jump into bed with you. I don't want our relationship to be about sex."

"You keep talking about sex. You must think about it a lot."

Maggie looked at Liz sidelong and raised a brow. "I do. Don't you?"

Liz laughed softly. "Yes, I do. You have no idea how hard it is to restrain myself."

"Oh, I do know because it's hard for me. But I want to be sure this time, because I can't hurt you again. I just can't."

There was a little squeak on the floor as Liz pushed her chair back from the table. She rose to take her dishes to the sink.

Maggie got up to remove the other plates from the table. "Are you worried?"

"Of course, I'm worried. Getting involved with you is a big risk, but... it's worth it."

When Liz turned, Maggie saw her younger self looking back. She saw the frank attraction in her eyes, but also the tenderness someone only shows a lover. Then Liz's expression changed. She became the adult, practical Liz once again, guarded and in control. Maggie so wished young Liz with that look of complete devotion and unconditional love would come back.

Chapter 15

On Saturday, Tony brought over Maggie's thrift shop purchases. Ironically, now that her winter clothes had arrived, the temperature had turned unseasonably warm. They sat on the deck to enjoy the nice weather and drink margaritas. Tony, who said he'd missed lunch, gorged on the salsa, guacamole, and chips Liz had set out.

"This happens every year," said Tony. "It gets cold enough for frost, and then it's hot enough for the beach."

"Looks like High October fooled us and came early this year," said Liz, replenishing the supply of chips. "I hope it's this warm when we go to Acadia next weekend."

"The warm weather never lasts. Prepare for anything."

"It's Maine. You know what they say: 'Don't like the weather? Wait a few hours.'"

Tony reached for a handful of chips. "So, Maggie, I'm working on the winter schedule for the State Theater. What do you think about a revival of *The Glass Menagerie*? I think you'd make a superb Amanda."

"Oh, Tony! I've *always* wanted to play that part!"

"It's a wonderful role. Slightly deranged faded beauty. Perfect for you."

When Liz snickered, Maggie gave her a dirty look. Liz ignored her and glanced at her watch. "Tony, why don't you stay for dinner?"

"Fred's down in Boston with some friends, so it's your good cooking or Lean Cuisine. Guess which I'll choose?"

Tony and Maggie kept Liz company on the deck while she grilled curried fish kabobs and vegetables. She listened to them debate the candidates to play the role of Tom.

Liz covered the fish kabobs with foil to stay warm. Maggie brought in the vegetables from the grill without needing to be asked. Although she overlooked the mess she created in her own room, Maggie had a sharp eye for things that needed to be done in the kitchen.

"This looks delicious." Tony sat down at the table. "Maggie, you have such a good deal here with Liz. She cooks, provides housekeeping and laundry service, and medical treatment. You should consider making it permanent."

"She hasn't asked me to move in, and I'm surprised I haven't already overstayed my welcome."

Liz brought in the rice from the kitchen. "You make a very good guest, Maggie, especially when you don't decorate the furniture with your clothes."

Maggie sighed and looked appropriately chastened. "I'm trying to be better."

"I know. Ellie told me there's been a big improvement."

Tony leaned over and patted Maggie's hand. "I sympathize, darling. I'm the slob in my relationship. Fortunately, Fred's not the neat freak that Liz is."

"She's not always neat. She tracks in sawdust from her workshop. It drives Ellie crazy."

"So, you're the odd couple," said Tony, heaping food on his plate. "All the more reason you should move in together."

"But what would I do with my apartment in New York?"

Tony raised his shoulders as if the solution were obvious. "Rent it. I bet you could get nice money for it. It's close to campus. Rent it to faculty instead of students. Then you won't need to worry."

Liz was amused that they were making plans for Maggie to move in without even consulting her. She decided to stay out of the conversation to see what developed.

"Liz might need that downstairs room for her strays," Tony continued. "You could move up to the second floor, now that your leg is mostly healed. That way, you can keep your mess contained and no one will see it. Or maybe you want to move to the third floor for the view."

Maggie frowned. "Tony, you know there's only one bedroom up there, and that belongs to Liz."

"I know." Tony poured himself another glass of wine.

"And who are these strays Liz takes in?"

"I'm exaggerating, of course. I only know of one, my friend who had prostate cancer. He couldn't work because the chemo made him too sick, and he lost his apartment for back rent. Liz took him in, no questions asked."

"Well, he's your friend, Tony. I didn't take in someone off the street."

"Maggie, I'm telling you, she fed the guy, gave him free medical care, waited on him hand and foot. He's doing great now." Tony crossed his fingers. "But you never know with cancer."

"Stop, Tony." Liz engaged his eyes to make sure he understood her message. "Chris is doing really well now. Let's be optimistic for his sake."

"You're right. Why even think the worst? Bad luck."

"Luck has nothing to do with it," said Liz, serious now. "One way a cancer survivor's friends can show support is by not talking about how bad things could be."

Tony squirmed under Liz's scolding. He nodded, but he obviously couldn't wait to change the subject. "So, Maggie, how about Amanda?" He picked up his fork and dug into his food.

"Amanda in *Menagerie* and then Nettie in *Carousel*? That will keep me busy for a while. I'll have to talk to my agent."

Tony's face darkened. "Leave him out of it. Let's keep this between us."

"Tony, you know I can't do that. I'm under contract."

"I hate dealing with agents. They're all bloodsuckers."

Liz interrupted. "Don't push it, Tony. Maggie wants to do the right thing. I don't think it's about the money."

Tony gave her a sly look. "Of course not. It's about the accommodations. Are you going to invite her to stay, or what?"

The direct question surprised Liz, and she didn't appreciate being forced to make a formal invitation, especially not in front of company. She glanced at Maggie who wouldn't look at her. "You're welcome to stay, Maggie, as long as you want."

Maggie seemed to sense Liz's discomfort. "We'll see," she replied vaguely.

***

Tony finally left around midnight. Liz wearily thought of the prospect of a pre-dawn date with the crew at Awakened Brews. Since Billy's death, she'd lost some of her enthusiasm for seeing them, but she pushed herself, knowing they were hurting too.

She was locking the doors to the deck and the porch when Maggie came out from rinsing the dessert dishes.

"It was kind to invite Tony to dinner. He's such a nice man."

"Yes, and a good friend. You know, he's right. You could stay with me during your plays. In fact, you can stay the whole winter, if you'd like. I'd be glad for the company."

Maggie smiled. She reached up and took Liz's face in her hands and drew it down to hers. "You're generous and very sweet, but I don't want to take advantage of you."

Take advantage of me! Liz thought loudly in her mind.

"You want me to kiss you, don't you? Come here, you." Maggie pulled Liz's face closer. She opened her lips as Liz's mouth touched hers. Liz put her arms around her as Maggie's tongue played in her mouth, but then Maggie released her lips. She leaned against Liz and nuzzled into her shoulder. "I'm sorry, Liz. My leg is feeling better, but I still can't stand long."

"Maybe we should sit down."

"Maybe we should each go to our own bed before we get into some mischief we might regret."

"If that's what you want."

"No, I want something else, but I'm not sure it's a good idea."

"I'll follow your lead."

Maggie gave her a quick, dry kiss. "Sleep well."

Liz watched her walk down the hall to her room. She wished Maggie would turn around and invite her in. When she didn't, she toyed with the idea of inviting herself.

No, you said you'd follow her lead.

Chapter 16

Maggie's thrift shop purchases would only get her so far. Although she was anxious driving the Audi, she took it into town to shop. To accommodate the summer tourists who were its best customers, the local department store stocked a little bit of everything from enamelware to deodorant. Among the varied offerings was overstock from top-name brands. Most of it was high-end sportswear for the outdoors. Maggie filled her cart with wool socks, long sleeve tees, flannel nightgowns, thermal underwear, and polar fleece zips. While she waited in the checkout line, she realized her purchases looked like she was planning to winter in Maine.

Maggie couldn't decide what to do about Liz's invitation, although she couldn't deny that her stay had been productive. She'd drafted the first third of her book and sent it off to her editor. The slower pace of life in Hobbs was conducive to research and writing. She felt calmer here, less likely to need a pill to soothe her nerves in order to fall asleep. The quiet and perfect darkness of the Maine nights quickly lulled her into deep, restorative slumber.

In Maggie's shopping basket were a few things Liz had asked her to pick up for their camping trip: skewers, box matches, and three sizes of batteries. These items would be added to "the camping box," a repurposed copy paper box with a lid. The contents were so tightly packed that it held a surprising amount, including tableware, enamel cups, aluminum foil, an ingenious index of herbs and spices with small portions of all their favorites, as well as cooking utensils. Liz went through the items carefully, checking them off her list. "The preparation is half the fun of camping," Liz explained to Maggie.

"Only to a Virgo."

Liz laughed. "You're probably right." She gave the camping box a final once-over. "Can you think of anything else we should bring?"

"Your guitar."

Once everything was packed and stowed by the garage door for a quick departure in the morning, Liz made a fire in the wood stove. To benefit from the warmth, Maggie sat on the love seat in front of the stove to read, while Liz stretched out on the sofa to read on her tablet. They almost never turned on the enormous television in the media room except to watch British dramas, old movies, and some sword opera series Liz was following. Their evenings were civilized and quiet, almost old-fashioned, despite the tablet on which Liz read. Maggie preferred to read ink on paper, real books that she could touch.

The scene reminded Maggie of Liz studying in their dorm living room. Then, as now, she liked to gaze over the top of her book and watch her friend unobserved. Stretched out on the sofa, Liz rested with an easy grace, looking perfectly relaxed. The little beer belly she liked to joke about was hardly noticeable when she was lying down, but her breasts made a discernible soft mound that looked very inviting.

Maggie imagined joining Liz on the sofa and nudging her arm around her. She wanted Liz, which she'd proven to herself many times when she awoke feeling the need to give herself pleasure, but she didn't lust for Liz like an adolescent. Perhaps that was the one gift of menopause—sex was important, but not the only thing. It wasn't a goal to strive for at the expense of all others. Things were moving in that direction. Maggie was confident that it would happen when the time was right, and then it would be deep, unhurried, and exquisitely sensual.

As Maggie continued to steal little glances at Liz over the edge of her book, she wondered why she was depriving herself. Why not enjoy the simple pleasure of Liz's arms around her? Maggie put her book aside and got up.

Ever the attentive hostess, Liz instantly sat up. "What do you need?"

Maggie shook her head. She took Liz's iPad, tugging gently because Liz, staring at her in confusion, wouldn't let it go. Finally, she did, and Maggie set it down. "Move over and give me some room." Liz rolled on her side to make more space. Maggie lay beside her and insinuated herself into the curve of Liz's body.

"What's this about?" Liz gently brushed Maggie's blond hair away from her face and curled it behind her ear.

Maggie shrugged. "I want to be close to you. You're nice and warm." Liz draped her arm around Maggie's waist and settled down behind her. "Remember how we used to do this and listen to music for hours?" Maggie asked.

With a few taps on her iPad, Liz began streaming some easy jazz. She reached around Maggie to put the tablet on the table. When the warm arm returned, Maggie pressed it closer and snuggled deeper into Liz's surrounding body. The soft music was mellow and calming. After a while, Maggie's eyes closed.

When she opened them again, it was dark in the room. The timer had switched off the lamps. Behind her, Liz was breathing deeply, sound asleep. Maggie gently patted her thigh to wake her.

Instantly, Liz sat up. She looked around, then sighed. "Good. No emergency."

"I would have let you sleep, but I didn't think you'd want to spend the night on the sofa."

"I was pretty comfortable, although I don't usually like people touching me when I sleep." Liz yawned. "I guess you're the exception." She got up. "We should go to bed. Early morning tomorrow." She reached out to help Maggie up and offered a sleepy embrace.

"You don't know how hard it is to let you go," said Maggie, clinging tightly to hold her there a moment longer.

"Oh, I do," said Liz, holding her closer. She kissed her forehead.

Reluctantly, Maggie released her and headed to her room.

Chapter 17

"Maggie," called a soft voice, reaching into her dream. Maggie opened her eyes. Although it was still dark, Liz was fully dressed. "I know it's early for you, so here's a cup of coffee to get you started." Liz left it on the bed stand. She went out and closed the door.

Maggie drank the coffee to clear her head. What a luxury to have coffee delivered to her bedside. She realized she'd been dreaming of sleeping in Liz's arms. The thought made her feel cozy and warm even though it was frigid in the room. Then she remembered there had been more to the dream, but there was no time to explore the sensations it had aroused. Liz was obviously in a hurry to leave, so that would have to wait.

After she finished the coffee, Maggie took a quick shower. She dressed, smiling as she laced up the new hiking boots Liz had picked out for her. They fit perfectly.

The drive north to Bangor provided a stunning view of the brilliant fall colors at their peak: vermillion, gold, deep maroon, and incandescent red. Maggie's eyes couldn't get their fill of the visual feast.

"Oh, look at that one!" she cried, pointing.

Liz patted her thigh affectionately. "I saw it. Let me drive."

Check-in was at three, so they had hours to spend exploring the park. After they took a ride around the park loop road and took in all the vistas, they had popovers and tea at Jordan Pond.

"Yours are better," Maggie said.

"You're so loyal."

"No, truthful."

They headed to the sand beach. It was warm enough to set up their sling chairs and enjoy the early autumn sun while they ate their sandwiches. Maggie was careful to cover herself with sunscreen without any instigation from Liz. She had adopted Liz's wide-brimmed fishing hat as her own. Liz had never asked for it back, so Maggie had decided to keep it.

They had pie and tea in Bar Harbor and afterward, browsed the shops.

That is, Maggie browsed the shops. Liz accompanied her to the first few, hovering impatiently while Maggie inspected the wares. Finally, Liz announced that she was going outside. Maggie guessed she would find someplace to sit and surf the internet while she waited. Less than twenty minutes later, Liz was back, looking insufferably bored.

"How many clothes do you need?" she asked, surveying the pile in Maggie's wagon. "Are you moving up here?"

Maggie turned to her with a little smile. "It's getting cold. I need something to wear."

They headed to the campground to check in. The miniature log cabin was even cozier than Maggie had imagined from the pictures on the website. She put the perishables in the refrigerator while Liz brought their bags into the bunk room.

Liz groaned as she threw the last of Maggie's bags up on the top bunk. "Still packing rocks, I see."

"I'm sorry, I didn't mean to turn you into a pack animal. I can help."

"When your leg is completely healed, you can be the pack animal."

"Somehow, I don't think you'd ever let that happen."

"Probably not."

While Maggie put away the kitchen items, Liz went out to start the fire, so they could have dinner before dark. The night before, Liz had carefully prepared their first camp meal: shrimp, andouille sausage, corn on the cob, and red potatoes, all carefully seasoned and wrapped in foil. Once the coals were the right temperature, she placed the packets on the grill. Maggie poured wine and handed a glass to Liz.

"Thank you. You're so attentive. You'd make a great wife."

"You think so?"

"Yes, too bad Barry didn't appreciate you. What was he thinking?"

Maggie considered her words before responding. Barry was such a sensitive topic. "I never knew what he was thinking," she finally said. "Maybe that's why I didn't catch on right away when he began the affair."

"Did you love him?" asked Liz.

Again, Maggie hesitated. This was dangerous territory, but she answered honestly. "I thought so at the time, and on some level, I did love him. Now, I realize I married him because everyone thought it was such a good idea."

"But you stayed with him all those years."

"I took my marriage vows seriously."

"Good little Catholic girl that you are."

"There's nothing wrong with that."

"If you say so." Liz plucked the packets off the grill with tongs. "Needs to cool a minute. Otherwise, dinner is ready."

On their outdoor table, they ate their campfire meal right out of the foil. The shrimp was juicy, the sausage spicy hot, and the corn tender and sweet.

"If I knew campfire cooking was this good, I'd let you make it for me every night." Maggie wiped her hands on a piece of paper towel. She couldn't take her eyes off the amazing sunset over the bay. "Look at that. How gorgeous! Thank you for bringing me here."

"I told you this is a special place."

"Maybe we should just move into this little cabin and hide from the world."

"Except the campground is closing next week, so they'll probably throw us out."

Maggie slipped her hand under Liz's hoodie and affectionately rubbed her back. "Then I guess we'd need to go home. Your house feels cozy too, especially when you make a fire at night."

"If you're going to be home during the day, I'll have to teach you to make a fire. It can get chilly in the house during the winter." Liz wrapped up the foil that had enclosed their dinner so the stiff wind wouldn't blow it away.

"You really do want me to stay." Maggie drew back a little so she could see Liz's face. "But what about my life in New York?"

Liz shrugged. "People move all the time."

"Maybe you should ask me to marry you." Maggie smiled to let Liz know she was teasing. In fact, she was only half teasing, and she was very curious to hear what Liz would say.

Liz eyed her for moment. "Don't you think we should have sex first to see if we're still compatible?" The glint in Liz's eye let Maggie know she wasn't serious.

But Maggie was when she said, "Yes, I suppose we should."

"Finish your dinner," Liz replied briskly. "I'm on KP duty tonight."

"KP duty! I haven't heard that expression since my Dad was alive."

"I think I got that expression from him. He liked me."

"Yes, he did."

After cleaning up from dinner, Liz built up the fire because twilight had brought a rapid drop in temperature. Maggie put on her parka and pulled her chair closer to fire.

Liz huddled deeper into her hoodie. "It's getting dark. Maybe we should tell ghost stories."

"Maybe you should get your guitar."

Liz went into the cabin to get it. She strummed a few chords, then launched into the introduction to "Who Knows Where the Time Goes."

"I thought you hated those old Judy Collins songs."

"Well, you're back, and you haven't left yet, so today, I don't mind them. Go on. Sing."

Maggie began to sing. Liz joined in for the chorus. Their voices blended, interwove, separated, and joined again.

Maggie smiled at Liz. "I've had many singing partners, but no one has ever sung that song with me like you do. Your harmony is perfect." She reached for the wine bottle to refill their glasses but found it empty. "I think we need to open more wine."

Liz went into the cabin to get another bottle, and Maggie picked up the guitar. When she finished the song, she saw that she was surrounded by faces illuminated by the campfire. They watched like curious forest creatures as they stood at the edge of the patio surrounding the fire.

Maggie beckoned to them. "Well, come on. You're welcome to join us."

An elderly couple took the two remaining chairs, while a young couple with a small boy went back to their cabin to get some sling chairs. When Liz saw they had company, she opened another bottle of wine to share.

The Judy Collins theme continued, but Maggie interwove it with the music of James Taylor, Carly Simon, Carole King, Joni Mitchell, and Joan Baez. The applause was enthusiastic. Other people came, bringing sling chairs, firewood, and more alcohol. Someone brought a bag of popcorn; another, a tin of cookies. When Maggie took a break, Liz led the group in classic Peter, Paul and Mary songs. As the impromptu concert wound down, Maggie began to sing Leonard Cohen's "Hallelujah," alternating verses with Liz. Everyone joined in for the chorus. Eventually, the alcohol ran out, and the fire had died down to embers. The other campers began to drift away, calling "good night" as they faded into the dark.

"I suppose we should turn in too," said Liz. "Great concert, Maggie. You certainly love to perform."

"I do. I admit it. But you were great too. We should start an act and sing in pubs."

"Oh, Maggie, any opportunity for an audience!"

Liz banked the fire. She offered her arm to Maggie as they headed up to the cabin. After Liz got ready for bed, Maggie went in to wash up and brush her teeth. When she emerged again, the door to the bunk room was shut tight.

Maggie sighed and got into bed, surprised to find it as spacious and comfortable as any in a luxury hotel. She settled down to sleep, but when she repositioned her pillow, she was transfixed by the glowing sliver of light under the pocket door to the bunk room. Obviously, Liz was still awake. Maggie pictured her scrunched up in the tiny bunk, her eyes glued to her iPad. It couldn't be comfortable in that cramped space. She regretted going along with the arrangement, which now seemed like such an overstated defense against the possibility of sex.

She wondered if Liz ever imagined making love to her. Maggie, of course, had devoted quite a bit of mental time to that subject. She'd drawn on her last experience with a woman, but that was years ago, and the memory of it had long since faded. On the other hand, the forty-year-old memories of making love with Liz had never dimmed. The memories of youth, lacking competition from other experiences, are always so vivid.

Maggie touched herself. She was already wet just from thinking about Liz making love to her. A few caresses brought the sensation into sharper focus. Yes, she was ready, but where was her lover? Reading medical journals? No. Not tonight.

Maggie knocked on the pocket door and pushed it open. There was Liz, reading on her iPad exactly as she'd imagined. She was still wearing her baseball cap and a pair of woolly hiking socks. She looked comfortable and boyish in an oversized T-shirt and men's knit boxers with a button fly.

"Come out of there," ordered Maggie, "I won't have you sleeping in that tiny bunk like you're a child. There's plenty of room in the bed."

"Are you sure?" asked Liz, pulling her knees practically up to her chin to get her long legs around the ladder to the top bunk. "I'm fine in here."

"No, you're not fine. Let's go." Maggie pointed in the direction of the bed.

Liz plugged in her iPad to charge, hung her ball cap on a peg by the door, and took off her socks.

"Thanks for sharing the bed," she said, getting in beside Maggie. "I have to admit it was a little tight in there." Liz moved to the far side and made herself small at the very edge. "Good night."

Maggie, lying beside her, was amazed that Liz sounded ready to nod off, while she was completely awake and stimulated. She molded herself around Liz, who became very still and quiet. Maggie pressed her breasts against Liz's back. Surely, that would give her the idea, but Liz didn't move a muscle. Maggie hooked her finger in the waistband of the boxer shorts and snapped it.

"These need to go away."

Fortunately, Liz didn't argue because Maggie had no idea what she would say if she did. With a sigh, Liz pulled down the boxers and dropped them on the floor.

"I can't wait any longer. I need you to touch me." Maggie raised her nightgown and guided Liz's hand between her legs.

"Right for the crotch," Liz whispered, teasing Maggie's ear with her tongue. "Don't you believe in foreplay?"

"What do you think we've being doing all this time?" Maggie managed to say despite the undulating waves of pleasure brought on by Liz's touch. She closed her eyes as Liz gently explored her with her fingers.

"You're so ready. What were you doing before I got here?"

"What do you think?"

Maggie felt Liz smile against her cheek, which made her smile too. She lost the smile and gasped a little when the exploring fingers found their way inside. She rolled her hips to invite them deeper.

"Don't you even want a kiss?" Liz added another finger and went deeper still.

"Yes, I'd like a kiss," murmured Maggie, focusing on the gentle drag of Liz's fingers deep inside her. Liz moved over her and began to explore her mouth with her tongue. Maggie thought of honey.

Maggie broke the kiss. "Fuck me!"

"I thought you hated that word."

"Oh, I like it in bed when I'm actually doing it. And if I don't tell you, you'll be too gentle."

Liz's hand moved more aggressively, her tongue in her mouth, her fingers deep inside her, expanding, opening her with each stroke. They withdrew and began caressing her outside, gentle, then intense, next gentle again. They slipped back inside. Tease, strike, caress, strike again. Maggie felt faint, but at the same time, completely conscious of the relentless assault on her senses. When she was least expecting it, the orgasm flowed through her, flashing the skin above her breasts and making it prickle. The sensitivity made her flinch from her lover's touch, but still the teasing fingers came back for more until Maggie had to beg her to stop.

When the spasms below finally subsided, Maggie tugged on Liz's T-shirt. "Take this off. I want to feel your skin on mine."

Obediently, Liz sat up and took off her shirt. Maggie pulled her nightgown over her head. When Liz took her in her arms, Maggie wanted to weep from the pleasure of feeling their bare skin finally touch.

Finally, after forty years.

"I've missed you." Maggie rubbed her cheek against Liz's breast.

"I've missed you too."

"Your breasts are larger."

Liz chuckled softly. "So are yours." She reached up to touch Maggie's breast, kneading the nipple gently between her fingers. She caressed the breast with her fingertips. Maggie heard a sudden, sharp uptake of air, not quite a gasp. Liz's body tensed. The caresses stopped for a split second, and Liz's touch became more deliberate as her fingers found their way around the breast. They moved to the other breast and prodded it in the same way. The exploration felt almost…clinical. Liz sighed and laid her head against Maggie's shoulder. Maggie lazily stroked her hair, which smelled faintly of wood smoke from the campfire. Her fingers wove the waves into ringlets.

"Liz, are you going to let me make love to you?"

"Yes!" Liz raised herself on her elbow. She kissed Maggie so profoundly it felt like she was trying to inhale her soul. Liz finally released her mouth. "You are so beautiful. Just as I remember." She delicately tested the cleft in her chin with her finger.

"Oh, Liz, your memory is foggy. Our bodies have changed. We were perfect then."

"We are perfect now."

"Let me make love to you. Come, sweetie, lie back. I remember what you like." She said it confidently as if no time had passed and nothing had changed. Her desire for Liz was so intense and her feelings so strong that nothing else mattered.

Liz used her elbows to pull herself up on the pillows. Maggie kissed her breasts and her little tummy, dawdling along the way to offer little kisses, treating herself to the slightly salt taste of Liz's skin. After a leisurely exploration of her lover's body, Maggie insinuated her narrow shoulders between her thighs and nudged them apart. She blew gently. Liz shivered. Maggie smiled at the memory of that long-ago time, when she'd given Liz Anaïs Nin's diaries to educate her about the possibility of oral sex. The memory competed with a present, so fully real, it was rubbing against her skin and pulsing in her ears.

Liz jumped at the barest flick of her tongue, exactly like that first time. Tentatively, Maggie tasted the woman who had awakened her to the love of women. The taste was strange, yet so familiar—salty, tangy, a hint of musk—the scent of something mysterious soon to be revealed. Maggie smiled as she found the rhythm. A delicate approach worked best with Liz. She was a person who was easily moved by small gestures, the lightest touch, the gentlest kiss. Maggie felt strong fingers combing through her hair, urging her on. "Yes, don't stop. Please don't ever stop." The climax came moments later, but it was powerful. Maggie struggled to hold on as Liz's back arched.

When it was done, she resettled herself into Liz's arms. "So quick. Just like when we were young. Do you need more?"

"Not right now. I'm too sensitive." Liz's arms, wrapped around her shoulders, suggested her strength. She kissed Maggie on the top of her head. "Let's sleep now."

***

When Maggie awoke, she found the other side of the bed cold and empty. Confused, she sat up. The door to the bunk room was open, and the light was off. The cabin was silent except for the soft hum of the refrigerator. She became aware of an orange glow through the window. She jumped out of bed and looked out.

Liz sat by the fire ring. She had built up the fire, and it was blazing and spitting sparks into the air. Bundled in her parka, hood up against the cold, Liz sat with her back to the cabin.

Maggie threw on her robe and went out to the front deck. "Liz?" she called, but Liz didn't turn around. The brisk wind off the water roared past Maggie's ears. "Liz!" she called again, louder this time.

Liz couldn't hear her, she realized, over the sound of the wind and the ocean. Maggie walked down the path to the campfire. In its light, she could see the water lapping against the shore, barely a few feet away.

Maggie sat down beside Liz.

"It's after three. What are you doing out here?"

"I'm thinking."

"Come inside. It's so cold."

Liz glanced back at the cabin. "Yes, it's cold." She got up, slid her arms out of her parka and draped it around Maggie's shoulders.

"No, then you'll freeze."

"The fire is warm when you get close enough."

The parka was warm from Liz's body. It smelled of her, not an unpleasant smell, just her familiar scent below a hint of laundry detergent. Maggie hugged the parka closer. "Thank you," she said. "You're very kind." She snuggled into the parka, and eventually, she felt warmer. "What are thinking about?"

There was a long pause. "The past...and the future."

"Are you sorry we made love?"

Liz turned to her. The tenderness in her eyes was painful. "How could I be sorry? I've wanted you for weeks...years...forty, actually."

"But it changes things."

"Yes." Liz nodded. "It was more than sex."

"Are you sure that's all right? You seem so upset." Maggie anxiously reached for her hand.

Liz gazed thoughtfully into her eyes. "I'm glad we finally made love. I knew it was going to happen and waiting for it was excruciating." She turned back to the fire, moving closer for the warmth.

"So, what's the matter?"

Liz stared into the fire. "All these years we've been apart...and now, who knows how much time we have left."

"Liz, you're scaring me."

"I'm sorry. I didn't mean to." Liz put her arm around her. Maggie could feel that she was trembling.

"Come inside. It's too cold out here." Maggie got up and reached for Liz's hand. Without a word of argument, Liz got up and followed her. She put her arm around Maggie's waist as they made their way up the path to the cabin.

Maggie reluctantly took off Liz's parka. The brisk wind and humidity from the water had been bone-chilling. She shrugged off her robe and got into bed.

Liz pulled her sweatshirt over her head. Her breasts fell loose, and Maggie longed to touch them. In a moment, Liz was in bed, covering Maggie's shivering body with her own. Liz's skin felt merely cool. Like her personality, her body temperature was steady and reliable. Maggie opened her legs wider so that her lover could lie between them.

"I'm not too heavy?" Liz gingerly let down her weight.

"No, it feels wonderful. Hold me tight and warm me up."

After Liz began to kiss her, the temperature rose rapidly.

***

Maggie felt someone gently shaking her arm. She opened her eyes to see that it was still dark. "Wake up, Maggie. We're going to watch the sun rise from Cadillac mountain. Here, put these on." Liz laid a pair of heavy sweatpants and a hooded sweatshirt at the foot of the bed. "Come on. You can crawl back into bed when we get back."

"You're crazy." Maggie reluctantly sat up.

"I know. That's why you love me."

"I do love you, or I wouldn't be doing this." Maggie pulled on the sweats over her naked body. "Promise I can go back to bed when we get back."

"You can go back to bed, but I won't promise I'll let you sleep." Liz put a cup of coffee into her hands. "Drink up or we'll miss the show."

As Liz navigated the narrow, winding road in the dark, she drove at a speed Maggie found unnerving. In some places, it was a sheer drop down the side of the mountain, which Maggie clearly remembered from the drive in the daylight. Finally, they reached the top of the mountain, where they found they had company. The summit parking lot was overflowing with cars and bicycles. People in colorful hiking clothes passed by in a steady stream as Liz found one of the last parking spaces. Maggie began to realize this was very special event.

"Come on, we can't be late for this." Liz took Maggie's hand. They walked along the rocks, past the summit to the other side of the mountain where the ocean below was barely visible in the dim light. Only the whitecaps over the dark expanse let Maggie know they were looking at the Atlantic. "This is where the sun first rises on the continental United States," Liz explained. "The first dawn in our country." She squeezed Maggie's hand and then held it. Soon, a sliver of light appeared over the ocean. It grew quickly, rising above the water and throwing streams of pink and lavender in its wake.

"My God!" breathed Maggie. "How beautiful!"

They watched until the sun rose in the sky.

Liz put her arm around her. "I'll take you into town for breakfast."

"No, take me back. I need to make love to you."

When they returned to the cabin, they peeled off their clothes and lay flesh to flesh. Maggie reveled in the feel of Liz's soft skin against hers.

"Please fuck me," whispered Maggie into Liz's ear.

"Is that your new favorite word?" Liz smiled against her cheek as she moved in her more forcefully. Maggie pulled up her knees to get more, and then, unexpectedly, she had an orgasm inside, something she'd never experienced with men no matter how long and hard they pounded into her. Then Liz stealthily moved down her body and used her lips and tongue to make her come again. Maggie nearly screamed with pleasure before she remembered that they were very close to other people in the campground, closer than they would ever be in Liz's house. She would reserve that particular pleasure for another time.

Liz was grinning when she raised her head. "Impressive," she said. "More?" She blew gently on Maggie's clitoris, which made her jump.

"No more. Get up here."

Liz returned to Maggie's arms and kissed her.

"I can smell my scent on your face."

"I've never forgotten your scent. It's very dear to me." Liz pulled her closer, and Maggie felt that she could never be happier than she was at that moment, safe and warm in her lover's arms.

Chapter 18

As Liz drove down from Portland, where they had stopped to have lunch, she stole glances at Maggie, who'd fallen asleep soon after they'd gotten on the highway. Liz had only herself to blame for exhausting her. They'd spent the previous day exploring the park, which included a brief hike, confirming without doubt that Maggie's leg was fully healed. Afterwards, she'd taken Maggie to an elegant, intimate dinner in one of Bar Harbor's best restaurants and followed that with a night of passionate lovemaking. It wasn't going to be easy making up for those forty lost years, but Liz would happily try.

Maggie awoke briefly. "I love you," she murmured.

"You're besotted."

"I am. I adore you." Maggie adjusted her seat and went back to sleep. She fell into such a stupor, she began to snore softly, which made Liz smile. In the early days of a relationship, everything seems charming, a new invitation to intimacy. Until the earplugs come out one night. In fact, there was little Liz didn't know about how Maggie slept, including her ability to have whole conversations while sound asleep. There was no need to be on their best behavior. They'd already lived together and knew one another's secrets.

But not all of them.

As Liz sped down I-95, she wondered how to break the news. It had been difficult to keep her discovery to herself, but once she decided not to say anything, she couldn't go back. Their Acadia weekend would have instantly turned into a disaster. At first, Liz was sure that keeping the information to herself had been the right thing to do, but as time passed, a little doubt had crept into her mind. No matter how she justified keeping the secret, she knew she'd lose Maggie's trust if she delayed much longer.

Maggie got a second wind when they arrived home and helped Liz unload the truck. They decided to leave all the camping gear in the garage until the next day, when Liz would be at home and could bring it in at her leisure. Only the refrigerated food needed to be put away. Once that was done, Liz opened a bottle of wine.

Maggie sprawled on the sofa. "Oh, Liz, I had such a wonderful time. Acadia is as beautiful as you said, but…" She sighed deeply. "It's so good to be home."

Liz savored the sound of the word coming from Maggie's lips. She hated that she was about to spoil Maggie's pleasure in the homecoming.

She tried to organize her thoughts and decided that building a fire would be a good delaying tactic. She had it down to a science. First, she crumpled newspaper, then built a little structure over it with kindling on the bottom and small logs on top. She twisted a few sheets of newspaper into a rope, held it under the flue, and lit it with a match. After it burned out, she touched a lit match to the newspaper under the kindling. It burst into flame and burned without smoke. Leaving the door partway open so the stove could draw air, Liz sat near the fire to make sure it was well established.

"You're so good at that," Maggie said, watching. "You always get a roaring fire on the first try. When I made a fire in Connecticut, I always filled the house with smoke."

"The secret is warming the air in the flue to create a draft."

"So I see. How did you get to be so smart?"

"I was born that way."

Maggie smiled. "Yes, I guess you were."

Liz picked up her wine glass and took a few swallows for fortification. "There's something I have to tell you." Unfortunately, her tone sounded more ominous than she'd intended.

Maggie sat up straight. "I'm listening."

Liz felt Maggie's anxious eyes on her but couldn't immediately find the words.

"What is it, Liz? From the look on your face, it's probably not something I want to hear."

Liz was wearing her neutral "doctor face," so Maggie was exaggerating, but she was right about one thing. This was definitely not something she wanted to hear. No woman ever wanted to hear what Liz was about to say.

"Well?" Maggie leaned forward a little.

Liz took a deep breath. "You have a lump in your breast."

Maggie's eyes widened. "What?"

"I found a lump in your breast."

Maggie's eyes shone with pure horror. Her hands began to tremble, but she managed to put down her wine glass before spilling red drops all over the carpet. "When did you find it?"

"The first time we made love."

"Where is it?"

"In your left breast." Liz demonstrated by showing the location on her own breast. "Here."

"You found it while we were making love?"

Liz nodded.

"And you didn't you tell me?" asked Maggie in an accusing voice.

"I knew it would only upset you."

"You should have told me!" Maggie's voice was shriller this time.

"I know, but I didn't."

Maggie got up and ran to her room. Liz winced when the door slammed. She waited a few moments before she got up and walked down the hall. She stared at the closed door. "Maggie, I'm sorry. It was selfish, I know. I didn't want to spoil our weekend. I knew you'd be upset when I told you."

No response.

Liz knocked softly. "I'm sorry."

This time the door opened.

"Of course, I'm upset. My mother *died* of breast cancer. I'm not just upset. I'm terrified!"

Liz took a deep breath. "I know you're scared. Everyone is scared to find a lump. It could be nothing but a cyst. Not all lumps are cancer. Even if it is, it's very small. Many breast cancers are indolent and never become dangerous."

"Listen to you, standing there, sounding like a doctor."

"I am a doctor." Liz raised her open hands. "How else should I sound?"

"Don't be such an idiot, Liz Stolz. Hold me!"

Liz took her in her arms and Maggie began to sob. Liz held her tighter, stroking her hair and her back to soothe her. Maggie leaned into her and held on tight, pressing her closer until there was no space at all between them.

In all, the crying bout lasted a good five minutes. When it was over, Liz fetched the box of tissues from Maggie's bed stand. Maggie's mascara had run, and dabbing her eyes had made it worse. "Excuse me." She ran into the bathroom.

Liz sank down on the bed, digging at her forehead with her fingertips out of pure frustration. No matter how she'd delivered the bad news, it would have been wrong. At least, Maggie had enjoyed the camping trip and had a few more days without worry. It made perfect sense to Liz, although she knew from years of dealing with breast cancer patients, none of this had anything to do with sense.

Maggie remained in the bathroom for some time. Liz finally got tired of waiting and returned to the living room and her glass of wine. She finished it, but it left her flat, even though it was excellent wine. *Maybe I should have told her right away.* She answered her own thought aloud. "I don't think so."

"You don't think. That part's true."

Liz looked up to see Maggie. She had taken off all her makeup. Without it, she looked pale but in Liz's eyes, still beautiful.

"I'm sorry, Maggie."

"You should have told me."

"Is that how you want to remember the first time we made love in forty years?"

"No, of course not." Maggie sat down on the sofa and nudged her way under Liz's arm. "You knew. How could you keep it to yourself? What a burden that must have been for you." Maggie stroked Liz's thigh, which Liz took as a sign of forgiveness. "That's why you were so moody after we made love. And when I caught you unawares, and you looked distracted. You were thinking about it."

"Yes."

"How could you stand it?"

"Doctors learn to keep secrets."

Maggie was quiet for a long moment. "You must be scared too." She took Liz's hand and held it tight.

Liz did a quick scan of her emotions, something she rarely did when medical issues were involved, but this was different. The patient was her lover, and that changed everything. Even so, it was easier to default to detachment. In any event, she wouldn't admit to her fears until she knew more. "No use getting scared before we know the facts. I'll save my anxiety for when we determine how serious it is."

"How serious is it?"

"I can't say without examining you, which I wasn't about to do during sex."

"But you tried." Maggie gently pounded Liz's knee with her fist.

"It was that obvious?"

"One thing you're not, Liz Stolz, is subtle. But I didn't realize you'd found something until now." Maggie sat up and cupped her breasts with her hands. "Where is it? I never felt anything."

Liz took Maggie's fingers and placed it over the spot. "There. Feel it now?" Maggie snatched her hand away like she'd touched fire.

"May I examine you?" Liz asked gently.

Maggie stared at her with alarm. Then a look of resignation crossed her face, and she nodded. She pulled her top over her head and unhooked her bra.

Liz entered the mental space where her fingertips could see. She carefully examined each breast and the armpit nodes. Fortunately, she found only the original lump.

"There's only one lump, and it's small, about the size of a cherry pit." Liz pinched her fingers together to demonstrate the size. "We'll need a mammogram to see if there are smaller lumps I can't feel. When was your last mammogram?"

"I don't remember. Three, maybe four years ago."

"Maggie! With your family history?"

"I know. It was stupid, but there was so much going on. I just forgot."

"Where was it done?"

"NYU Medical. I got free healthcare there."

"I'll call tomorrow to get your last mammogram. We can go to Southern Med. I know the breast radiologist there. She'll read it right away." Liz handed Maggie her top and bra and kissed her. "Let's forget about this for a while. What do you want to do about dinner? There's not much in the house."

"I don't feel like eating."

"I understand, but you need to eat, and so do I. Let's go out. I don't really feel like cooking."

"You know what I feel like doing? Fucking. I'm miserable, and I want to feel good again." Maggie reached up and gently touched the little pucker that had formed between Liz's brows. "Don't look at me like that. It's how I feel."

Liz took her hand. "Okay, let's go upstairs."

Once the elevator door closed, Maggie began to kiss her so passionately that Liz forgot to press the button for the third floor. They stood there for a long time, tongue kissing like two adolescents until Liz finally realized the elevator hadn't moved and pressed the button to go up. Maggie slid her hand down Liz's jeans as the elevator rose.

"It doesn't take much for you, does it?"

Liz smiled. "I'm not like this for every woman." The door opened. "But I can't walk with your hand in my pants."

Maggie withdrew her hand and suggestively sucked her fingers, which made Liz want to kiss her again. While she did, she held the elevator door open by pure force.

They shed their clothes on the way. Flannel shirts and jeans made a colorful trail to the bed. Liz almost tripped balancing on one foot to pull off her sock. She ripped off the duvet, and they flopped into a heap, lips pressed together, hands roaming everywhere.

Maggie took the lead. Liz loved it when she became a lioness. It always came as such a shock when she burst into her body, taking exactly what she wanted. That, juxtaposed against the delicate touch of her lips and tongue, could drive her to distraction. Liz was disappointed that she came so quickly, but it allowed her to focus on Maggie's needs, who had clearly demonstrated by example how she wanted to be loved in return. She moaned loudly when she came, gripping Liz's shoulders with her fingers like pincers.

Then came the deluge. Liz knew to expect it. Women had a wide variety of responses to discovering a lump in their breasts: alarm, stoicism, anger, bravado, terror, but inevitably, it always ended in tears. When Maggie began to sob, Liz cradled her against her shoulder and stroked her hair until the sobs devolved into sniffles.

"Will I lose my breasts?" Maggie's voice was mournful.

"Let's not jump to conclusions. It's just a tiny lump in one breast. We don't even know what it is yet."

"But you're concerned."

"A breast lump is always a concern, but it could turn out to be nothing. Every woman's breasts are lumpy, full of mountains and valleys. We just don't think about them that way."

"But my mother–"

"Maggie, you're not your mother. Even if you share a gene mutation, it doesn't mean you'll get breast cancer. And it doesn't mean the lump I found is cancer. Let's just wait and see. All right?"

Maggie began to cry again. Liz gathered her close. This was going to be a long night. It wasn't that she was unsympathetic, but she had been through this with many women and knew what to expect. Of course, none of them had been her lover, which complicated everything. She suddenly had new compassion for the partners of her breast surgery patients.

Liz was suddenly filled with overwhelming anger. Its source was diffuse. She was always angry when it came to cancer, angry because it stole so many young lives, angry because it caused so much pain and suffering, and especially angry because sometimes, no matter what she did, cancer won. She was also furious at the injustice of it. She had waited forty years for Maggie, and now this.

If Liz thought about it too much, she wanted to scream, throw things, and cry. Instead, she would roll up the anger and store it for a time when she had more privacy. The last thing she wanted to do was transmit her negative feelings to Maggie, who needed all the positive energy she could get.

"Liz, I love you."

"I love you too," said Liz, hugging her closer. "What do you say I go downstairs and defrost some of that beef barley soup I made last week?"

"I'm not hungry."

"You have to eat. I have to eat."

"Okay."

Liz got dressed and went downstairs. It was actually a relief to have a moment alone. Mechanically, she prepared their dinner. While she patiently waited for the microwave to defrost the containers of soup, she heated some frozen sourdough rolls in the oven. She leaned against the counter while she made plans for the mammogram and needle biopsy. She could justify involving herself in the testing, but she would recuse herself from any treatments. They were too close now that they were lovers.

She could probably do the biopsy the next day. She'd take Maggie to Southern Med. If necessary, she could even do it in the office, but she liked to have imaging available to guide the needle—less risk of causing unnecessary injury or pain.

Focusing on planning the tests was easier than allowing her own feelings to seep into her mind and dampen her energy. She needed to be cheerful and strong for Maggie. Drawing on her training in detachment was the best way to maintain her equilibrium. She'd spoken the truth when she'd told Maggie it could be nothing. Just a cyst. How many lumps had Liz removed that were perfectly benign? Fortunately, many. But Liz had a bad feeling about this one based on nothing but gut instinct, and that worried her. A physician's uncanny sixth sense was too often right. Dead right.

The microwave pinged and Liz divided the soup into two oversized mugs shaped like giant coffee cups. She microwaved each until the soup was boiling hot. By then, the rolls were done. She put everything on a tray and headed to the elevator.

Maggie had been crying while Liz was downstairs. That was obvious from her reddened eyes and the mountain of used tissues on the floor by the night stand.

"Eat something," urged Liz. "You'll feel better." She set the tray on the little table by the window and opened the drapes. Maggie got up and came to the table. "I often eat here when I'm alone," Liz explained. "Seeing the ocean calms me, especially after a hard day."

"It's beautiful." Maggie managed a little smile.

"After we eat, I'll bring your bags up."

Maggie gave her a questioning look.

"I assumed you'd want to move up here…now, that we're lovers."

"I'm honored to be admitted to the master suite."

The weak attempt at humor heartened Liz. "But if you want your own room, you can stay where you are."

"Of course, I want to sleep with you, Liz. I need to be near you, especially now." Maggie dipped her spoon into the soup. It was still steaming, so she sipped it gingerly. The vapor fogged her glasses, and she took them off. "I'm ravenous now that I can smell how good your soup is."

They ate in silence, hungry despite, or perhaps because of the emotional episode. The conversation had been draining, and it had been hours since their lunch on the road. The thick soup was nearly a stew, filled with chunks of beef, vegetables, mushrooms, and barley. It was hearty and satisfying.

"Have I ever told you you're a great cook, Liz?"

"Yes, but thank you. It's always nice to hear compliments."

"I like that we cook together. We nourish and nurture one another."

Liz's spoon stopped on the way to her mouth as she paused to consider what Maggie had said. "I like that too."

"Will I have my treatments here?" The change of subject revealed what Maggie really had on her mind.

Liz put down her spoon, debating whether to continue the conversation about the lump, especially while they were eating. She decided that Maggie was unlikely to let it go until all her questions were answered. "We can do the diagnostic tests here. If you need treatment, I'd like to take you to Yale, where the surgeons and oncologists are first rate. We could also go to Dana-Farber or Sloan Kettering, if you'd rather go back to New York."

"Whatever you think is best, Liz. I trust your judgment."

"Thank you, but I don't want you agreeing with me because of our relationship."

"Is that what you think?" Maggie gave her a hard look. "You are the smartest person I know. Sophia has been filling me in about your career. I even have your book, and now, I suppose I'll have to finish reading it."

"You have my book? I could have given you a copy. I have a whole carton of them in the storage space."

"Never mind. I didn't want you to know I was reading up on you. The irony of it. You, considered the best in the field, are suddenly my doctor."

"There are brighter lights in my field…Susan Love, Kristi Funk…"

"Don't be modest, Liz. Remember, I know you."

"Do you want more soup? There's plenty more in the freezer."

"And don't change the subject."

Chapter 19

Maggie awoke disoriented and had to remind herself that she was in Liz's bedroom on the third floor. At first, she didn't realize she was alone because the king-sized bed was so enormous. She reached out to touch where her lover's body had lain during the night to confirm that she was really gone. She so wished Liz hadn't chosen today of all days to slip away unannounced.

Maybe Liz thought it was kind to let her sleep. During the night Maggie had awakened many times seeking comfort. Although Liz was obviously exhausted from the long drive and the emotional conversations, she awoke instantly. Without protest, she held Maggie and murmured soothing words: "It will all be all right…Don't worry…I'm here for you." Maggie remembered the sweetness of their lovemaking, tender and sensitive beyond imagination.

Maggie slipped on the flannel shirt Liz had given her during the night when she'd complained of being cold. She found a pair of Liz's workout pants hanging on the back of the closet door. The legs were too long, so she rolled them up. She decided to take the elevator because she was groggy from lack of sleep and didn't trust herself on the stairs.

Liz was in the kitchen talking on her phone. She nodded to Maggie but turned around as she headed out to the porch to continue her conversation. Maggie's eyes followed Liz as she walked away because she looked so different this morning. She was wearing a tailored suit with a skirt, heeled pumps, jewelry, even makeup. The word that instantly came to mind was "professional." Maggie wondered why Liz was so dressed up. She never had office hours at Seacoast Women's Health on Mondays.

Maggie mimed apprehension when Liz returned to the kitchen. "And who are *you*?"

Liz deadpanned. "You don't recognize the woman who made love to you last night?"

"Of course, I do," said Maggie, accepting a kiss. Liz sat down beside her.

Maggie patted her knee and let her hand find its way under the skirt. "I like it when you wear skirts. You should wear them more often." Liz's disapproving look was intimidating, so Maggie withdrew her hand. Clearly, Liz was all business this morning.

"I set up an appointment for a mammogram at ten thirty. Alyson Gagnon will meet us there to read the films," Liz waved dismissively, "... images, I should say. Everything is digital now. You can always tell the old-timers. We still call them films."

Maggie felt a little rush of anxiety. The pleasant sensations of the night's lovemaking and the comfort of sleeping in Liz's arms had almost blotted out the memory of the previous day's dreadful revelations. Now, they engulfed her mind like an angry wave.

"That was the ambulatory surgery clerk I was speaking to. I reserved a room for a needle biopsy."

Maggie found it hard to swallow the coffee in her mouth. Finally, she got it down. "Today?"

Liz reached for Maggie's hand. "I thought you'd want to know as soon as possible."

Yes, she wanted to know, but then the lump would be named, assigned to a category. Its identity would become a fact instead of a possibility. She wasn't sure she was ready for that.

"Are you doing the biopsy?" Maggie asked in a small, hopeful voice.

"If that's all right with you. Otherwise, one of the other surgeons at Seacoast Women's Health can do it but not today. We'd have to schedule it."

"No, I want you to do it. No one else."

Liz nodded and began to describe the procedure until Maggie asked her to stop. She'd already read about it in Liz's book. The thought of her lover sticking a needle into her breast was unnerving. Just a few hours before, she had tenderly kissed and caressed that breast. How could she separate herself from her feelings like that?

"Will you still love me if I lose a breast?" asked Maggie. Her voice was shakier than she'd expected.

Liz's eyes widened a little, but otherwise, it was impossible to know what she was thinking because she was wearing her doctor face. "We seldom do full mastectomies if we can possibly conserve the breast, usually only if the tumor is very large in relation to the breast or the patient insists."

"Why would a patient insist?" Maggie asked. It made no sense.

"Fear mostly. Or she doesn't want to do radiation. We always recommend radiation after a lumpectomy."

"I read that in your book."

Liz arched a brow. "Then, how did you miss the part about conserving the breast?"

"I didn't. But when I think of breast cancer, I think of my mother. She lost both breasts and the chest muscles and some of the muscles in her arms. It was a horrible, ugly mess." She closed her eyes tightly as if she could banish the terrible memory of her mother's ravaged chest from her mind.

Liz feigned a shudder. "Unfortunately, I remember those days. We were unnecessarily brutal until we knew better." Liz put her arm around Maggie's shoulders and gave her a little hug. "Don't worry. It's different now," Liz said in that calm, reassuring voice she used when she was explaining something medical. "Finish your coffee. I'm going to give you some light anesthesia for the biopsy. You shouldn't eat anything until afterwards. If you're up for it, I'll take you out to lunch in Portsmouth."

"But can I have another cup of coffee?"

"That's fine, but no solid food, and take it easy on the cream." Liz glanced at her watch.

"Yes, I know. I need to pay attention to the time. Just let me have another cup of coffee."

Maggie showered downstairs and made some effort with her appearance. She always liked to make a positive first impression, and she'd be meeting Liz's colleagues today and wanted them to like her. Intellectually, she knew it was ridiculous, but that's how she'd been raised—to please people in order to be treated well in return.

As Liz drove to the hospital, Maggie had trouble finding a topic of conversation unrelated to their mission, so there was silence.

"The radiologist and I had a thing for about a year," Liz announced out of the blue. She said it casually, as if she were talking about her favorite restaurant in town. "I'm telling you in the interest of full disclosure."

The thought made Maggie uneasy. "Another ex?"

"The relationship wasn't serious enough for her to be an ex. Although evidently, Alyson thought so."

"She'll be reading my mammogram. Isn't that a little…odd?"

"She's the best breast radiologist I know. She'll also be helping with the ultrasound during the needle aspiration."

"So, I'll get to meet her."

"I hadn't planned on a formal introduction, but I'll ask her to come down during the imaging. Most women never meet the radiologists who read their mammograms. Medicine has become so disjointed and compartmentalized. I absolutely hate it."

"But you stay."

Liz sighed. "Yes, I stay, and it's not for the money. I probably shouldn't say this, but I have more money than I can ever spend in this lifetime."

"Why shouldn't you say it?"

"In case you're only interested in me for my money." Liz briefly glanced at her. Her tone was light and playful, but for a split second, Maggie worried Liz was half serious.

"I was raised to marry up and climb the social ladder. My mother had identified Barry as a good catch."

"From her point of view, he was. Football star, National Honor Society, engineering student at a good school, destined to go straight to the top of the corporate ladder."

"If we had been born twenty years later, you could have been the perfect catch. From a wealthy family, Phi Beta Kappa, promising pre-med destined for a brilliant career in medicine…"

"I doubt your mother would have seen it that way even twenty years later. Maybe not even now."

"No, she was a devout Catholic. She was appalled that gay people were fighting for equal rights, especially after finding out about us. I'm sure gay marriage would have killed her, if she wasn't already dead."

"Maybe we should get married just to spite her."

"Oh, great. What a good reason to get married."

"You did propose to me the other night. Actually, you suggested that I propose to you."

"I was only kidding."

"Uh huh." Liz turned into the hospital entrance and swung into a parking space a little too fast for Maggie's nerves. She turned off the engine and yanked up the parking brake. "We're here."

Maggie got out of the car and scrutinized the place. Southern Med was tiny compared to NYU Medical Center or any New York hospital for that matter. She was relieved to see that everything in the Women's Imaging Department looked brand new.

"You'll need to check in at that window." Liz pointed to an opening in the wall. "I'm sure Alyson will extend professional courtesy for reading the mammogram, but you'll have to provide your insurance card for the imaging."

"Of course." Maggie felt slightly insulted that Liz should think otherwise. "I have insurance. It pays for an annual mammogram."

"So, why didn't you have one?"

"I already told you."

"I'll stop. I hate doctors who preach too." She patted Maggie's shoulder. "I'm going to find Alyson. Be right back."

The patient manager who took Maggie's information was a graying, pleasant woman about her age. "Your previous mammograms just arrived a few minutes ago. Dr. Stolz called NYU, and they came right away. She must have some pull there."

After Maggie answered all the questions about her medical history, the patient manager directed her to the waiting room. "It shouldn't be more than a few minutes' wait. They're right on schedule this morning."

Maggie checked her phone while she waited. There was a text from Sophia. As usual, it was brief, dashed off by a harried oncology resident on the fly. *Mom, when are you going home? That leg should be healed by now."* Five heart emoticons.

She dreaded answering that text and explaining everything that had happened…so much in just the last few days. She wrote: *Don't worry. Everything's fine. I'll call later.*

Instantly, a text came back. *I'm on a long shift until tomorrow. Call after 6 pm Love, S.* More heart emoticons, now in multiple colors.

Maggie looked up to see Liz approaching. Beside her was a slender woman with long, strawberry blond hair in a ponytail. Both wore white coats. As they came closer, Maggie could see the green Southern Med logo on the pocket of Liz's coat and "Elizabeth A. Stolz, M.D., Dept. of Surgery" embroidered in blue thread above it. She thought back to the night Liz had come into the waiting room in her shorts and T-shirt. Now, there was no doubt she was really a doctor. "The actor creates the character, but the costume seals the deal," Maggie's old acting coach used to say.

In this costume, Liz was smooth and professional. "Maggie, I'd like you to meet Alyson Gagnon. She's going to be reading your mammogram."

"Hello, Ms. Krusick." Dr. Gagnon extended her long, elegant hand and gave Maggie a warm smile. Her eyes were a compelling shade of green. Her skin was flawless. There was only one word to describe her: stunning. "Dr. Stolz was telling me all about you. I'm so sorry I missed you in *Mama Mia.* I really wanted see it, but I just never got there."

She's charming as well as beautiful, thought Maggie, *and at least a decade my junior.*

"Ms. Krusick?" the technician called.

Liz tapped her lightly on the shoulder. "Go with her. We'll be in the technician's booth. It's wired for sound. Yell if you need anything."

As the technician threw her breast around the imaging plate, Maggie remembered why she hated mammograms. Fortunately, it wasn't quite as bad as some she'd had in the past.

She heard Liz's disembodied voice say, "You're doing great, Maggie. Hang in there."

The process was repeated until Dr. Gagnon spoke through the intercom. "All right, Ms. Krusick. Take a break. I think we have all the shots we need. Let me take a quick look to be sure." The technician came out to release her from the torture instrument. She flipped the hospital robe over Maggie's shoulder to cover her naked breast.

"It won't be much longer." She smiled reassuringly. "I think we have what they need."

The sound in the technician's booth cut off. Maggie watched the two doctors hunched over a screen. The blue light reflected on their intent faces. Dr. Gagnon picked up a magnifying glass and moved closer to the source of the light. Then, she handed the magnifier to Liz, who leaned forward, evidently to get a better look. When she stood straight, her face looked pinched. Eventually, she noticed Maggie watching her through the glass and managed a weak smile.

The sound switched back on with a slight hum. "Okay, Maggie. We're done here. You can get dressed now. I need to talk to Alyson for a few minutes."

Chapter 20

Liz flipped the switch to turn off the speakers in the technician's booth. She tapped the microphone to make sure the sound was off.

"Let's get out of here," said Alyson. "I don't trust these sound systems."

In the elevator, Alyson leaned on the button for the third floor. "There's no way I can grade that lesion any lower than a 4C. Liz, you need to biopsy it." She gave Liz's arm a little squeeze of sympathy. "You found it when you were making love to her? How did that make you feel?"

"Like I'd been punched in the throat." Liz was surprised to hear herself speak so openly about her reactions, even to Alyson with whom she had literally been naked.

Alyson soothingly rubbed her back. "Oh, baby, I'm so sorry. You wait forty years for her and now this!"

Liz cleared her throat to make sure it was solid before she spoke. "But if we hadn't had sex, we wouldn't know about the lump."

"Small consolation to you."

"I tried to see if there were any more masses…without being obvious, of course."

Alyson's expression changed from sympathy to amused skepticism. "It's pretty hard not to be obvious while you're doing a breast exam. Did you really think you could get away with it?" The elevator pinged when it reached the floor. "I'll go over everything again and write up my notes. Needle biopsy at eleven thirty, right?"

Liz nodded and accepted Alyson's quick kiss. After Alyson exited the elevator, Liz pushed the button for the first floor.

She found Maggie, looking lost and anxious in the waiting area.

"Come with me. I know a place where we can speak privately." Liz guided her to the elevator with a hand at her back.

As soon as the elevator doors closed, Maggie asked, "It's bad, isn't it? I saw it on your face."

"I didn't realize you were watching us."

170

"Liz, you have a very expressive face when you're not guarding your feelings."

"I try to control it in medical situations. Maybe you can give me some pointers on being a better actress."

Maggie smiled weakly in response. "At least, you look like a doctor today." She touched the embroidery on Liz's pocket.

"It's the white coat. Wait till you see me in scrubs. You'll have an orgasm on the spot."

"Thanks, but it doesn't turn me on. I've seen enough doctors to last a lifetime, and now, it seems I'll be seeing a lot more of them."

Liz gave her a sympathetic look and a quick kiss. She led her to the hospital office the doctors at Seacoast Women's Health shared. She was the only one of the practice's surgeons in the hospital that morning, so they had it to themselves. Liz gestured to the sofa and Maggie took a seat.

Liz sat down beside her and put her arm around her. "The news isn't all bad. There's only one visible lesion on the mammograms. It's very small, well under two centimeters."

"Stop being optimistic for my sake. I need you to be completely honest with me."

Liz sighed as she considered how to explain the situation. Of course, she would be honest with Maggie, but there were always ways to make the news sound less ominous. "It's unlikely it's a cyst," Liz said gently. She brushed a lock of blond hair away from Maggie's eyes. "Alyson and I agree it needs to be biopsied. Like you, I was hoping it would turn out to be nothing, and it may still turn out to be nothing. The best news is there aren't more masses, and the one we found is very small. I only found it because I've done so many breast exams."

Liz's phone pinged. She pulled it out of the pocket of her white coat and scrutinized the screen.

"That's Alyson. The previous procedure finished early. We can go down now and get it over with, or we can wait until the scheduled time. Your choice."

"That's fine," said Maggie with a sigh. "I wish it could all be over. It's like a bad dream. I keep hoping I'll wake up from it."

"I know. I wish we could all wake up from it."

As they set up the IV drip, Liz steadied herself with the thought that a CNB was a simple procedure that she had done literally hundreds of times. She knew that performing it on Maggie was skirting the bounds of medical ethics, but she flatly told her conscience to mind its own business.

When Alyson came in, Liz felt calmer and more confident. Ostensibly, Alyson was only there to give advice on needle placement. Liz knew her real motive was to offer moral support in this potentially difficult situation.

As Liz watched Alyson study the mammogram on the screen, she wondered why she had refused her proposal. Alyson would have made a good partner. Not only was she beautiful and intelligent, her support was reliable and completely sincere. A wisp of strawberry blond hair had escaped Alyson's ponytail. Her elegant fingers reached up to loop it around her ear.

Maggie reached for Liz's hand, distracting Liz from her admiration of Alyson.

Liz explained what would happen next. "The sedative will make you sleepy. I'll spread some topical anesthetic on your skin. It will be icy. Hopefully, by the time I inject the local anesthetic, you'll be out cold."

"Sweet dreams," said Alyson in a genuinely kind voice. "Liz is great at this, and don't worry. I'm here to keep an eye on her."

Maggie nodded off quickly, but Liz waited a moment for the local to act before beginning. When a patient was under, it was difficult to know the level of numbness. She'd rather wait a few minutes than cause unnecessary pain.

Liz quickly located the mass with the ultrasound wand.

"You're very good with that thing, Liz," said Alyson. "Maybe you missed your calling."

"Forget it. Radiology is the most boring discipline I can imagine."

"Everything in medicine is boring to a surgeon."

"At least, I see my patients once in a while instead of staring at a screen all day."

"Hey, hey, be nice. I'm here for you."

Liz positioned the needle for insertion. They both trained their eyes on the ultrasound screen, where they could see the needle entering the breast and penetrating the mass. "Bullseye." Liz aspirated a core and repositioned the needle to take another sample. She repeated the process with another syringe. "That should give them plenty to work with." She handed the syringes to the technician, who took them to the instrument area to discharge them into the sample vials. "Okay. That was easy enough. Shut off the drip. We're done here."

The medical assistant approached to wipe up the gel and cover the breast with a sheet.

"I've got to go." Alyson gave Liz a pat on the shoulder. "Let me know when you get the path report. I'll shoot over mine this afternoon."

"Thanks, Al." Liz stripped off her gloves. "Join us for lunch? We're going to that place you like in Portsmouth."

Alyson's eyes lit up. "The one that makes those delicious Cuban sandwiches?"

Liz nodded.

Alyson glanced at Maggie, who was just opening her eyes. "No, I think your patient will need all of your attention today. Another time." She gave Liz's arm a quick pat and left.

Liz looked into Maggie's hazel eyes, which were desperately trying to focus without her glasses. "Hey there. How are you feeling?"

"Is it over?" asked Maggie in a sleepy voice.

"All done. You did very well. But I want you to lie there for a moment until you feel well enough to sit up." She carefully put Maggie's glasses on her face so she could see.

"How long will it be until we find out?" Maggie gazed around the room, blinking as she acclimated herself to her surroundings.

"Couple of days, a week at the most. They're pretty quick in that lab. I also requested a second evaluation from another lab. That's one reason I put you under. Being poked with one syringe is bad enough, never mind two."

"I think I can sit up now." Liz slipped her hand under Maggie's back to help her sit up. "I'm still a little woozy. Can I just sit here for a minute?"

"Of course, you can. Take your time." Liz patted her thigh. "We're the last ones using this room until one o'clock. No one is going to rush us out."

"Wow. That sedative was powerful!"

Liz nodded. "Most of the younger docs use only local anesthetic. That's the trend because there's less risk. You weren't really out cold, just sedated. I figure the poor patient is terrified enough by the prospect of having cancer. No need to cause more pain and anxiety."

"You're a very good doctor, Liz. I wish all those fertility doctors I saw were as considerate and gentle as you."

"I'm not sure all my patients would agree that I'm gentle."

The technician, a young, dark-haired woman, who'd remained to tidy the room chuckled softly. "Don't let her fool you, Ms. Krusick. Her patients love her. That's why she gets so many surgeries even though she claims to be retired."

"Someday, Sandy, I really will retire and fool you all. You'll see."

The technician laughed out loud. "Yeah, right. I'll believe it when I see it."

❊❊❊

While Maggie dressed, Liz headed to the Seacoast Women's Health office to drop off her white coat. Maggie was waiting when she returned to the first floor. She gazed vacantly ahead, apparently lost in her own thoughts.

Liz had to tap her shoulder to get her attention. "Hungry?"

"I'm starving. You wouldn't let me eat any breakfast. Remember?"

"I'll make it up to you. You'll like this place."

Maggie was quiet as they drove to Portsmouth. Liz let her have the privacy of her thoughts. So much had happened in only a few days, and Maggie had a lot to digest. After they crossed the bridge and navigated the multiple lanes of traffic merging to get off the exit, Liz reached over and patted her thigh. Maggie compressed her lips and gave her a sad look. Liz could see she was on the verge of tears.

"Don't worry. It will be all right."

"I hope so."

"I promise."

"Don't make promises you can't keep."

Liz nodded. "I'll keep this one."

The restaurant was one of the many eateries along Congress Street in downtown Portsmouth where Liz often ate when she had business at Southern Med. They ordered the Cuban pork sandwich. Maggie raved about it and completely finished hers except for some of the bread which she left on her plate "for her figure." She had noticeably perked up since she'd eaten. "Excellent. You may bring me here again."

"As you wish, Madam." Liz bowed her head.

"So, how does this Alyson fit into the picture?"

"I've been waiting for you to ask that question."

"She's gorgeous."

"Yes, she's very attractive. Surgeons always get the prettiest girls."

"And why is that?" Maggie carefully folded her napkin and set it down beside her plate.

"Well, you know. We're the cowboys of medicine. Make a lot of money. Prestige."

"Amazing that women still fall for that."

"Surprisingly, they do." Liz nodded to the waitress who was handing her the check. She gave it a brief glance, decided it was correct, and put her credit card in the sleeve.

"So why aren't you and Alyson still together?"

"She was more serious about the relationship than I was. She wanted to get married. She proposed to me and even bought me a ring."

Maggie's face produced a theatrically perfect look of shock.

"Yes, I know. That part didn't go over very well. If anyone's going to do the proposing, it will be me."

Maggie nodded. "But apart from offending your butch sense of propriety, what made you reject her proposal?"

"I don't know exactly. Alyson is wicked smart. Very athletic. Runs marathons. Loves to hike. As you said, she's quite attractive." Liz stopped to gauge how Maggie was receiving this information. So far, she didn't look very disturbed, but she knew that Maggie, the actress, was incredibly skilled at disguising her feelings. "Something was off. I can't say exactly what it was. Maybe I'm just not the marrying kind."

An emotion Liz couldn't define crossed Maggie's face. She glanced around, looking suddenly anxious to leave.

Chapter 21

Maggie listened to the water in the shower beat against the wall in the bathroom while she tried to drift off to sleep again. She remembered lying in Liz's arms and falling asleep against her breast.

Breasts. *You've got to stop thinking about breasts!* Maggie told herself. She'd never thought much about her own until now. They were something that sat on her chest and gave her tops and dresses an attractive, feminine line. Barry hardly bothered with them, joking from time to time that he didn't mind that she wasn't "big." He wasn't a "breast man," he'd said. Neither was Tom. Maybe that's why Maggie had come to disregard them.

They were obviously important to Liz who lavished attention on them. Sometimes Maggie felt she could come from nipple stimulation alone. When she'd said as much, Liz explained that the nerves in the nipples connected to the same part of the brain as those in the clitoris. Liz was a font of information about sex. "Comes from living with a gynecologist for years. I never knew women's bodies were so complex until I met Jenny. They certainly didn't teach us much in medical school."

The water in the shower cut off. The hair dryer droned for a few minutes. Liz always made quick work of her hair—a casual blow dry, then a brush through the uncooperative gray waves that had replaced the sleek, chestnut hair of her youth.

Liz strode into the room completely naked. Although, she was a bit slack around the middle, she still had a strong body, muscular arms and back, and a tight backside. Her long, shapely legs could be in a pantyhose ad. Maggie watched her dress through her eyelashes. Liz yanked up her panties and wiggled her way into a cotton bra. She stepped into a pair of dress pants. Now that summer was over, she'd put away the shorts and dressed "office casual." The suits came out for her appointments with her surgical patients at Seacoast Women's Health. Although Liz looked more like a doctor, there was a part of Maggie that missed the Liz-on-perpetual-vacation who had treated her broken leg.

Liz bent down and pressed her lips to Maggie's temple gently, as if she were kissing a sleepy child. "I love you." Liz nipped her ear a little with her lips. "Have a good day."

"I love you too." Maggie turned her face up to offer a kiss.

In four strides, Liz was out the door. Maggie listened to her feet pounding down the stairs.

Now that it was dark in the morning, Liz dressed before getting her coffee at Awakened Brews and walked on her lunch break. Maggie had become attuned to the rhythm of Liz's life. She knew which days Liz operated at Southern Med and saw her surgical patients in York. When Liz had evening meetings, Maggie had dinner prepared in time for her to eat beforehand. Today, Ellie was coming to clean, so Maggie had set her phone alarm for eight.

When she'd wondered aloud how to explain to Ellie that she'd moved into the master suite, Liz had laughed. "Ellie has seen a lot of people come and go in this house," said Liz. "If she has an opinion about your sharing my bed, she'll never let on." That only made Maggie think of Alyson. No doubt, there had been others.

She'd meant to ask Liz about the ring. Was it a big, showy diamond? Maggie never had one. Barry was only a student when he'd proposed, and the engagement ring he'd given her was puny. He'd tried to make up for it with an anniversary ring years later. Maggie had sold them after the divorce for a pittance.

Although thinking of Alyson and Barry distressed her, it was more comfortable than thinking about breast cancer. Whenever someone mentioned those words, Maggie had a flashback to walking in on her naked mother. Pat Fitzgerald was an old-fashioned Irish Catholic, always modest, even around her adult daughters. Maggie was shocked to see the devastation of her mother's body—the muscles sliced away from her chest wall, her underarm hanging flabby and empty, her ribs visible under a thin layer of skin, still angry and red years after the surgery.

The anticipation of the worst-case diagnosis was stealing all of Maggie's peace. The pathology reports would arrive soon. Liz had said she wanted to read together, side by side, before discussing the results or making any recommendations. As much as Maggie wanted to know, she dreaded hearing the verdict. She wanted to be prepared, so she picked up Liz's book where she'd left off, but she couldn't concentrate. She couldn't focus on anything. The mind chatter was incessant and exhausting. So far, only sex had been powerful enough to drown it out.

"You need to calm down about this," Liz advised when Maggie complained that she couldn't sleep. "I know it's hard waiting for test results, but this is just the beginning. If you have cancer, you'll be living with this for the rest of your life. You need to learn to cope with the anxiety."

Maggie had to draw on her skill as an actress to hide how much Liz's blunt assessment had hurt. Later, when she'd had time to think about it, she realized that although the words sounded harsh, they were sound advice.

"What do you suggest…to help me cope?"

"Some people try meditation…or yoga…you could join a support group…lots of things. I have some pamphlets in the office. Do you want me to bring them home?"

Maggie shook her head. What could pamphlets do? Nothing.

"If it gets really bad, I can write a script for anti-anxiety meds, but that's the solution of last resort."

"Sex is a good distraction. And it's harmless."

"Yes, but we can't spend all day in bed," said Liz, "as much as I'd like to."

Maggie took the memory of that conversation as a cue to get up. She turned off the alarm app on her phone. Her plan was to be showered and dressed before Ellie showed up. Fewer questions that way.

She was hard at work in the office space Liz had created in a small room on the third floor when Ellie appeared around nine thirty. From the window, Maggie watched the old Subaru Forester pull into the driveway and park in front of the garage. A few minutes later, she heard steps on the stairs. Ellie poked her head in the door.

"Good morning, Dr. Krusick." Ellie continued to address Maggie formally no matter how many times Maggie had asked her to call her by her first name. "I'm sorry to disturb you, but do you mind if I clean the downstairs guest room for the next guest?"

"Certainly not. I won't be using it any longer."

"Yes, Liz called to let me know you've moved upstairs."

How like Liz to smooth things over by taking charge and addressing the issue directly.

"So, you'll be staying a while..." Ellie's little smile was canny. "If you don't mind my saying so, Liz could use the company. She has a full house with her summer visitors, but no one comes in the winter. It can get pretty lonely up here."

It was the most personal thing about Liz she'd ever heard come out of Ellie's mouth, but she knew Ellie adored Liz, and her intentions were completely benign.

"We all need companionship." Maggie tried to sound vague.

"Yes, everyone needs someone special." Ellie glanced around the little office space. Liz had brought up a folding worktable from the basement, a retired office chair and a two-drawer file cabinet. "Will this be your office now?"

"For the moment," said Maggie.

"You could use something on the walls to cheer it up. It's very bare."

"Yes, maybe I'll enlarge some of the photographs I took in Acadia."

"Scenes of the outdoors would be nice." Ellie, nodded in approval. "Do you have any laundry for me to do?"

The laundry was now intermingled in the hamper in the master bath.

"Ellie, I don't need you to do my laundry. I can take it out of the hamper."

"No, problem. I can throw it in with Liz's clothes."

"If it's not too much trouble. Thank you. Let me know when it's done, and I'll sort it."

"No need. I'll sort it. I can tell the difference." Of course, anyone could tell Liz's simple cotton underwear from Maggie's lace panties and bras.

After she left, Maggie realized that, apart from being engaged in a movie or having sex, the conversation with Ellie had been the first time she'd forgotten the dread that now hung over her life and occupied her every waking moment. She picked up her phone and called Tony.

A mellow baritone answered the ring. "Hello, stranger. Are you back in New York?"

"Nope. Still in Maine. Something came up to hold me here."

"Oh, I bet I know what." Maggie could hear the smile in Tony's voice, almost a giggle just below the surface.

She lowered her voice, even though she knew Ellie was downstairs and couldn't possibly hear. "I bet you don't, but what you suspect also happened."

"Aha! I knew it! Congratulations, girlie. Liz is quite a catch. Tell me everything!"

"'I' don't kiss and tell. Sorry, Tony."

"I bet you are, and I can't wait to hear all about it."

"How about lunch at that place you like? Afterward, we can go to the shops. I need more warm clothes."

"Are you moving in up there?"

Maggie laughed to deflect the question. "I'll tell you later."

❋❋❋

The Omelet Mill was closed on Tuesdays, so Tony recommended a more upscale restaurant called The Gypsy Queen. "As the name suggests," Tony explained, holding his open hands near his face and wiggling his eyebrows, "it is très gay."

"Sounds like fun."

"The food is good. I always appreciate good food. Hint. Hint. I'm angling for another invitation to your house for dinner."

"You could invite us to your place, you know."

After a brief pause, Tony said, "We don't have enough room in the condo to entertain, although Freddie's not a bad cook when he puts his mind to it."

There was a short wait for a table because the last of the "leaf peepers" were still in town. Within a week, Webhanet's population would be reduced by half. "I can't wait for them all to leave, so we can have our town back," Tony grumbled as the waitress finally led them to a table.

They ordered iced tea and settled down to read the menu. Tony recommended the Hungarian mushroom soup. "The chef's mother is Hungarian, and it's supposed to be totally authentic. The haddock sandwich is also good."

They both ordered the Hungarian mushroom soup and decided to spilt a fish sandwich.

"This is delicious," said Maggie after she tasted the tangy soup. "I think you may have better restaurants up here than we have in New York."

"Oh, I'm sure you have more variety, but Maine's become a foodies' paradise. Great chefs. Amazing local ingredients. You won't go hungry… now that you've moved up here."

"I never said that."

"Actions speak louder than words, and now that you've conquered the warrior queen, how can you bear to go home?" He leaned forward and spoke in a confidential voice. "Was it as good as everyone says it is?"

"Was what good?" asked Maggie, playing dumb.

"The sex, Maggie! How was the sex?"

"You think I'd tell you? And who's everyone?"

Tony raised his hands and mimed exaggerated ignorance. "I can't really say."

"You're full of it."

"Of course." He wiggled his brows Groucho Marx-style again. "But you do have the look of a woman who's been getting great sex."

Maggie rolled her eyes.

"Well, you do. And you haven't gone back to New York yet, so you must want to stay. Just move in with her. She invited you to stay. I'm a witness."

"I'm staying for the time being, until some things get sorted out."

"I'm telling you, Maggie, just rent the damn place in the Village, or sell it. You could get a fortune for it."

Maggie's mind balked at the thought of giving up her snug little apartment. It had been her safe haven after the sale of the house in Connecticut. She'd decorated the apartment in an avant-garde style in a deliberate rebuke to the expectations of her Connecticut friends, who were all addicted to HGTV.

"I may need a fortune, so I'll keep that in mind."

Tony looked up from his soup. "Why?" His dark brows came together in a puzzled frown.

Maggie lowered her voice. "I might have some big medical bills on the way."

"Oh, no. I'm sorry. What's wrong?"

"Liz found a lump in my breast." There. She'd finally told someone.

"Oh, my God! No! That's horrible!" For once, Tony's reaction didn't seem over the top.

Maggie nodded. "It is horrible, and I'm scared to death."

Tony reached across the table and took her hand. "Oh, honey, I'm so sorry. So, so sorry."

"Thank you." Maggie swallowed hard in the hope of blocking the tears, but her eyes filled anyway. She dabbed them with her napkin and left some mascara on the cloth. "Liz did the biopsy on Monday. We should know more in a few days."

"If it's any consolation, you couldn't find a better doctor than Liz. She's famous for that, you know."

"So, I'm discovering. But now, it's complicated because we're lovers, not just friends."

"Why should that matter?" Tony tilted his head and frowned.

"Medical ethics, apparently."

"Don't worry. Liz will figure it out. She knows a lot of people."

"Yes, and everyone is an ex."

Tony laughed. "So, you've met Alyson. Yes, she's quite something. That was a close call."

"You didn't approve?"

Tony shook his head. "It would have never worked. Despite her feminine looks, personality-wise, Alyson is as butch as they come. They were too much alike. And I'm not sure Liz was ready to settle down again. She and Jenny have a messy, complicated relationship."

"I've heard. And I've met Jenny."

Tony finished his soup and pushed away the bowl. "At least, you know what you're getting yourself into."

***

Maggie managed to get home in time to start dinner, although she hated to mess up the pristine kitchen Ellie had just cleaned. When Ellie moved upstairs to clean the bedroom, Maggie got her chicken and leek stew started.

She'd always associated stews with fall, a dish to celebrate the change of seasons. In New York, the transition was so gradual. The heat of summer slowly gave way to cooler temperatures. The leaves in Washington Square Park turned a dingy yellow and drifted to the ground. In Maine, the air suddenly became crisp. The leaves turned from deep green into a riot of brilliant colors. The air was filled with the comforting scent of wood smoke. As Liz had said, High October was spectacular.

Although the day had been warm, the weather service predicted a chilly evening and warned about the possibility of a hard frost. It had been years since Maggie had lived in a suburban house and needed to worry about bringing in houseplants. She'd nearly forgotten what a big event the first real frost of the season could be.

When Liz came home, she barely gave Maggie a kiss. "I've got to cover my tomatoes!" She ran upstairs, taking the steps by twos. Moments later, she returned in jeans and a hoodie and headed straight out to the garden. Maggie watched from the kitchen window as Liz draped plastic sheets over the tomatoes. She secured the plastic around the perimeter with rocks. In all, the rescue operation took a little over fifteen minutes. Liz was back in the house in time to pay Ellie. She always paid cash to spare her housekeeper the trouble of cashing a check.

When she returned to the kitchen, she kissed Maggie and apologized for her abrupt entrance. "How was your day?"

"I went to lunch with Tony."

"That's good. I should introduce you to more of my friends."

"If it's all the same to you, I don't think Alyson and I are ever going to be tight."

Liz laughed. "I never thought so, but I do have some friends who have never been in my bed," said Liz, putting her arms around her. "Maybe we should throw a little 'welcome Maggie to Maine' dinner party."

"Let's wait for the results of the biopsy, if you don't mind."

When Liz tensed, Maggie instantly knew she was holding something back. She could practically hear the gears turning in Liz's brain as she tried to find the best way to word what she had to say. "One came today. I sent it to that lab because they're so fast."

Maggie took a deep breath. "And…?"

"And I told you, I wouldn't discuss it until I read both reports."

"Liz, that's not fair. If you're going to keep things from me, I'm going to have to find another doctor."

"Be patient, Maggie." Liz tightened her embrace. "I want to get all the data and evaluate it, so I can give you the best advice possible."

Maggie eased herself out of Liz's arms so she could look at her face. "Liz, please. What did it say?"

"Well, it's not the best news, but not the worst either."

"And that means what?"

"It is cancer, but very treatable. I should get the other report very soon. Then I'll explain everything. I promise."

Maggie swallowed hard, trying to stop the tears. She wanted Liz to see that she could cope, but the sob escaped anyway. Liz pulled her close. "Oh, Maggie, I'm so sorry."

Chapter 22

Liz stared at the screen until her eyes watered and her vision blurred. She blinked, hoping the offending numbers would change, but they were still the same. She felt a blunt pain in her throat exactly like when she'd found the lump.

She exhaled a deep sigh and sent the report to the printer to make a copy for Maggie's file. Then, she printed a second copy and put it in her pocket. She'd use it later to explain the results to Maggie.

The news wasn't all bad. Maggie's Ki-67 was relatively low, so the cancer was slow-growing. Technically, it fell into the Luminal A category, which meant targeted endocrine therapy would be effective, and Maggie could probably skip chemo. Liz forwarded the report to Beverly Birnbaum, the chief of oncology at Yale New Haven, through the secure portal with a note saying she'd call in the morning.

She closed her laptop and checked the time. Three o'clock. She picked up her cellphone and found Maggie in her favorites. As the call rang on the other end, Liz imagined how she would break the news.

"Well, hello there, Dr. Stolz. You don't usually call me from the office."

"I'm on official business."

"You are?" Maggie's voice was full of playful doubt.

"Yes, I hope you haven't started dinner yet because I want to take you out to celebrate the good news." Liz bit her lip, hoping she didn't sound too optimistic, and Maggie would get the wrong idea.

"You got the other pathology report," Maggie guessed correctly. Liz could hear the sharp intake of air, a little gasp to brace for bad news.

Liz spoke in her usual medical tone to calm her. "Yes, I just got the report on the sample I sent to the lab I really trust. It's top-notch but really slow. In fact, I'm surprised it came back so fast."

"What's the verdict?"

"It agrees with the other report. But let's have a really nice dinner at a very special place I know. Then, we'll have an after-dinner cognac, and I'll explain it all to you. Deal?"

"You're going to feed me a delicious dinner and then ply me with alcohol to deliver your bad news?"

"I told you it's good news. It's all in the interpretation. Now, put on something nice. This is a classy place. Five diamonds, as is fitting for my best girl."

"I'd better be your *only* girl." The warning note in Maggie's voice was playful, but Liz heard the slight edge.

"You are. Scout's honor."

"Liz, you were never a Girl Scout."

Liz laughed. "No, but it sounds good. I'll make the reservation for six. I'll come home first, so we can take the Audi."

"Good. That means I can wear a dress."

Liz imagined Maggie in one of her little black dresses. "Yes, please. You look very sexy in a dress."

"Dr. Stolz, can your staff hear you?"

"No, I'm alone in my office. My door is closed."

"Good. Then they won't hear you gasp when I tell you I like to wear dresses because I feel more open to you." Maggie adjusted her voice to be low and sexy. "It makes me think about how much I like to feel you inside me...deep inside."

Liz felt a quick flush of arousal. She closed her eyes to concentrate the feeling. "Maggie, please. Don't torture me. I have to work for another hour."

"Okay. No phone sex in the office. I'll be ready when you get here."

"To go to dinner, right?"

Maggie laughed. "You'll see." Liz could practically see her wink. "Yes, to go to dinner, but that doesn't let you off the hook for later."

After she ended the call, Liz took a minute to gather her forces before seeing her next patient. Her genitals had responded to Maggie's suggestions with heightened sensitivity even though she knew it was only a tease.

Maggie's seductive voice could drive her crazy. To tamp down the desire, Liz reviewed her next patient's file before heading to the examination room.

***

They ordered the seasonal tasting menu, which included a demitasse of wild mushroom soup, venison sliders, haddock ceviche, a selection of raw and grilled oysters, and roasted beet salad. Each tasting was paired with a wine. The entrée was local pork tenderloin medallions and spiced apples. They passed on the dessert, real Indian pudding, and ordered cognac instead.

Liz leaned forward to speak in a confidential tone. "Professor Krusick, you look especially fetching tonight."

"You're just buttering me up for your bad news." Maggie glanced away and took a sip of cognac.

Liz frowned. "You keep expecting bad news."

"Isn't cancer always bad news? Well, go ahead. All that alcohol has gone to my head. I won't feel a thing."

Liz collected her thoughts and cleared her throat before delivering her little speech. "Your tumor is slow-growing. It's estrogen sensitive, so it should respond to endocrine-based treatments. It might also be responsive to Herceptin, but we need to wait for the results of the FISH test. You probably won't need chemo, but I sent the report to the chief of oncology at Yale. Bev Birnbaum is a brilliant woman. I trust her implicitly. I'm ninety-nine point nine percent sure, she won't recommend chemo."

"But you will take out the lump."

"Yes, and if you agree to be treated at Yale, I'll call Ellen Connelly in the morning. She trained under me, and she's an excellent breast surgeon."

Maggie looked at her intently. "I want *you* to do the operation."

Liz shook her head. "You don't really, and even if we were just friends and not lovers, I wouldn't agree."

"You're supposed to be the best."

"There are other surgeons who are just as good as I am, and a lumpectomy is a pretty simple procedure."

"Then why won't you do it?" Maggie looked determined. Her tone was insistent.

Liz wondered how she could make her understand. At this point, it went beyond medical ethics, which were an abstraction, in any case. Liz tried to explain in the most direct, visceral terms. "Maggie, I love your body like it's my own. Cutting your breast would be like cutting my own flesh."

"You had no trouble stabbing me with that needle."

"That was different. And it's not true that I 'had no trouble.' I was shaky because it was you and not some anonymous patient. You don't want a shaky surgeon, do you?" Liz picked up her butter knife and mimed a shaky hand holding a scalpel.

"I get the point."

Liz put down the knife.

The discs on Maggie's gold bracelet tinkled softly as she moved her hand across the table cloth and took Liz's. "I just realized how hard this is for you."

"It's not hard," protested Liz.

"Oh, Liz. I'm sure you can fool a lot of people, but you can't fool me. You're trying to be so professional and strong, but inside, it's got to be really difficult."

Liz succeeded in contorting her mouth into a defective smile. "We both need to be strong to get through this." From the corner of her eye, she caught sight of the waiter hovering. She released Maggie's hand and motioned to him to come forward.

***

Liz was brushing her teeth when she heard Maggie's phone ring. Who could be calling at this hour? It was after ten.

"I'm sorry, honey. I know I promised to call you, but things got so busy."

The caller on the other end was speaking. Liz rinsed out her toothbrush and tried to ignore Maggie talking the other room, but Maggie's voice was distinctive. From her theatrical training, she had perfect elocution that was hard to ignore, and her voice carried. "I'm staying here for a while. Liz has been a very good friend. It's been a tough time."

It was quiet for a moment while Maggie listened. Then she said, "No, Tom's out of the picture. Let's just say he took an unhealthy interest in one of his female students."

Liz sympathized. That had to be so difficult to admit. She began to feel guilty about eavesdropping, so she put on her pajamas and headed downstairs. She soon had company. Maggie, still on the phone, had followed her. Instead of muting the call, Maggie held the phone against her hip to muffle the mic.

"It's Sophia. I told her about the lump. Would you please explain the situation to her? You two can talk doctor talk together."

Liz sighed in exasperation, but she took the phone. "Hello, Sophia," she said warmly. "How are you?"

"I was better before Mom told me about the lump. What's going on?'

Liz put the phone on speaker, so Maggie could hear both ends of the conversation. "The tumor is small, less than two centimeters. It's Luminal A." Liz recited the data on the report from memory, surprised as always, that such information lodged in her brain, and she could report it verbatim afterward. She spoke in the sort of neutral voice she would always use with a colleague, but she sensed the growing anxiety on the other end of the call.

Liz drew a breath and paused for questions. When there were none, she continued. "I've asked the chief of oncology at Yale New Haven to review the report and give me her opinion. I've suggested to your mother that she go to Yale for both the surgery and the oncology consult."

"Why not Sloan Kettering? It's closer to home for Mom."

Liz made an effort to be patient. After all, it was a good question, and this was Maggie's daughter. "Sloan is a great cancer center, but it's also enormous, and the strong focus on research means patients often get lost in the system. Don't get me wrong. They do very good work there, but I know the people at Yale because I used to work with them."

"Honey, I told Liz I'd go to Yale if she thinks that's the right thing."

There was a sigh with a hint of exasperation through the speaker. "Dr. Stolz, would you mind if I spoke to my mother alone?"

"Of course, not. And please…call me Liz, everyone does."

"Thanks, Dr. Stolz…I mean, Liz."

"Would you like me to send you a copy of the report? I can send an encrypted email. Your mother will call you with the key."

"Yes, that would be great."

"Your mother will also give you my phone number and email address. Feel free to call me anytime."

Liz handed the phone back to Maggie, who mouthed "Thanks." Liz shrugged and headed to the media room. She opened the liquor cabinet and poured herself a glass of cognac. In the face of so many things she couldn't control, she felt the need for something orderly. She loaded a CD of Faure's "Pavane." The soothing music worked its magic, and she soon felt much calmer.

Eventually, Maggie wandered into the room. "I thought I might find you in here."

Liz turned down the music. "All the good liquor is here in the cabinet, in case you ever need it. Cognac?"

Maggie shook her head. "No, thank you. I think I've had enough alcohol for tonight." She sat down beside Liz on the sofa. From her frown, Liz surmised the remainder of the conversation had not gone well, but she decided not to pry and sipped her cognac in silence.

"She can be so stubborn sometimes," Maggie finally said. "She's always been terrified that something will happen to me, and I'll suddenly disappear, so she wants me where she can see me." Maggie gave Liz's glass a covetous look. "As a matter of fact, I think I will take you up on that cognac."

Liz got up to pour it.

"Sophia wants me to go to Baylor for treatment."

"Baylor! No disrespect to Sophia, but there are much better places. Will you go?"

"No, of course not. The girl's been an oncology resident for five minutes and thinks she knows everything."

"Unfortunately, arrogance is a common quality of young physicians. They have yet to be humbled by their own ignorance."

"In Sophia's case, it's bravado. She's so unsure of herself." Maggie took a sip of cognac. "After I said I wouldn't go to Baylor, she pushed for Sloan Kettering."

Liz shrugged. "Sloan is a very good cancer hospital. I won't deny it."

"But you want me to go to Yale."

"I have some influence at Yale because I worked there. The health care system today is like a maze that no one knows how to navigate, not even doctors. The only way to get good care is for someone knowledgeable to advocate for you. I can do that for you at Yale."

"You say you trust these people."

"I do, and I know their work. I've seen it firsthand. If the situation were reversed, I'd go to Yale."

"That's recommendation enough for me." Maggie drained the last of her brandy. She took Liz's empty glass out of her hand. "I'll rinse these out and wash them in the morning."

Liz followed Maggie into the kitchen. "We should go to bed. It's almost midnight, and I have office hours in the morning."

While Maggie carefully rinsed out the glasses in the kitchen sink, Liz leaned her chin on her shoulder and put her arms around her waist.

"I just want you to hold me tonight," said Maggie with a sigh.

"I can do that."

"Liz, you're so solid. Why did I ever give you up?"

"I don't know. Why did you?"

"I don't know either, but I'm not making that mistake again."

Chapter 23

As Liz sped down the highway, the rain beat steadily on the windshield. Although the wipers were going full tilt, the visibility was poor. Liz's eyes remained carefully trained on the road ahead. In the beginning, the speed at which Liz drove frightened Maggie. Now, she knew that Liz was a careful driver and hardly noticed anymore.

"If you're uncomfortable staying with Jenny, we can stay in a hotel," Liz said. "I'm sure I can still get reservations. Maybe I can get one of those suites with a kitchen."

"It's too expensive."

"I don't mind spending the money."

Maggie wasn't sure why Liz was bringing this up again. They had discussed where they would stay during Maggie's surgery and recovery and had agreed that Jenny's house would be more comfortable than a hotel. It was close to New Haven without being in the city. While Jenny was at work, they would have the run of the place. And after all, it was Liz's house too.

"I'm sure it will be fine," said Maggie, unwilling to discuss it again, but she certainly didn't look forward to spending a week with Liz's ex, especially not after Jenny's unpleasant visit in September.

"You don't sound like you're sure." Liz glanced in the rear-view mirror as she cut into traffic for the merge onto I91.

"It's not always easy being around Jenny. Sometimes, she acts like she owns you." Maggie bit her lip. She hadn't meant to say so much.

"Believe me. That's only since you've come on the scene. Weird."

"This is what we planned. It will be fine."

"I'll do my best to keep Jenny in line, but if it gets uncomfortable for you for any reason, we're going to a hotel. You have enough to worry about, and so do I."

Liz took backroads to avoid the traffic in New Haven. As they passed small farms and acres of undeveloped land, Maggie was surprised to see this part of Connecticut was still so rural. Where she had lived with Barry to be near his job, it had been so congested.

"We're almost there." Liz obviously meant to sound encouraging, but it had the opposite effect. The closer they came to their destination, the higher Maggie's anxiety level rose.

Finally, they turned onto a long drive leading to a Colonial-style house right on the waterfront. Maggie just stared. "This place is enormous. Oh, my God! That view!"

"Now, you see why we didn't want to sell when I decided to move to Maine. The trouble is, Jenny may never be able to get the money together to buy me out, so I may be part owner forever."

"Doesn't that bother you?" Maggie tried to sound as neutral as possible. It definitely bothered her.

Liz took their bags out of the backseat. "It's just money. Stop worrying. It has nothing to do with us." But Maggie wasn't so sure.

Liz brought the bags in. "I'll bring them up later. First, let me give you the nickel tour."

Although it was a dreary day, the interior of the house was painted and furnished in light colors, which made it look bright and sun-splashed. The open floor plan allowed the rooms to merge into one another. The cook could easily talk to guests in the dining room, the living room, or the library. The entire wall on the waterfront side of the first floor was glass—windows and French doors. It provided a picture-perfect view of Long Island Sound, which today looked like a stormy watercolor seascape. Maggie instantly saw the inspiration for the wall of glass in Liz's bedroom. She was stunned by the size of the house and the sheer beauty of the view.

"How could you bear to leave this place?"

"The house and the location are great, but the neighbors are as stuck up as they come…when they're here. Most of the houses along the water are just weekend and summer homes for people who are obscenely rich." Liz headed toward the stairs. "Come on. Let me show you where our room is."

Although Maggie offered to help, Liz carried all the bags upstairs.

"Jenny has the room with the best view, of course, but I think you'll be very comfortable in this room. I'll leave you to unpack while I see what's in the refrigerator."

A few minutes later, Liz returned, bringing up the garment bag. "As I suspected, the cupboard is bare. Would you mind if I ran down to the supermarket to pick up a few things? Cooking is the least I can do while Jenny is putting us up."

"I can cook."

"No. You are the patient, and you will follow doctor's orders. That means I'm cooking tonight." Liz gave her quick kiss. "I'll only be gone a short time. Maybe you should get some rest."

The fatigue was nearly overwhelming after the long drive and the stress of anticipating her visit with the surgeon in the morning, but before Maggie lay down, she unpacked for both of them. She carefully hung Liz's suits and dress blouses in the closet. She arranged their underwear and casual clothes in the empty drawers in the dresser.

When everything was put away, she turned off the light and lay down on the enormous mahogany four-poster. As she adjusted the pillow, she noticed Liz's mark carved into one of the head posts, which meant that Liz had built it. Maggie was surprised that Liz would leave it behind. She took such pride in her work and was so protective of the furniture she built.

It was chilly and damp because of all the rain, so Maggie pulled up the afghan from the foot of the bed. She was dozing lightly when she heard a female voice calling though the house. "Hello? Hello? Liz! Where are you?"

The door opened, and Jenny poked her head in. "Oh, Maggie, you're resting. Sorry to disturb you."

"No, it's all right." Maggie sat up and switched on the bedside lamp. "Come in."

Jenny came in and sat down on the bed. "Maggie, I'm so sorry. It's nice to see you again…despite the circumstances. Welcome."

Maggie didn't know how to respond to this warm reception. She managed a theatrical smile. "Thank you for letting us stay with you."

"*Mi casa es su casa.*" Jenny's Spanish accent was surprisingly good. "Actually, it's Liz's house too, but let's not get technical." Jenny looked around. She glanced at the clothes hanging in the open closet. "Where's Liz?"

"At the supermarket getting dinner makings."

"Oh, I should have guessed. I thought we'd go out to dinner, but the truth is, I miss her cooking. She usually got home earlier because she'd operate at the crack of dawn and see patients in the early afternoon. I loved to come home to those delicious smells from the kitchen. Heavenly, actually. People always assumed I was the nurturing one because of my specialty, but it's Liz. She's very maternal. You should see her with kids."

Maggie, who never woke up well, was overwhelmed with this blast of information.

Jenny patted her hand. "I'm sorry I interrupted your nap. I should let you rest."

"I dozed a little. I should get up."

"Come down and join me for a drink. Martini?"

"Wine, I think. Except not–"

Jenny laughed. "Yes, Liz told me the Châteauneuf was too much for you. Not everyone appreciates it. Don't worry. I have some California wines. Come on. It will drive Liz crazy to come home and find us talking about her."

They settled in the library. The wine Jenny selected for her, a pinot noir, was perfect. They sat side by side on a sofa facing the sound.

"It's so beautiful here."

"Isn't it? That's why I'm glad Liz hasn't forced me out. If I could afford it, I would stay here forever."

"Thanks again for letting us stay while I have my surgery."

Jenny settled back into the corner of the couch and gave Maggie a critical look. "Don't worry. A lumpectomy is a pretty simple procedure. I hear Liz has you booked in with Ellen Connelly for tomorrow morning. Liz trained her, so you might have to put up with a little hero worship."

"I don't care so long as she's a good surgeon."

"No one better, except Liz herself. And Bev Birnbaum is great too. You'll love her. Straight talker. She'll let you know exactly what she thinks."

"Liz said she probably won't recommend chemo."

"Probably not. I saw your labs."

"Liz sent them to you?" Maggie felt uncomfortable. She wasn't sure she wanted Jenny knowing so much about her.

Jenny smiled, obviously to reassure her. "She often asks my opinion about her breast cases because of the hormone component. That's a subspecialty of mine. I'm sorry. Didn't she ask you if it was all right?"

"No," said Maggie, frowning. "She didn't."

Jenny looked nonplussed for a moment. "Technically, it's not a HIPAA violation because she was consulting me as another physician, but as a personal matter, she should have asked your permission." Jenny patted her hand. "Don't worry. It's all in the family." That remark only made Maggie more uncomfortable.

A few minutes later, Liz came through the door. Jenny got up and Maggie followed her into the kitchen.

Liz was busily unpacking the groceries. Jenny kissed her. "Welcome home, sweetie. How about a martini?"

"Thank you, but I won't sit with you. I need to get dinner going."

Jenny began mixing the martinis. "How was your trip?"

"Not bad, considering the weather."

"I see the makings of chicken piccata," observed Jenny, watching Liz lay out the ingredients.

"I found the capers you like. The very tiny ones." Liz began beating the chicken breasts thin with a meat mallet.

"You're so sweet to look for them for me." Jenny put her arm around Liz's waist and gave her another kiss.

"I have my moments." Liz dipped the cutlets in beaten egg and dredged them in seasoned flour.

Maggie, relegated to the role of bystander, asked, "Can I help with something?"

Jenny gave Maggie a dismissive glance. "No, sit down. We've got it covered. Would you like some cheese and crackers to munch on before dinner? Let me get you something."

Maggie sat on a stool at the kitchen island, nibbling on cheese and crackers while Liz prepared the meal.

"Has Liz made this for you before?" asked Jenny. "Her piccata is her pièce de résistance!"

"Stop, Jenny. It's not that special."

"You see, Maggie? Dr. Stolz is occasionally capable of modesty."

"Knock it off, or you can cook for yourself, and we'll go out."

"All right," said Jenny, slinking away. "I'll behave."

Maggie listened to them banter and realized they were like a long-married couple. She believed Liz when she said that their sexual relationship was in the past, but in some ways, sex was the least of it. They had an easy, uncomplicated intimacy. Maggie envied them all those years of sharing milestones as well as the small moments of sorrow and joy that together make a life. Forty years of separation could never be made up in this lifetime. No matter what her relationship with Liz became, they could never reclaim all those lost years.

Chapter 24

Ellen Connelly was one of those pale-haired, freckled women with hazel eyes whose features are indistinct even with makeup. Such people can look wholesome or bland, depending on the tastes of the beholder.

Liz wondered why she was thinking about her protégée's looks instead of helping Maggie provide an accurate medical history. Maggie had stumbled a few times trying to answer Ellen's rapid-fire questions, and Liz had jumped in to provide the information. Because Ellen had worked under her, it would be so easy to dominate the consultation, but Liz wanted Maggie to take the lead in directing her treatment.

Ellen was close to the end of the patient interview sheet. Liz knew she was winding down because she had designed the questionnaire when she was at Yale.

"Can you think of anything else, Dr. Stolz?" Ellen looked a little anxious, as if she were still Liz's subordinate.

"No, Dr. Connelly, I think you've covered everything."

"I'll examine you now, Ms. Krusick," said Ellen, getting up. "This way." She opened a door that led to an examination room. "There's a gown there. Opening in the front, please."

The door closed and Liz imagined Maggie wrestling with the examination gown. Whoever invented that absurd garment should be hanged by it in hell.

"I'm surprised you didn't do the lumpectomy yourself," Ellen said. "It's such a simple procedure. Why come all the way down here?"

"Call me old-fashioned, but I believe in that particular dictum of medical ethics."

Ellen nodded. "We should all follow it, but many don't."

Liz thought of Jenny, who'd performed an abortion on her own sister without a second thought. Afterwards, she'd bragged that it was a feminist act while Liz stared at her in amazement. "What if something had gone wrong? How could you ever forgive yourself?" Jenny had merely shrugged.

Ellen interrupted Liz's thoughts. "But you will scrub in, won't you? You still have privileges here." The look in Ellen's eyes was clearly a challenge.

"No, I trust you, Ellen, but if you feel the need for supervision, I will definitely scrub in."

They exchanged a look of agreement. "Good. I'll see you in the OR tomorrow."

Liz instantly regretted taking the dare, and she suspected the invitation had less to do with courtesy and more to do with Ellen showing that she now had mastery of the team. It was obviously very important to her to prove to her mentor that she'd succeeded. She seemed to have missed the fact that Liz had spent years training and coaching her and took real pleasure in seeing her success.

Agreeing to scrub in also meant Liz would have to deal with everyone's expectations. Most of the current staff had worked under her and would be watching to see if she was still sharp.

But the real reason Liz didn't want to be in the OR was she didn't want to watch Ellen cut open Maggie's breast. Even Liz's detachment had limits.

Ellen knocked on the door to the examination room. "May I come in?

Liz followed her in, and her heart went out to Maggie. It wasn't enough to be overwhelmed with anxiety. Now, the poor woman had to cope with the indignity of trying to cover herself with the skimpy, uncooperative exam gown.

Liz moved to Maggie's side and took her hand, while Ellen studied the mammogram on the screen. "Let's see. Left breast, two o'clock 4CM FN."

Maggie looked anxious. "What does that mean?"

"It's medical code for the location of the mass," Liz explained. "We think of your breast as a clock. In your case, the position of the tumor is at two o'clock and it's four centimeters from the nipple." She smiled to reassure Maggie but stepped back so Ellen could begin the examination.

Ellen brushed aside the paper gown and gave the breast in question a critical look before she began. For good measure, and also to make a comparison, Ellen carefully examined the other breast and both armpits.

Maggie shut her eyes tight while her breasts were being palpated. Her jaw was set hard, as if her doctor's touch was painful. Finally, Ellen drew closed the flaps of the gown.

"All done, Ms. Krusick. You can get dressed now." She left the room. The door latch engaged with a sharp click.

Maggie sat up and leaned against Liz, who soothingly stroked her hair.

"I know. It's humiliating."

"No, that's not it. It's that all this makes it so real."

"I'm going to scrub in tomorrow. Do you mind?"

Maggie's arms around Liz's waist pulled tighter. "No, I want you there."

Eventually, Maggie let go, and Liz left to give her privacy while she dressed.

"It's textbook, Liz," said Ellen, as Liz sat down in the visitor's chair. "You should have done it in Maine and not dragged the poor woman down here."

"I just couldn't," said Liz. Ellen stared at her, but then she nodded. "I'll open with your method for nipple conservation in case we need to do a mastectomy later."

"I hope you use it most of the time. It does less nerve damage."

"Oh, I do. Just letting you know I haven't made any radical changes around here."

When Maggie emerged from the examination room, she looked unsettled, so Liz focused on the torrent of information Ellen was conveying. "We'll do the surgery at eight o'clock tomorrow morning. It's a quick procedure that lasts only fifteen minutes to a half hour. Max forty minutes. We'll keep you in recovery until the anesthesia wears off and you can sit up. Then Dr. Stolz can bring you back to Dr. Carson's to rest. Don't worry. We'll give you plenty of medication for the pain." Ellen rose and extended her hand. "See you tomorrow, Ms. Krusick."

Maggie turned to Liz on the way to the car. "She's a cold fish, isn't she?"

"Unfortunately, surgeons often have poor patient management skills. Our involvement is brief, so some surgeons think it's a waste of time to develop a rapport."

"But you're wonderful with your patients."

"I wasn't always. In the beginning, I had to force myself."

Before she sat down in the driver's seat, Liz unbuttoned the waistband of her skirt. "Maybe Jenny's right about the beer."

Maggie laughed for the first time that morning. "I think your little belly is adorable."

"Well, if you want to see me in suits more often, I'm going to have to lose it."

Liz started the engine, then sat for a moment, debating whether to visit her mother. It had been months since she had seen her, and it would be a shame not to take advantage of being nearby.

"I probably should stop in to say hello to my mother while I'm down here. You can come along, or I can drop you off at Jenny's."

Maggie's reply was instant and cheerful. "No, I'll come with you. I've always liked your mother."

Liz wondered how much she should tell Maggie about the many twists and turns in her relationship with her mother. After being disowned, Liz was finally welcomed back into the family, but things with her mother had remained rocky. There were months when they didn't speak. Then they were back to being as close as ever—her mother completing her sentences and practically reading her mind.

Maggie listened carefully as Liz gave her a quick overview of where things stood. Monica Stolz had been a widow for over thirty years. Fortunately, Robert, Liz's youngest brother, who'd never married, lived with their mother and looked after her.

Monica had turned eighty-five in the spring. Her mind was sharp, especially on the subject of politics. Liz often thought her mother had missed her calling and should have run for office herself. In fact, Monica was too used to being the boss and giving orders. She would have failed miserably at the give and take of politics. To keep up with her mother's obsession with politics, Liz had to read all the political stories that showed up in her newsfeed before their morning phone call.

Unfortunately, conversation, even political debates, had become increasingly difficult because her mother was losing her hearing. Once considered a great beauty, she was too vain to use a hearing aid.

Maggie nodded, absorbing the information. "You're lucky to still have your mother, and how many people our age can go back to the house where they grew up?"

"She'll never sell that place and she'll never leave it until they carry her out in a body bag. Unfortunately, she doesn't have the money to keep it up. My brother has a good income, but it's too much even for him. The taxes are killing them."

Maggie was silent for a few minutes as she gazed out the window. "Do you think she'll remember me?"

"Once I provide her with some context. Don't be surprised if you get a chilly reception. I told her how our relationship ended. Years after the fact, but I told her. Despite her issues with me, she's fiercely loyal to her kids, so of course, she always takes my side."

"Then maybe I shouldn't go with you."

"It will be fine. Let me call and see if it's a good time to come over. We can bring her lunch from the Chinese restaurant."

Liz roused Siri and asked her to call her mother. The phone rang and rang until the answering machine picked up. No doubt their entire conversation would be recorded. "Hello, Elizabeth!" sang a cheerful voice through the dashboard when Monica finally picked up the call.

Maggie and Liz exchanged a smile. "Hi, Mom. I'm in the neighborhood and wondered if I might drop by for lunch. I'll bring Chinese food, and if you don't mind, I'd like to bring along a friend."

"Really? Who?"

"You remember Maggie Fitzgerald. From college?"

There was a long silence. "Oh, that Maggie!" The disapproval in her tone was obvious.

"Yes, that Maggie. We're staying with Jenny for a few days. I knew you'd kill me if you found out I was down here and didn't stop by."

"Well, I wouldn't kill you, Elizabeth. You're my daughter."

"Just kidding, Mom. See you later."

Maggie looked anxious after Liz ended the call. "Your mother didn't seem too happy about seeing me. Maybe you should drop me off at Jenny's and go alone."

"Don't worry. It will be fine." Liz sounded confident, although she was a little anxious herself.

When they were in college, Maggie had been Monica's favorite among Liz's friends. Maggie would put on her best theatrical performance for Monica and charm her. Monica, who was something of an actress herself, used to selling top corporate clients on the family design and decorating business, was easily charmed.

Maggie always came along when Liz went home on weekends or for holidays when it was too expensive to go to Syracuse. They slept in Liz's room, where they squeezed into one of the twin beds and slept with one ear awake, ever alert in case they needed to change the sleeping arrangements at a moment's notice.

Ironically, Monica had once considered Maggie a good influence on her daughter. Maggie had presence, whereas young Liz was awkward and unsure. The tallest girl in the class since seventh grade, Liz stooped, whereas Maggie had a bearing that came from learning how to carry herself onstage. Maggie knew how to dress and make herself attractive, while Liz preferred threadbare jeans and T-shirts.

Maggie woke Liz from the memories by asking, "How long will it take us to get there?"

"Oh, about an hour and change, depending on the traffic." Liz glanced at Maggie and caught her chewing her lip. "Are you sure you're up to it? You've been on an emotional roller coaster the last few weeks."

"Yes, it's been a wild ride, but your mother will be so disappointed if you don't come." Maggie frowned. "It's been so strange. One day, everything's fine. The next, you have cancer."

"You had cancer, but you didn't know it."

"But everything is different now. My life is suddenly *about* cancer."

Liz reached over and patted Maggie's thigh. "No, it's not," she said in a perfectly serious voice. "It's about fucking." She raised a brow and gave Maggie a naughty grin.

Maggie's mouth momentarily opened in shock, then she laughed until tears came to her eyes. "Stop it, Liz! You're going to make me wet myself."

"Don't you *dare* ruin my leather seats!"

❈❈❈

Liz tried to hide her embarrassment when Maggie walked into the venerable, old farmhouse. No doubt, Maggie would compare it to her memories of the place in its heyday. The drapes in the family room hadn't been updated since the 1960s. The 1980s kitchen appliances still functioned, so they'd never been replaced. Everything looked dated and shabby. Here and there were signs of actual neglect—a leak in the ceiling that had never been repaired, a bare light bulb hanging from wires since the renovation project had been interrupted years ago.

Maggie gave Liz a look of sympathy and a gentle smile that communicated, "We'll talk about it later." Despite the uncertainty in Monica's voice when Liz announced she was bringing Maggie, the greeting they received was enthusiastic, even operatic. Monica made such a fuss over Maggie that Liz was left to stand aside with an arched brow to wonder what had suddenly come over her mother.

Liz set the table in the kitchen and distributed the Chinese food, while her mother held Maggie captive in the family room, regaling her with stories of the family business in its prime. The visit was going well until Maggie revealed that she had been the house guest of her old college friend since the trampoline accident. Liz could feel her mother's eyes boring into her back as she scooped out the fried rice.

Instead of addressing the issue directly, Monica called to Liz from the other room. "Elizabeth, make sure you use the nice flatware." Liz sighed, weary of being told what to do as if she were still a child.

After lunch, Liz cleared away the dishes, loaded the dishwasher, and washed the pots left over from the previous night's dinner. She scrubbed the counter around the sink, trying to remove the brown stains around the faucet. Whenever she came, she tried to tidy a little, but the entire house was such a mess it was merely a gesture.

After a few hours, Liz noticed Maggie's act beginning to unravel from fatigue. She suggested that it was time to go.

Monica tried to delay the departure with extended farewells and opening a new line of political conversation. She plied her daughter with a box of chocolate chip cookies she had baked. Liz tried to refuse them, pleading the need to cut back on sweets for her figure, but Maggie stepped in and graciously accepted them.

"I'd never refuse your wonderful chocolate chip cookies, Mrs. Stolz. Thank you so much!"

Monica stood by the door to wave goodbye. Liz waited until they were down the driveway to ask, "Were you shocked?"

Maggie gave her a quick, anxious look, obviously weighing how much to say. "Honestly? I was a little. She is so frail…and old. She was such a beauty."

"A lot can change in forty years."

"But what happened to the house? It used to be like something out of a magazine. Remember when it was featured in *Town and Country*?"

Liz remembered. "The money from the sale of the business ran out. It had been poorly invested, spent on the wrong things. Robert tries to do the maintenance, but it's too much for one person. Without hired help to keep the place up, it's falling apart."

"Can't you help them?"

"I do. I give them money to make repairs. They spend it on things that make no sense, like rebuilding the cupola on the barn. It's all about appearances. Meanwhile, the floor is rotting under the downstairs toilet. Sometimes I do the work myself to make sure it gets done. I replaced the kitchen faucet a few months ago. There's so much that needs to be done; it's a losing battle."

"Your mother is rather hard of hearing."

"Let's be candid. She's half deaf."

"She seems lonely."

"She tells me she's not old enough to go to the senior center. She snubs the neighbors' lunch invitations although she's known them since I was in grade school. She thinks she's too good for them."

"That's a shame." Maggie sighed.

"I know, but there's only so much I can do."

Maggie reached out and touched Liz's arm. They rode in silence until Liz switched on the radio.

Chapter 25

Maggie awoke feeling sweet and sexy from dreaming about Liz making love to her. Then, she realized it was the day of the surgery, and her eyes flew open. Her heart began to hammer. She remembered that Liz would be in the operating room and told herself that everything would be all right. Curling deeper into Liz's embrace caused her to stir. She reached up and cupped Maggie's breast, the healthy one, as it happened, and kissed the back of her neck.

"I dreamt you were making love to me," whispered Maggie.

"Maybe I was." Liz nibbled Maggie's ear as she lifted her nightgown and caressed her from behind. "That must have been some dream! You are so ready." She penetrated deeply before exchanging her fingers for her thumb so she could stroke outside at the same time.

Maggie closed her eyes and enjoyed the sensation. Liz had been revealing her skills as a lover gradually, surprising Maggie with the amazing things she could do with her clever hands and mouth. But the pleasure Maggie experienced when they made love had less to do with Liz's technique than her incredible sensitivity to her responses—the slightest tightening of her muscles around her fingers, every nuance of her breathing, the way her back arched or her legs parted to ask for more.

Liz switched and went deep again. "Yes, like that. Don't stop." Maggie came on the inside moments later.

After Maggie's breathing returned to normal, Liz fended off her attempts to return the favor. "Go back to sleep. It's still early. I have to be sharp in the OR today."

When Maggie woke again, it was to her lover's kiss, a soft press of her lips against hers. Still in a groggy haze, Maggie sat up. There was a steaming cup on the bed stand. "Black, because of the surgery, but I thought you might need a caffeine jolt to get into the shower."

"I thought I wasn't supposed to eat or drink anything."

"Clear liquids are allowed up to two hours before surgery. Drink fast."

"I love you," said Maggie, raising her face for another kiss.

As Maggie sipped the coffee, she watched her lover head off to the shower and felt very lucky to have literally stumbled back into Liz Stolz's life.

She felt even luckier when she lay on a gurney in the hall outside the surgical suite and felt strong fingers intertwined with hers. The pressure wasn't aggressive. It was sure and comforting.

"Why do you love me?" asked Maggie.

Liz thought for a moment. "I don't know. Do I need a reason?"

"No, I guess not."

"Do you know why you love me?"

"Yes. I do."

Liz gave her a quizzical look, but moments later, Dr. Connelly appeared, smiling broadly. How could anyone look so joyful about cutting up someone's body? Did Liz look like that when she greeted her patients before surgery?

"I'm going to mark the breast we are operating on today. It's to make sure we're operating on the right one. The marker comes off with some isopropyl alcohol. Dr. Stolz knows." Ellen opened the gown and drew some figures on Maggie's breast with a black marker. She patted Maggie's arm. "Don't worry about a thing. Dr. Stolz will be there watching me like a hawk!" She smiled and headed off through the double doors.

Maggie frowned. "She's certainly cheerful."

"We encourage surgeons to look cheerful and optimistic before a procedure to allay the patient's fears. I'm afraid Ellen learned that particular lesson a little too well. Too bad she can't apply it in the exam room."

"Will you really be watching her?"

"Yes, but only because she keeps teasing me about it. But don't worry, I made sure she's the best breast surgeon in the country."

"After you."

Liz smiled and kissed her forehead. "Yes, after me."

The nurse came to start the sedative drip. Maggie watched her land the needle in her vein on the first try.

When they were alone again, Liz took Maggie's hand. "You'll be asleep in no time. The nurses will prep you. I need to scrub." She gave Maggie's hand a reassuring squeeze, then raised it to her lips and kissed it.

"I love you, Liz."

"Me too. See you in a few minutes. It's a very short procedure."

That was the last thing Maggie remembered before opening her eyes again. Liz was standing there in surgical scrubs.

"When are we going in?" Maggie asked.

Liz chuckled and patted her thigh. "It's all over. Ellen got great margins. You may have a little dimple in that breast, but otherwise you'll hardly know we were in there."

"You were in there too?" Maggie was surprised, especially after hearing all Liz's protests about being involved in the surgery.

Liz looked momentarily sheepish. "Ellen insisted I inspect her margins. That mentor-protégé thing can be hard to shake. I think she just wanted to reassure me that she'd gotten it all."

Maggie felt a little spasm of anxiety. "Does she know we're a couple?"

"Of course. Everyone here knew about me and Jenny too. When we bought the house, we decided we should come out to our coworkers. Is that a problem?"

"No, I guess not."

Liz ran her fingers down Maggie's cheek. "This is way too much conversation for someone just waking up from anesthesia. I'm going to get dressed. They'll be throwing us out of here soon. Here's Linda to get you ready for discharge."

A moment later, a middle-aged, blonde nurse came in to remove the IV lines. "How are you doing, Ms. Krusick?" Her voice was cheerful, and her smile warm.

"I'm so glad it's over. That was quick!"

"Dr. Connelly is fast, but very thorough. Dr. Stolz trained her well."

"Did you work with Liz…uh…Dr. Stolz?"

"I sure did…when I was still an ER nurse. She's a phenomenal surgeon. We really miss her." Linda frowned and looked thoughtful. "I never understood why she quit. Guess she just got sick of it. A lot of them do. Then they retire early to play golf."

Maggie couldn't imagine Liz retiring to play golf. In fact, she didn't know if Liz played golf.

"Dr. Stolz practices family medicine in Maine," Maggie said proudly.

Linda smiled, but Maggie could tell it was old news to her. "I bet she's a great family doctor. She's so smart. Good to her patients too." She smiled at Maggie and lowered the gurney to sitting level with a few taps of her foot. "Think you can make it to the chair with my help?"

Maggie nodded, although she was still quite woozy and unsteady on her feet. She leaned heavily on the nurse as she moved toward the chair. "Take it easy. There's no rush." Finally, Maggie made it to the chair. The nurse gave her a gadget with a little ball in it and a breathing tube. She explained that Maggie was to raise the ball with her breaths until it reached the mark on the side of the tube. "It helps to push out the anesthesia and clear your lungs. It will also get rid of that groggy feeling." Maggie took a deep breath and blew into the gadget. Raising the ball with her breath was harder than she'd expected.

"Deep breaths!" Linda watched Maggie struggle to raise the ball in the tube. Maggie tried harder. The ball went up a little farther each time.

The nurse began to strip the gurney. "Maine is beautiful. I love it up there. My husband and I go to Camden every fall."

Maggie let go of the mouthpiece. "Yes, it is beautiful. I've enjoyed the fall up there."

Liz came back, looking smart in her tailored suit.

"Thanks, Linda. I can take it from here. You finish your paperwork. I can go over the post-op drill later, when she's more alert."

"Are you sure? Doctors make lousy nurses."

Liz laughed. "So I've been told, but I have learned a few tricks since becoming a GP."

"Take good care of your patient there. She's still pretty dizzy from the anesthesia."

"I'll take her out in a chair. She'll be fine."

Linda gave Liz a critical look. "Haven't changed a bit, have you? Still doing that tough love routine."

"Always works, doesn't it? People rise to the occasion."

Linda shook her head. "Don't let her push you around, Ms. Krusick. She can be like a bulldozer sometimes. Nice meeting you." She gave Liz a disapproving look before she went through the double doors.

Liz had brought Maggie's clothes from her locker. She yanked closed the curtain for privacy. Maggie had chosen the softest flannel shirt from her thrift shop haul because Liz had encouraged her to bring a button-down shirt, explaining that it might hurt to lift her arm at first.

"It's a pretty quick recovery," said Liz as she helped Maggie get her arm into the sleeve. "A lumpectomy is not really much of a surgical procedure. You're working outside the body cavity, so there's no big vascular involvement. Breasts are mostly just fat anyway. But it's a sensitive area because it's so densely innervated."

Maggie listened to Liz casually discuss the operation. It almost sounded as if she were dismissing the importance of it. "That's easy for you to say. It's not your breast."

"I didn't mean it that way." Liz narrowed her eyes. "I'm only saying how lucky you are to get away with a simple procedure because your tumor is tiny. Otherwise, we probably would have sampled some nodes, which means you'd have an incision in your armpit too."

The lecture reminded Maggie of how the fertility doctors used to talk to her. "Thanks for your thoughts on the matter. It's pretty damn uncomfortable, if you want to know the truth."

Liz evidently missed the sarcasm. She frowned with concern. "Ellen called in a script to the pharmacy. We'll pick it up on the way to the house." An orderly arrived with a wheelchair. "Here's your ride. I'll get your discharge papers from Linda and then get the car. I've got your purse."

By the time, the orderly brought Maggie to the entrance of the hospital, she regretted being sharp to Liz. She felt even more guilty when Liz helped her into the car, gently arranging the shoulder strap behind her back, so it wouldn't bind or pull on her breast and cause her pain. "All good?"

"Yes, and thank you."

"Just doing my job." Liz went around the car to get in the driver's side. "We'll stop for your meds first. Once we get you home, we'll take a little walk to get the anesthesia out of your system. Then, it's nothing but rest for you for the rest of the day. I'll watch old movies with you, if you feel up for it."

"Sounds divine, but do you mind if I take a little nap? I'm suddenly very tired."

"A walk on the beach will cure that. The salt air will wake you right up!"

When Liz pulled up to the pharmacy window, she was able to provide Maggie's date of birth without a moment's hesitation.

"How can you remember my birthday after all these years?"

Liz shrugged. "Physicians are trained to remember details."

When the time for payment came, Liz handed the clerk her credit card.

"Liz! You don't need to pay for my prescriptions!"

"Why not? I'm closer to the window. Besides, it's only seventeen dollars."

The clerk returned with an electronic tablet, which she handed to Liz. "Ms. Krusick will have to sign for the Percocet. It's the new law in Connecticut." Liz passed the tablet over to Maggie, who signed it with the stylus. Finally, the clerk handed over a white bag containing the pills and a receipt five feet long.

"Do you need the pharmacist to explain anything about these medications?" the young woman asked politely.

"No, thanks. I'm a physician. I can explain it to her."

❋❋❋

As Liz had predicted, a leisurely walk on the beach helped Maggie feel more alert, and she could breathe more easily. Her chest felt much less congested. They sat on a bench near the water's edge and watched the wake from passing boats roll up and slap the sea wall. Despite the slight crispness in the air, Maggie enjoyed the play of the wind in her hair. "It's so beautiful here. How could you ever bear to leave it?"

"It wasn't easy, but I wanted to establish the practice in Maine while I still had the spit to do it. In five years, I might not have the energy to take on something so ambitious."

"Oh, I'm sure you would. That nurse, Linda, said, a lot of surgeons get sick of it and retire to play golf. Why didn't you?"

"Well, I don't play golf," Liz replied with a grin, "so that was never an option. I thought about quitting medicine. Then, I read about the shortage of doctors in Maine. Of course, that's mostly in rural areas, so buying the practice in Hobbs didn't really help."

"Your intentions were good." Maggie glanced around. They were alone on the beach, so she felt free to lean against Liz's shoulder. "Thank you for all your support today. I'm sorry I was snappish."

"Surgery is stressful, and you don't need to keep thanking me. I'm happy to do it for you."

"Would you do it if we were still just friends, not lovers?"

"Of course, I would."

Maggie raised her head and studied Liz's face. "I believe you would."

They sat on the bench until the damp wind off the sound became too chilly. As they headed back to the house, Maggie threaded her arm through Liz's. "Forty years ago, I never would have dared to do this."

"Women have always walked arm and arm. Think of all the great cinematic scenes with women walking with linked arms. It's almost as if political awareness of lesbians spoiled an innocent pleasure and made it somehow dirty."

"You don't think much of gay activism, do you?"

"I didn't say that, but I think critically and don't toe the party line."

"No, you've never been a follower."

Liz opened the side door. The warm air wafting out from inside was welcome. Liz offered to make sandwiches and nodded in the direction of the library. "Go sit down and enjoy the view while I make them."

After they finished eating, they decided on a Meryl Streep festival. First, *The French Lieutenant's Woman*, then *Sophie's Choice*. By the time Stingo was crossing the Brooklyn Bridge, Maggie had fallen sound asleep.

She awoke to the sound of Liz and Jenny in the kitchen. They were speaking softly to avoid waking her, but Jenny's merry laughter had cut through her sleep. Again, she felt a twinge of jealousy at their easy domesticity. Whenever they were together, it was as if they had never parted. Maggie got up from the sofa and went into the kitchen on stocking feet.

"Here's our patient!" announced Jenny in a cheerful voice. She embraced Maggie gingerly, careful to keep away from the breast where the lump had been removed. "I heard it was a huge success. Congratulations!"

"Thank you." Maggie stifled a yawn. "I'm so glad it's over."

"I'm glad you're awake, but I'm going to shoo you and Liz out of my kitchen while I finish dinner. Go watch the news or something."

Liz winked behind Jenny's back and pulled the dish towel off her shoulder. "All yours. Remember, the fish only needs fifteen minutes. Don't overcook it."

"Liz likes her salmon like sushi on the inside," Jenny explained. "Now out of here. Both of you!"

Jenny's dinner of herb-encrusted salmon, scalloped potatoes and green salad was excellent, and Maggie freely offered genuine compliments.

Liz smiled in Jenny's direction. "Jenny has about five or six dishes that she cooks really well. Once in a while, she makes them to impress company."

"Thanks, Liz. I love you too." Jenny gave Liz a filthy look.

"I know you do."

Maggie watched them, still unable to decide how to read their banter and sexual innuendoes.

When they were getting ready for bed, Liz volunteered to sleep in another room, so Maggie would have plenty of room to make herself comfortable.

"No, you don't. I want you right here where I can keep an eye on you."

"There are five bedrooms in this house," Liz explained artlessly.

"That may be, but you're sleeping in this one…with me."

"Yes, ma'am." Liz gave her a brisk salute and slid into bed beside her. "Wake me if you have pain, and I'll get your meds for you." She switched off the bedside lamp, punched her pillow a few times, and rolled over.

"Why did you ever break up with Jenny? You seem so good together."

Liz leaned up on her elbow. "It was mostly physical from the beginning. Friends with benefits that lasted longer than either of us expected. As much as I enjoyed the sex with Jenny, I don't think I was ever in love with her."

"Is that why you never married?"

"Maybe."

It was quiet for a long moment.

"Are you in love with me?" asked Maggie.

"You need to ask?" Liz was smiling. Maggie could hear it in her voice.

"Yes, I'm asking. Are you?"

"I've always been in love with you."

Chapter 26

Beverly Birnbaum was a small, birdlike woman with cinnamon-colored hair and piercing blue eyes. Liz had known her since they were residents together in the 1980s. She was the kind of old-school physician who liked to look her patients in the eye and hear their complaints firsthand. She still did physical exams to make sure her patients were fit for chemo and to catch any changes the labs missed. In short, she was like Liz. And they were both New Yorkers who'd grown up immersed in the cultural life of the city, so it was no wonder they had gravitated toward one another and become the best of friends.

Bev was superb at communicating complex medical information in terms a layman could understand, so there was no need for Liz to translate for Maggie. Instead, she listened intently, absorbing the details of the post-op pathology report, although there was really nothing new beyond a precise measurement of the excised tumor.

"I'm not recommending chemo," said Bev. "It's unnecessary because you have a low-risk cancer, and chemo won't make the risk any lower. We will put you on hormone therapy. I'm waiting for the FISH test to see if you're a candidate for Herceptin."

Liz sighed as she listened to Bev explain the side effects of the drug. The damage caused by cancer drugs could be significant, and in the course of selling a treatment, some doctors glossed over the harm they could do. Not Bev. She wasn't the kind who presumed on her patients' trust.

It pleased Liz to hear Maggie asking so many questions. She was paying attention and not taking Bev's advice uncritically. Too often, Liz saw the good Catholic girl she remembered from their youth. Surviving cancer took grit and sometimes aggressive self-defense. Some doctors were too willing to fill a patient's veins with drugs that did more harm than good or cut into the body unnecessarily. That's why Liz had chosen all of Maggie's physicians carefully. They were all conservative, like she was, and practiced "less is more" medicine.

217

Beverly suggested that she could direct the treatments through the cancer unit at Southern Med. "Once we come up with a protocol and treatment plan, your treatments can be administered anywhere. If you're a candidate for Herceptin, Dr. Stolz could give you the injections. Does that work for you, Ms. Krusick?"

Maggie nodded. "I prefer that Liz be here for this, so Maine it is."

"I do recommend you do genetic testing. That will help you assess your future risks."

"We sent a sample," said Liz. "It will take a couple of weeks. The lab is backed up, as usual."

"Let me know the results. If there's anything significant, we'll talk."

As they waited for the elevator, Liz scanned the instructions for Maggie's radiation treatments at Southern Med. "Are you satisfied with this strategy for treating your cancer?"

"Yes, completely. So far, you've picked excellent doctors for me."

"They are the doctors I would pick for myself if I were in your situation."

"If they're good enough for you, they're good enough for me."

The elevator opened on the first floor. Liz pointed to the exit. "Ready for our foray into Manhattan?"

Maggie nodded. "It will be good to check on my apartment and get more winter clothes. I'd like to have my winter coat in case we go out. I feel silly wearing my parka over a dress." Liz smiled at the mental image. It was an entertaining sight, but not uncommon in Maine, where warmth was more important than style.

They had a long walk to the car because the doctors' parking lot had been full when they'd arrived. Liz clicked open the car door with her key fob. "Have you decided what to do about the apartment?"

"Are you really sure you want me to move in with you?"

"How many times do I need to ask?" asked Liz, sliding into the driver's seat.

Maggie adjusted her seat belt to avoid her sore breast. "I don't want to sell the place while the market is down. If I rent it, I'll have to clean it out. Let's wait until after the radiation treatments."

"Hedging your bets?"

"Liz, I'm being practical. You like that. And be nice to me. I've had a hard week."

"Trying to play the sick girl card? Doesn't work with doctors. Good try, though." She winked, then backed out of the parking space.

✳✳✳

Maggie's one-bedroom apartment on East 9th Street was tiny, as most apartments in the Village were, but it was cleverly furnished with built-in storage cabinets and bookcases designed to utilize every bit of space. There was a little desk, a miniscule television, and a table for two in the kitchen alcove.

Liz looked around. "Nice place. Cozy." By that she meant "cramped." Although Liz had lived in "the city" when she was in college and medical school and for the two years when she was a visiting professor at NYU, she'd become accustomed to more living space. She was sure she could never live in a city again.

Maggie dropped her handbag on the bed. "I'm glad I cleaned up the place before I left for my Webhanet gig. Otherwise, you'd be witnessing me in my natural state."

"Oh, I can imagine. I remember our dorm room. Face it. You're a slob, Maggie Fitzgerald."

Maggie lightly punched her on the shoulder. "Make yourself useful and get my suitcases down from the top shelf in the other closet."

"I knew it! Back to my job as your pack animal."

"Stop complaining. You signed up for this," said Maggie screeching the hangers over the rod as she decided which clothes to take with her. "You're the one who won't let me lift anything heavy until my breast heals."

While Maggie was organizing what she wanted to bring to Maine, Liz prowled around the apartment. The galley kitchen was tiny, but it had full-sized appliances.

"Do you actually cook in here?" she called to Maggie in the other room. "I can't imagine how."

"I've given some big faculty dinner parties here," Maggie called back. "You'd be impressed."

"Where do they sit?"

"Wherever they can find a place."

Liz picked up a photograph of two dark-haired young women. Maggie's daughters, she guessed. Attractive. There was a picture of Maggie's brother, Kevin with a grown child. Although forty years had passed and Kevin would now be in his fifties, Liz instantly recognized him. He was the most accepting of Maggie's family members. He'd tagged along that summer when Maggie and Liz desperately wanted to be alone. Liz always suspected he had a little crush on her, the infatuation adolescent boys seemed to form because she could talk about boy things: fast cars, super heroes, and fishing.

There were more family photographs in the hallway. Maggie had always been an excellent photographer and was especially good at taking revealing portraits. A dramatic black-and-white photograph of Maggie's mother, Pat, showed an old woman, wrinkled, sculptural, but still proud. Here was Liz's nemesis, shriveled by age and brought down by cancer. As Liz gazed at the picture, she found that her anger with this woman had lost its power. Pat was nothing but a woman of her time. She had been brought up to hate homosexuals and lesbians because her religion told her so. Like every woman who grew up during the war, she had been encouraged to marry up and wanted the same for her daughter.

Liz straightened the frame on the wall out of a need for order rather than respect. There was another photograph nearby, showing one of Maggie's daughters with a small child.

"You're a grandmother?" Liz called into the other room. "You never told me."

"You never asked."

"How many do you have?"

"Just the one." Maggie came out of the bedroom. "Katrina. Isn't she beautiful?" She leaned her head against Liz's shoulder. "That's Alina, by the way."

"How do you think your daughters will react when they find out you're hooked up with me?"

"I don't know. They'll probably be shocked."

"Shocked? Why?"

"They had a very sheltered upbringing because their early life was so traumatic. They're not your conventional young women. But you can be sure, I raised them to be feminists!"

"Sheltered feminists. Isn't that an oxymoron?"

"Not exactly. Think about it."

Liz did, but she was still puzzled. Sometimes, the things Maggie said baffled her.

***

By dinner time, an enormous suitcase, a stack of garment bags, and boxes containing books and personal items stood waiting beside the front door. Liz surveyed the pile with raised brows. "Good thing that hatchback in the Audi has a lot of room. I thought you said you weren't sure about moving in with me."

"Oh, there's lots more where that came from."

"I was afraid you'd say that."

"Come on. I know a wonderful little Japanese restaurant, and tonight is my treat!"

As they ate the most amazing noodle bowls Liz had ever tasted, they talked about the possibilities for the apartment. Maggie explained that the mortgage was paid off, so the only cost was the condominium common charge. When she quoted the figure, Liz almost choked on her food. The monthly fee for the tiny apartment was more than a quarter of what Liz paid in real estate taxes for the entire year!

"But it's good to have a New York base, especially if I can get some good theater roles. My agent is working on it."

"Tony offered you parts in his productions." Liz tried to snake a noodle into her mouth without spraying the savory broth all over her blouse.

"I know. But it's not the same as being on a New York stage."

"Chauvinist! We have great local theater in Maine."

Maggie reached across the table and patted Liz's hand. "I'll take the parts Tony offered me…so long as I'm well enough."

"You will be," Liz replied confidently.

***

As they sat reading side by side in bed, Maggie asked, "Will you be comfortable here for the night?"

Liz closed the cover of her iPad. "Well, to be honest…your mattress is like a coroner's slab, and I haven't seen a cockroach in twenty years. If I find out you've brought them home in your luggage, there will be hell to pay."

Maggie laughed. "Give me this," she said, reaching for Liz's iPad. Maggie took Liz's face in her hands and pulled it closer.

"You're being very aggressive tonight, Professor Krusick."

"Sometimes, a firm hand is what you need, Dr. Stolz," said Maggie, leaning forward to kiss her. Her phone rang.

"Let it ring," said Liz, but Maggie picked it up and looked at the display.

"It's Sophia. I have to take this. I promised I would call after we saw the oncologist."

Liz retrieved her iPad and slunk down in the bed. She tried not to intervene when Maggie reported skewed and sometimes incorrect information to her daughter. Finally, Liz lost patience. "Give me that phone."

Maggie shook her head.

"I said, give it to me!"

Maggie rolled her eyes, but she handed over the phone.

Liz recited the statistics from the labs and explained Beverly Birnbaum's treatment strategy. She could almost hear the worry in her listener's mind. "Do you want a copy of the labs, Sophia? I'll be happy to send them to you when I get back to Maine."

"No need. Mom can give me a copy. Alina and I are coming to visit her. We already booked our flights to New York."

"Does your mother know about this?"

"No, it's a surprise."

"Well, maybe you'd better tell her because we're heading back to Maine in the morning. Here. I'll put her on." Liz handed the phone back to Maggie. "They're coming to New York."

"What!" Maggie got out of bed and went into the other room. Her voice was muffled but agitated. She returned to the room and looked at Liz with pleading eyes. Liz reached for the phone.

"We'll pick you up on the way home. Reroute your flights to Boston. I'll pay the transfer fee."

"Dr. Stolz, I don't want to impose."

"You're not imposing. I'm used to house guests, and I have plenty of room. Text me your flight information after you've made the arrangements." Liz handed the phone back to Maggie. "Convince them it's okay. We're not staying here with your roaches."

Maggie gave her a filthy look, but she convinced Sophia to reroute their flights to Boston.

Maggie was distant when she returned to bed. Liz nibbled at her ear, but Maggie rolled away, pulling her legs up to her chest.

"What's wrong?"

"I'm not ready for them to come into our life."

"We'll handle it. They're your kids, and they're worried about you."

"Sophia asked if I'd told Barry yet about the cancer. I asked why."

Liz let out a long deep sigh at the mention of Barry. "I'm sure she means well. We'll sort it out when they come."

"They have no idea I was ever involved with a woman."

"Well, then I guess you'll have to tell them."

Maggie groaned.

Liz pulled her closer, careful to avoid the breast where the sutures had been removed. "Don't worry, Mag. We've got this."

Chapter 27

Liz was pacing again in front of the flight announcement board. The flight from New York to Logan had been delayed another hour. Finally, Liz plopped down in the seat beside Maggie. "If I had known they weren't going to reroute their original flights, I would have picked them up at LaGuardia or told them to fly into Portland!" Liz scowled. "Obviously, they're not very savvy when it comes to travel."

Like all mothers, Maggie bristled at hearing her children criticized, but in this case, she couldn't fault Liz. She'd been so patient through this unexpected detour from their plans. They had raced to Boston to meet her daughters' flight only to find there was a two hour delay. Now, the ETA had been revised again.

"I'm sorry, sweetheart." Maggie patted Liz's thigh. "It was a bad plan to begin with. If they had told me, I would have told them to wait until we got back to Maine."

"Where do they sleep when they visit? Your apartment is microscopic."

"They don't usually both visit at the same time. If Alina comes with her husband, they stay in a hotel. Sophia sleeps on the sofa in the living room. It pulls out."

"Cozy, I bet," said Liz in a cynical voice.

Maggie looked at her. "You're pretty crabby today."

"I just drove for almost five fucking hours on not very much sleep. I'm not used to sleeping in such a small bed. We've been away for almost two weeks. I just want to go home."

"I know. I want to go home too."

Liz glanced at her watch.

"We have time to get something to eat. Let's go upstairs and see what we can find."

After a long wait, the hostess at the crowded hamburger restaurant led them to a table. The aisles were cluttered with luggage, so navigating their way required close attention. Liz sank into the chair with a sigh. "This place is so fucking noisy."

"Liz, watch your language. I brought up my girls to be ladies."

Liz grunted in amusement. "I bet you did, Maggie. Good, little Catholic girls like you."

Maggie frowned in disapproval. "There's nothing wrong with that."

"All right. I'll try to be on good behavior." With a sullen expression, Liz slumped in her chair.

"Yes, please try. Sophia idolizes you. She keeps telling me how famous you are. How brilliant. How she can't wait to meet you."

"In that case, I'll do my best to jump off my pedestal as soon as we meet. I don't deal with hero worship very well."

"Oh, Liz, enjoy it. It's so sweet that she looks up to you."

The waitress came to take their drinks order. Maggie ordered seltzer; Liz, the IPA on tap. After the waitress departed, Liz studied the list of beers on the back of the menu. "I don't know much about the microbreweries in Boston, but they seem to have a slew of them."

"I thought you were cutting back on the beer, so your skirts will fit."

"Later. I need alcohol to fortify myself for the arrival of your brood."

They ordered the restaurant's signature dish and were surprised that, despite the crowd, it arrived so fast. Liz was silent while she demolished the hamburger. Maggie knew from past experience that when Liz was hungry, she became irritable and snappish. And sure enough. It was like a miracle. After eating, Liz became much friendlier. She ordered one of the local beers and sipped it while Maggie finished her hamburger, less the bun, having put it aside to save a few calories.

"I downloaded the United App so I can keep track of their flight." Liz pulled out her phone. "No change, which is good." She raised her crossed fingers. "At this rate, we might be home by midnight."

"You're such an optimist."

"I always expect delays when I travel. I used to love it. In my heyday, I was invited to speak at a lot of medical conferences. After 9/11, travel became a nightmare. I never enjoyed it after that."

"So, it's true what Sophia says about you. You are famous."

"Yes, I have a storied past." Liz sighed. "The renowned Elizabeth A. Stolz, super surgeon and breast cancer guru." She raised her beer glass.

"The recovery room nurse. What was her name? Linda. She said she didn't know why you quit."

"That's bullshit. They all know why I quit. A new administration came in. They were all about cost cutting. They filled all the top spots with accountants and professional administrators, kicked out the doctors. I was always locking horns with them. Then came the lawsuit. That was it for me."

"What is this lawsuit you keep talking about?"

"It was a high-profile case, an actress who makes her home on the Connecticut Gold Coast. I can't tell you who because of confidentiality. I did a lumpectomy on her. She knew going in that radiation was part of the plan, but when the time came, she refused it. Bev wanted her to do endocrine-based therapy. She refused that too. Then she turned around and sued me because of a recurrence."

As Maggie listened to the story, she found herself wondering if she would have a recurrence even though she was following doctor's orders to the letter. But a recurrence was always a possibility. They'd said her mother was cured, but the cancer came back. Then it killed her.

"But you were cleared of wrongdoing."

"Of course, I was. The case was thrown out because she hadn't followed doctor's recommendations, but it was in the courts for three years before it got resolved."

"A long time to have that hanging over you." Maggie noticed the waitress eyeing their empty plates. "I think they would like us to leave."

"I think you're right." Liz took out her wallet.

***

When the United flight from New York was announced, Maggie had to nudge Liz awake. She'd said she felt sleepy after devouring the hamburger, but Maggie knew it was the beer. She let Liz lean her head on her shoulder, despite the stares from some people in the waiting area. If she was going to be with a female partner, she'd have to learn to tolerate some public disapproval.

Finally, the number of the girls' flight flashed on the overhead display. "Sweetheart, wake up. Their flight arrived."

Liz woke with a start and sat up straight. "Oh great. My mouth feels disgusting." She dug into her pocket and came up with a tin of mints. She popped a few into her mouth and offered the tin to Maggie, but she was too excited to notice.

Finally, the disembarking passengers began coming through the gate. Maggie anxiously watched for her daughters. It was a commuter flight so it emptied quickly. "There they are!" she said and jumped up from her seat. She waved vigorously. Her daughters' faces lit up when they saw her, and they rushed in her direction.

"Mom!" Alina threw her arms around Maggie.

"Take it easy, honey. Mom's still a bit sore."

"Oh, I'm sorry. You look great! I was so worried when Phi told me."

Sophia carefully hugged and kissed her mother. Then she introduced herself to Liz. "Dr. Stolz, it's an honor to meet you."

Liz assumed her most professional demeanor. "Pleased to meet you too, Dr. Krusick, but I insist you call me Liz. Everyone does." She offered her hand, and Sophia solemnly shook it. "Can I carry anything?" asked Liz.

The Krusick daughters each offloaded a bag on Liz. "We went carry-on all the way," Alina explained. "It became too complicated to check the bags with the flight change."

They headed for the street where they caught the shuttle bus to the parking lot. Maggie felt bad watching Liz trudge ahead as she and the girls caught up on their news. "Liz, come back!"

"I'm fine," Liz called, walking backward. "I'll meet you there." She strode off on her long legs toward the car. The engine was running, and the trunk open and waiting when they finally caught up to her. Liz stood by to help load the luggage in the trunk. "Sorry, it's so tight back here, but your mother took over all the space."

Alina surveyed the pile of suitcases and garment bags. "What's all this? Are you moving in, Mom?" She was joking, of course, but the question landed a little too close to home.

"I'll tell you later, sweetie." She gave Alina a quick hug around her shoulders.

Liz helped Maggie's daughters arrange their bags in the back. When they were all packed, the rear compartment was full to the roof.

While they waited in the line to pay for parking, Alina sat forward so she could talk to her mother. "I'm so excited to go to Maine. I've never been there."

Maggie gazed at her daughter with worry. "Oh, honey, don't you remember? Daddy and I took you both to York when you were a little girl. We went to the zoo where they have the white tigers."

Alina had that blank expression on her face she often had when encouraged to think about her childhood. Everything about her early life in a Romanian orphanage was so traumatic, she tended to block out the good memories as well as the bad.

Maggie remembered how her heart broke to see those two little girls coming down the ramp from the plane. They were just toddlers. Each held a hand of the sympathetic flight attendant. They looked so bewildered and lost, clinging together when she and Barry tried to pick them up. They refused to be separated and stared at their new parents suspiciously. When she'd finally hugged them, they didn't respond at first. Only gradually was she able to teach them to accept affection. They insisted on sleeping together in the same bed until they were teenagers. It was a miracle they were as intact as they were.

"Yes, I think I remember the tigers, Mom," said Alina after a long period of reflection.

"I definitely remember the tigers," said Sophia, who was a year older. "And we went to the beach. We found those little green crabs and the pink starfish under the rocks." She nudged her sister. "Don't you remember, Ali?"

Thank God for Sophia, Maggie thought. What a tough, little thing she was. In the orphanage, she'd had to fight for her own survival and her sister's. At first, Maggie thought she'd blocked the horrible memories of the orphanage, but Sophia had told her adopted mother about the nightmare of their early life without emotion. "Our parents died in a car accident. Our grandmother gave us up because she was too old to care for us and didn't have enough food for herself. I could see how it broke her heart to leave us there." It broke Maggie's heart too, just to listen.

When Alina spoke, her voice was small and childlike. "Can we go to the zoo, Mom? I want to see the white tigers again. I really don't remember them."

"Liz? Can we take them to the zoo?"

Liz glanced in the rear-view mirror to engage Alina's eyes. "I'm sorry, Alina, but the York Animal Kingdom closes in September. It's only open in the summer. If only you had come a few weeks ago."

Alina looked so disappointed Maggie worried that she might cry. She never knew what memory, no matter how inconsequential, might trigger a deluge.

"A few weeks ago, we didn't know Mom had cancer," said Sophia in a matter-of-fact voice.

"So that's what it takes to get you two to visit," said Maggie, trying to inject some levity into the conversation.

"Does Dad know you're sick?" Alina asked.

"I told him," interjected Sophia. Of course, she would tell Barry. She'd always been especially attached to her father. Sometimes, it seemed she was still hoping against hope for a reconciliation between her parents. "Dad said he was really sorry to hear it. He asked if there was anything he could do."

Maggie glanced at Liz to see what effect this conversation was having on her, but Liz's eyes were firmly fixed on the road ahead. Fortunately, Alina changed the subject to Katrina, her daughter. She showed Maggie new pictures on her phone. Maggie could never see enough photos of her beautiful granddaughter, who had dark hair like her mother, but enormous blue eyes like her father.

They stopped in Kittery for dinner at a trendy restaurant Alina had found on a travel app. Liz didn't look impressed with either the food or the service, but she paid the bill without complaint. When they finally arrived home, Maggie could see how tired Liz was when she brought in her daughters' luggage. She proved her fatigue when she asked Maggie if she would mind leaving the things she'd brought from her New York apartment in the car overnight. "Hopefully, I don't get your roaches in my car. With our winters, maybe they'll freeze to death."

Liz showed Alina to the seashore room. Sophia liked the moose on the quilt in the Great North Woods bedroom and asked if she could sleep there.

Maggie sat on the bed while Sophia unpacked her bag. "Thanks for coming, sweetie."

"Of course, we'd come, Mom. We couldn't let you go through this alone."

"I'm not alone. Liz has been there every step of the way."

"You're lucky to have such a good friend."

Maggie sighed. Was this the moment to tell her?

No, better do it tomorrow after a good night's sleep.

Chapter 28

Liz was keeping an eye on the eggs and bacon in the frying pans while Maggie and her daughters devoured her blueberry muffins in the breakfast room. She was listening to them debate whether to head up to Cape Elisabeth to see the Portland Head Lighthouse or to Gray and the Maine Wildlife Park. Morning had brought the gift of a brilliant High October day, not a cloud in the sky, crisp, but warm enough to get by with a sweatshirt.

"But Mom, I want to see the moose," Sophia said petulantly. "I've never seen a moose."

Liz observed that like most adult children, Maggie's daughters regressed slightly in their mother's presence. That is, until the mothers aged to the point when they became the children, like Monica Stolz.

Alina had a different agenda. "Let's go the lighthouse. I want to take some photos with my new camera."

Liz delivered the first batch of over-easy eggs to the table. "Yours are coming right up." Liz was tempted to kiss the top of Maggie's head as she went by, but she remembered they had company and caught herself just in time. She returned to the kitchen for the plate of bacon.

"Your muffins are incredibly good," Alina called after her. "Do you always get such good meals here, Mom?"

"Yes, Liz is a very good cook, although you wouldn't have known it from the meals she made in college."

"Liz, if you've known Mom since college, why has she been keeping you a secret?" Apparently, Alina's journalist's instincts had sniffed out a story.

In the kitchen, Liz almost broke the yokes of her over-easy eggs as she flipped them. "You'll have to ask your mother that question."

Maggie slid smoothly into theatrical poise. "We lost touch after I married Dad."

Good answer, thought Liz. *True, but sufficiently vague.* She took the heated plate out of the oven with a pot holder and put the eggs on them. "Sorry for the wait."

Maggie looked up and smiled at her. "It's always worth it when you cook for me."

Liz struggled to keep a straight face when Maggie surreptitiously rubbed her backside. She looked up and noticed Sophia studying her. Liz smiled to disarm any curiosity on Sophia's part and took her seat at the head of the table. "If you don't mind driving around a bit, we can probably take in both the Wildlife Park and the Portland Headlight. We can end our adventure at my favorite seafood restaurant in Portland. What do you think?"

Alina jumped at the idea. "Yes! Perfect!"

"Mag?"

"I'll go along with whatever the girls want to do." Maggie gave each of her daughters a smile.

"Okay! Eat up. Then showers. Let's be on the road by nine." Liz dipped the corner of her toast into the yolks of the eggs, reluctantly spoiling their golden perfection.

When Maggie and Alina went up to take showers at the same time, Liz was glad that she'd agreed to the architect's suggestion of a backup water heater.

While Liz cleaned the cast iron pans with kosher salt, Sophia cleared the table. She stayed to watch Liz clean the muffin pan. "I always wondered about the right way to do that."

"I don't know if it's the right way, but it's the way I do it," said Liz, rubbing oil into the surface of the pan.

Sophia nodded thoughtfully. "Thanks for looking after Mom, first with the broken leg and now this."

Liz realized that Sophia had waited for this opportunity to speak privately. "That's what friends do."

"I'd say what you're doing is above and beyond the call of friendship."

Liz stood straight, putting her a head taller than tiny Sophia. She studied the young woman's face to see if she suspected something, then decided it was an innocent remark.

"As you can see, I have plenty of room here. And your mother couldn't drive. I'm used to house guests. I have them all summer."

"Still. It was nice of you. It was so lucky she was here when she found the lump."

That comment told Liz that Sophia had no idea about their relationship or the circumstances under which the lump had been discovered. "Yes, lucky," Liz repeated, arching her brow slightly.

"Don't you think she should consider chemo?"

"No, I don't," replied Liz bluntly.

"I have enormous respect for Dr. Birnbaum. I've read her papers, but…"

"But what? You think you know better?" The remark had flown out by reflex. For years, Liz had needed to put snotty residents in their place. But this was Maggie's daughter.

"No, I don't," stammered Sophia, "but she's my mother, and I want her to be cured."

Liz leaned back against the counter so that she looked less intimidating. "As we both know, 'cure' where cancer is concerned is a relative thing." She bent down a little so her face was closer to Sophia's. "Do you love your mother?"

"Of course, I do!"

"But you think we should pour toxic, heavy metals into her veins for no appreciable benefit?"

"It could save her life."

"Yes, it could, but in this situation, it's like using the atomic bomb when a rifle shot will do."

"Don't you believe in chemo?"

"Oh, I believe in it when there is no better treatment. Or to shrink tumors in advance of surgery."

"Is Dr. Birnbaum considering Herceptin?"

"Yes, we're still waiting for the results of the FISH test. But when Dr.

Birnbaum was telling your mother about the potential for cardiac damage, I began to wonder, is it really worth it? Is a small statistical increase in long-term survival worth wrecking your heart?"

"If you're the one who survives, it is."

Liz nodded her agreement.

"I know surgeons are skeptical of medical solutions," said Sophia.

"Guilty as charged. I often think surgery is the only honest branch of medicine."

"Surgeons kept doing mastectomies long after lumpectomies were shown to be just as effective."

She's a sharp kid. Liz looked at Sophia with new respect.

"Yes, we did, and that was wrong. Sometimes, we keep doing things based on habit rather than data. No disrespect, Sophia, but chemo in early-stage breast cancer is one of those bad habits."

Sophia gave her a long critical look. "I truly respect you, Dr. Stolz, but she *is* my mother."

It was on the tip of Liz's tongue to say, and she *is* my lover. Instead, she took a deep breath. "If you want to talk your mother into chemo, go right ahead, but I don't agree with you, and I will make my opinion *very* clear."

"I'm sure you will," replied Sophia tersely. "I'm going to take a shower."

Liz was fuming as she finished loading the dishwasher. She wished Maggie would get on with coming out to her daughters because it was becoming more awkward by the minute.

Maggie breezed into the kitchen. "I'm sorry I left you with all the dishes." She raised her face to offer a kiss. The one she received in return was perfunctory.

"It's fine," said Liz in a surly voice.

"What's the matter?" Maggie drew back to see her face.

"Sophia and I disagree about chemo for you."

"I'm not doing it," said Maggie with conviction.

"Then, you tell her. She's annoyed with me, I think."

"Liz," said Maggie, nudging her by the shoulder so she would turn around. "Try to be patient. Dealing with adult children is like walking on egg shells."

"I'm trying, but it's not easy." Liz tried to give Maggie a hug, but she heard footsteps on the stairs and instantly took a step back.

Alina bounded into the room. "I'm ready to see the moose!"

❃❃❃

Liz and Maggie trailed behind the young women as they walked down the small mammals trail. Maggie reached out and gave Liz's hand a little squeeze.

"Thank you so much for bringing us here. The girls are having a great time." Her daughters squealed in delighted horror as the fisher cat snarled at them. "Look at them. It takes so little to entertain them. They were so deprived as little ones. If their grandmother hadn't taken them when they were babies, they would be much worse off."

"That was a big undertaking for you and Barry. Adopting abused children from another country was very brave."

"I know you're not a big Barry fan, but he wasn't the worst person. He was a very good father. The girls adore him."

"Oh, I'm sure he excelled in the pater familias role. It completely plays to his male ego."

Maggie stopped walking, forcing Liz to stop as well. "Sometimes, Liz, you are so unforgiving."

"Why should I forgive him? The man stole you from me, and it took four decades to get you back."

"He didn't steal me, Liz. I went willingly."

"Then maybe I should be angry at you," said Liz in a cool voice, "but I blame you less. Your mother blackmailed you into staying in Syracuse. Barry played along and benefited from having a trophy wife. The dicks always win in the end." Liz hadn't meant to sound so angry or bring up the past, but sometimes the old wounds still ached in the present, no matter how often she said to Maggie that she'd forgiven her.

Maggie glanced anxiously toward her daughters. "Let's save this conversation for another time. I don't want the girls to hear you."

Liz let out a long frustrated sigh. "You will tell them soon? About us?"

"Yes, I'll tell them before they leave. I want them to get to know you first. And I haven't seen them in months. I want some bonding time before I lower the boom."

***

Alina had the opportunity to get some great shots of the Portland Headlight. She noticed that Liz was interested in technology and let her try her camera. Then she had a hard time getting it back. Alina showed her how to take high definition shots of the ocean. She said the afternoon light was perfect. Alina had also taken some amazing photos of the wildlife in the game park and showed them around at the table while they ate dinner in the Old Port.

On the way home from Portland, Sophia and Alina fell asleep in the back seat. Liz gazed at them in the rear-view mirror. "I guess the old ladies wore them out."

"Their convoluted travel yesterday must have been exhausting. And we stayed up so late last night."

Maggie gazed into the back-seat area before putting her hand on Liz's thigh. "I think the sensitivity where they operated has calmed down." She lightly tapped her breast to make her point.

"Are you trying to tell me something?"

Maggie smiled. "I've missed you."

"Maybe our young friends will decide to make an early night of it."

"More likely, they'll get a second wind and raid your wine cellar."

"That's what it's there for."

As Maggie had predicted, her daughters felt refreshed after their nap and were looking for sweets. After a feast of seafood, they had declared themselves "too full" to have dessert, but then they discovered Liz's stash of local ice cream in the freezer and changed their minds. Liz offered them hot fudge that could be heated in the microwave, nuts and whipped cream. Sculptural sundaes were the result. Sophia built a skyscraper for her mother.

"I couldn't possibly," Maggie protested.

"Please, Mom," Sophia pleaded. "I made it just for you."

"Oh, all right, if Liz will help. Bring another spoon."

There was quiet in the breakfast room while the ice cream was being consumed. Then Alina said, "When are you going home, Mom?"

Maggie glanced anxiously at Liz. "I don't really know, darling."

Sophia primly offered more information. "Mom's having her treatments up here. Dr. Stolz will be overseeing them."

"That's really nice of you, Liz." Alina was distracted, trying to rescue the whipped cream landslide cascading down her mountain of Black Raspberry Explosion ice cream.

"Your mother elected me her doctor. I don't really have a choice." The sundae was really good. Liz reached for another spoonful.

"Isn't it a conflict to treat your friend?" Sophia sucked hot fudge from her spoon.

"Now that her leg is healed, I'm not really treating her."

"But you did the core needle biopsy."

Liz put down the spoon. This interrogation was getting serious. "What's a CNB?" she said lightly. "It's like lancing a boil."

"But you did it." Sophia's eyes held a challenge.

Liz returned it. "What's your point, Sophia?"

"Don't you think someone else should be overseeing her treatment?"

"Actually, Bev Birnbaum wrote the protocols. I'm just arranging for them to be executed."

Alina stopped eating, realizing there was a confrontation underway. She put down her spoon and looked from Liz to Sophia.

"Phi, why are you being so hostile? Liz has been so kind to Mom. Stop it."

"Don't you think it's weird that Mom is letting an old college friend she hasn't seen in forty years take so much control over her life?"

Maggie set the melting sundae on the table and reached under the table for Liz's hand. "Sophia, I thought you admired Liz."

"I do. In my world, she's a god."

"Then what's this all about?" Maggie gave her daughter a hard look.

"There's something going on here that I can't figure out. I want to know what it is." Sophia sat back and crossed her arms on her chest. Her dark eyes firmly held Maggie's.

Liz drew breath to say something, but Maggie squeezed her hand under the table, so she sat back.

"Liz is a great doctor, and I trust her."

"That's not what I mean, Mom. Something's going on between you two. What is it?"

The long, tense pause that ensued was as brittle as glass.

"We're lovers." Maggie gripped Liz's hand.

"What?" Alina blinked as if sand had blown in her face.

"We're lovers," Maggie repeated. "We were lovers in college. Grandma wouldn't let me go back to school to be with her. She said they wouldn't pay for college unless I gave her up. I never wanted to leave her. I've always loved her."

Alina stared at them. "Mom, you're kidding. Right?"

"No, I'm serious. Absolutely serious. And for the first time, *I'm* in control of my life. Except for the fucking cancer, that is."

Liz couldn't keep her brows from shooting up. Evidently, the young women were also shocked. Mouths open, they both stared at Maggie. Probably, they'd never heard the F-bomb escape their mother's lips.

"Liz, would you please give me some time alone with my daughters?"

Liz felt conflicted. Should she stay to support Maggie or go and give her the privacy she'd requested? She silently prayed that her decision was the right one. "No, Maggie. This conversation concerns me too. I'm staying." Under the table, Maggie squeezed her hand.

"You can ask your father," Maggie said. "He knows all about it."

"Mom!" exclaimed Alina.

"Don't 'mom' me."

"That's crazy!" Alina repeated.

"It's not crazy to be with the person you love." Maggie fiercely gripped Liz's hand under the table. "Is it crazy for you to be with Jeff?"

"He's my husband."

"And Liz is my partner."

Oh, shit, thought Liz. *Now they're going to ask me what my intentions are, and I don't have an answer.* As if they'd heard her thoughts, they both trained their eyes on her.

Chapter 29

Maggie saw that her daughters' eyes were riveted on Liz. She pulled her hand, linked in Liz's, up to the table top and stared back at them defiantly. "It's true. You see? We're a couple." She could feel Liz glancing at her, waiting for cues. Maggie heard a buzzing in her ears exactly like when she told her parents about Liz. Maybe her daughters would never speak to her again.

Then something unexpected happened. Alina went to her mother and put her arms around her. "I love you, Mom. I just want you to be happy. Really. I don't care who you love."

Sophia continued to glower at Liz.

Liz steadily held her gaze. "I'm sorry I'm no longer your hero. Now that we've gotten past that, maybe we can be friends."

Sophia approached, her eyes never leaving Liz's. "Take good care of my mother. That's all I ask."

Then they were all talking at once and hugging. Meanwhile, the ice cream was melting, and Liz suggested they go back to it.

"Mom, have you really known Dr. Stolz since she was seventeen?" asked Sophia.

"Liz," Liz interjected.

"Liz."

"Yes, and she was very much like you, sweetie, very serious. A brooding philosopher quoting existentialists at every opportunity." She gazed at Liz fondly, seeing the younger version clearly in her mind's eye. As much as she sometimes missed that girl, this gray-haired woman, who laughed quickly, was even better.

Liz slapped her thighs. "Does anyone want champagne? I think we should celebrate."

"My God!" exclaimed Alina, clutching her belly. "I couldn't eat or drink another thing!"

"I'll have some champagne," said Sophia brightly. "We should celebrate that Mom finally found someone!" Maggie hadn't known her daughters had been concerned until now. Her eyes followed Liz as she went into the kitchen, and she could see that her step was a little lighter.

"When's the wedding?" Alina asked just as Liz returned to the room with the champagne. Liz's look of apprehension was instant and obvious. Of course, they had joked about getting married, but now it was a serious question and a real possibility.

Maggie affected calm. "We need to get through the treatments first." Out of the corner of her eye, she could see Liz visibly relax.

"Of course," agreed Alina in a sympathetic voice. "It's a lot all at once."

Maggie looked at her daughter, surprised as always that someone who'd endured such trauma had such quick perceptions, but her younger child had always had wisdom and emotional depth beyond her years.

Fortunately, the girls' second wind blew out early. They both went off to bed, leaving Maggie and Liz with a half empty bottle of champagne losing its fizzle.

Maggie reached for Liz's hand. "That went better than I expected. What do you think?"

"It only took you forty years, but you finally came out. Congratulations."

"I'm sixty years old. What am I waiting for? There's no time to waste." She sighed. "Especially now that I have cancer."

Liz sat up straight and gave her a firm look. "The cancer is gone. The radiation is just a precaution to kill any stray cells."

"You always sound so confident and optimistic when you talk about my cancer. Are you sure it's not just for my benefit?"

"I am confident," said Liz in an upbeat voice. "Your prognosis is excellent."

Maggie squeezed Liz's hand. "Promise you'll always tell me the truth about my condition. Promise me."

"I promise, but you need to promise you'll believe me and not second guess everything I say."

"Deal," said Maggie.

"You picked up that expression from me."

Maggie smiled. "Yes, I did. We're growing into each other…like tree roots."

Liz kissed her, then pinched her thigh lightly. "Let's go up to bed. Someone propositioned me earlier, and I expect her to make good on her offer."

Maggie had been so grateful when Dr. Connelly had cleared her to take a real shower. Now, in Liz's enormous bathroom, she enjoyed the deliciously hot water spraying on her chest. She didn't hear Liz step into the shower behind her and was startled to feel her arms suddenly around her waist.

"We're too old for this," said Maggie, enjoying the wet embrace. "What if we slip and kill ourselves?"

"Then we'll die happy." Liz reached for the soap and lathered Maggie's buttocks. "Want to try something new?" she asked in a seductive voice on a warm breath in her ear.

Maggie's eyes widened when she realized what the question implied. She was shocked and titillated at the same time. "Not tonight, but another time, I might take you up on it." She turned and lathered up her hands to wash Liz in return, sensually lingering over all the sensitive places.

Despite her obvious impatience, Liz finally agreed to wait until they were in bed to make love. She was especially careful not to touch or bump the breast where the lump had been removed. Maggie was grateful because despite her brave words, the surgical site was still tender.

She loved Liz's exquisitely gentle lovemaking almost better than when she was forceful, but it was hard to decide which she liked better, and after all, why did she have to choose? It was all wonderful, especially the intimate kiss between her legs. Her male lovers never did that. Well, Barry had a few times when they'd first married, but only because she'd asked. Tom, never. She took herself to task for thinking about men while Liz's sensitive tongue was doing amazing things. Finally, she just gave in to the sensation and let the climax flow through her. The skin above her breasts flushed with heat.

Liz cradled her and whispered endearments while Maggie caught her breath, but she was still excited, and she could feel how much her lover wanted her after almost two weeks of abstinence. "It's a good thing I'm right-handed, so I don't have to worry about my sore breast," Maggie whispered into Liz's ear as she slipped her fingers inside her. Maggie loved to explore inside, a place of mysteries that was always changing. She especially liked to feel the muscles contract around her fingers, holding her inside. "I love you so much," Maggie whispered into Liz's ear.

Liz moaned softly and rolled on her back to invite her deeper.

The knock at the door made them both jump.

"Mom?" Sophia's voice. Maggie reluctantly withdrew from Liz and sat up.

"What's the matter, honey?" called Maggie.

"Alina won't stop crying."

"What the fuck?" exclaimed Liz in an angry whisper.

Maggie laid a finger on her lips. "Shhh. This happens sometimes when there are big changes. It triggers the trauma of that horrible orphanage. It was really difficult when Barry and I separated."

Liz sighed. She got up and put on her pajamas. Maggie slipped her nightgown over her head. "I'm coming, honey." She kissed a scowling Liz. "I'll be back soon," she promised and lightly tweaked her nipple. "Don't go away."

Maggie went out into the hallway and closed the door behind her.

"I'm sorry, Mom. I let her into my bed and the crying stopped for a while, but now's she's having a full-blown panic attack."

Maggie cringed. Alina's attacks were terrifying to witness. Her child paced and panted until she declared she couldn't catch her breath and she was dying from suffocation. No one could comfort her during these times, not even Barry, whom Alina adored. He would stand there, watching with wide, frightened eyes, his hands at his side—helpless, as they all were.

"She went off her meds without telling her doctor," Sophia explained. "I said that was stupid, and that made her cry harder."

"It was stupid, but it was also stupid to say that. You're a doctor. What were you thinking?"

Sophia looked sheepish. "When it comes to my family, I don't think like a doctor."

"Well, maybe you should!" Maggie hadn't meant to sound so harsh. "Never mind that now. Let's see what we can do." She headed downstairs, followed by Sophia.

Alina was pacing back and forth. When she saw Maggie, she threw herself into her mother's arms, pressing against the newly-healed breast wound. It hurt, but Maggie gritted her teeth rather than flinch in case Alina would perceive it as a rejection. That would definitely send her over the top, and it would be hours before she came down again. She led Alina to the bed and sat down beside her. "It's all right, sweetie. Mommy is here." Alina buried her face in Maggie's shoulder, again bumping the tender spot in her breast. "Please be gentle, sweetheart. Mommy's still a little sore from the surgery."

Alina's head shot up. "Oh, I'm so sorry, Mom," she said in a mournful voice.

Her response came as a relief to Maggie because it meant Alina wasn't so deeply into the attack that she couldn't think of someone else. Maggie gently brushed Alina's hair away from her eyes.

"Why did you go off the Zoloft?" demanded Sophia in an angry voice.

"I told you. I was feeling better, and I was tired of feeling like a zombie all the time."

"*This* is better?" asked Sophia, hands on her hips.

"I was doing it gradually…like the website said."

"You were following advice from a website instead of asking your doctor?" asked Sophia, incredulous. "That's nuts."

"Now, now, girls. That's enough!" Maggie raised a hand in Sophia's direction. "Sophia, please be quiet."

"Do you have your medicine with you?" Maggie asked.

Alina shook her head. "I threw all the pills down the toilet at home."

Sophia stared at her sister. "You flushed psychotropic drugs into the water system? How stupid is that!"

"Mom, get her out of here," begged Alina.

"It's *my* room!"

"All right!" said Maggie, raising her voice. "That's enough. Both of you! You're grown women. Now, act like you are."

At least, the argument had completely snapped Alina out of the panic attack. She glowered at her sister, which meant she was grounded enough to feel anger.

There was a knock at the door, and Liz poked her head in. "Is there anything I can do?"

"Come in, Dr. Stolz...Liz," said Sophia. "My sister went off her meds without talking to her doctor."

Liz stepped into the room. "What was she taking?"

"Zoloft."

"I may have some."

"You do?" asked Maggie, surprised. "I didn't know you took antidepressants."

"I don't. You'd be amazed at what family docs carry around in their bags...just in case. Let me see what I have." She left.

Maggie eased Alina down on the bed. "Sophia will stay with you tonight. Won't you, honey?"

Sophia made a face, but she nodded.

Meanwhile, Liz had returned. "What's your usual dose?"

"Fifty milligrams," volunteered Sophia.

"Thank you, Sophia," Liz replied in a patient voice. "I was asking your sister."

"She's right," said Alina, nodding. "Fifty milligrams."

Liz glanced at the label of the brown pharmacy bottle. "I happen to have fifty milligram pills. I can give you enough to last until you get home. Then I want you to see your doctor. Maybe you need an adjustment or a different medication but going off an antidepressant abruptly is not a good idea. Do you understand?"

"Yes," replied Alina in a meek voice.

"Good." Liz turned to her sister. "Sophia, please get your sister some water from the bathroom. There are paper cups in the dispenser." Sophia left to get the water. "Alina, do you need a sedative to calm the anxiety? I have some clonazepam."

"What's that?" asked Maggie.

"An anti-anxiety drug and sedative," said Sophia, returning to the room.

"Yes, please. I really need to sleep," said Alina. "I'm exhausted."

Liz shook out a pill into Alina's hand. She counted out some pills from the bottle of Zoloft. "That's enough for the next few days, but I want you to see your doctor when you get home. Promise me." Alina nodded. Liz watched while she downed the pills. "Okay," she said, closing her bag. "Do you think you can sleep now?"

Alina nodded. Liz patted her arm. "That's good. Don't worry. Your mother and I are here for you, and so is your sister. Right, Sophia?"

"Yes, I am." Sophia got into bed beside her sister.

Maggie breathed an enormous sigh of relief, marvelling at how her daughters responded to the sure authority in Liz's voice.

"All right, now, let's all get some sleep." Liz got up from the bed. "Good night, ladies."

When they were upstairs, Liz put her medical bag on the dresser. "Thank goodness those pills weren't expired. I have to check my bag more often."

"You were amazing!"

"Excuse me while I take off my cape," said Liz with a quick laugh. "I'm glad I was able to help, but what were you fighting about?"

"It was really just a sisterly spat. They don't usually argue, they're so tight. They needed to be to survive in that orphanage."

Liz pulled off her slippers and got into bed. "What's Alina's diagnosis?"

"PTSD, anxiety disorder, depression. You name it. It was hard when they were growing up."

"Is Sophia on medication too?"

"I don't think so. Sophia always seemed to deal with the bad memories better."

"She made herself responsible for their survival. That probably gave her a purpose and helped her keep her balance." Liz shook her head. "What am I saying? I'm not a shrink. I have no idea."

Maggie got in beside her. "Where were we?" She slid her hand into Liz's pajama pants.

"Oh no." Liz trapped her hand through the fabric with a strong grip. "I can't go back to sex that easily, especially not after all that. Let's try again after your brood leaves."

Maggie felt a little hurt when Liz rolled over and pulled up the covers, but she snuggled against Liz's back. "I love you."

"I love you too," said Liz, "but you sure do have a crazy family."

Chapter 30

The patient jumped when the buzzer on Liz's watch sounded. She'd set it to remind her to pick up Maggie for her radiation treatment. "Don't worry, Mrs. Delaney," Liz assured the elderly woman. "That alarm has nothing to do with you." Liz finished entering her notes into the office system and escorted her patient to the front desk.

"You're all set, Mrs. Delaney," Ginny said with a smile. "Happy Thanksgiving."

"Thank you, and you too, Dr. Liz. Enjoy your turkey."

"You bet I will."

Ginny gave Liz a firm look. "You need to leave. And I mean now."

Liz gave the counter a quick pat. "Thanks for holding down the fort. Have a great turkey day."

"Jeanine is on this weekend," Ginny reminded her.

"I know," Liz called over her shoulder. "Thanks."

Liz had organized her schedule so that she could take Maggie to York for her radiation treatments. This was the last. Afterward, they would head to Nathan's to celebrate and enjoy their last quiet evening before their guests arrived. To their surprise, everyone they'd invited for Thanksgiving had accepted. Liz's brother, Robert, was bringing their mother up from New York. Maggie's daughters were coming, but at least this time they'd planned a reasonable itinerary and were renting a car at Logan. Alina was bringing along her husband and their daughter. Tony and Fred had also accepted the invitation.

As Liz drove home, she reflected that the guest list would certainly make for an interesting mix of characters. Maggie had begun writing a play about a woman coming out in her sixties. Maybe she could find some inspiration in this motley crew. Tony doubted the play would ever have a wide audience but had promised to consider it for the Short Plays Festival at the State Theater. Maggie had also been invited, at Tony's instigation, to teach as an adjunct at the University of New England. She hadn't accepted yet, but she was seriously considering it. Liz hoped she would take the post because it would give Maggie another anchor in Hobbs.

Liz turned into the driveway. As soon as her headlights hit the house, Maggie came out the front door. She looked smart in a wool dress and her best winter coat. "Hello there, lover," she said, getting into the car. She kissed Liz. "Last one. Thank God!"

"I'm sure it's a relief to have this part behind you."

"I'll be glad when it's all over."

"You'll probably be on Tamoxifen for a while."

"That's not so bad," Maggie replied cheerfully, "just a pill in the morning."

Maggie's treatment options had become limited when the FISH test predicted she wouldn't be a good candidate for Herceptin. Liz had mixed feelings because she always felt that, where cancer was concerned, the more weapons in the arsenal, the better.

While Liz waited for Maggie, she chatted with Alyson, but as soon as the timer on her watch sounded, she headed straight to the nuclear medicine waiting room.

Maggie was beaming when she emerged through the double doors. "All done!"

Despite all the people in the waiting room, including a few of her patients, Liz put her arms around Maggie. "Congratulations!" When Liz looked up, she saw that everyone was smiling at them.

Maggie wanted to celebrate at Nathan's because it was the scene of their first official "date." Liz, who liked to try new places, would have preferred to go elsewhere, but she felt nostalgic when they were seated at the same table they'd shared on the night of the Judy Collins concert.

Liz admired Maggie across the table, secretly proud to be with such an attractive woman. "Have I told you how beautiful you look tonight?"

"No, but your eyes told me," Maggie gave her a warm smile. "You look pretty good yourself. I like it when you dress up for me."

"It's a special occasion."

Maggie smiled and patted Liz's hand. "You're always finding special occasions, Liz. Any excuse to cook a special meal or open an expensive bottle of wine."

"Why not? Life is short."

A shadow crossed Maggie's face. "Let's not bandy about that particular sentiment. I'm still a little sensitive on that topic."

"Of course." Liz compressed her lips. "I'm sorry."

The waiter brought the elderberry martinis they'd ordered, and Liz raised her glass. "Congratulations!"

"Thank you." Maggie tasted her drink. "I'm not a big martini fan, but these are so good!"

"The tourists love this emphasis on local ingredients," said Liz. "And I have to admit, I'm not immune to the hype. You'll be sampling some of our best local produce on Thanksgiving."

"Yes, I've seen you sneaking in your bags of goodies…your private stash out there on the screen porch. That squash is the size of a toddler!"

"The rind of a Blue Hubbard is so thick, you have to cut it with an axe."

Maggie looked skeptical. "That's just one of those Maine tall tales."

"I'm not kidding. I'll show you tomorrow. I picked a big one because we need a lot of food for all those people."

"You should be flattered the girls want to spend Thanksgiving with us."

"I am, of course, but they're really coming to see you."

Maggie's eyes sought the tableware. "This is the first time in years. The girls almost never come for holidays."

"Really?" asked Liz, surprised. "Why not?"

"Barry and I had joint custody. In the beginning, the girls mostly lived with me because they were still in school. I kept the house until they were in college. After I moved to New York, it was tough competition—Barry's big house in Palo Alto, his trophy wife cooking perfect food. Then there was my place—a cramped apartment in the Village with a tiny kitchen."

"They can't be that shallow, can they?"

"It was my mother. She stopped inviting us for holidays because Barry and I were separated and planning to divorce. That was a scandal. You don't get divorced in an Irish Catholic family."

"Why didn't your father step up? Or your siblings?"

"Mom ruled the roost. If she said I was the black sheep in the family, I was, so they ostracized me."

"That's incredible! Barry was at fault. He's the one who had the affair."

"I know, but my mother didn't see it that way. She thought it was my fault that I couldn't hold my husband's attention."

"Why didn't you explain about male menopause?"

"Oh really, Liz. She would never understand. She was married to my father until the day he died."

"So, you married a man you really didn't love, got shafted by him, and she still disapproved?"

Maggie nodded. "I'm afraid so."

"It's so unfair."

"I know, and it never ends. My mother has been dead for over five years, but I can still feel her disapproval. When I realized we were heading for a relationship, I could hear her voice in my head: 'Stay away from that girl.' She would be so upset to know we're back together."

Liz nodded. "I'm sure my mother's not overjoyed either, although she hasn't said anything…yet." She sighed. "How is it that we're old enough to be grandmothers, and our mothers still occupy so much space in our heads?"

Chapter 31

Liz took the day before Thanksgiving off. She rose at dawn and went straight to work on the food preparations. Maggie had gotten up early too because the enormous Blue Hubbard squash had to go into the oven early, and she wanted to watch Liz prove that it had to be opened with an axe. Shivering, Maggie stood on the deck while Liz cracked the squash into sections with a hatchet she reserved solely for the purpose. "One of my most specialized food utensils."

In the kitchen, Maggie scooped out the seeds from the orange flesh to toast with spices while the squash roasted. It would take most of the day, but the heat from the stove was welcome because the weather had turned cold enough for snow flurries.

The squash was done just in time for Maggie to get her pies in the oven before the first round of guests arrived.

Liz's brother, Robert helped his mother into the house. "Smells good in here," Monica announced. "Someone has apple pie in the oven."

"It's Maggie." Liz took her mother's coat from her. "She's making the pies."

"I'm glad she's doing something to help you." Monica's tone was tart and she frowned in Maggie's direction.

Maggie shot Liz a quizzical look. Liz just shook her head. She never knew what would come out of her mother's mouth, but where her partners were concerned, her comments were almost never good.

While Liz scooped the cooked squash out of the shell to process for soup, Maggie helped get Liz's mother settled into the downstairs guest room. Afterwards, she entertained Robert and Monica in the living room. Liz prepared the brine for the turkeys and set them out on the porch, which had become a makeshift refrigerator to hold all the extra food.

As a foil to the next day's orgy of poultry, Maggie had prepared two big trays of lasagna to feed the crowd, but once her daughters and granddaughter arrived, Maggie was distracted. Fortunately, Liz managed to remember to put the lasagna in the oven on time. She was glad to hear the chorus of praise, especially from Maggie's daughters, now that she'd heard the sad history of their holiday celebrations.

❊❊❊

On Thursday morning, there was a crowd in the kitchen. Monica was cutting the red cabbage, wearing the surgical gloves Liz had provided so her hands wouldn't turn purple. Maggie's daughters were assigned to the task of peeling and chopping the vegetables. Robert hauled the turkeys out of the brining solution and trussed them for smoking on the grill, while Liz kept an eye on her cranberry sauce bubbling on the stove and made the stuffing.

Maggie was in charge of appetizers and entertaining everyone during dinner preparation. More guests arrived. Although Tony and Fred could be flamboyant at times, they made a charming and witty addition to the guest list. They could talk about anything from movies to national politics. Tony's comic impersonations of famous actresses were irresistibly funny. Even Robert, who was a Harley-riding, deer-hunting traditional male, couldn't resist laughing.

Liz had to leave the gathering from time to time to check on the turkeys. Depending on the weather, the temperature in the grill could be hard to control. The colder outside, the longer it took to cook the birds. Fortunately, the day had warmed to a pleasant crispness, and the turkeys were done right on time.

Liz carved one turkey while Robert carved the other, and Maggie finished the gravy. Liz breathed an enormous sigh of relief when everything came to the table at the same time. The only football fan in the group, Maggie's son-in-law, responded to repeated demands to tear himself away from the game and showed up just as everyone was sitting down.

With so many helpers, kitchen cleanup was quick. The guests sat in the living room to enjoy their food comas and watch *The Wizard of Oz*, while Maggie and Liz got the pies ready to serve.

"I think this is the best Thanksgiving I've ever had," said Maggie, setting out the tubs of ice cream on the counter to soften.

"Oh, you must have fond memories of Thanksgiving when you were young."

"Yes, of course, I do, but my mother was never the great cook Monica is, so the meal was never this spectacular. You certainly outdid yourself." Maggie checked to make sure everyone was occupied, then kissed Liz. "Thank you for inviting my girls."

"I hope they're having a good time."

"Sophia told me it's the best Thanksgiving *ever*."

Katrina came into the kitchen and tugged at Maggie's skirt and raised her arms. "I'm sorry, sweetie, but Grandma has a hurt and can't pick you up right now."

Liz gave her a quick critical assessment followed by a look of sympathy. "Still that sore? Radiation is hard on the skin."

Maggie nodded. "The baby doesn't understand. She squirms, and it really stings."

Liz looked down at the pouting, dark-haired toddler. "Will you come to me, Katrina?" Liz knelt and reached out for her. The little girl clung to her grandmother's legs with a suspicious look. "Please?" begged Liz. The child smiled shyly and nodded. Liz hauled her up to her hip. "I know," said Liz in response to Maggie's look of surprise. "Kids like me. Go figure. But it comes in handy for a family doc."

The party was still going strong when Monica signaled to her daughter that she was ready to go to bed. Liz accompanied her mother to the downstairs guest room to lay out towels for her and turn back the bed. She lowered the hand shower on the rod.

"Was dinner okay, Mom?" Liz lifted Monica's bag to the luggage stand so she could reach the contents more easily.

"Everything was delicious, dear."

"I'm so glad I had Maggie's help. It made everything so much easier."

Monica turned and gave Liz a firm look. "Yes, she's certainly made herself at home here."

Liz was startled at first. She studied her mother with an uneasy feeling as she waited for what might come next. "She's doing her treatments up here so I can oversee them."

"You'd better watch out, Elizabeth."

"Watch out for what?"

"She couldn't be bothered with you when you were young. Now that you've made something of yourself and have some money, she shows up."

Liz straightened to her full height, which dwarfed her mother. Her mother stood straight too, not to be outdone.

"Maggie didn't 'show up,' Mom. She had an accident and came to my office for treatment."

"Likely story."

"It's true."

"I don't trust her. She's only here because she needs you to take care of her."

"That's not true." Despite her anger, Liz tried to modulate her voice.

"And she now has her kids parked here too."

"They're only visiting for a few days. I invited them."

"Uh huh."

"Mom, can't you be nice to my friends for a change?"

"Just be careful." Monica's tone held a strong note of warning.

Liz swallowed her anger. "Do you need anything else, Mom?"

"No, thanks. I'll be fine," Monica said in her most pitiful martyr's voice. "You go back to your guests."

Chapter 32

With visitors, Liz could be as upbeat and cheerful as a camp counselor, but around her mother the next day, she was terse and standoffish. Only Maggie noticed something amiss. She was glad when Monica and Robert left on Friday morning at first light. The farewells were cold and strained, leaving Maggie to wonder what had transpired between mother and daughter. Liz had volunteered to open the office, so any extended conversation would have to wait.

On Saturday, Maggie's daughters departed in their rented van for the airport after a leisurely breakfast. She was sad to see them go, especially Katrina, the adorable little one, who had stolen her heart. She wouldn't see them at Christmas because the girls had promised Barry they would spend the holiday in California. Maggie would miss them, but the idea of a quiet Christmas alone with Liz was appealing. Maybe they would have snow. The flurries on Thanksgiving Day had been a tantalizing harbinger of the Maine winter. Maggie imagined the yard covered in a white blanket, snowflakes gently falling, as she and Liz watched from the porch, listening to Christmas carols and drinking mulled wine.

The only thing spoiling Maggie's dream of the perfect Christmas card was Liz's moody introspection, which persisted after she came home from the office that afternoon and through dinner. She spent most of the weekend in her home office, glued to spreadsheets on her computer screen because year-end filings were fast approaching. At least, that's what she said. Most of the time, Liz was an open book. She said exactly what was on her mind, not as hurtfully nor as tactlessly as when they were young, but she was usually forthcoming, so her silence puzzled Maggie.

When they were in bed, Liz lay with her hands clasped behind her head, staring at the ceiling. Maggie, beside her, debated whether to probe the reason for Liz's withdrawal. "Liz, what happened between you and your mother?" Maggie finally asked.

"Nothing important."

"I don't believe you. You've been in quite a mood since she left."

There was a long silence before Liz spoke. "It's my problem. I'll deal with it." Liz rolled over and gave Maggie her back.

Maggie tugged at her shoulder, but she wouldn't budge. "You've made it our problem. Now, tell me."

"No. Go to sleep."

Maggie sighed. "Please, talk to me."

"No. It's been a very busy weekend, and I'm exhausted. I have to get up early tomorrow and need to sleep." Liz pulled the duvet up to her chin.

Maggie crept closer for warmth, but didn't dare touch her.

She was relieved when Liz tenderly kissed her temple as she always did before she left in the morning. Most mornings, Maggie pretended to be asleep, but today, she opened her eyes.

"Come back and give me a real kiss."

Liz let out a big sigh, but she returned and kissed Maggie on the lips this time. "I'm sorry about last night. My mother can really get under my skin." She gently stroked Maggie's cheek with her fingertips. "How about we go out to dinner tonight? I need to talk to you about a few things."

"But we have all that turkey."

"It will keep. Besides, I'm sick of turkey. Aren't you?"

"I'll make some turkey pies today and put them in the freezer. We'll be glad for them on busy nights during the winter, when you're rushing off to one of your meetings."

"Smart," Liz agreed.

After Liz left, Maggie felt cold. She pulled up her knees and hugged herself in an attempt to get warm. She sensed that whatever Liz's mother had said had introduced doubt into something that had once seemed so sure, so reliable, and unquestioned. Why now, when Maggie needed to believe in it so much? It was lonely enough living with cancer.

Maggie's mind would give her no peace. She tried to keep herself busy by making the turkey pies. She chopped mountains of carrots, celery and onions. The whole kitchen smelled of them. After the pies were in the freezer, Maggie cleaned up the kitchen. Ellie was coming the next day. After the initial embarrassment at having Ellie discover the disaster in her room, Maggie was careful never to leave a mess for her again.

It was nearly four o'clock when she finished washing everything and putting it away. She raced upstairs to shower before Liz came home. She was dressing when she heard her phone ringing in her little office. "Dammit!" She ran into the other room, grabbed the phone, and switched to her theatrically polite greeting.

"Maggie Krusick?" asked the caller.

"Yes, this is she."

"Hi. It's Bev Birnbaum from Yale."

Maggie was puzzled. Why would her oncologist be calling? "Oh, hello, Dr. Birnbaum. How are you?"

"I'm fine, thank you. Just calling to see if you have any questions."

"Questions? About what?"

There was a surprised silence. "Liz hasn't talked to you yet?"

"No," said Maggie, drawing out the word. Her mind went into an instant panic. What hadn't Liz told her?

"Well, I'll let her discuss it with you, but call me if you have any questions. I'm happy to talk to you."

Maggie thanked Dr. Birnbaum and ended the call. Stunned, she sat down on the bed and put her face in her hands. *No, don't cry*, she told herself. *Now, more than ever, you need to be strong.* She heard the front door open, and moments later, Liz was walking up the stairs.

"Hello, sweetheart," said Liz, coming into the bedroom. She frowned when she saw Maggie still in her bra and panties. "Not ready to go to dinner yet?"

"No, I was just getting dressed."

"Okay." Liz looked confused. "Take your time. I'll be downstairs."

She left, and Maggie mechanically pulled on her skirt and sweater. She sat down at the vanity in the dressing room to put on her makeup. Her mind was stunningly empty because she didn't know what to think. She was afraid to imagine whatever new horror had prompted Bev Birnbaum's call. She couldn't believe that Liz had failed her…again. Her hand shook as she tried to put on her lipstick. She had to put the tube down and deliberately steady herself.

"Maggie!" Liz called up the stairs. "I'm getting hungry!"

"I'm coming!" Maggie finally succeeded in applying her lipstick. She always managed to put on her makeup before a performance, even when an occasional bout of stage fright made her shaky. She'd get through this too, even if she had to draw on every bit of skill as an actress. She couldn't waver now. Everything was much too fragile.

As Maggie came down the stairs, Liz gazed at her with that frank look of admiration she always gave her when she was dressed up to go out. The powerful desire Maggie felt for Liz when she saw the attraction in her eyes was the same. Everything was the same except Maggie knew Liz had failed her.

"Are you ready now?" Liz bent to give Maggie a kiss, but Maggie held her back with a hand on her shoulder.

"In a minute. First, I have to ask you something."

Frowning, Liz stood straight. "Sure. What is it?"

Maggie spoke in the calmest voice she could muster. "Why does Dr. Birnbaum think you should have discussed something with me?"

Liz's face darkened. The furrow between her brows deepened and she took a deep breath. "Your genetic tests came in."

"When?"

Liz hesitated for a moment. "On Friday."

Maggie nodded, glad, at least, that Liz had told her the truth. "But you didn't tell me." Her voice was only faintly accusing because she actually felt numb inside.

"No, I didn't. We had a houseful of people, and I wanted some time to do more research before we discussed the results."

Maggie braced herself. "It's bad news."

"It's not the best news. You tested positive for the BRCA2 gene. I'm guessing you inherited it from your mother. Your siblings and their children should probably be tested too."

Maggie squeezed her mind to remember the implications of having the BRCA2 gene. All she could remember from Liz's book was that it wasn't quite as bad as having the BRCA1 gene.

Liz reached out to put her arms around her, but Maggie pushed her back with an open palm against her shoulder. "You should have told me right away. This isn't the first time you've kept something from me. How can I trust you?"

"You can trust me not to blurt out information before I have time to think about it."

"You mean, before you have a chance to put your spin on it."

"No, I mean, before I have all the facts."

"Give me the bottom line."

"The bottom line is you have an increased risk of malignant cancer. A fifty percent chance of getting breast cancer, and a seventeen percent chance of ovarian cancer. You also have a higher risk of pancreatic cancer and melanoma."

Chapter 33

Liz could feel the force of Maggie's disappointment in the pressure of her hand against her shoulder. She could see the anger and fear in those stormy, hazel eyes. All Liz wanted to do was to hold her and tell her everything would be all right, but the firm hand held her back.

"Why couldn't you just tell me?" demanded Maggie in a voice about to break. "I trusted you!"

"I'm sorry, Maggie. I was waiting for an appropriate time to tell you. That's what I would do with any other patient."

Maggie pounded lightly on Liz's shoulder with her fist. "I am not any other patient! You say you love me!"

Although Liz was tempted to defend herself again, she focused on calming Maggie, whose restraining hand finally fell to her side. She crumpled against Liz and began to cry.

"I'm sorry," Liz said, holding her close.

"Don't be sorry! Just *talk* to me!"

Liz increased her grip to show she'd heard the message. "Let's sit down."

"No," said Maggie, straightening. "Let me get myself together." She left, heading upstairs, Liz guessed, to mop up the ruined mascara.

With a sigh, Liz headed to the living room and slumped on the sofa while she waited for Maggie to return. Obviously, blurting out the fact that Maggie had a genetic mutation while they had all those people in the house wasn't a good idea. Her intentions were good. She'd only been trying to avoid upset and drama in the middle of a family holiday. Never mind that she'd needed to stuff down her own feelings about the news to avoid communicating her fears. Why couldn't Bev have waited for her to get back to her as she'd asked?

Maggie was upstairs for some time. What next? Would they go out to dinner as planned? Or should Liz think about ordering take-out from the Thai restaurant?

She had her answer a few minutes later when Maggie reappeared, makeup repaired and looking as attractive as ever. Liz often marveled at her ability to transform herself so completely, but after all, she was an actress.

"I'm ready to go to dinner," Maggie announced in a haughty tone that Liz found confusing until she realized Maggie had retreated into full actress mode.

"Are you sure?" asked Liz. She didn't want to risk an emotional scene in a public place. Too many people in town knew her. "I can pick up Thai food or pizza."

"I'd like to go to a nice restaurant while you tell me the bad news," said Maggie in a testy voice.

"I said I'm sorry." Liz's tone was equally testy. Her patience was beginning to unravel.

"Yes, you did. Let's go." Maggie picked up her purse and opened the front door. "Let's take the Audi and drive like civilized people. I don't feel like indulging your adolescent fantasies tonight."

Liz winced. She was about to call Maggie on the bitchy remark when she decided it was best not to argue. "I'll get my keys."

Liz pulled the Audi out of the garage. Maggie opened the door to the passenger side and got in.

"Where do you want to go to dinner?" asked Liz.

"La Scala. I feel like Italian food."

As they headed toward town, there was silence in the car. Finally, Maggie said, "If we're going to make this relationship work, you need to share information, not squat on it like a bear in the woods until you figure out what to say."

"I have the right to think things over and formulate a reasonable response, not blurt everything out the moment I know something. That's irresponsible."

"When it comes to me and my health, you have no right to withhold information. Even Dr. Birnbaum was surprised."

"She said that?"

"No, I could hear it in her voice, but she wouldn't let on about why she was calling."

"At least, she got that part right. I asked her to wait until I got back to her." Liz turned on to Route 1.

"How long did you expect her to wait? You sat on the report for almost four days! That's why you were hiding in your office. It had nothing to do with year-end accounting."

"Now, there, you're wrong. It was about the books. As managing partner, it's my responsibility."

"If it hadn't been bookkeeping, it would have been something else." Maggie's voice was suddenly flat as if she'd run out of feelings. "You just couldn't face me."

"I didn't want to ruin your weekend."

"Your mother already ruined the weekend, and you wouldn't tell me about that either."

"My mother is my problem."

"Your mother is *our* problem. My cancer is *our* problem. That is, unless you still consider yourself single."

"No. I don't."

"Then act like we're a couple and talk to me." Maggie sighed. "I have a knot in my stomach. Let's stop arguing or I won't be able to eat."

"Good idea."

Liz was grateful that Maggie had set the ground rules before they reached the restaurant. There would be no discussion of 'the thing' until they finished their dinner.

The house grappa at La Scala was particularly good. It stung the tongue a little, but not too much. Liz held the glass of colorless liquid up to the light to admire its clarity. "So, what would you like to know about your condition and prognosis? Ask me anything, and I will answer your questions to the best of my ability."

Maggie gave her an impatient look. "I can read all the medical stuff in your book. I want to know what you think I should do...not as a doctor who looks at facts and figures, but as the woman who says she loves me."

Liz put the glass down and studied Maggie's face. "I can't tell you what to do. It's your body."

"Then how am I supposed to decide?"

"We'll go down to Yale and hear what Ellen and Bev have to say. We'll call the team together and go over all the options."

Maggie's expression changed from completely adult indignation to an almost childlike look of bewilderment. "Liz, I need you to tell me what to do. I'm scared."

"It's all about risk," said Liz in a very rational tone, the one she used in the office when patients were becoming panicky. "We need to assess and weigh the risks…"

"Bullshit! This is my life we're talking about!"

Liz glanced around to see if their conversation was attracting the attention of the other diners. She deliberately lowered her voice. "I know. It's very personal. For me too, but we have to be objective."

"You be objective. I'll be scared." Tears began to roll down Maggie's cheeks. She blotted them with her napkin. "I'm sorry," she murmured. "My mother thought she was doing the right thing. She did whatever the doctors told her, and she still died from this."

"We should go," said Liz. "We can talk about this at home." She reluctantly left the half-full glass of grappa on the table because it was too strong to throw down.

Maggie waited in the lobby while Liz paid the bill. In the parking lot, she stood silently waiting for Liz to find her keys and click open the doors. As soon as Maggie was inside the car, she began to sob. Liz opened the glove box and found a few napkins from Awakened Brews and offered them to Maggie. A police warning for speeding fell out on the floor. Liz stuffed it into her pocket.

"Tomorrow, I'll call Bev and Ellen to set up a meeting. We should probably have a gynecologic surgeon on the team. I'll call Jenny."

"No, thanks. I don't want your ex-lover anywhere near me."

"Okay," said Liz drawing out the word. "We can ask one of Jenny's partners. There are some outstanding surgeons in that practice."

"Why do we need a gynecologic surgeon?"

"In case you elect to have a prophylactic oophorectomy." Maggie stared at her. "To have your ovaries removed...to lower your risk of ovarian cancer. Really. It's not a big deal. Most oophorectomies are performed laparoscopically."

Maggie let out a tiny cry of dismay.

"What's the matter? Did I say something wrong again?"

"You talk so casually about cutting up my body."

Liz raised her shoulders. "I'm sorry. I'm a surgeon. That's how we talk." Liz rubbed her forehead from pure frustration. She glanced over to see if Maggie had any response, but she was huddled into her coat. Liz couldn't clearly see her face. "So, can I start planning a team meeting?"

"Sure. If that's what you want," said Maggie in a listless voice that left Liz confused.

When they arrived home, Maggie went upstairs to get ready for bed. Liz remained downstairs to build up the fire as she usually did before turning in for the night.

"Yes, you can set up a meeting," Maggie said as Liz got into bed, "but find someone other than Jenny. I don't want her involved."

"I'm sure I wouldn't want Barry to have any say over my medical treatments."

"You hate Barry."

"No, I don't. Not anymore. I couldn't care less about him."

"When Sophia put him on the phone on Thanksgiving, he said he was sorry to hear about the cancer."

"That's nice, I guess." Liz said it because it was expected, but she still hated to think that Barry still existed, never mind had any contact with Maggie or her daughters.

"It's really hard to hear people's condolences.... It's like they assume I'm dying."

"Despite all we can do now, cancer is very frightening to people. That's part of why I didn't say anything while everyone was here for Thanksgiving.

If you thought it was hard hearing Barry's condolences, imagine what my mother would have to say."

Liz wove her arm under Maggie's shoulders. Although, she still wasn't a fan of snuggling while she fell asleep, she sensed that Maggie needed more than the usual reassurances. In response, Maggie moved closer. Her freshly washed hair smelled of a summer's day, grassy and warm.

"I'm sorry I didn't tell you right away," said Liz. "I needed time figure out how I felt about it. I didn't want my concerns to wash over on you."

"What are your concerns?" Maggie's voice sounded very loud in the dark.

Liz thought for a moment. "I expected the surgery and radiation to be the end of it. Now, we're looking at a different set of problems, but at least, we know what we're dealing with and can prepare."

"You keep approaching this like it's a problem to solve."

"It is."

"Liz, I don't know to explain this to you. It's really great having a doctor as my friend, but right now...right now, I need you to be my partner."

"I'm not doing a good job?"

"Oh, you're sweet and attentive, but you keep trying to manage my feelings. I just want you to be honest and tell me how you feel."

"I did."

"No, you told me your opinion as a doctor. How do you *feel*?"

Liz scanned her emotions to come up with an honest answer. "I'm frightened. I didn't expect this either. BRCA mutations are pretty rare. You might think it's easier because I'm a physician and know what we can do to fight this cancer. But I also know what happens if it doesn't work."

"So do I," said Maggie, snuggling closer as she tugged at Liz's waist. "Hold me. Hold me very tight."

Chapter 34

Maggie could see the generational divide as she sat in the conference room at Yale New Haven. The two younger women, Ellen Connelly and Jenny Carson's partner, Melissa Katz, brought only their iPads to the meeting. They had presentations ready to go on the smartboard. Liz and Bev Birnbaum had pads and pens poised to take notes.

"Let's get started, ladies," Dr. Birnbaum said to open the meeting. "I'm sure you're all busy today."

The other women at the table nodded.

"Dr. Stolz has asked for this tumor team to review the options for Ms. Krusick, whose genetic testing came back showing she's BRCA2 positive." Dr. Birnbaum glanced at Liz. "Dr. Stolz is here as her PC, so—"

Liz interrupted. "I'm here as Ms. Krusick's partner, but functionally, I'm her primary. I know we wouldn't ordinarily include the patient in one of these meetings, but Ms. Krusick wants complete transparency regarding her case. So, please express your opinions as openly as you would if she weren't here, and you were talking to me."

Dr. Katz gave Liz a mildly disapproving look, which led Maggie to think she wouldn't be following this advice. Although she'd seemed pleasant enough when they were introduced, the intense woman with dark hair and eyes had a permanent furrow between her brows.

"I'm sure you've all done your homework and read the case history, but I'll do a quick summary anyway," said Dr. Birnbaum and launched right into it. As Maggie listened to the facts of her case summarized as if she weren't there, told in the medical shorthand that doctors evidently used with one another, she felt an odd detachment. So much of what was said she didn't understand, but she felt it would be impolite to interrupt. She'd ask Liz to go over everything later. The last thing Maggie wanted to do was embarrass Liz in front of her colleagues or make a fool of herself. She especially didn't want to draw attention to herself because Liz had made it obvious on the way down to New Haven that she was only being included in the meeting as a courtesy. Clearly, Liz was trying to do damage control after withholding the test results.

The details began running together, but instead of listening to the medical debate, Maggie found herself observing how the doctors conducted themselves. She'd had a brief stint playing a female doctor on a daytime soap opera. Then, her only role models had been other actresses playing doctors or the few female doctors who'd treated her during the fertility treatments. Now, she could see how they really behaved in their natural setting. Immersing herself in these observations was comforting and helped her muster the objectivity she needed as each of the specialists at the table outlined their recommendations.

Dr. Birnbaum advocated observation, more frequent imaging and continuing the daily Tamoxifen indefinitely. She mentioned adding aromatase inhibitors, but she was careful to explain in detail the damage they could do to her bones and joints. "However, they're something to consider. We will put you on a schedule of CA 125 tumor marker blood draws to monitor the levels. There's a lot we can do to keep an eye on the situation."

The surgeon looked Maggie right in the eye when she spoke, which Maggie appreciated but found disconcerting. She dared not blink while Dr. Connelly was speaking. "I'm trying to read you, Ms. Krusick to see how much risk you're willing to tolerate. If the idea of a recurrence terrifies you so much you'll never be able to sleep at night, my recommendations will be different."

Maggie glanced at Liz, who nodded, but didn't intervene. "I'm scared, but somehow, I manage to sleep. I like to sleep."

Everyone laughed.

"If you were really anxious about recurrence, I'd recommend a prophylactic double mastectomy followed by reconstruction."

Maggie actually flinched at hearing those words. She glanced at Liz, who remained as impassive as a boulder.

"Some BRCA2 women elect to go that route," continued Dr. Connelly. "Since it's a relatively rare mutation, I personally haven't had many patients face that dilemma, so I don't have much experience to gauge whether that's a wise decision. A lot depends on you. If you really want to prevent the cancer from ever coming back, removing the tissue in which it grows is your safest bet. But even the best surgeon can't remove every last cell, so it's not iron-clad insurance."

"So, what do you recommend, Dr. Connelly?" Maggie asked.

"I'm with Dr. Birnbaum so far. I'm guessing Dr. Katz is going to recommend removing your ovaries and tubes. We have a lot of ways to treat breast cancer as long as we find it early enough. Ovarian cancer is a tougher opponent because it's harder to detect."

Dr. Katz nodded. "Yes, and we can remove the ovaries and tubes laparoscopically, so the recovery time and scarring are minimal."

"One reason I'm not pushing the mastectomy route," continued Dr. Connelly, "is I know Dr. Stolz will watch you like a hawk. She'll make sure you get to all your imaging appointments. Right, Dr. Stolz?"

For the first time since the meeting had begun, Liz smiled. "You can bet on it."

Maggie agreed to let Dr. Katz schedule the surgery to remove her ovaries.

"It may have to wait until after the holidays," said Dr. Katz in an apologetic tone, but it will be soon after the new year."

Dr. Birnbaum summarized the results of the meeting.

"I recorded the meeting," said Liz, reaching for her phone, "...in case, we forgot anything." She tapped the app to turn it off. "Thanks, ladies. I appreciate your time."

Dr. Birnbaum escorted them to the elevator. She gave Liz a hug as the door opened. "We'll be in touch." She offered her hand to Maggie. Then she opened her arms and pulled her into an embrace. "Enjoy your holidays and don't worry about a thing! Let us do the worrying."

Easier said than done, thought Maggie as she mentally reviewed the meeting on the way to Guilford. They'd agreed that staying the night at Jenny's was more sensible than driving round trip back to Maine. Maggie had given in to Liz's request to stay an additional day, so that she could visit her mother. The relationship between mother and daughter had been strained since Thanksgiving, but Liz had half-forgiven Monica. Maggie understood. If her mother were still alive, she'd want to make peace too.

Liz was quiet as she drove, and Maggie allowed Liz her introspection. She had plenty to think about herself. The fact that all the doctors on the team had been fairly low-key about their recommendations helped ease her mind. No one seemed to be rushing toward any dramatic interventions. Maybe the risk wasn't as great as it seemed. She glanced at Liz, who was deep in thought.

"Do you agree with the recommendations of the doctors?" Maggie asked.

"Yes, mostly."

"Liz! You promised you'd talk to me."

"That doesn't mean I have to tell you absolutely everything I think."

"No."

Liz turned into the driveway and parked in front of Jenny's garage, but she didn't get out. "What do you think of Melissa Katz? Jenny thinks she's phenomenal."

"I wasn't impressed with her bedside manner."

"For your ears only, she sucks. Don't say anything to Jenny, please."

"My lips are sealed."

"But I'm glad you're electing the RRSO," said Liz, shutting off the engine.

"The what?"

"Short for Risk-Reducing Salpingo-Oophorectomy....when they remove your fallopian tubes and ovaries for prophylactic reasons."

"I don't need my ovaries. They didn't do me any good when I was trying to have children. They can go."

"Bilateral mastectomy would reduce your risk of breast cancer recurrence to ninety percent."

"Then maybe I should consider it."

"We do conserve the nipples now, so the cosmetic results are better. We've been working to preserve sensitivity. That was one of my research interests. Unfortunately, we're not there yet. After a mastectomy, the best case scenario for the recovery of sensation is about fifty percent. In some women, it never comes back."

Maggie had read that in Liz's book, but that was before the results of the genetic tests. Then it had been a mere abstraction rather than a real possibility. No feeling in her breasts? That sounded terrible. Liz enjoyed them so much and so did she.

"Could you fall in love with a woman with fake breasts?" asked Maggie. "Honestly, Liz."

Liz shrugged. "I don't know. I've never been faced with that possibility."

Maggie couldn't believe what she was hearing. "YOU DON'T KNOW?"

Liz looked alarmed when she finally realized the implications of what she'd said. "That doesn't apply to you. I thought you were asking a theoretical question to which I gave a theoretical answer. Obviously, I already love you."

"No, it's not obvious, and you gave an honest answer."

Liz stared at her anxiously. "I'm sorry. I didn't realize what you were asking."

"Take me home," said Maggie. "Right now."

"Okay, but it's a long trip back to Maine."

"I don't want to go to Maine. I want to go home…to New York."

With effort, Liz spoke in a calm voice. "Maggie, please. Be reasonable."

"No, I will not be reasonable. I don't want to be reasonable. I want to go home!"

Liz got out of the car and slammed the door. Maggie got out on the passenger's side.

"This is asinine," said Liz angrily. "I'm not going anywhere."

"I'm not kidding, Liz," Maggie said. "Take me home right now, or I'll call a cab to take me to the train station."

"This is insane."

"*Now*, Liz." Maggie got back into the car and shut the door.

Chapter 35

Muttering the F-word and several other choice profanities, Liz swung into the driver's seat. She started the engine and backed out of the driveway so fast the gears complained.

"Liz, take it easy."

"I should take it easy? You're nuts. Absolutely fucking nuts," she added for emphasis.

Maggie did not reply. In fact, she said not a single word as Liz sped down I-95 toward New York City. She stared forward, watching the traffic ahead like a mute sentinel.

The silence finally unnerved Liz. "Does this mean we're breaking up?"

"Were we ever together?" Maggie's voice was chilly.

"I thought we were. I guess I missed something."

"No, we're not breaking up," said Maggie. "I don't know what we're doing. I only know I need to be away from you for a while."

"Why? What the fuck have I done wrong?"

"Liz, please, your language."

"Fuck my language! What have I done wrong?"

"You don't know if you could love a woman with fake breasts."

"So? What does that have to do with you?"

"I am thinking about having a double mastectomy."

"But you told everyone you weren't interested."

"I know, but I'm really afraid. My mother died from breast cancer. It came back even after they told her it was cured."

Liz frowned and focused on the road. She was silent for a few minutes. "You said you were fine with observation and imaging."

"Dr. Connelly didn't pick up how scared I really am. I guess I am a pretty good actress."

"So, you fooled Ellen. Brava. Great performance. Why didn't you at least tell *me*?"

Maggie spoke in a quiet, surprisingly young-sounding voice. "I wanted you to think I'm brave."

Liz turned on to the bridge ramp and accelerated unnecessarily to get ahead of another car. Out of the corner of her eye, Liz saw Maggie anxiously gripping the ring over the door.

"I know you're brave. You never have to put on an act for me."

"I know. Maybe I'm putting on an act for myself."

Liz glanced at her, but the heavy traffic required her complete attention, so she instantly returned her eyes to the road. "Look, this is crazy. Let's go home."

"No, I need some time. I love you, but I need to think. Everything happened so fast. Us. The cancer. Please just give me some time."

"All your things are in Maine."

"I'll manage. If I need something, you can send it to me."

"You're going to stay *that long*?"

"I don't know," replied Maggie vaguely.

When they arrived, Liz double parked while she carried Maggie's bags up to her apartment. They'd only brought enough for a few nights at Jenny's, so there weren't many. Liz was able to bring everything upstairs in one trip.

"Are you sure you have everything you need?" Liz asked doubtfully, surveying the small pile of bags.

"I have my laptop and clean clothes. I live here, Liz. I'll be fine." She reached up and gave Liz a quick peck on the cheek.

"That's it?"

"Go." Maggie pulled her by the arm toward the door. "Go, or you'll hit rush hour traffic."

❊❊❊

Liz swore loudly in the car on the way back to Connecticut. She played the final act of *Ariadne auf Naxos* with the volume blasting, hoping to drown out her own thoughts. She was rude to other motorists, flipping the bird to a few on the way. She drove much too fast on the Merritt, practically mowing down the cars in the left lane.

Finally, she arrived in Guilford. Her heart sank when she saw Jenny's car in the driveway. Now, she'd have to explain why Maggie wasn't with her. Jenny was the last person she wanted to know about the argument.

Jenny, it turned out, had gotten home only moments before. She still wore her suit, but as usual, had stepped out of her heels when she'd walked in the door.

"Hello, sweetie," she said greeting Liz with a quick kiss. "Where's your friend?"

"She needed to do a few things in New York, so she asked me to drive her down."

"Oh?" Jenny cocked a perfectly arched brow. "What things?"

Liz shrugged. "I don't know. Things." She'd tried to sound casual about it but hadn't quite succeeded. Jenny's blue eyes studied her intently.

"Aren't you nice to drive her all the way down to the city? So accommodating."

"Yes, I know. I'm wonderful."

"You are. I hope she appreciates you." Jenny gave Liz another kiss, then she took Liz's coat and hung it in the closet. "I was just about to mix up some martinis."

"Oh, yes. I could use one."

Jenny gently pinched her cheek. "I bet you could. You have that I'm-dying-for-a-martini look."

Liz took off her shoes and suit jacket and followed Jenny into the kitchen.

"How did your tumor team meeting go?" Jenny asked, taking the martini pitcher and the liquor out of the cabinet.

"Fine. Just as I expected. They recommended observation, imaging, and testing. Tamoxifen, and maybe AIs. Bev is still mulling it over."

"Sounds about right," said Jenny, measuring off the gin. "The tumor was low grade. How did Melissa do?"

"You mean, apart from having the bedside manner of a seaworm?"

"Yes, she's not Miss Personality. We only keep her for surgeries. You know most surgeons are zeros at personal interaction."

"I beg your pardon," said Liz with mock indignation.

"Don't pout, Liz. You're the exception, of course." Jenny ran her fingers gently down Liz's cheek, but Liz made a face and moved away. Jenny shrugged and went back to mixing the martinis. She added a dash of vermouth and crushed ice to the pitcher. She stirred the mixture gently with a glass rod. "What does Melissa want to do in Maggie's case?" Jenny opened a jar of olives and speared a few on plastic daggers, which she set in the glasses. She took another olive and popped it into her mouth.

"An RRSO."

Jenny nodded. "Sounds like a good idea." She turned to Liz. "There's some of that cheese you like in the fridge. Will you get it for me?"

"Sure." Liz took out the cheese and a box of crackers from the bin and mechanically began to slice the cheese. She arranged the slices and the crackers on a plate. She took a jar of hot pepper jelly out of the refrigerator and spooned some into a small bowl. When they'd lived together, this had been their favorite afternoon snack on the rare occasions when they were both home.

"I've become a lightweight since you moved out," said Jenny. "I need to eat something when I drink."

"I find that hard to believe."

"Believe it. It's true." Jenny popped another olive into her mouth and put away the jar.

They took their drinks and snacks to the library and sat down to admire the fading light over the sound.

"So, what's really going on between you and Maggie, Liz?" Jenny put her feet up on the sofa.

"Nothing."

"Bullshit. I know you too well. Did you scare her away with your overbearing Teutonic personality?"

"No." Liz sighed. "I don't think it has anything to do with me. She has a lot to absorb. She just doesn't want me breathing down her neck while she thinks things over."

"Uh huh. I don't believe you."

Liz shrugged. "Don't. See if I care."

Jenny peered directly into Liz's eyes. "She's worried about you. I could sense that she's insecure where you're concerned."

"Oh, what a crock."

"The lady doth protest too much."

Liz ignored her and took a big swallow of her martini.

"Let me guess," said Jenny, putting her feet in Liz's lap. Liz noticed that the toes were perfectly manicured and painted an elegant pink. "I would appreciate a foot rub," said Jenny. "Miserable day. Two primas." Liz put down her glass and absently began to massage Jenny's foot. "Mmmm. Feels good."

"Thanks."

"Maggie doesn't think she's enough for you, especially now that she may lose her breasts."

The insight was so succinct and so on the mark that Liz paused the foot rub to take a double sip of her martini.

"Score!" said Jenny triumphantly. "She's right, you know. She's not enough for you. I'm sure the nostalgia goes a long way in holding your interest, but not that long. She's not your equal, Liz. Not even now when you're just a country doctor, which we both know is pure fraud."

"That's enough, Jenny!" Liz released her foot and moved to the other side of the sofa. "I won't allow you to speak of Maggie in that way."

"Sorry. I'll mind my manners." Jenny sat back and sipped her drink.

They finished all the snacks. Liz got up to replenish the tray when she realized she hadn't brought in anything for dinner. "Should I call the Thai place for takeout?"

"I feel like sushi tonight," said Jenny, sprawling on the sofa. "That new place is really good, and they deliver. The menu is on the back of the pantry door."

Liz went back to the kitchen to get it. "The usual?"

"No, let me see. They have some good specialty rolls."

After a brief debate, they compiled a list. Liz called to order the rolls.

"Like old times," said Jenny when Liz got off the phone. "I really miss it."

Liz was a little anxious to see where this was heading, but not curious enough to wait for Jenny to say more. She made a quick escape into the kitchen to make another round of martinis. "This is my last," she said, bringing in the pitcher. "I have to see my mother tomorrow, and I can't deal with her AND a hangover."

"No, we don't want that. There's some hummus and cut up veggies in the fridge. Eat more cheese and crackers."

After the sushi was delivered and devoured, Liz felt sated and mellow. She left Jenny downstairs while she went up to put on her pajamas.

"I'll clean up the kitchen," she said when she returned.

"Oh, leave it. Maria can deal with it in the morning." Liz was surprised that Jenny still had the same housekeeper. She'd always been so critical of the people they hired to do things around the house.

"At least, let me put the food away."

"Go on, do your efficient German thing." Jenny waved dismissively. Her speech sounded slurred. She had switched to Saki after the martinis, and Liz suspected she'd had at least one too many.

Liz put away the cheese and the few pieces of maki that remained. She returned to her seat and suddenly found Jenny straddling her legs.

"Liz, you know what your problem is? You need boobs." Jenny began unbuttoning her blouse.

"Stop, Jenny," Liz protested weakly.

Jenny opened the front catch of her bra and her breasts sprang loose. And what breasts they were, creamy and soft, the pink aureoles each as large as a sand dollar, the nipples big and pert. Liz felt her crotch lurch as Jenny took her hand and brought it to her breast.

"Come on, Liz. You love my breasts. Don't you just want to caress them and suck on them? You like that. I know you do. You love boobs. You *need* them."

"Jenny, you're better than this."

"Better than what? It's not like you're married to her."

"Jenny, don't. Please."

"You know you want me."

Liz cringed. Yes, she did want Jenny, not because it was Jenny, but because her body was familiar and beautiful, and it aroused her to think of sucking on those beautiful orbs of perfect, white flesh and entering that warm, wet vagina. She had opened and caressed that welcoming place for years. Jenny loved penetration almost as much as Maggie did.

Liz's mind started working in staccato:

Maggie.

No.

Yes.

Stop.

Liz withdrew her hand from Jenny's breast. "I'm sorry, Jenny. I love you. I will always love you, but we can't have sex tonight."

Jenny pouted. Liz slid out from under her.

"I need to go to bed." Liz got up to leave.

"You're making a big mistake, Liz…getting in so deep with that woman," Jenny called after her. "Her prognosis isn't good."

Liz turned around. "It's not that bad either."

"You know the chance of recurrence is high. Very high. Are you sure she's a good investment?"

"Now, that's really low, Jenny. Don't make me question our friendship." She didn't wait to see Jenny's reaction. "I'm going to bed," she said resolutely.

Chapter 36

Liz was glad that Jenny had already left before she came down in the morning. Next to the coffee maker, Liz found a note scribbled on a free Save the Children notepad.

> Dear Liz,
>
> I'm so sorry about last night. Please don't hold it against me. I'm just looking out for my best friend. Would things be different if I said I might be ready to move to Maine?
>
> > I love you.
> >
> > Jen

"Are you kidding me?" Liz crumpled the note and flung it into the trash. "You'll be lucky if I ever speak to you again."

Liz showered and dressed, relieved to put on jeans after wearing her professional costume for the previous day's meeting. She loaded her bags into the car and headed to her mother's. She stopped at the town bakery on the way and picked up some of the cheese Danish her mother liked.

When Liz arrived, Monica was listening to a cable news political show. Monica was wrapped up in it and told Liz that she wanted to watch it until the end. The TV was still blaring while Liz made coffee in the old-fashioned drip coffee maker.

"Mom, you should wear your hearing aid," Liz said, handing her mother a mug of coffee. "The TV's so loud."

"I can hear you just fine when you're in the room. It's only when you go into the other room that I can't hear you."

"That's because you read my lips when I'm in the room."

Liz sliced the Danish into manageable pieces.

"Thanks for bringing this," Monica said, taking a bite. "It's my favorite."

"I know." Liz helped herself to a small slice of the sweet, sticky treat.

"I don't know how much longer that bakery will hold on," said Monica, shaking her head. "The supermarkets are putting the little shops out of business." She sighed. "Everything changes."

"It's the one thing we can always count on." Liz finished her piece of Danish. She had to admit the pastry was far superior to anything from a supermarket. She wanted to lick her fingers, but settled on washing her hands in the sink, which was filthy again and full of dishes.

"Where's Maggie?" Monica asked, as if she'd just noticed her absence. "Didn't she come down with you?" Monica's voice sounded almost hopeful.

"She's in New York. She needed to take care of some things." That certainly wasn't a lie. Liz made it a policy to tell her mother the truth because lying to her never worked. Somehow, Monica always managed to extract the facts like some back room spy.

"Is she going to move in with you?"

"I don't know," Liz replied casually. "We'll see."

Monica shook her head. "I don't know if that's a good idea, especially now with that cancer."

"Thanks, Mom. When I want your opinion, I'll let you know."

"Well, do *you* think it's a good idea?" Monica's blue eyes peered intently into hers.

"You know, Mom, I'd really like to have a nice visit with you, so let's drop this discussion. Okay?"

"You don't need a sick woman to take care of. I think you should reconsider."

"Mom, I don't care what you think," said Liz impatiently. "Now, leave it alone!" Liz instantly regretted shouting at a frail, elderly woman, but Monica could push her buttons like no one else. "I'm sorry, Mom. I didn't mean to raise my voice. I just don't want to talk about it. Okay?"

Monica glowered at her like a dog threatened with having its bone taken away.

"Mom, please try to understand," said Liz in a more modulated tone.

"I understand just fine."

"No, I don't think you do. I care about Maggie. I love her."

Monica frowned. "That's what I'm worried about. I don't want you to get hurt again."

Liz sighed. "Mom, I'm fifty-eight years old. I can look after myself."

"I wish I believed that. You're too good. You always lead with your heart. I'm your mother. It hurts me to see you hurting." Tears came to her eyes.

Liz sighed. "I know, Mom. You want to protect me. I appreciate it, but I need to do what I need to do."

"She has cancer."

"I know. I found the cancer."

"She needs someone to take care of her."

"Yes, she does. And who better than me? People do that for those they love. She takes care of me too. Very good care, as a matter of fact."

Monica shook her head. "Elizabeth, I hope you know what you're doing."

"I do, Mom. I promise."

***

When Liz left her mother's house, she didn't get far. She pulled off the road at the end of her mother's street and tried to figure out where to go. She really wanted to drive to New York and pound on Maggie's door, but she knew she couldn't. That would only bring back memories of her youthful persistence and make Maggie anxious. She'd asked for time to think, and if there was hope for their relationship, Liz needed to give it to her.

Liz knew she should head back to Maine, but she hoped Maggie would change her mind and want to come home. Just in case, she didn't want to leave the area. She considered returning to Guilford. Sober, Jenny would be full of apologies, but then there was the note. Liz had no intention of addressing the possibilities that raised.

The frustration and fear was overwhelming. The hollow ache in her chest kept getting bigger. It felt too much like that summer when Maggie left and never come back. Paralyzed by indecision, Liz watched the traffic drive by until she realized she had lost track of time. She glanced at the dashboard. Ten minutes had somehow disappeared. But she had discovered one thing. She needed to talk to someone—someone who would listen without judgment. Liz summoned Siri and asked her to call Bev Birnbaum.

Bev's voice was cheerful when she answered the call. "Liz? Hi. Did you have more questions?"

"No, but I need to talk."

"Talk," replied Bev bluntly.

"I mean, in person."

On the other end, Bev laughed softly. "I'm off today. Come to the house."

"I'm just leaving my mother's. It will be an hour, at least."

"Don't rush. I'll be here."

Bev's unquestioning kindness brought tears to Liz's eyes. She swallowed the lump in her throat and cut an errant tear from her cheek with her fist. She started the engine and turned back on the road, already thinking of what she would say to Bev. She could navigate without thinking. She had driven back and forth from her mother's to Connecticut for years, not only when she'd lived in Guilford, but all the way back to when she was a surgical resident with Bev decades ago.

Finally, she turned onto the Birnbaum's driveway, only a few doors from the house she owned with Jenny. The Birnbaum's house was more modest than the other houses on the street. The quaint Tudor-style reproduction didn't really fit in with the Colonial theme of the neighborhood either. The dark wood contrasted dramatically with the stucco. Liz rang the bell. The plank door with iron straps opened.

Bev wore a heather wool cardigan that brightened her pale face. The cinnamon hair color had become too much of a contrast to her skin. Liz wondered when Bev would finally give up dyeing her hair. In her field, she never had to worry about snotty residents, or maybe she did. The young were always snapping at their heels in an endless cycle of replacement.

Bev stepped out on the porch. She couldn't look over Liz's shoulder so she looked around her. "Where's Maggie?" She glanced at the car. "Did you leave her at Jenny's?"

Liz shook her head. "She's back in New York."

When Bev's eyes searched hers, Liz could see that she understood. "Come in." Bev reached for her hand and gave it a little tug.

Liz followed her into the house, which felt oppressively warm. The thermostat in the Maine house was always set low to conserve fuel, so what most people considered a comfortable room temperature seemed sweltering to Liz.

They passed through the dining room. There was a menorah on the sideboard. Liz remembered that Hanukkah was approaching and Christmas. Without Maggie, the holidays would be dismal. Liz didn't want to think that far ahead.

Bev tugged at her elbow. "Sid's in the sunroom. Go say hello."

Liz went out to the solarium and stood in the doorway. Bev's husband of thirty years was completely bald. He'd recently retired from Yale, where he'd taught twentieth century European history. He always said he'd come by his knowledge honestly. His father was a Holocaust survivor.

"Sid," said Liz to get his attention.

Sid looked up, his pale, blue eyes smiling. "Liz," he said with warm affection. "So good to see you again."

"Coffee's ready!" called Bev. "Come in and sit down."

Liz sat at the old farm table. She'd helped the Birnbaums find it at an auction, when an old farm that had been in the same family since Colonial times was being sold for development. The legs of the table were as big around as Liz's thigh. It was solid and fit perfectly into the deliberately old-fashioned kitchen.

Liz listened to the comforting sound of the coffee pouring from a glass carafe. Bev pushed the cup across the table. She still used real coffee cups and saucers instead of mugs. She poured herself a cup of coffee, added some milk, and slid the pitcher across to Liz.

Bev sat studying Liz for a long time. Finally, she said, "Go on. Talk."

Liz thought for a long moment, trying to decide where to begin. If she were a patient, she'd be imposing by unnecessarily taking up a doctor's time, but Bev had learned early in her career to listen to patients. Cancer patients often had a lot to say. Bev remained unhurried and relaxed, sipping her coffee while she waited for Liz to find words. Liz could hear her swallow in the silence of the kitchen. The only sounds were the old clock counting away the minutes and the low hum of the refrigerator.

Finally, Liz said, "Maggie asked if I could fall in love with a woman with reconstructed breasts."

Bev sat up. That had definitely gotten her attention. Her eyes widened. "What did you say?"

"I said I didn't know."

Bev took another swallow of coffee. Her dark eyes gazed at Liz without judgment.

"Could you?"

"I already love Maggie. It's a moot point."

Bev shook her head. "No, it isn't. She was asking if you'll find her attractive even if she loses her breasts. She needs to hear you say it out loud… that you'll love her no matter what."

"I know that now."

Bev leaned on her hand. "How will you feel if Maggie elects a double mastectomy?"

Liz drank her coffee in silence as she thought about Bev's question. "I would find it difficult. I would miss her breasts. Because I've performed mastectomies, I would always be aware of the difference between a natural and a reconstructed breast. I would mentally see its structure when I touch it. I would know the sensation in the conserved nipples is minimal, so it would be difficult to go through the charade of stimulating something that I know can't feel much."

Bev flinched almost imperceptibly, but her brown eyes were kind as she studied Liz's face.

"That would be terrible for you and for Maggie."

Liz nodded and looked away. She felt so guilty now that she'd admitted the truth. "It sounds so selfish."

"Doesn't matter. It's how you feel."

"Jenny said I should leave Maggie because of her prognosis."

Bev gave Liz a sharp look. "That's a really shitty thing to say. Jenny should be ashamed of herself."

"She's jealous. But yes, it was shitty. I was shocked."

"Keep her away from Maggie. She doesn't need to hear that kind of negative talk."

"Oh, I agree. And I don't need it either. It's hard enough to keep up a good front."

"But Jenny has a point. Maybe you should end it now. It might be easier for Maggie to deal with her cancer alone than have to worry about you and your issues."

"Issues," Liz repeated in a disparaging tone. "We already had enough baggage—the past, her mother, my mother, her traumatized kids, her snotty oncologist daughter *demanding* her mother have chemo. I'm not sure I'm ready for this."

Bev sighed. "You don't really have much choice now."

"No, I can't run out on her...not while she's going through this."

"So, what are you going to do? Run out later? When she's not looking?"

"No, of course not."

"Then you'll have to decide. She's giving you an out if you want to take it."

"What kind of friend would I be if I abandoned her now?"

"Liz, this isn't about you and your sense of honor. This is about Maggie. She'll need a lot of support from you. You'll have to keep telling her how much you love her, how beautiful she is, how sexy. If she elects a double mastectomy, you'll have to forget all you know about reconstruction and make love to her like you would any other woman."

"I don't know if I can do that."

Bev sat back in her chair. "That's an honest answer. It's a step in the right direction."

"I always thought the husbands and boyfriends who ran out on my cancer patients were shallow and selfish. Now, look at me."

"Liz...don't be so hard on yourself."

"Well? Look at me!"

"I am. And I see a woman who's struggling to find her way."

Liz twirled her teaspoon and stared at her distorted image in the bowl. "How do you do it? I cut out the cancer, but you help them decide what to do next. When to go on...or when to stop."

Bev sighed. "I knew early on that my life in medicine would be about helping people face death, but it's also about helping them face living with cancer. Not only the patient, but the families too."

"How do you help them live with the fear?"

"I tell them they have to learn to live with it, or it will eat them up worse than the cancer."

"I'm afraid."

"I know you are."

"I can't show my fear to Maggie. She's already terrified."

"But you have to deal with your fear. That doesn't necessarily mean burdening her with it. You can talk to other people."

Liz nodded. "I know. That's why I am talking to you."

Bev got up to refill their cups. That was the downside of regular coffee cups. They needed to be refilled too often.

"Maggie says I sound like a doctor when I talk about her cancer."

"You are a doctor. How else should you sound?"

Liz chuckled. "That's exactly what I said!"

"But I understand what she means. When threatened with a loved one's medical crisis, you retreat into your professional role, where you feel comfortable and in control. It's easier to talk about treatment protocols than the fact that someone you love may be dying. I did the same thing when Sid had prostate cancer."

"I knew you would understand."

As if he'd heard them talking about him, Sid came into the kitchen. "That coffee smells good." He looked from Liz to his wife. His face lit up when he saw her, and the smile spread across his face like a bead of oil in hot water. Liz recognized that smile. It was the smile that Maggie gave her when she came home at the end of the day. It had no other reason for being other than pure joy at the sight of her.

Sid took a cup from the cabinet. "I'll just get myself some coffee. I don't want to break up your hen party."

Bev shook her head after he left. "Two department chairs at Yale New Haven sitting here, and he talks about a hen party."

"He's only kidding. He has nothing but respect for you. He worships you."

Bev got up to pour herself another cup of coffee. "Are you in a big hurry to get home?"

"No, I took time off because I knew I'd be visiting my mother, and I wanted a couple of days to do any damage control with Maggie after our meeting."

Bev stirred sugar into her coffee. She put down her spoon and looked at Liz. "Why not stay the night? I'd enjoy the company. You know that Sid loves to talk to you about the war and the stories your father told you."

Liz nodded as she considered the invitation. "Yes, thank you. I think I will. It will be nice to catch up."

When they finished their coffee, Bev invited Liz to take a walk along the inlet. Over the years, Liz had spent many afternoons here, walking along the tidal river, while she and Bev talked about medicine or personal things—their families and plans for the future. Sometimes, not talking at all.

Liz hooked her arm in Bev's. "You've been married to Sid for a long time. What do you talk about when you know everything about your partner?"

"It's hard sometimes. We take each other for granted. Sometimes he doesn't listen to what I say, but there's no problem with his hearing. But we try to keep it fresh. We go on date nights. We leave each other little love notes. He still brings me flowers for no reason at all. He makes blintzes for me on Sunday morning."

"I envy you. Almost everyone we know is divorced. You and Sid are the exception."

"If it's going to last, it has to be more than sex, but that's important too. Sid can't get it up anymore, but he always makes sure I'm satisfied."

Liz wasn't sure she wanted to know that about Sid, but Bev had always been completely open about sex, something her patients and Liz appreciated.

Bev gave Liz a penetrating look. "The Tamoxifen's not affecting her libido, is it?"

"No, no. Thank God, that's not one of our problems." Liz pulled her friend's arm closer. "You should have been a shrink."

"I thought about it…when oncology got too depressing. They desperately need more psychiatrists. It's not a growing field. Except mental illness can be worse than death sometimes."

Liz suddenly remembered Alina's panic attack. "I think you're right."

"So, what are you going to do? You can't be in this halfway, Liz. It's all or nothing."

Liz nodded and stared out over the water. "She asked me to marry her. She was joking, of course, but also half serious."

Bev's eyes narrowed. "It's pretty early for that."

"Maybe, but I've been waiting for her for forty years."

"Just don't be impulsive. You're one of those people who thinks herself into analysis-paralysis, and then jumps in with both feet, just to make a decision. Remember when you retired?"

"That only looked impulsive," said Liz. "I knew I wanted out at the top of my game. Wielding a scalpel past your prime is pure ego. My eyes aren't as sharp. Robotic surgery is for kids raised on video games. My hands are stiff when I wake up, especially in the winter. It was the right thing to do."

"I'm sure you'll do the right thing now. You always do."

They came to a bench at the waterfront. Bev suggested they sit down. For a long time, they sat without speaking as they looked at the sound. Liz reached out, took Bev's hand, and gave it a friendly squeeze.

"Thanks for this," she said.

❊❊❊

Liz was driving through downtown Guilford when she spied the jewelry shop. Terry Piotrowski, the owner had always steered her in the right direction. When Liz needed a gift for Jenny, Terry always helped her choose exactly the right thing. Maybe she could help her find something for Maggie to cheer her up. A peace offering.

Terry instantly looked up when Liz walked in. "Dr. Stolz," she said, reaching out her hands with a warm smile. "I haven't seen you around town for ages."

"That's because I moved to Maine. I quit my job at Yale New Haven and bought a little family practice in a small town up there."

"Oh, I LOVE Maine," said Terry. She gave Liz a curious look. "I haven't seen Dr. Carson in here either. Did she move to Maine too?"

Liz shook her head.

Terry nodded, understanding.

Liz gazed around the store. It looked the same since the last time she'd been there, when she'd bought diamond earrings for Jenny's birthday. That was the last jewelry she'd bought for Jenny, or anyone else for that matter.

"How's the jewelry business?" Liz asked cheerfully.

"Surprisingly good. The chains haven't knocked us out yet. We try to keep the line fresh. We maintain a stable of custom jewelers, and we brought in this collection of genuine Irish jewelry. It's an exclusive. You can only order this line directly from Ireland or from us. Want to see?"

"Sure. Why not?" Irish jewelry didn't really interest Liz, but she politely listened while Terry reviewed the offerings in the new line.

"We went with this company because they only use the best stones and 18-carat gold. Look at this." Terry reached in and took a ring out of the case. "Isn't the design unusual? These beautiful Celtic knots are set with small diamonds and a perfect solitaire in the center." She put it on a velvet pad so Liz could see it better.

"Is this an engagement ring?"

"Yes, that's what it's meant to be. It comes with a matching wedding band."

"Nice. Are the diamonds good quality?" Liz held the ring under the light to inspect it more closely.

"This particular stone is at the top of the GIA grading. It's almost two carats and comes from Canada, so it's ethically sourced."

"Beautiful." Liz put on the ring. It fit perfectly. She knew Maggie wore the same size because she'd left her ring on the window sill while preparing dinner. Out of curiosity, Liz had tried it on.

"Is someone getting engaged?" Terry's voice was hopeful.

"Maybe. How much is this?"

Chapter 37

Maggie's phone pinged, and she saw the text from Liz flash across the screen. "How are you?"

She wondered how she could answer the question without going into extended explanations. The truth was ugly. Maggie had hardly slept since she'd been back in New York, despite being in her own bed for the first time in months. Since Liz had become her lover, she'd never spent the night apart from her. She knew Liz didn't like people touching her when she slept, but after the lump had been discovered, Liz had held her every night until she fell asleep.

But now there was no Liz with her strong arms and warm body an arm's length away. There were only the cold sheets and the too-firm mattress, bought at a time when the firmer, the better. "Like a coroner's slab," Liz had said. Remembering those words, Maggie felt doubly chilled.

Maggie stared at the text. Liz would worry if she didn't respond. Maggie needed some space, but she didn't want to be cruel.

"I'm okay," Maggie wrote back. She added a red heart emoticon.

Liz responded with a red heart.

Maggie finally got out of bed. She brewed a cup of strong tea and sat down at the little round table in the kitchen foyer. It was progress. Yesterday all she could do was lie in bed until noon. She'd read and watched old movies on the tiny TV. She'd never changed out of her pajamas, never showered. When she finally realized around four that she was hungry, she'd ordered Chinese food delivered.

As she sipped the tea, she gave her surroundings a critical look. The tiny apartment seemed so cramped after the spaciousness of Liz's house and the privacy of the woods. Even though all the windows were tightly closed, Maggie could still hear the noise of the city. Before spending time in Maine, she'd found the constant buzz of activity comforting, especially on the nights when she couldn't sleep. It soothed her to know that all around her people were still awake. Today, it only reminded her of how alone she was in this vast sea of humanity.

Maggie decided that brooding over feeling alone was ridiculous when she had so many friends in the city she hadn't seen for months. She unplugged her phone from the charger and called the number of her best friend in the NYU theater department. A moment later she heard Laura Maglione's dramatic contralto.

"Maggie Krusick! Where the hell have you been?"

"I was in Maine doing summer stock."

"Yes, I think you told me before I left for my cruise. How was it?"

"Can you come over for coffee? I'll tell you all about it."

"I can be there in an hour. Give me some time to put myself together."

That was the standard line from theater people. No self-respecting woman of the stage ever went out in public without "putting on her face." But Maggie had been changed by her stay in Maine and Liz's easy disregard of social convention. She decided not to rush to put on makeup. She had known Laura for years and suffered with her through breakups from their respective male partners. Maggie decided it was about time to show the woman she called her best friend her true face.

Maggie found some refrigerator cinnamon buns. She put on her glasses to scrutinize the purple date stamped on the bottom, happy to discover they hadn't expired. She set the oven to preheat, whacked open the can on the edge of the counter, and arranged the buns on a pan. She put on a pot of coffee only to realize there was no cream. Fortunately, she remembered that she'd stashed some packaged creamers in the cabinet for emergencies.

"Smells good in here," Laura said, appreciatively sniffing the air when she entered the apartment. She was a lithe, tall woman with stunningly white, long hair. She'd been a model before she studied modern dance—one of Martha Graham's last crop of students. She often talked about it to lord over her peers, who'd studied with lesser lights. "Martha always said…" Laura liked to say. Her specialty in the theater department was choreography. Maggie, who loved modern dance, quickly gravitated toward her.

"Hey, girl." Laura caught Maggie in an embrace, one of the few straight women she knew who gave full body hugs. "Why haven't you called me? I've been sooooo worried about you."

Maggie pulled the cinnamon buns out of the oven and set them on a rack to cool while she poured Laura a cup of coffee. She refilled her own cup and added double sugar because she needed the energy.

"I'm sorry. I just didn't have time. When I was doing *Mama Mia* in Webhanet, it was eight shows a week."

"So ambitious of you. I can't imagine returning to the stage at our age."

"Well, maybe it wasn't the best idea for me either. I fell during a trampoline stunt…"

"Oh, my God! Were you hurt?"

"I broke my leg…right above the ankle." Maggie pulled up her caftan to show her where. "Fortunately, the theater manager took me to the local family practice."

"He took you to some local doctor! Why not just call an ambulance?"

Maggie raised a finger. "Wait! That's where the story gets interesting."

Laura leaned on her hand. "Do tell."

Maggie joined her at the little table in the kitchen alcove and passed the plate of cinnamon buns.

Over the next hour, She told Laura the entire story from the trampoline accident to the meeting of the tumor team. By the time she finished, they'd drained the entire pot of coffee and devoured all of the cinnamon buns.

"My God! That's quite an adventure. How long did you say it was since you'd seen this Liz?" Laura picked up the crumbs from the plate with her fingertip.

"Forty years."

"And how long have you been lovers?"

"Six weeks."

"That's pretty quick work, Maggie. You don't waste any time."

"At our age, there's no time to waste."

"No, especially not for you." Laura gave her a quick guilty look. "That came out wrong."

Maggie shrugged. "Not something I haven't thought myself."

"Oh, Maggie, I know so many breast cancer survivors. Some of them had it years ago. It sounds like your doctors are optimistic."

"They are, but you know how doctors are. They never tell you the whole truth."

"Maybe that's because they don't know themselves."

That was a possibility Maggie hadn't considered. Maybe Liz was guarded because she didn't know the answers. Of course, she didn't. She was a doctor, not God. But Maggie had been brought up to think doctors *were* God.

"So, how long are you going to keep Liz away?" Laura studied Maggie. "It's not over already, is it?" she asked, raising a brow.

Maggie was anxious for a moment. Laura was one of the few people who knew about her affair with Katherine Gleason, the woman with whom Maggie had had a fling that summer years ago. She'd sworn Laura to secrecy about the affair and never revealed Katherine's name, although she was so tempted. There was an unspoken agreement in the theater to honor the privacy of those who were still in the closet. Maggie had assured Laura that falling for a woman had been a momentary lapse, and she was still completely straight.

"Is it over?" Laura asked again, prodding with an intense look.

"No, it's not over," said Maggie. "And in fact, I haven't really been fair. Liz has been nothing but kind to me." Laura's open and interested look made Maggie want to keep talking about Liz. Conversation about her made her somehow nearer. "She's such a good person. The townspeople adore her. She was there every step of the way for me with this stupid disease. You'd like her, Laura. You really would."

"Is she the one?" Laura asked gently.

Maggie was startled by the question. "The one what?"

"To finally sway you…" Laura said, wiggling her brows, "…to the dark side?"

It took Maggie a moment to figure out what Laura was trying to say. "You mean, to loving women?" Maggie laughed. "Oh, she did that forty years ago!"

"So why has it taken you so long to be honest with yourself? I've known for years."

Maggie stared at her. "It was so much easier to be straight, like everyone else."

"But Maggie, have you ever really been happy? Now, tell the truth."

Maggie shook her head.

"So? Maybe, here's your chance."

It sounded so easy and uncomplicated when Laura said it. Why wasn't it that way in life?

"The cancer changed things. I don't want Liz feeling she has to stay because she feels sorry for me."

"If she discovered the lump the first time you were together and stayed, I doubt that's the reason."

Maggie thought about it. "You're right."

After that, Laura filled Maggie in on all the department gossip. Rumor had it that the chairman had gotten a lucrative offer from Northwestern and might be willing to risk losing his tenure to take it. That meant there would be jockeying to see who would fill his role. As Maggie listened to Laura recount the political machinations behind the scenes, she was surer than ever that retirement had been a good idea.

After Laura left, Maggie finally took a shower and got dressed. She scanned her emails and texts, including one from Sophia wanting to know about the tumor team meeting. Rather than write all the details in an email, Maggie called her daughter.

"You're not going to go for a bilateral mastectomy, are you, Mom?" asked Sophia in a worried voice.

"I don't think so. It seems very drastic. Don't you think?"

"It is, and once you do it, you can't undo it. Besides, implants have their own risks. What does Dr. Stolz say?"

Maggie smiled. No matter how many times she'd heard Liz ask Sophia to call her by her first name, Sophia insisted on formality.

"She agrees with the other doctors."

"You know she'll keep an eye on you and be after you for all your imaging and labs. Is she there? Can I say hello?"

Maggie's breath caught. Usually, she kept her troubles from her daughters because of the girls' difficult history. It had been so hard to break the news when she and their father had decided to separate, but she also hated to keep things from them deliberately. The repercussions of that could be much worse.

"She's not here. I'm back in New York."

"Oh! Didn't she come down with you?"

"No, I'm alone. I needed some time to think. So much has happened. I need to catch my breath."

"Yes, a lot has happened. You're still going to move to Maine, aren't you?"

"I don't know. We'll see."

"But it could be good for you, Mom. Dr. Stolz seems like a good person. It's obvious she cares for you. That guy, Tom was a real dick."

Maggie bit her tongue to prevent herself from scolding her daughter. Sophia seldom used foul language, but when she did, it was definitely for emphasis. The word choice to describe Tom was tantamount to three, maybe even four, underlines.

"He's out of the picture, honey. Let's just forget him, if you don't mind."

"He never deserved you, Mom." Maggie's heart was warmed by her daughter's loyalty, but she'd already known she could always count on it.

After she got off the call with Sophia, Maggie spent some time looking over the condominium bylaws to see what her rights were regarding rentals. She was relieved to see there were no major restrictions. Next, she went around the apartment taking mental inventory of the items that would need to be moved or put in storage if she decided to rent it.

So many of the things she had once treasured—mountains of books, linens for formal entertaining, high-end pots and pans only useful for cooking in a huge kitchen—had been donated or sold for ridiculous prices in tag sales when the Connecticut house was sold. The girls' childhood memorabilia had already been passed on to them. The few valuable items from her parents were in active use rather than stored away in a curio cabinet. Maggie had already done her last meaningful purge. Rather than feel depressed by this idea, she felt lighter, glad that she felt no need to inflict the stuff she had collected on someone else.

She was in the kitchen washing the dishes and almost didn't hear the knock at the door over the running water. Only a few people had the code to get into the building. Thinking it might be one of her neighbors, wondering where she'd been for months, Maggie opened the door without looking though the peephole.

In the hallway stood Tom Meier.

"I just saw Laura Maglione on campus," Tom quickly explained. "She told me you were back in town."

"Apparently, I am."

"How are you?" asked Tom cautiously.

"I've been better."

"What's the matter?"

"I've had some health issues."

"Oh? Anything serious?" He frowned with concern.

"Potentially. But so far, I seem to be okay."

"That's good. May I come in?"

"I'm kind of busy right now," said Maggie, thinking of the piles of books and files all over the apartment. There was hardly any place to sit down.

"I could really use a sympathetic ear. There's a lot going on." Tom gave her his lost boy look, and Maggie felt sorry for him.

"All right. Come in." Maggie stood aside and gestured for him to enter. "Would you like a cup of coffee?"

"I thought you'd never ask."

"I'll have to put on a new pot. It will take a few minutes."

"I have time."

Maggie and Tom spent the next hour catching up on their lives since their abrupt goodbyes in Maine. Old habits die hard, and it was difficult for Maggie to cut him off, even when he went on and on about how much he hated his department chair. She patiently listened to his concerns, as she always had when they were a couple, and as she listened, she realized that most of their conversations had been about him. When she was married, most of her conversations had been about Barry. She frowned as she recognized the common denominator. Tom seemed not to notice her change of expression. He just went on talking.

"You know, I've been thinking…" Tom began with a sly look.

Maggie raised a brow. Thinking had never been Tom's strong suit.

"I was an idiot to take up with a student. Nowadays, I was opening myself up to serious liability. She could have filed a formal complaint against me."

"Will she?"

"I hope not."

"But she's past tense?"

Tom gave her a quick, sharp look. He shrugged. "It's over. She ended it."

"What did you expect? You're old enough to be her grandfather! What makes old men think they're entitled to all the young girls? You played the power card as her teacher. That's never a good idea."

"When I was in graduate school, all the professors were screwing their female students."

"Times have changed, Tom, in case you haven't noticed."

"Who needs kids? You and I were great together. We like the same movies, the same restaurants, we had great sex…"

"*You* thought we had great sex."

Tom's eyes widened. He looked both shocked and insulted. "But I always tried to pay attention to your needs."

"My needs," Maggie repeated cynically. Tom was strictly a penis-in-vagina kind of guy. She almost never had an orgasm during intercourse. With Liz, she came every time. "What's your point, Tom?" she asked impatiently.

"Maybe…just maybe, you'll find it in your heart to forgive me?" Tom gave her his most penitential look.

"I doubt it, but maybe someday, way in the future, we might be friends."

"Really, I'm sorry," said Tom.

There was a sturdy knock at the door. This time, Maggie checked through the peephole. Liz's blue eyes peered back. Maggie took a quick step back even though she knew she couldn't be seen.

She waited until her heart stopped racing before she unlocked the three locks and opened the door.

"Liz! I thought you were on your way back to Maine."

"I was. I changed my mind," said Liz with a scowl.

Maggie realized why Liz was scowling when she followed her line of vision to the kitchen alcove where Tom sat.

"You have company." Liz frowned menacingly in Tom's direction. "I'll come back later." She turned to leave.

"No. Wait!"

Chapter 38

Maggie's grip on her forearm was like steel pincers. Her eyes pleaded with her. Liz dropped her arm to her side to reclaim it from Maggie's grasp because it was becoming painful. She took in the scene in a glance, annoyingly reminded of the day she had first met Tom Meier and almost shot him as an intruder.

"Hello, Dr. Stolz," said Meier. "How nice to see you again."

Liz continued to glower at him. Maggie looked anxious. "You don't have your gun, do you?" Maggie whispered under her breath.

"No, I can't carry it here," Liz whispered back. "No reciprocity."

"Aren't you going to come in and join us?" Meier asked cheerfully. "There's more coffee."

"Get rid of him," Liz whispered. "I need to talk to you."

Maggie replied with a severely disapproving look.

"I mean it," said Liz.

Maggie remained silent.

"Meier, I need to talk to Maggie about something important. Would you mind?"

"Liz, that's rude!" whispered Maggie.

"Too bad."

Meier's chair made a little scratching sound on the floor as he pushed it back. "Actually, I was just leaving." He made himself small by hugging the wall as he slipped by Maggie to get out the door. Liz's eyes followed him down the hall as he hurried to the elevator.

"What was he doing here?"

"What are *you* doing here? I thought you agreed to give me some space."

"I did, but I need to talk to you before I go home." She frowned. "This is not how I imagined it would go."

Maggie put her hands on her hips. "Well, maybe you should come in and say what you have to say."

Liz stepped into the apartment, and Maggie closed the door behind her. "I'd like to give you a kiss, but I'm a little afraid. You look like you want to kill someone."

"The thought crossed my mind." Liz raised a brow. "You can kiss me. I promise I won't kill you or anyone else." She smiled to confirm that it was safe to approach.

"Oh, Liz!" Maggie threw her arms around her neck. "You really scare me sometimes."

Liz bent down to kiss her, and it didn't take long for the kiss to become much more than a friendly greeting. Liz reached out to the wall for support.

"I guess you missed me a little," said Liz.

"You know I did. Come in and sit down." Maggie tugged on her arm to lead her to the sofa. On the way, Liz surveyed the boxes full of books in front of the half-empty bookcases.

"Are you packing?" Liz asked in a hopeful voice.

"I'm organizing my things in case I decide to lease the apartment."

"Really? Are you moving? Where are you going?"

Maggie gave her a hard look. "Don't play that game with me, Liz Stolz. You know exactly where I'm going."

"Just making sure I understand." Now that Liz had the chance to look around more carefully, she saw there were stacks everywhere, piles of paper, files, books. This was not going to be a quick process. Maybe she should make arrangements with her partners to spell her for a few more days.

"So?" Maggie tapped her arm to get her attention. "What did you want to tell me?"

Liz cleared her throat to buy herself some time and to make sure her voice was strong and solid. She took a deep breath. "I want you to know that I will respect any choice you make regarding your treatment, including prophylactic surgery. When the surgery is done right, the difference between a natural breast and a reconstructed breast is hard to detect. If anyone, you'll be the loser because the sensitivity in the–"

"Liz..." Maggie interrupted. "I know all that. I read your book."

"I think a double mastectomy at this point is overkill. That's not to say, I haven't agreed to perform it when patients have asked. It's your body and your life. If the idea of a recurrence is so terrifying that you'll never stop thinking about it, then have the surgery, and I'll support you." She reached out and took Maggie's hand. "What I'm trying to say is I will love you with your natural breasts or without them. It's you I love, not your body parts."

Maggie laid her open palm against Liz's cheek.

"Why couldn't you say that when I asked?"

"You caught me off guard. I didn't think."

"You gave me a spontaneous answer. Maybe that's how you really feel."

Liz sighed. "I have to be honest. If you decide to have the mastectomy, I will really miss your breasts." To Liz's surprise, her eyes filled, and her voice thickened. She swallowed hard in order to continue. "I love your body, but I will give up anything so that you can be happy."

"It's hard to be happy when you're terrified. But one way or the other, I'm going to have to learn to live with this disease. It's not a nightmare that I can wake up from. It's going to be there every day."

Liz nodded. "Yes, it will."

Maggie looked directly into Liz's eyes. "I trust you and your doctor friends. All their recommendations sound reasonable."

"I appreciate your trust," Liz replied, "but you're still at high risk for a recurrence."

"I know, and the double mastectomy would lower the risk, but I love you, and you take such pleasure in my breasts. Why should I deprive you or myself unless it's truly necessary? Maybe someday I'll need to make that choice, but not today."

"As long as you're making your decisions based on what's good for you."

"I am, and I'm aware of the risks. Liz, I'm willing to take a lot of risks… as long as I know you'll be by my side."

Liz cleared her throat. The moment to say what she'd come to say had arrived, but for some reason, she was fumbling for words. "I have something for you," she said more gruffly than she had intended.

Maggie's eyebrows rose. Her eyes followed Liz's hand as she searched in the pocket of her jacket. The receipt from the jeweler fell out on the floor. Liz snatched it up quickly, hoping Maggie wouldn't see it, but she turned sharply and searched Liz's face.

"Are you crazy?"

"Yes, I think I must be." Liz held out the shiny, black box. "Here. It was made in Ireland. I thought you would like that."

Liz watched carefully as Maggie opened the box. Her eyes widened and her mouth fell open. When she looked up, her eyes were bright with tears. "Are you sure you're not doing this because you feel sorry for me?"

"Right. I just blew a lot of money because I feel sorry for you."

Maggie looked surprised at the impatient tone. Then, she smiled. A single tear ran down her cheek. "Aren't you going to say something?"

"You mean, I have to say the actual words?"

"Yes, I think you do. Don't you?"

Liz took a deep breath. Her hand was shaking when she reached for Maggie's. "Margaret Mary Fitzgerald, will you marry me?"

"Yes, Elizabeth Anne Stolz, I will marry you."

"There's only one condition." Liz snatched back the box. "I am not marrying a woman who still has her ex-husband's name. You have to go back to your maiden name."

"You're kidding."

"I am not. I may have gotten over my jealousy of that prick, but I won't marry you if you still have his name."

"What if I don't want to go back to my maiden name?"

Liz shook her head. "No deal." She closed the box and put it in her pocket.

Maggie looked defiant. "What if I wanted another name?"

Liz eyed her. What game was this?

"What if I wanted to take *your* name?"

Liz had never considered that idea. "Maggie Stolz?" she said aloud purely to hear the sound of it. "Not bad." She nodded. "My mother will die when she hears it."

Maggie made a face. "Let's hope not. Despite the grief she's caused you…and me, I don't wish her any harm." She reached out her open hand. "Can I have my ring back now?"

Liz mimed debating the question. Then she smiled and pulled the box out of her pocket. She put the ring on Maggie's finger.

"Fits perfectly. How did you manage that?"

"Remember when you took your ring off to mix chopped meat for meatballs? I tried it on."

"Oh, but you are sly, Liz Stolz." Maggie held her hand up to admire the ring. "So, when should we have this event?"

"Tomorrow. Before I change my mind."

"No, you don't. I want to invite my family. And I'm sure it takes time to change your name."

"Not long. I have connections."

"We're not getting married tomorrow, but we will soon." Maggie gave her one of those Maggie the cat smiles.

"No, Maggie. No big wedding and NO white dresses."

Maggie continued to smile.

FIVE YEARS LATER

Epilogue

Bev Birnbaum frowned slightly as she looked over the paperwork in the folder. The frown made Maggie a little anxious, although she already knew there was no cause for concern. Liz had been copied on all the reports and had reviewed them with her beforehand. Officially, Cathy Pelletier, the other female member of Hobbs Family Practice was Maggie's doctor, but Liz managed all the care related to her cancer. Somehow, the two doctors never tripped over one another in the process.

"Your MRIs and mammograms look great," said Bev. "Your tumor markers are low. Everything looks perfect. Congratulations, Maggie. It's been five years, and you are now officially a survivor." Bev clicked open her pen, ready to take notes. "So, the Tamoxifen is still working for you. No new side effects? No increased vaginal dryness? No decrease in your libido?"

Maggie glanced at Liz, who suddenly found the ceiling tiles extraordinarily interesting.

"No," Maggie assured her doctor. "Everything is fine in that department."

Liz continued to stare at the ceiling. Bev looked over her glasses in Liz's direction. "Liz, did you have anything to add?"

Liz sat up straight. "No, as Maggie said, she's tolerating the Tamoxifen well."

Bev glanced at Maggie. "A good thing. Unfortunately, you'll probably be on it for the rest of your life."

"It's gotten me this far without a recurrence. I'll take it forever if I need to."

Bev gave her a warm, encouraging smile. "I'm going to miss seeing you. Both of you."

"You could come to Maine," said Liz. "You know you're always welcome."

"I know, and I'll get there. This summer, I promise. I have a lot of catching up to do in my retirement." She closed Maggie's file and moved it to the side of her of desk, a casual thing, but to Maggie, an act with great significance. "What about you, Liz? Are you going to go through with selling your practice to your partners?"

Liz raised her shoulders. "They can't seem to get the money together, and honestly, I'm not ready to let it go. We keep getting offers from the local health network. I'll close the practice down before I sell it to them."

"Liz will never retire," confided Maggie behind her hand.

"Oh, I don't know." Bev gave Maggie a doubtful look. "Now that she's finally getting her money out of the Guilford house, she might think differently. The two of you might want to travel the world."

"We did think about buying that little cottage in Ireland," said Liz, "but I don't want to be tied down to one place."

"You live in Maine, where it's always cold, and you want to buy a house in Ireland, where it always rains? How about someplace sunny and warm?"

"Like Tuscany?" Maggie nodded enthusiastically to encourage this line of thought.

"Exactly."

"Bev, don't encourage her," warned Liz. "She doesn't need any encouragement."

Bev got up ."I'll see you at Jenny's wedding next month."

"At least, she's wearing a white dress." Maggie gave Liz a hard look.

"Oh, for God's sake! Still?"

Bev looked from Liz to Maggie. "Well, she did wear white. It just wasn't a dress."

"Thanks, Bev. And Jenny is the last person who should wear white. Fortunately, her little plastic surgeon fiancée doesn't know any better."

"And you're not going to tell her." Maggie elbowed Liz.

"No, I'm going to take the money and run. Although I will miss the place. Those views of the sound! But I'm sure she'll let us stay there when we visit."

"Are you going back to Jenny's place tonight?" asked Bev as she walked them to the elevator.

"No, our camping gear is packed and we're heading straight up to Acadia," said Liz, "...to celebrate High October and our anniversary."

"But I thought your wedding was in May."

"It was," said Maggie. "We celebrate another anniversary."

Liz grinned. "A consummation devoutly to be wished."

"That line's about death, Liz," said Maggie. "Thanks, but no."

Bev gazed at each of them fondly. "Yes, I'll really miss you two."

"All the more reason to visit," said Liz.

Bev opened her arms. Maggie fell into them, enjoying the warm hug.

"You promised you'll come to Maine. I'll hold you to it, you know," said Liz, planting a kiss on Bev's cheek as the elevator door opened.

When they reached the ground floor, they headed out to the doctors' parking lot. "Glad that's over?" Liz asked, clicking open the doors to Maggie's Forester.

"You have no idea. I love Bev, and I really hope she comes to visit us, but I never want to see the inside of her office again."

"Understood." Liz opened the door to the driver's seat.

"I could drive. It *is* my car."

"I'll drive." Liz's tone left no room for argument.

Maggie smiled to herself as she got into the car. Liz liked to think she was in charge, but Maggie knew better. And why let on?

Maggie adjusted her seat and sat back to enjoy the ride.

Also by Elena Graf

OCCASIONS OF SIN

For seven centuries, the German convent of Obberoth has been hiding the nuns' secrets—forbidden passions, scandalous manuscripts locked away, a ruined medical career, perhaps even a murder. In 1931, aristocratic physician, Margarethe von Stahle, is determined to lift the veil of secrecy surrounding her head nurse, Sister Augustine, only to find herself embroiled in multiple conflicts that threaten to unravel her orderly life.

LIES OF OMISSION

In 1938, the Nazis are imposing their doctrine of "racial hygiene" on hospitals and universities, forcing professors to teach false science and doctors to collaborate in a program to eliminate the mentally ill and handicapped. Margarethe von Stahle is desperately trying to find a way to practice ethical medicine. She has always avoided politics, but now she must decide whether to remain on the sidelines or act on her convictions.

ACTS OF CONTRITION

World War II has finally come to an end, and Berlin has fallen. Nearly everything Margarethe von Stahle has sworn to protect has been lost. After being brutally abused by occupying Russian soldiers, Margarethe must rely on the kindness of her friends to survive. Fortunately, the American army has brought her former protégée, Sarah Weber, back to Berlin. As Margarethe confronts painful events that occurred during the war, she must learn both to forgive and be forgiven.

THE MORE THE MERRIER

A HOBBS CHRISTMAS STORY

Maggie and Liz have been dreaming of a quiet Christmas since they got back together after being separated for forty years. This year they are determined to celebrate a romantic holiday alone. Their plans of sitting by the fire, drinking mulled wine, and watching old Christmas movies get scuttled by surprise visits from friends and family. The Christmas chaos provides some holiday cheer and a touching lesson in the real meaning of Christmas.

THIS IS MY BODY

The new rector of St. Margaret's by the Sea Episcopal Church has a secret. Lucille Bartlett was a rising star at the Metropolitan Opera, but she disappeared from the stage and no one knows why. Philosophy Professor Erika Bultmann is a confirmed agnostic, who doesn't have much use for religion, but she is fascinated by Mother Lucy. When Erika returns to her summer cottage in Hobbs to finish her last book before she retires, Lucy is drawn to the enigmatic professor, but she wants much more than a casual affair. When Lucy's secret is revealed, she needs Erika's support more than ever. Can they put aside their differences and find common ground?

LOVE IN THE TIME OF CORONA

It's midwinter in Maine, and the biggest problem is a snowstorm. Only Liz Stolz, the senior doctor of Hobbs Family practice, is paying attention to the strange virus in China that's roiling the financial markets. She tries to alert the town leaders to the potential danger, but police chief, Brenda Harrison, is distracted by Liz's new physician's assistant, Cherie Bois. Brenda's interest repels Cherie. The friends are pushed together during the lockdown. Friendships and relationships are strained as they act selflessly and selfishly out of love, faith, and duty. Can they find new strength and forge deeper connections through helping one another and the town survive?

About the Author

In addition to the books in the Hobbs series, Elena Graf has published three historical novels set in Germany during the Weimar Republic and the Nazi era. *Lies of Omission*, the third volume in the Passing Rites series, won a Golden Crown Literary Society award for best historical fiction and a Rainbow Award. The fourth volume, *Acts of Contrition* also won a Rainbow Award and a Goldie.

The author pursued a Ph.D. but ended up in the "accidental profession" of publishing, where she worked for almost four decades. She lives in coastal Maine.

If you liked this book and would like more stories about the people of Hobbs, Maine, write to the author at elena.m.graf@gmail.com.

9 781733 449205